WE WHO
HAVE
NO
GODS

WE WHO
HAVE
NO
GODS

A NOVEL

LIZA ANDERSON

BALLANTINE BOOKS

NEW YORK

Ballantine Books
An imprint of Random House
A division of Penguin Random House LLC
1745 Broadway, New York, NY 10019
randomhousebooks.com
penguinrandomhouse.com

LIBRARY OF CONGRESS CATALOGING-IN-PUBLICATION DATA
Names: Anderson, Liza author
Title: We who have no gods : a novel / Liza Anderson.
Description: New York, NY : Ballantine Books, 2026.
Identifiers: LCCN 2025032252 (print) | LCCN 2025032253 (ebook) |
ISBN 9780593976319 hardcover acid-free paper | ISBN 9780593976326 ebook
Subjects: LCGFT: Witch fiction | Fantasy fiction | Fiction | Novels
Classification: LCC PS3601.N544295 W4 2026 (print) | LCC PS3601.N544295 (ebook)
LC record available at https://lccn.loc.gov/2025032252
LC ebook record available at https://lccn.loc.gov/2025032253

International edition ISBN: 979-8-217-09455-4

Printed in the United States of America on acid-free paper

1st Printing

FIRST EDITION

BOOK TEAM: Production editor: Loren Noveck • Managing editor: Pam Alders • Production manager: Erin Korenko • Copy editor: Hasan Altaf • Proofreaders: Alice Dalrymple, J. J. Evans, and Julie Ehlers

Chapter-opening illustrations: Liza Anderson
Shutterstock illustrations: ekosuwandono (crow), Abramova Aleksandra (church window), Unleashed Design (textured background), aPhoenix photographer (glitter texture)

Book design by Ralph Fowler

The authorized representative in the EU for product safety and compliance is Penguin Random House Ireland, Morrison Chambers, 32 Nassau Street, Dublin D02 YH68, Ireland, https://eu-contact.penguin.ie

For my mother,
who is nothing like this

Part I

THE ARENA

I

The Acheron Order maintains the boundary between the world of the living and the world of the dead. Behaviors and individuals that threaten this balance are to be eliminated.

—William Ruskin, *A History of the Acheron Order* (New York, 1935)

That man, there, was looking at her funny. Having worked in this restaurant for the better part of a decade, Vic Wood knew the weight of men's eyes on her back. Most of the time she hardly noticed the touch of a curious glance between her shoulder blades.

This was something else.

A mousy man of about sixty sat alone at the bar. To the untrained eye, he looked profoundly normal. Dashes of gray streaked his brown hair, and he wore a crisp button-down under a suit the color of drab carpeting. But pallid tweed spoke as loudly as any other clothing. He was rich. The outfit—dull and perfectly tailored—was the kind of plain pricey the wealthy deployed to avoid undue attention from the masses. Where the nouveau had not yet learned the dangers of flaunting their luck, old money hid itself well. Best to fit in and keep your head attached to your shoulders. Vic clocked him on sight.

A useful skill, when tips paid the rent. Isolating the haves from the have-nots.

When her mother died eight years ago, Vic had taken the first job she found that would hire a sixteen-year-old lying about her age. She spent two years waiting tables in a shitty restaurant for half-decent pay. Hands up her skirt and dirty jokes were part of the game, and Vic learned to play along. She got tough and hoped that one day her and her brother's survival wouldn't depend on her ability to smile when she wanted to scream.

Once they moved to Austin, she upgraded to Le Curieux Gastro-pub, an upscale fusion joint that sold lifestyle as much as food. The restaurant hired for hot, young, and cooler-than-you, so Vic looked the part. She left her curly black hair loose around her face and learned to ignore it when it fell in her eyes. When a new makeup style came into vogue, Vic practiced in front of a mirror until she could apply it without thinking. She amassed an all-black wardrobe fit for the uniform requirements but interesting enough to push the envelope a little.

Vic rose through the ranks quickly. It didn't hurt that most of the staff worked on a temporary basis. College kids crammed service jobs into the gaps between semesters. Vic enjoyed the descriptions of campus life they brought with them, even if she felt a twinge of jealousy at their adventures.

In all her years of waiting tables, hundreds of men had sat at that bar, and hundreds of eyes had watched her from across it. None of them had felt quite like this.

Henry would have called her paranoid. That was a favorite word of his to describe her. Suspicious, cynical, always looking for the worst and usually finding it. The man at the bar was just a man at the bar, her brother would have said.

As if Vic didn't have good reason to be wary of strangers.

This man was too clean, too pressed, too pale. Muted, like a photo printed without enough ink. His eyes, as nondescript as the rest of him, followed Vic with too sharp a precision—as though she were a specimen ripe for dissection.

The familiar warning sounded in the back of her brain.

She approached him, her spine pin-straight, and slid a rag across the bar to give her hands something to do.

"Can I get you something to eat?" Vic spread her service smile wide, and an expression flashed across the stranger's face as fast as an animal darting in front of a headlight. Recognition, she would have sworn, if it had appeared on any other face.

Was this the man she'd been waiting for? Had the time finally come?

"I am not staying."

He had an odd voice, Vic thought. Accented in a way that avoided accent, as if he had taken great pains to excise any hint of identity from his speech.

"You let me know if you change your mind," Vic replied. The hair on her neck stood on end, and she turned to leave.

A clammy hand slipped around her wrist and gripped tight. Vic tamped down the urge to wrench her arm from his grip. Eyeing the damp cloth hanging in Vic's hand, he pulled away, his lip turned up in disgust. Her skin echoed the wet pressure of his palm. She shivered.

His eyes clung to hers, and Vic couldn't look away.

"On second thought . . ." He slapped the counter like he meant to kill an insect. "Is there anything you recommend?"

Vic couldn't move. Why couldn't she move?

"Everything's good here," Vic heard her voice answer. "I'm partial to the ragout."

The stranger hummed a noncommittal note and kept his snakelike gaze on hers.

"Have you worked here for a long time?"

"Since I was eighteen." The words fell from her tongue without hesitation.

"Will you stay here?"

Vic tried to break eye contact. She didn't like the questions, the artificial calm in his voice. She didn't like that she couldn't stop her words from spilling out.

"Will you continue to work in this restaurant?" the stranger repeated, an edge to his tone.

"I don't have any reason to leave."

A bead of sweat swelled on the stranger's forehead. Glistening in the amber light of the bar, it rolled into his eyebrow and hung there, a dewdrop on the end of a rotten leaf.

"You did not go to university, did you?" he asked.

"No."

"Why not?"

Vic tried to shake her head, but her muscles were locked. She wanted to tell the stranger to go to hell and take his prying questions with him. She wanted to scream in his face to leave her alone.

But memories floated to the surface, and Vic could not send them away.

"I couldn't go to college," she said, her voice weak and quiet. "I had to take care of my brother."

"Why?"

"I'm the only person who can."

It had been eight years since Vic last saw her mother. Eight years, ten months, sixteen days, and about half an hour, to be precise. Meredith Wood had thrown a rushed "remember to feed your brother!" over her shoulder and slipped out the front door of their apartment for the last time. She worked the late shift at a nearby hospital, and her lifelong disinterest in punctuality left her practiced at hasty goodbyes. After three days of watching the door, Vic called the hospital.

Fifteen minutes later, she hung up on an increasingly concerned hospital administrator, who explained in a deep Southern drawl that they had no record of a Meredith Wood. She was very sorry, dear, but she couldn't find that name anywhere.

Not a full day had passed before Henry, only ten years old and small for his age, sidled into the living room, chewing on his lip. He'd spilled their mother's secret, and Vic's life had fallen apart. Men were coming for Henry, people he said could do things Vic couldn't. *Witches,* he'd said. *Mom called them witches.*

"But surely you want more than this?" The stranger gestured to the space around them, though his eyes remained locked on hers.

No, Vic wanted to say. She was happy, she'd swear.

For the last eight years, Vic had done just as her mother had asked.

Henry is special, her mother had told her again and again. *Take care of him.*

Vic had been taking care of Henry even before their mother vanished. When Meredith dragged them across the country, lying about working long hours at whatever hospital needed the staffing that month, Vic had made him dinner and helped with his homework and made sure his clothes were clean. She'd stayed up with him when he was sick and walked him home from school every afternoon.

Vic had done well. Henry would graduate high school in a few months. He was safe and happy and no strange men had come to take him away from her.

And that was enough for Vic.

The stranger's lip twisted, his skin sallow in the light. "You're nothing like your mother, are you?"

No, Vic thought instantly. She was not. Where Meredith beamed bright and lively, Vic was combative and cold. Where Meredith had taken up as much space as possible, Vic had folded herself to fit in the cracks her mother left behind.

But he shouldn't know that. He shouldn't know any of that.

"How do you know my—"

He cut off eye contact, and Vic dropped against the bar like a puppet with its strings cut. A nearby couple looked at her in alarm, but Vic righted herself quickly, backing away in confusion.

"Are you okay?" one of her co-workers whispered as Vic passed. "It looked like you fell."

Vic couldn't get her bearings. She'd been wrung out, hung to dry, and left behind.

"Nothing happened." Vic wiped sweat from her neck.

Something had passed between her and the stranger who knew her mother. Looking at him had twisted her up inside. Only seconds later, and the memories were already drifting away. Vic couldn't recall exactly what he'd said or how she'd felt, but she retained the slimy feeling in her gut.

All her planning. Hiding, avoiding new people, keeping her life as small as possible. All of it had worked for a time. But it was over now. Vic could see that clear as day. Just as Henry had warned when he had been a frightened child, looking up at her like she could fix it.

They had come at last.

She cast a glance backward. The stranger rose from his seat. Reaching into his coat pocket, he extracted a thin leather wallet and removed a single bill. He folded it with care, running a blunt fingernail along the crease as if he had all the time in the world. He leaned forward to ease the bill under his half-empty wineglass, and Vic caught sight of a carmine stain against his crisp white sleeve. His cuff had come undone, revealing a thin strip of skin and markings more intricate and alien than any writing Vic knew. A circle, letters in an alphabet she didn't recognize. Bloodied marks only just beginning to scab.

They were carved into his skin.

Vic bolted.

II

Magic, to commandeer the layman's term, has existed alongside time since its inception. Early understandings of magic viewed the world as a binary split between chaos and structure. Magic, then, was the organization of the world's natural tendency toward chaos. Men trained in the ancient arts could warp the unorganized energy around them into something tangible. They could, through the use of conduits and ritual and their own innate abilities, bend reality. According to the old wisdom, the world yearned for chaos, and men gave it what it wanted. This chaos, once widespread, spawned vicious creatures that hunted and killed humans en masse. These were the dark days, long before the rise of the Acheron Order.

We know now that magic is neither inherently chaotic nor inherently structured. Magic is simply energy, rooted in the physical plane whence it originates.

Modern practitioners discovered that there are two distinct physical realms: the world of the living (which these theorists, rather geocentrically, called Earth) and the world of the dead (Orcus, a term they borrowed from the Romans). To maintain balance and preserve human life, the two worlds must be kept separate.

But the realm of the living and the realm of the dead were always connected, and would always be connected, because men would always die.

—William Ruskin, *A History of the Acheron Order*
(New York, 1935)

Weakness, that was the shaky feeling in Vic's hands. An awareness of her own vulnerability settled cold across her skin, brought to the surface by the stranger. She had stared into his dull brown eyes and felt, for the first time in years, small and fragile.

It was true that Vic's survival instincts were . . . overactive. For years, she had watched the shadows like something might leap from them at any minute. She lived her whole life thinking she heard footsteps behind her, always a touch faster than her own.

After her mother's death, mastering her weakness became Vic's obsession. It took her first to the track, where she learned to run. But soon it insisted she find a gym, then a dojo, then a gun range. She could outsmart her weakness. She could prepare, and she could fight, if she needed to.

By the time Vic hit twenty-five, she'd spent almost a decade learning to fight anything that came her way.

But she didn't know how to fight a stranger who carved his own skin.

Vic rushed home after he left, making no excuses to her colleagues for her absence. But the restaurant would forgive her, and if they didn't, Henry mattered more anyway.

She wrenched open the door to the apartment she shared with her brother and sped into the hall.

"Henry!" Vic shouted, twisting toward the living room.

"In here, Vic."

"We need to get out of here," Vic said, breathless, as she stormed in. "A man came to the restaurant. I think they found us."

Henry didn't move. His eyes slid to the corner behind her.

Vic spun, her heart pounding.

The stranger from the restaurant sat in a velvet wingback chair in a dark corner of the room, untouched by the late-evening lamplight. His legs were crossed, and he examined his nails as he spoke.

"We've been looking for you for a long time," he said, his voice bored and low.

"You let him in?" Vic asked Henry, panic in her throat.

Henry shook his head without taking his eyes from the stranger.

"Get out," Vic told him, moving to stand between the man and her brother.

"My name is Nathaniel Carver," he said. "I am an Elder of the Acheron Order, and I will not take instructions from you."

"This is my house," Vic said. "Get out."

"I will leave once I've said my piece."

Vic looked to the doorway beside him, weighing her chances of subduing him long enough to escape with Henry.

"I assume, given the intensity with which you have avoided this conversation," the stranger, Nathaniel Carver, began, "that you already know what I aim to say."

A muscle in Vic's jaw jumped. This wasn't happening. It couldn't happen. She'd been careful.

"Henry is a witch of his mother's line. He must come with me to Avalon Castle and be trained in the ancient arts."

"He's not going anywhere with you," Vic said, reaching back for her brother's arm.

The stranger watched her movement.

"The dramatics are unnecessary," Nathaniel said. "I will not hurt him. Or you, for that matter, unless warranted."

"Our mother died in the service of your 'Order.' You can't have him."

A knowing flash in the stranger's gaze was the only hint that her words had surprised him.

"What do you know of the death of Meredith Wood?" he asked, leaning forward slightly. The disinterest was gone from his tone.

Vic had the distinct sense that her answer to this question was important, though she didn't understand why. What Vic did or didn't know mattered to this man.

"I know she left and didn't come back," Vic said. She did not add the single fact that made her confident that her mother was no longer alive: Meredith would never have left Henry behind. Vic, maybe, but never Henry.

"And what do you know of how she spent her days?" Nathaniel asked, sharp eyes narrowing.

"She lied about being a nurse," Vic said.

"She fought monsters," Henry said behind her, his voice quiet.

Nathaniel's gaze widened a fraction.

"So you know enough," he said. "That's annoying," he added, almost to himself.

Vic's hand tightened around her brother's wrist, readying him to run. But she had no escape plan. She had no idea what this man was capable of, and she would not risk her brother's safety testing it.

"I should not need to inform you that Meredith committed a very grave sin by telling you that," the stranger said. "Nor should I have to remind you that spreading such knowledge would result in strict consequences."

Vic wanted to roll her eyes. Like she would go around telling everyone about the secret society of witches her dead mother belonged to. Monsters hiding in the sewers, hunted by a woman in scrubs. Vic would have laughed if she weren't so terrified.

"Time is of the essence, I'm afraid," Nathaniel said. "Our newest class of recruits began training last week. Henry must join them."

"He will not," Vic said through her teeth.

"He is a witch. He belongs to the Acheron Order," Nathaniel said, his annoyance clear.

"He belongs to me," Vic said.

Nathaniel watched her for a long moment.

"Do you know what becomes of witches who are never trained, Ms. Wood?"

When Vic said nothing, he went on.

"No, Meredith would not have told you that. I see."

His lips curled in a malevolent imitation of a smile, amused at Vic's expense.

"Whether your brother can hear the language of the ancients is not in dispute. It's preordained, in his blood. Sooner or later it will express itself, if it hasn't already. In the best of outcomes, witches who are not trained risk exposing themselves to the human world, and in doing so endanger the stability upon which we all rely. In the worst of cases, unchecked abilities lead to chaos. Chaos is untenable, Ms. Wood."

Nathaniel rose from the chair slowly and approached the siblings, stepping into the light.

"The Order is tasked with the righteous mission of preventing such chaos," he said, looking down his nose at Vic. "It was not only monsters your mother hunted."

Vic swallowed. She didn't feel Henry's hand on her shoulder until he squeezed it, and she couldn't stop herself from imagining him dead, murdered by a shadowed figure that looked an awful lot like their mother.

"I've compiled instructions on how to find and access the castle." The stranger addressed Henry as if he hadn't just threatened his murder. "Inside you'll also find information on the upcoming courses and training requirements, a suggested packing list, and the like. For your eyes only, of course."

In his empty, outstretched hand, a thick envelope materialized, and Vic heard her pulse in her throat. Magic, real and pure as day, in front of her. She had pictured it for years, ever since Henry told her his secret. She'd waited for her brother to show his abilities, watching him out of the corner of her eye. But she had never seen it before tonight.

"Do let me know if you have any trouble getting there." At that, the stranger's eyes flashed to Vic.

Henry had a puzzled expression on his face.

"Why would you go to my sister's work?" he asked. "If you knew where we lived, why would you go there first?"

Nathaniel watched Henry's face and said, "I wanted to see what kind of woman Meredith Wood's daughter had grown into. I meant no harm."

He turned his back on the siblings and marched from the room, his staid leather shoes making no noise on the linoleum.

Vic waited, breathing hard, for the sound of the front door shutting behind him, but it never came.

Silence filled the room for a long moment, until Vic rushed forward to make sure he was gone. She looked out the peephole, into the open-air hallway leading from the parking lot to their apartment door, but the world outside was empty and quiet. There was no sign of the stranger.

Vic walked back to the living room, her mind racing.

"We have to get out of here," she said to Henry. "We have passports; we can leave the country. I have enough saved for a few months. We can start somewhere new—"

"Vic . . ." Henry sat on their faded leather couch, running his palms over his jeans, an anxious habit neither of them could break.

"You're right. Leaving the country is a bad idea. Too complicated, too much security. Somewhere remote, then, off the grid."

"Vic," Henry repeated.

But Vic felt the past catching up with her, collapsing against the present like a wave breaking over the shore. The day her mother disappeared had been the worst day of her life, and she fought to shake the sense of history repeating itself.

That phone call—*Sweetheart, is there someone I should call?*—hung in Vic's mind. She had felt very small that day. Small and wrong and out of her depth in a thousand ways. The nervous feeling in her hands redoubled, and Vic fought the urge to rub them together, to hit something.

Henry raked a hand through his too-long blond hair, the same shade as their mother's. A combination of trust and entreaty made his face childlike when he looked up at Vic, though now he stood half a head above her and rarely ever needed to look up. To Vic, a part of Henry would always be ten years old, turning to the older sister who could fix anything.

Men are coming for me, he'd told her all those years ago, in an apartment hundreds of miles away now. *Mom told me. In case anything happened to her, she told me to run.*

"Vic," Henry repeated, and she snapped back to the present. Henry's eyes were wide with concern, and Vic forced her body to still. He spoke slowly, carefully. "I think the jig might be up."

"Wait a second—"

"I think I should go."

"No," Vic said, shaking her head. "No way, not when we've been hiding from these guys for eight years." She pointed an angry finger at the door. "Not when they're threatening to kill you if you don't go."

"What if he's right?" Henry asked. "What if it's the safest place for me to be?"

"Did you forget what Mom told you?" Vic asked, exasperated. "She told you to *run.*"

Henry paused to think, his forehead pinched. "I'm not sure that's what she meant," he said, and it was Vic's turn to frown. "I've been trying to remember. I was so young when she died, the conversation isn't clear anymore."

" 'Run' is pretty clear, Henry."

"She said that men were coming, yes. But she also said that I would be safe at the castle. The castle," he repeated.

"I thought you made that part up," Vic said. He'd been a child. Of course he would conflate something terrifying with what he knew— fairy tales, fantasy. There were no castles in the United States.

"I did, too," Henry admitted. "But Nathaniel said he would take me to Avalon Castle. And then I remembered. That was real, she really said the part about the castle."

Not for the first time, Vic raged internally at her mother. Why did she confide only in the youngest child? Why couldn't she have given Vic the tools to understand the threat? Instead, Vic was forced to rely on a warning passed through the ears of a fourth grader, and she'd been out on a limb ever since.

"And if I can learn," Henry went on, "then I can protect us. We won't need to look over our shoulders every day. You can be normal, and I can be like Mom."

Like Mom, Vic wanted to scoff. She remembered all the strange things that trailed her mother. The faucet starting a second before she touched it, electricity bounding out of outlets and into Meredith's fingers without hurting her. Muddled looks in strangers' eyes when they gave up arguing and let Meredith do what she wanted. She'd even heard hints of the organization her mother worked for, whispered conversations when Vic was supposed to be sleeping. Vic had written it off—first because Meredith was her mother and the strangeness surrounding her was normal to a child who knew nothing else, and later when maturity cast doubt on Vic's early memories. But then Henry told her his story, and Vic realized she'd been right all along.

Vic put her head in her hands and rubbed her temples. "You haven't even finished high school."

"You dropped out of high school," he pointed out.

"I wouldn't recommend it," she said.

"Look at our choices here," Henry said, his voice low. "If it's death or training, I'm going with the second one. At least then I might be able to fight back."

How were those their choices? Just that morning, Vic had driven Henry to school, complaining about his oversleeping and missing the bus and an eighty-degree January in Austin and shouting at the traffic on the highway. Her biggest concern had been the asshole in front of her, and Henry had shaken his head at his irascible sister and her inability to control her temper. Now, like a bomb dropped in her lap, it was death or training. Be hunted or learn how to hunt.

Vic couldn't imagine her life without Henry. Even worse was the idea of him wandering into a dangerous situation, into a world where men cut strange marks into their skin and disappeared without a trace.

"Where is this place, anyway?"

Henry tore open the envelope and thumbed through the materials Nathaniel had left. "Somewhere in New York," he said. "Look."

He pushed the paper toward Vic, but she stared at it with confusion.

"What?" Henry asked. He flipped the page back to look at it again. "What do you see?"

Vic didn't see anything. The paper was as blank as the wall behind her.

"Fucking magic," she groaned under her breath, and Vic felt her world spinning away from her. There was really no choice, at the end of the day.

Vic sat up straight, set her shoulders, and came to a decision.

"We'll leave on Monday."

Henry nodded, solemn, then frowned. "Wait, did you say 'we'?"

"Yes. I'm coming with you."

"*What?*"

III

When men first found fire, they prayed to it. They stared into it, night after night, until it spoke to them. These men listened and they learned until they could see the filaments that bound the world together. Strands of life hung in the air like strings tying matter to itself, and if men pulled hard enough against these connections, they could wield them. They bent, they plucked, they toyed and twisted just to see what would happen if they snapped. And then, long before men's mouths could mold the shape of words to name them, they broke them.

Pulling energy apart, forcing it together, created chaos out of perfect order. A harmony untouched across time immemorial suddenly unraveled. Disorder spread like a sickness, and with it came the beasts. Beings unseen by the eyes of men began to hunt them in the dark. The nascent species barely survived the onslaught. Those who did learned better than to mess with the fabric of reality. They crafted mythologies to explain the chaos and rejected the practices that had borne it. They huddled around fires and ignored the voices when they came.

—From the archives of E. Henry Aldous (1875)

"You know you don't have to do this," Henry told his sister. Vic rolled her eyes and kept driving.

They had been on the road for two days. Vic and Henry got along well by sibling standards, but the thirty-hour drive between Austin and upstate New York was testing their limits.

Vic was sick of Henry's irrational optimism about the Order. He couldn't stop himself from speculating aloud about every little detail that awaited him—the food, the training schedule, the other recruits. Vic, with less humor each time, asked every hour on the hour whether he would prefer to turn around and drive anywhere else.

"We could go west," she said. "I know you've always wanted to see the Pacific. We could go do that instead."

"Can it, Vic."

"You know it snows in New York, right? Big icy sheets of it. We're not going to New York City. This is upstate. Basically Canada. Whole lakes freeze over, and you have to scrape ice off your car if you want to go anywhere."

Henry sighed, deep and beleaguered. Vic considered suggesting he abandon his pursuit of witchcraft for the theater. "Vic, please."

"They have a regional delicacy called a garbage plate. A *garbage plate,* Henry."

Five hundred miles ago, he might have laughed at that. By the time they hit Pennsylvania, Vic suspected he was ready to throttle her.

Once Henry convinced himself Meredith *had* told him he'd be safe at the castle, to him it was a done deal. If their mother said it, well, her word was gospel. Henry had tried to persuade his sister to stay home, though half-heartedly. He settled on forcing Vic to promise that she would only drive him—once they got there, he insisted, she would turn around and leave.

Vic suspected he secretly appreciated her decision to tag along. Whether he was scared of making the journey alone or apprehensive about leaving his closest confidante half a continent behind, he didn't say. But Vic sensed her presence was a comfort to him.

"Vic, you are literally driving me insane." Henry set his head against the window and closed his eyes.

An annoying comfort perhaps, but a comfort all the same.

"I'm trying to prepare you for your future."

"I want to die," Henry moaned.

"You just might. Who knows what these people get up to in the wilderness? Maybe it's a human trafficking ring. Or a sex cult."

"It's not a sex cult." Henry sighed without opening his eyes. "We've been over this."

"As far as I can tell, the sex cult evidence is inconclusive."

"Mom said I'd be safe at the castle," Henry said. Case closed. Mom said the castle was safe, and he trusted Mom.

Where Henry got this trust, Vic had no idea. Their mother had, as far as Vic was concerned, thrown him into the deep end just as much as Vic. They both shared the consequences of their mother's secrets. But Henry viewed Meredith through a lens of optimism and good intentions. Vic was unfamiliar with the concepts.

An unnamed weight pressed against Vic's chest as she watched the trees fly by through the windshield and the reality of her situation settled upon her. She was driving her brother across the country to a castle where strangers would try to teach him witchcraft, and they were almost there.

In the dead of January, the landscape in the Northeast was impossibly bleak. A somber sky hovered close overhead, pressing Vic to the ground like a hand against her neck. Trees held empty branches heavenward, and cast-aside remnants of days-old snow littered the shoulder of the highway, smeared with dirt and compacted into clotted mounds of ice. Gone was the kudzu-covered South, where winter rarely knocked. Vic had entered a colder, meaner place. The sun began its descent too early, and darkness engulfed them before the dashboard clock read five P.M.

They followed the instructions Nathaniel had left, which Henry had copied by hand so Vic could read them. When they peeled off the highway, they thrust forward into a kind of darkness unknown to city dwellers. Twin beams cut a thin path ahead of them, and the rest of the world fell into blackness.

Vic slowed to a near crawl, not trusting her worn tires on the slick pavement. Any concern Vic might have had about oncoming traffic on the single-lane road fled when she heard the crunch of ice beneath the tires. No one had driven this way in days.

Her hands wound around the steering wheel as her shoulders climbed toward her ears. Henry shifted in his seat, his eyes darting across the windshield as if expecting a castle to materialize on the side of the road. His knuckles turned white in his lap.

Out of nowhere, he shouted, "There! Right there, turn right!"

Vic followed where he pointed but saw nothing.

"Can you not see it?" Henry asked.

"I can't see shit."

"Pull over. We can trade places."

Vic looked askance at the heaps of worn snow on the shoulder and opted to park in the middle of the lane. The brakes ground out a rumble as she wrenched to a stop on the ice.

Henry cracked open the passenger-side door and clambered out, reaching his arms overhead and stretching like a cat. Vic unclipped her seatbelt and climbed over the center console to take his seat.

"Seriously?" Henry asked, looking in from the driver's side.

"I don't fuck with the woods."

"You're a child."

"What I am is not getting eaten by a forest monster."

He shook his head, grabbed the wheel, and shifted into drive. The tires jumped and spluttered on the ice before the car lurched forward. When they reached the part of the forest Henry had pointed out, he veered off the road—directly into the trees.

Vic shouted and braced for the crash, but an instant before impact the trees disappeared. As she stared, a road appeared before her eyes, leading into the forest.

She supposed Henry had seen it the whole time.

That was magic, wasn't it? Vic had witnessed it herself. One second a row of trees stood sentinel in front of the car—so tactile she could see the bark sloughing off—and the next, gone.

Asphalt gave way to stone, and the car rattled along, oblivious to Vic's anxiety. About a half mile down the strange driveway, lights glittered out of the darkness like stars. Golden lanterns lined the path, and when the road curled, Vic heard her own sharp intake of breath.

A magnificent stone structure loomed at the end of the road. A giant of rich gray stone, Avalon Castle crouched at the base of the forest, and Vic once again felt time collapsing around her. A dozen spiked turrets stretched to the sky. Hundreds of arched windows glowed bright in the black night. She thought of cathedrals, of candlelight and horror stories.

Fear scrambled up Vic's spine as she stared at the castle. It resembled less a building than a living thing. A great stone dragon, lying in wait.

"Holy shit," Henry breathed.

The structure could have housed an entire university, a whole town. Vic wondered how many people lived within its walls, hiding in the mountains. Hundreds? Thousands?

Elaborately carved arches narrowed above a colossal wooden door. Even at a distance, Vic knew that door would dwarf her.

Henry pulled to a stop in front of the entrance, and Vic wanted to demand he turn around. Keep driving. Leave.

The materials Nathaniel had left said the Order was founded in the seventeenth century and that Avalon was completed in 1824. The castle had barely seen two centuries. So why did Vic feel as though she stared into the wizened face of history itself?

Vic jumped when Henry opened his door, his eyes never leaving the castle. Reaching over, Vic pulled the keys from the ignition and stowed them in her pocket. She took a deep breath, pushing her panic down until it quieted, and followed her brother into the night.

A frigid wind pierced the cheap material of her jacket. The thin faux leather was never intended for a real winter.

Vic had told Henry she would stop here. She'd sworn to take him just as far as the front door. Turn around and head back the way they'd come.

But Vic had also promised their mother she'd keep him safe, and the front door beckoned like a siren.

Vic threw a look at the black edge of the forest as she mounted the stone steps to the entrance. Shadowed gaps among the trees could hold anything, and the longer she watched, the more she imagined movement right outside the limits of her vision. Vic tore her eyes from the darkness before she could convince herself it stared back at her.

Henry shouldered the massive door inward, and Vic was struck by his confidence, like here was his birthright and he had come to claim it. In his eyes, she guessed maybe it was.

The door creaked open, and the entryway shone like a sun in the middle of the forest.

Vic crept in behind him. As soon as she crossed the threshold, the door swung shut with a thud so heavy Vic jumped.

A carved ceiling soared high overhead, buttressed by an ornate cascade of arches meeting at the top. The floor, walls, and ceiling were all stone, though a massive antique rug carpeted the floor. Staircases spiraled from either side of the hall, leading to a shared landing at the center.

A middle-aged man in a three-piece suit waited on the landing with his hands on the railing.

"Henry Wood," he said with a smile. "Welcome to Avalon Castle."

IV

Though humankind writ large forgot the magic they'd used to break the world, sects of men who remembered, who retained the mastery of all life, swore to rid the world of the chaos their ways had created. Rules, structure, organization: These became their escape route. With each generation, they fought to fix what they'd broken. With each generation, they failed.

But the world thrived under chaos. Men built for the sky. They stored food in unimaginable quantities and broke the landscape into discrete, nameable parts. Though the beasts remained on the fringes, waiting for weakness, humankind persevered.

Thus emerged a radical alternative. The new order ought to be balance, not restoration. They would never fix what was broken, but the world, it seemed, *could* live on the knife's edge between chaos and control.

This approach won out in the end, once its proponents outlived everyone who opposed them, and they took up their mantle of sitting by and waiting for the world to end. It nearly did, a few times, and they stopped it, as they promised they would.

Here was the origin of the Acheron Order. They sat at the end of history, looking backward. They fell into the shadows and allowed the world of men to forget what they had done. All the same, they kept their power. They nursed it through the centuries, kept it fresh, kept it vital. A condensed kind of power, held tight in the hands of a few. They lorded it over the world they had saved long after it had forgotten them.

—From the archives of E. Henry Aldous (1875)

"And you've brought a guest."

The man's genteel smile widened when his eyes fell on Vic. Henry, noticing his sister for the first time, shot a wide-eyed look back at her.

The man descended the staircase like nobility from another time.

He wore a suit of rich ivory, with a shirt and tie in darker shades of cream. A teal kerchief completed the anachronistic ensemble. Even at a distance, Vic knew his clothes were expensive, probably bespoke. Wavy hair couldn't decide between black and gray, though Vic guessed he couldn't be much older than fifty. He could have been a golden-age star, some Hollywood legend kept ageless in a castle. He was strikingly handsome.

Vic stepped forward with a hand outstretched. "Victoria Wood," she said. "I'm Henry's older sister."

"I remember," he said with a smile. His eyes were a soft gray, like blue eyes drained of their vibrance. "I knew your mother quite well once."

"That makes one of us," Vic said with a sardonic smile, and an odd curiosity flashed across his face.

Henry angled around her to shake the man's proffered hand. The stranger looked between the siblings before introducing himself.

"My name is Max Shepherd," he told them. "I'm one of the Elders in the Order."

Nathaniel, too, had introduced himself as an Elder. Though this man didn't look old enough to be the elder of anything. Vic's confusion must have shown on her face, because Max laughed—a happy laugh, charming against the austere backdrop of the castle.

"It's more a title than a descriptor. And I'm flattered. There are twelve of us."

"Mr. Shepherd," Henry cut in. "I know the documents Elder Carver provided stressed secrecy, but my sister was concerned about my safety."

"A perfectly understandable concern," Max replied lightly, watching Vic.

"Yes," Henry said. "Before last week, we didn't have any idea—"

"Before last week, you were hiding from us."

"Our mother had given Henry reason to believe he wasn't safe," Vic said, her eyes narrowed, but the man, Max, nodded.

"There's no need to apologize. It was a misunderstanding. Your situation is . . . unique."

Henry stood up straight and continued, "I know that outsiders aren't allowed in the castle, but we were wondering if she—"

"Of course you can stay," Max said, his eyes on Vic. "The Order owes a great debt to Meredith Wood. Her kin is our kin."

Vic frowned at the ease in his words as her head spun. Years of hiding from these people, and she was welcomed inside without question? It didn't make sense.

Henry must have thought the same thing, because he went on, "Elder Carver wrote that humans are never allowed at Avalon. He threatened us with consequences, he said that—"

Max waved a hand to dismiss these concerns. "Rules are made to be broken," he said in an airy tone. "Come with me."

"But the car is—" Vic pointed feebly behind her, unsure of what exactly her complaint was. None of this was what she'd expected.

"All will be taken care of. Please, come."

He didn't ask for the car keys.

Max strode toward the twin staircases, and Henry followed without pause. With an anxious glance back the way they'd come, Vic hurried after them.

The corridor, as ornate as the entrance hall, had arched ceilings scattered with intricate stonework. Paintings dotted the otherwise bare walls, and the floor dipped down in the center, an impression formed under thousands of footsteps.

"Avalon Castle is the Order's home, and has been for two centuries," Max said. "The castle functions as a training ground for new members, houses the archives, and provides a meeting place. The main structure consists of five wings, excluding the tunnels and exterior buildings. It comprises more than five hundred rooms, including a half dozen libraries, an amphitheater, training areas, and of course lodging, all built around a courtyard, which is lovely in the sun but rather abysmal at present."

Vic surveyed a thin corridor as they passed, half expecting to see a stream of people appear—wearing robes and perhaps pointed hats—but no, only empty stone. Hard and cold and glossed with a thin layer of condensation. If Vic ran a hand along the wall, she imagined it would feel like the pockmarked side of a cave.

"Where is everyone?" she asked.

Henry sent her a warning look.

What? Vic mouthed. Henry ignored her and turned back to Max, who extracted a fine golden pocket watch from the front of his vest, then snapped it shut.

"The castle's inhabitants have settled into their rooms for the night. Order members are generally discouraged from wandering the halls during midnight hours." Before Vic could ask why, he continued, "Only a small number of active members live in the castle full-time. As I'm sure you can tell, the castle was built to accommodate many times more people than currently live in it. Even at the Order's height, we never had enough members to fill this place. Regardless, there are fewer witches remaining than many would prefer."

"Did something happen to the rest of the witches?" Vic asked. Her mind jumped to witch hunts, to violence and persecution. Women's bodies roasting on the spit.

Henry shot her another look. As if it were impertinent for her to ask pressing questions when assessing his safety was her only goal. She rolled her eyes, and Henry scowled at her. Vic thought Henry would have kicked her if Max didn't have a clear view of both of their feet. Max chuckled.

"Nothing so macabre as what you're thinking," he told Vic in that easy way of his. "It's simply that fewer witches are born these days."

"When does training start?" Henry asked.

"Two weeks ago," Max said. "You'll be the last to join, since we had such trouble tracking you down, but there's no need to worry about being behind. Everyone starts with the basics."

They entered a wide hallway lined with doors, and Max came to a halt about midway down.

"You may join if you like," he said to Vic.

"Join?" For an instant, Vic thought he meant the Order, and her mind raced. All this emphasis on secrecy, everything her mother hid from her because she wasn't born like Henry. She'd never expected to be invited inside, let alone welcomed to sit at the table.

"Classes," Max clarified. "In the morning, you may go with your brother."

"Oh, but I'm not—" Vic shook her head.

"I know you can't use magic. But if your aim is to guarantee your brother's safety, it would be a worthwhile use of your time. There's no better way to learn what we do here."

Obviously Vic would stay with Henry if given the chance. The prospect of leaving him here—driving back to Texas with an empty passenger seat—had hung like a specter over her all week. But she wasn't sure she understood what Max was suggesting.

Vic replied, "I won't be able to do anything."

"We'll see about that." Max gestured to the door in front of them. "This is the entrance to your rooms."

The thick wooden door was, like everything else Vic had seen in this castle, more extravagant than it needed to be and out of place in this millennium. Delicate carvings of foliage covered its face, and a red glass knob glittered against the oak like a single drop of blood. Apartment 241, according to the brass numbers fixed at eye level.

"I assumed it would make you more comfortable to be housed together," Max said.

"I thought you didn't know I was coming."

Max merely smiled and pressed a pair of barrel keys into Henry's palm. "You should find everything in order within. Please don't hesitate to let me know if there's anything I can do to make you more comfortable." His eyes held Vic's as he continued, "Allow me to recommend against wandering the halls after dark without an escort."

As he spoke, a door behind Max flew open and hit the wall like a fist. Vic jumped. She stared as the door slammed itself shut with equal force.

Max winced without turning around. "The castle has a mind of its own, I'm afraid." He gave the siblings an encouraging smile. "I will see you both soon. Please let me know if you need anything."

Max walked away, and Henry set the key into the lock and entered the room. Across the hallway, the door that had moved of its own accord stood motionless.

While her brother explored the new space, Vic hesitated, then chased after her strange new acquaintance.

"Max, wait!" She jogged to catch up with him.

He turned with his eyebrows raised. "Yes, Victoria?"

She drew up beside him and paused. "What does the Order *do*, exactly?"

"Did Nathaniel not explain this when he visited?" Max asked.

"He didn't explain anything to me," Vic said.

"The Order maintains the balance between the world of the living and the realm of the dead. The Veil keeps the two worlds separate, but it's like a complex membrane. Sometimes things that don't belong in our world manage to cross. That's why the Order was formed, to strengthen the Veil when it weakens."

Vic fought to keep up. "What happens if the Veil breaks down?"

Max paused with a finger on his chin. "I suppose without a boundary the worlds would blur together. The dead would walk among the living, killing freely. It would be cataclysmic." He said it casually, like an academic prospect—an interesting idea worthy of discussion over dinner and drinks, rather than a horrifying potential future best avoided at any cost.

"And my mother, she was a part of this?" Vic asked.

Max's brow wrinkled as he watched her. "Meredith Wood became a member the same year I did. Her death was a terrible tragedy."

"What happened to her?" Vic said.

"Stay, Victoria," he said. "And find out for yourself."

With that, Max nodded good night and left Vic alone in the hallway.

Her mind swam as she approached the apartment. When they'd left for the castle two days ago, Vic's best hope was that this was some kind of joke. That they'd wander the Northeast for a few days before Henry realized he'd been duped, that magic was, of course, made up, and that they could return to life as it was before. But as Vic had watched the castle blossom from the darkness, she realized her worst fear lay in front of her. Henry would enroll, he'd train, and he'd become different from her, as different as her mother had always been. Vic would be cast out, without her brother and alone in the world.

And her mother. A curiosity Vic had long repressed flared to life. What had Meredith done to end up here? And why had she left it behind?

Had this place killed her, or was something—someone—else to blame?

The apartment door opened into a decent-sized living space, with a sitting area before a stone fireplace on one side and a kitchenette and breakfast room on the other. The table was set with two dishes under domed silver covers. Steam billowed when Vic lifted one to reveal a plate laden with chicken breast, asparagus, and a baked potato, as well as a glass of wine and cutlery. Vic grunted and replaced the cover, uncomfortable with the prospect of mystery food appearing hot and ready in front of her.

Henry, on the other hand, threw himself into the opposite seat with a mumbled "I'm starving." Vic stopped him with a hand on his arm, not sure if the food was safe to eat. He leveled a flat stare at her. "They would not bring me all the way here to poison me."

He was probably right. More likely, if the Order was planning something nefarious, they would wait until they'd extracted whatever they wanted from him.

Vic removed her hand and perched on the seat beside him. She watched her brother dig in through narrowed eyes.

Henry groaned as he bit into his chicken. "You have to try this, it's delicious," he said around a mouthful.

"How did you turn out so trusting? I practically raised you."

"Exactly," Henry agreed, waving his fork for emphasis. "So I saw firsthand it never did you a lick of good to be so suspicious of everybody all the time."

"Criticize me all you want, but we're alive, aren't we?"

Henry laughed to himself as he ate. Vic picked at her food before taking a cautious bite of the chicken.

"It's good," Henry said. "Admit it."

"It needs garlic," Vic said, and he rolled his eyes.

After she finished eating, Vic cleared her dishes and looked around the apartment. On the other side of the main room sat a heavy armchair and a love seat in front of the hearth. A low fire burned behind the grate. Most of the walls were papered a deep red, although one displayed bare stone. It was cozy and more than a little medieval. Again, Vic marveled at the relative youngness of the castle. Creating a scene like this was intentional. Someone had meant to conjure images of feudal castles, of lords and ladies and ill-fated peasants and the academia of old, although expanded by a few sizes and accompanied by the modern comforts of electricity and forced-air heating. Vic wondered why they'd gone to the trouble.

At the back of the apartment she found two bedrooms, each with its own en suite. That was an upgrade—back home, she and Henry shared a bathroom.

Vic jolted when she saw her suitcase on a luggage rack in the second bedroom.

How had they gotten into the car? How had they beaten her and Henry to the room?

But Vic shook the questions from her mind. She knew witches

lived in the castle. She knew they used magic to do things she didn't understand yet. She had to stop being surprised by the simple stuff and focus on what mattered.

A wooden four-poster bed occupied the center of the room, matching a similarly opulent chest of drawers. Thick carpets lay one over another atop the stone floor. An upholstered chair and a table sat before a window concealed behind heavy drapes—red, like the rest of the room.

Vic caught sight of herself in a gilded mirror hanging in the hallway and released an audible groan.

"You good?" Henry called from the kitchen.

"No. I'm mad at you for not telling me I look like a tumbleweed," she called.

Henry's head popped over the back of his chair as he twisted to look at her. "I like your hair," he decided after a quick appraisal. "You look like Medusa."

"That is not the compliment you think it is."

Vic returned to the mirror and patted down the errant curls. Her reflection looked different in a golden frame. She looked almost stately, frowning into such an expensive thing.

Inspecting the row of books on the mantel, Vic found they were for show rather than substance. Hardback copies of boring books— the kind people bought in box sets with no intention of breaking their spines. She wanted books on the Order, or on magic more generally, but no such luck.

"What did you say to that Elder earlier?" Henry asked from behind her.

"I asked about Mom."

"What did he say?"

Vic hesitated, then said, "Nothing interesting."

"Are you really thinking about staying?" When she only shrugged, he came to stand behind the couch. "You're worried you won't be able to get your old job back?"

After her disappearance in the middle of a shift last week, the restaurant owner had yelled at her. Vic had yelled back. It hadn't ended well.

"To be honest, I hadn't thought about that at all," Vic said. She wasn't sure she wanted to go back. It had been years since she'd grown tired of the routine monotony of restaurant life. Nathaniel's questioning last week hadn't helped.

"You could do something else," Henry suggested.

"Have any ideas?"

"You could get a job at the dojo?"

Vic liked fighting, probably more than she liked anything else. It was her escape, her obsession. She wasn't sure if she wanted to turn that into a job.

Vic shrugged again and twisted to face her brother. "How are you feeling about this place?" she asked.

"Excited?" he said with a cautious smile. "I remember everything Mom said about me being special, me having purpose. For a long time I kind of wrote it off, but now I feel like it might be true."

"She said you were destined for great things," Vic said.

"This has to be what she meant, right?"

"Right," Vic agreed absentmindedly.

"We'll see tomorrow, won't we?" Henry asked, a sigh in his voice.

Vic nodded as he left for the bedroom, and she stared into the flames as they danced.

She wondered what that felt like, to feel destined, to feel like she was in the right place.

V

The Lumen, the distinctive feature visible in all witches, is characterized by a luminescence of the iris. It is visible from birth, though only under specific conditions. The appearance of the Lumen varies between practitioners. Scholars have yet to determine a link between Lumen appearance and the abilities of the witch in question.

—William Ruskin, *A History of the Acheron Order*
(New York, 1935)

Heeding Max's warning about wandering the castle should have been easy. But being cloistered in an unfamiliar space brought back memories. Her mother had done something similar to Vic as a child, and often. Meredith would bring Vic to a random building—sometimes claiming it was a doctor's office, or an administration building, or a still-under-construction wing of a new hospital—put her in a room by herself, and tell her to wait.

Vic had disobeyed this instruction only once.

Her mother had left her in a supply closet. Vic remembered sitting cross-legged on a big orange bucket turned bottom-up into a makeshift stool, reading a library book from a town they'd left the week before. Vic finished the book, flipped the plastic-coated cover shut, and started picking at the edges, but Meredith did not come back. Vic waited for what felt like ages as boredom sank its teeth into her.

She would only look outside for a moment.

Meredith could not have gone far.

The door wasn't locked, and it swung open easily. Fluorescent lights gave the speckled linoleum a pallid tone, made grayer with age and grime. Looking to either side of the hallway, Vic saw no sign of her mom.

Vic didn't call out for her, afraid that Meredith would scold her for leaving her hiding spot. But Mom shouldn't be angry with her, Vic reasoned. She had waited for a long time.

When a light flickered at the far end of the hallway, Vic followed it. She crept forward, her small feet padding against the hard floor.

She'd almost reached the bend when she heard it.

An awful sound came around the corner, and Vic slammed to a stop. A low growl quivered in the air. Then, a wet slap. And another, the growl getting louder, and Vic realized that was the sound of footsteps, the footsteps of something much bigger and stronger than she. Loud and wet and inhuman.

Vic plugged her fingers in her ears and screwed her eyes shut. She could feel it, whatever made that horrible sound, as it came closer, the growl growing into a roar. Closer and closer until it was about to round the corner.

There was a splatter and a shriek, and Vic's shrill scream echoed in the empty hall.

Someone shook her, hard. Vic's eyes flew open, and her mother's face was inches from hers, wearing an expression of fear completely foreign to Vic. Her ears rang. Meredith was yelling at her, deep lines carving the skin of her forehead. Meredith screamed at Vic for not staying put, for putting them both in danger. Her fingers dug into Vic's arm as Meredith dragged her from the building as fast as the child could run.

The ride home was quiet. Meredith wouldn't speak to her, and Vic stared out the window in a glaze of panic she would not shake for weeks.

Vic did not cry. Nor did she complain the next time Meredith left her behind.

In the years since her mother died, Vic often wondered why she hadn't realized sooner that Meredith lied about how she spent her days. And Vic never figured out what made that sound, though it echoed in her mind throughout the years that followed—in the shadowed corners of unfamiliar rooms, in the back seat of the car when she drove alone at night.

Twenty years of life gone by, and Vic hadn't learned a thing. With a furtive look at Henry's closed door, she slipped into the hallway.

The castle now lay dark and still. Moonlight reflected off the snow outside and cast long shadows in front of her. Vic clutched her phone out of habit. Fat lot of good it would do her here. She didn't know if the Order intentionally cut visitors off from the outside world, or if the lack of signal was an unintended perk of the castle's location in the middle of nowhere. Not that she had anyone to call. The only person she would ever ask for help had come with her.

Dozens of doors identical to her and Henry's lined the hallways, the pattern only occasionally broken by an arched window or a gilded painting, either of which would have looked more at home in the Renaissance wing of a museum than hidden in the mountains of New York. Vic watched to see if the portraits' eyes followed her as she passed, but none did. The paintings hung motionless, right where they belonged. In one, a man in velvet held a serpent in an out-stretched hand as if it were a glass of wine best swirled before tasting.

Some places buzzed with life even after their inhabitants took their leave. A well-loved home never really felt empty. Vic tried to imagine such life in this place. Generations of young witches eager to master their mysterious abilities—huddled on their way to class, books tucked against their chests, heads thrown back in laughter. But when she looked down the vast stone passageways around her, Vic could not conceive of revelry or joy in a place like this. The air felt thick with some other kind of history. Some empty and cloying thing.

Vic wondered how much time her mother had spent here. She wondered if Meredith felt more at home here than in any of the tem-porary residences she'd shared with her children.

Rounding a corner, Vic expected to find the staircase Max had led them up earlier. But another narrow hallway unraveled in front of her. Vic turned around when she realized she was lost.

The hallway behind her led straight back. The turn she'd taken seconds ago was gone.

Vic spun slowly, incredulously. Hallways did not move of their own accord.

But the castle had a mind of its own, Max had said. And it wanted her to continue.

Vic fought panic as she ventured forward. Maybe the castle *was* a great stone dragon, like she'd imagined outside. Maybe it would eat her.

Winding down hall after hall, she searched in vain for something she could use to find her way back to the apartment. She paid too much attention to the empty space around her, expecting noises where there were none, until she came upon a break in the endless maze of passages. On either side of Vic, hallways spilled into an open landing like a knot of roads meeting at a junction. An iron railing kept Vic from the edge, and her jaw dropped.

Opposite her loomed a stained-glass window that must have been thirty feet tall. Like the arched ceiling above it, it curved to a point. Thousands of glass pieces came together in a style she'd never seen, far too modern for the churches of old. Countless individual fragments, none of which was larger than Vic's fist, were lit from behind by moonlight. Near the center of the image, a woman cloaked in indigo clutched something to her breast, slumped onto her knees. Squinting against the low light, Vic caught a sliver of green between the woman's fingers. A box, maybe, or a jar. The woman's other hand lay limp at her side, her fingers loose around a thin disk of the same vibrant hue. The lid. Out of the woman's chest poured a black shadow, which crept across the frame like spilled blood. The monster ate its way through the image, all pointed edges and fangs, depicted in crude, sharp shards. The icy railing pressed against her hips as Vic leaned forward, and she saw that the woman's eyes were closed. The expression on her face might have been exquisite relief, or anguish.

It was beautiful. And wrong.

Around the edges of the window, the landscape outside peeked through clear pieces of glass. Miles and miles of unbroken woodland, above which a pale moon cast anemic light on the treetops. The evening's gloom had cleared, and the clouds shifted to reveal a tapestry of close-knit constellations.

Something moved outside.

Where the forest edge met the castle grounds, a shadow darted from the trees.

Vic barely had time to focus on it before it disappeared in the direction of the castle, but what she saw was horrible. The thing wrenched itself across the ground with unnatural speed—too large to be a person, too fast to be an animal. It pulled itself forward with tendrils of something intangible, as thick and dark as smoke creeping under a doorway.

Her breathing came fast and hard as it dawned on her that that *thing*—whatever it was—was heading toward the castle.

She stepped away from the railing and hurried back the way she had come, fighting the knot of anxiety in her belly as it crystalized into something sharper. A familiar fear given an unfamiliar face.

When she stumbled back into the hall leading to their apartment, Vic rushed to the correct room number with a sigh of relief.

Reaching for the doorknob, Vic froze.

The scarlet handle lay under a thick coat of dust and left a sooty print on her palm. But that wasn't right. It would have taken ages to accumulate that much dust. Years.

Apprehension wrapped around Vic's spine as she twisted the knob and pushed the heavy door inward. The room within was not their apartment, and Vic had the impossible realization that the castle would let her return when it was ready, not when she wanted to go back.

But Vic did not believe in buildings making decisions for her.

She found herself in an octagonal supply room with no windows. She turned on her phone's flashlight and gasped when the beam lit rows of weapons. Some of them Vic knew her way around—swords, knives, lengths of rope—and she recognized others, like Japanese throwing knives, a katar, a scimitar. But many she could only guess the use of. A long strip of thinly hammered silver, a whip without a handle.

She knelt in front of a cabinet full of dark, flat stones, tapping idly on the glass. The stones glistened in the low light, all arranged in neat lines, and Vic noticed a wide array of colors and textures. It looked more like a geology exhibit than a weapons case, and Vic was more interested in the blades.

Vic ran her finger along the pristine edge of a short sword at eye level. The metal sang as she touched it, slicing the skin too fast for her to notice. She sucked a drop of blood from her finger and marveled at the perfect condition of the blade. The upkeep required to maintain this many weapons—

Vic jumped at the sound of footsteps. Two sets of them, approaching from behind a door on the other side of the room. She fumbled to shut off her light and slid into the hallway. She sank into the shadows lining the wall and hoped whoever was in there wouldn't walk her way.

Her heart leaped in her throat. She forced herself to breathe quiet, slow. She couldn't afford to panic.

"I can keep putting them down easy enough," a man said from the room Vic had left. His voice had a roughness Vic associated with disuse, and it rumbled through her chest and landed behind her navel. The skin on her arms prickled in instinctive awareness that the owner of that voice was a dangerous person. She heard heavy footsteps, followed by the shuffling sounds of someone putting away their gear. "But this is only going to get worse if we don't address the source of the problem."

"I am quite familiar with your opinion on the subject," came a clipped response. Vic recognized the second voice as Nathaniel's.

At the unusual sound of scraping metal and a wet drip, curiosity got the better of Vic. Careful to step quietly, she eased forward until she could peer around the doorframe. The men had left the door behind them ajar, and a sliver of light lit the space enough for Vic to see.

Nathaniel's appearance was as bland as Vic remembered, but the figure beside him could not possibly blend in anywhere. He stood a head taller than Nathaniel, and he was filthy. A layer of some grime Vic couldn't identify covered his head and shoulders in the dim light. Unruly brown hair fell in front of his face, concealing it from view.

He couldn't be real. Broad-shouldered and dressed in black, he looked like he'd stepped out of another age. He was too big, too much for modern society. Someone of his stature would be more at home in a Roman temple, lording over worshippers and carved out of stone.

Rapt, Vic watched the giant remove a harness from between his shoulders. It was hung with short blades, a few inches long and nestled along the length of leather. His head still bent, the behemoth separated a single blade from the sheath. Vic took an involuntary step back when she recognized the dark liquid that dripped from it. Blood, black and thick like it had sat still too long.

At the sound of Vic's foot hitting the stone floor, the giant's eyes shot up.

His hair fell back as he straightened, revealing the most arresting man Vic had ever seen. A short beard obscured a square jaw. He had the rough look of someone equally likely to have grown facial hair on purpose as to have grown it over the course of that day, and the beard—like the rest of him—lay under a layer of blood. He had wide cheekbones and a prominent nose, a brow set heavy over eyes Vic caught and held.

His eyes were blue, pale but so bright they almost glowed in the darkness. Vic thought of ice and sky and coal. Broken glass on asphalt after a crash. The flashes remembered in the aftermath of something life-changing.

Vic's breath stuck in her throat as she stared at him, caught like a fish on the end of a line.

Nathaniel fell silent when he followed the man's gaze to Vic, but she couldn't tear her eyes from the man watching her.

"Who are you?" His voice skittered across her nerves like the bang of a drum, and Vic swallowed. She felt too aware of herself, like all the blood in her body had rushed to her skin, thrumming with tension.

"Victoria," she answered in a voice she was glad did not waver.

Was that all she could think to say? Her name? But she was mesmerized, cold and hot and frightened and excited all at once.

The stranger raised his eyebrows, and the muck on his face split.

She felt him assessing her, his eyes roaming over her face like he was looking for something. Vic chided herself to snap out of it, to think about the situation like the fighter she was. The man could see Vic better than she could see him, which put her at a disadvantage. But the hallway was to her back, and she was probably faster than he was. She could run—if the castle let her—and find the apartment again. Lock the door and hope he didn't bang it down.

"Victoria," he repeated, and the sound of her name in that deep voice sent a thrill through her. "Of course." He turned to Nathaniel. "This is Victoria," he said.

"Victoria Wood," she added in a bolder tone. "My brother, Henry—"

"Her brother is here for training," Nathaniel said, watching her with a stupefied scowl.

"And she just decided to tag along?" the stranger asked him.

"She was not invited."

"I was told my presence here would not be a problem," Vic said.

"Who told you that?" the stranger asked. Pale eyes watched Vic with such intensity she wanted to look away.

"Max," Vic told him.

"Max must have warned you about creeping around the castle after dark," he said in a low rumble, still expressionless. "This is a big castle. Mostly empty. All sorts of things hide in the hallways at night, none of which would be very kind to you, Victoria." He repeated her name in a mocking tone, and Vic scowled as the word ran down her spine.

"I can take care of myself," Vic said.

"I'm sure you believe that," he said with an almost imperceptible smile. "But things change fast here. You never know what will happen."

"I'm fine."

"For now," he said, looking at Nathaniel. "But I recommend you be on your way back wherever you came from when the sun comes up."

"Max told me I was welcome to stay in the castle."

"Max lied."

He turned his back to her and strode out the door.

Vic exhaled as she looked to Nathaniel, struck by the memory of finding him frightening only days ago. Compared to the behemoth, Nathaniel was almost comforting.

Nathaniel's lip slipped into a sneer before he followed the other man's path out of the room.

Vic stood rooted to the spot for the time it took her to draw two gasping breaths. Then she spun on her heel and ran.

This time, when Vic pulled open the door to the apartment, she fell forward into the living room and slammed the door behind her.

VI

We who have no gods know alone the secrets of man.

As an initiate of the Acheron Order, I pledge fealty to the ancient tradition. I give my life to the maintenance of Balance, to the keeping of the worlds apart.

I will guard the Order's secrets. I will adhere to her rules. I will not expose myself or my compatriots to the human world. I will respect her Elders, and I will obey their commands.

I understand the penalty for disregarding these strictures is death, and should I break my oaths I will embrace my demise as the necessity that it will be.

—From the Acheron Order's Rites of Initiation
(as recorded by E. Benjamin Thomas, 1867)

"It is precisely this ability to understand that separates the worthy from the *undeserving*."

It was afternoon the next day, and Vic's first encounter with the occult was off to a tedious start.

The class of recruits had gathered in a lecture hall about twenty feet underground. Four rows of rounded tables rippled out from a lectern at the center, occupied by an angular, angry-looking man of about seventy whose eyes kept drifting to Vic as he spoke.

He had introduced himself in a droning voice as Elder Thompson before proceeding headlong into a lecture on the history of the Acheron Order, which had—Vic checked her watch—been ongoing for seventy-five minutes.

Vic had been late. She'd slipped into the back of the room five minutes after the lecture began, cursing herself for not waking up earlier and cursing her brother for leaving without her. Max had left a note with directions on the kitchen table, which she'd barely seen on her way out of the apartment and which had proved woefully inadequate. The labyrinthine passageways of the castle had done their best to slow her down, and by the time Vic fell into her seat in the gothic lecture hall she was sweating, irritable, and out of breath.

She sat in the back, uncomfortable after her decade-long absence from formal education. Though none of Vic's experiences in the public school system had prepared her for a classroom like this. The ceiling sloped down, as the rest of the room did, toward the Elder, who stood behind a wooden pulpit that must have weighed a thousand pounds. The exposed stone walls had no windows, only sconces that flickered with candlelight and looming oil portraits of important-looking men. Behind the Elder hung four empty blackboards.

Henry had taken a seat in the front row, and Vic watched his blond head bobble as he nodded along to Elder Thompson's lecture while taking vigorous notes. He had a stack of books beside him, and Vic wondered where he'd found them.

The room was half full with several dozen other recruits, all of whom threw looks back at Vic every few minutes. Their expressions ranged from curious to outright hostile, and Vic had no idea how they knew she was different from them. But they knew.

Vic hardly noticed the attention, distracted as she was by something much stranger.

Posted like guards along the back wall were three hooded figures standing ramrod straight, obscured by lengths of black cloth that wrapped around their heads and draped down their bodies, belted in place with gleaming metal bands around their waists and necks. The hoods ended lengthwise below their noses, preventing them from looking anywhere but the ground. In gloved hands they held silver trays piled with leather-bound books. The trays must have been heavy, but the figures stood perfectly still.

"It is the belief of the Acheron Order that witches are the descendants of those who first developed the ability to hear and use the Universal Language, that energy that radiates through all matter, living and dead. . . ."

Vic barely heard the Elder over her curiosity about the robed figures. What were they doing here? Why were their faces covered? And why was no one else looking at them?

"Calling it a language is something of a misnomer. Though it is spoken aloud, heard, and repeated, it possesses no vocabulary, no syntax. There is no way to teach the Universal Language to someone who was not born, as we were, with the ability to understand it. . . ."

The door closest to Vic opened, and a figure slipped through. Vic kept her eyes on the Elder and wished she'd brought something to take notes with. The thought hadn't even occurred to her.

"Thus, it is more akin to an additional sense. Like the ability to see and hear, the Universal Language is innate in all our kind, as natural to us as breathing. Spells and ritual and all that you learn here will merely enable you to manipulate this energy, this language of the natural world, and to do so with control and ease. . . ."

Someone slid into the space beside Vic, though there were ample empty seats throughout the room and plenty in the back row.

"Psst," the woman whispered, and Vic turned. She noticed her eyes first. Deep brown, the color of clay soil, they reminded Vic of childhood afternoons spent playing in the heat. "Are you Vic?"

Vic nodded, wondering how she knew her name. "And you are?" Vic whispered.

"Late as hell," the woman replied. She flattened the wrinkled front of her red sweater, though the wool crumpled again as soon as she released it. "Has he given instructions for the practical portion yet?"

Practical portion? Vic wondered. She had assumed the classes would be like this, lectures, not that they would actually be expected to practice.

Vic shook her head, and the woman slumped with relief.

The Elder's tone grew serious. "As you proceed with your training, all of you should keep in mind the danger of overestimating yourself. You are born with these abilities, yes, but you were not born with the tools to master them." His gaze landed on Vic and the woman beside her. "Each of you has a limit. Learn it, and you have a chance."

Vic swallowed.

"Now," the Elder began. He straightened his papers. "Almost all of you," he said, with a lingering look back at Vic and her strange seat-mate, "are recruits in Level One of your training. As such, you're still focusing on the transport and structure of inanimate objects."

The woman beside Vic groaned.

"Your task today involves the invocation of the Universal Language with the goal of dissolution. Materials will be provided in the training room. Please pick up a spell book from the trays at the back on your way out."

He meant the trays the people were holding, Vic thought as the room filled with the shuffling sounds of the recruits packing their things. Vic followed the woman beside her when she stood, and they walked with the rest of the class toward the exit.

She stood on tiptoe to find Henry, who remained stuck behind the throng, but she could only make out a mop of blond curls near the back. Mumbling under his breath, a passing student knocked his shoulder against Vic's, and she stumbled.

"Hey!" Vic exclaimed. She caught herself and spun toward him.

"You're in the way," the man grumbled.

More surprised than angry, Vic stared at his retreating back. The woman beside Vic was watching her closely, and she nodded toward the door when she caught Vic's eye.

Vic followed her into the hallway, frowning at the strange looks she received from the other students.

"You didn't tell me your name," Vic pointed out as they proceeded down the windowless hall. Symbols scoured the length of the walls like claw marks. Some were elaborate, set in circles as wide as an arm's length, while others were small and rudimentary, as if someone had hacked at the stone with a knife.

"Sarah," the woman said, throwing a smile over her shoulder. "We're going in here."

They'd stopped at a door labeled with a bronze 1. Inside was clearly a practice room, with a high, beamed ceiling and scuff, char, and chip marks covering the stone floor. The space was open and empty, save a dozen or so small tables littered throughout, each occupied by a wicker basket full of . . . rocks?

The students, as if accustomed to the routine, split into groups of two and sat around the tables. Henry paired up with a tall, dark-haired boy and sat near the front with an apologetic look at Vic. She suppressed the sting of Henry leaving her to her own devices and reminded herself that she was glad he had always been good at making new friends.

Sarah gestured for Vic to follow as she took a seat in the back.

"Okay," Sarah said to herself as she opened a spell book in front of her, "let's see if I remember how to do this."

Vic opened her own book and stared, dumbfounded, at the writing within it.

"This is not English," she said. As a matter of fact, it didn't look like language at all. It was a mess of hatch marks and symbols unconfined by lines or paragraph structure.

"The Universal Language," Sarah said as Vic looked at her book upside down, "and that won't help."

"The Elder made it sound more like a concept than a real language," Vic said, dropping the book back on the table.

"It's a bit of both," Sarah said. "Written out, it's like an expression of something otherwise ill defined. Like an instinct. It's hard to write—pretty much only the Elders and the Mages can actually write a spell book."

Around her, recruits began to make strange noises. Staring at their spell books with brows furrowed, they read aloud in a language Vic had never heard before.

"How do they all know it?" Vic asked. She squinted toward Henry to see if he was speaking in the strange tongue, too, but another recruit blocked her view.

"It's actually the first test," Sarah said. "They give you a few pages of a simple book, and you're not allowed to come to lessons until you decipher it."

"Huh," Vic said. "I'm glad I skipped that day." Otherwise, she thought, she'd be sitting in the apartment all afternoon, staring at scribbles.

A booming crack came from beside them, and Vic's hands flew in front of her face on instinct as a small cloud of dust consumed the two recruits at the nearest table.

"Show-off," Sarah muttered, still staring at the page in front of her.

"Was that supposed to happen?" Vic whispered. As the dust cloud cleared, Vic saw that one of the recruits' egg-sized rocks lay shattered on the table. The recruit, a young blond woman, beamed at the brown-haired girl beside her, who wore a sour expression.

"'Transport and structure of inanimate objects,'" Sarah said, repeating Elder Thompson's earlier description of Level One in a mocking soprano. "You're supposed to destroy it."

"That's the first level, then. Destroying rocks?"

Sarah laughed. "That's like step one of Level One. Next week we'll have to chuck them across the room."

"Are all the levels rocks-based?"

Sarah shot Vic a look. "Of course not."

Vic really wished Max had left her more helpful instructions.

Two of the shrouded figures hurried over to the table to clean up the debris.

"Who are they?" Vic whispered.

"Servants," Sarah replied, almost spitting the word. "Non-magic humans employed by the Order."

"And that's their uniform?" Vic asked, eyeing the bottom half of the hooded woman's face, the only part of her skin Vic could see.

"For secrecy, they say. So the servants can only see what's right in front of them, what needs cleaning. But really I'd guess it's more of an exercise in humiliation. Reminds them of their place."

Vic made a disgusted face.

"Unfortunately, you will get used to it," Sarah muttered.

The servant closest to Vic finished clearing the shattered rock and bustled to a nearby table when a crashing sound signaled another recruit's success.

"They got the shrouds reduced for the summer months a few years back," Sarah went on. "More breathable fabric, you understand. That's what amounts to social progress in the Order, I guess." Sarah didn't bother to keep her voice down, and a few of the surrounding recruits glared at her.

"Are they the only non-magic humans in the castle?" Vic asked, and she felt a pit in her stomach at the thought.

Sarah looked at Vic and raised her eyebrows. "Not anymore."

Comforting.

The recruits at the table nearest them were watching Vic and Sarah. Both women were white and thin and looked to be about twenty, and both wore identical expressions of high-minded offense.

"Do you mind?" the blond one asked. "We're trying to concentrate."

But the brown-haired girl was watching Vic with a curious expression, like she'd finally been given permission to stare.

"If you can't concentrate with me talking, you'll never make it—" Sarah said, but the brown-haired recruit interrupted her.

"What are you doing here?" she asked Vic in a haughty voice, and Vic felt her hackles rise. She cast a look at Sarah, who was frowning at the recruit.

"Right now I'm watching y'all break rocks," Vic replied.

"No, what are you doing *here?*" she repeated, slow and emphatic like Vic was hard of hearing. Or an idiot.

"Are you stupid?" Sarah asked. "She's watching you guys break rocks."

Vic huffed a laugh at the shocked indignation on the two recruits' faces.

"Ignore them," Sarah said to Vic. "Dipshit and Pipshit over here are just surprised by the new animal in their enclosure."

"Lily and Claire," the blond one corrected, like Sarah's failure to refer to them properly was the insulting part of her statement.

"I wouldn't bother learning their names," Sarah said, still addressing Vic. "A lot of the recruits don't make it past Level Four."

"Why is that?" Vic asked, ignoring the other two.

"Eh, it's the first time in training you have to go from the concrete to the abstract. Instead of using spells other people have written, you have to think of your own. Some just can't hack it."

"But I thought all witches had to be trained. That they're dangerous if they can't control themselves." Vic remembered Nathaniel's threat, that if Henry endangered the Order they would put him down like a rabid dog.

"Sounds like fearmongering to me," Sarah said, shrewd eyes on Vic. "You really only need to know the basics to not be dangerous."

So Nathaniel had lied. Vic had *known* he was slimy. She leaned forward as another suspicion occurred to her.

"What about these kinds of markings?" Vic asked, pointing at the unreadable writing in the spell book Sarah held. "Would you ever cut them into your skin? What would that do?"

Sarah looked confused, but answered, "Some witches will mark themselves with a spell if they want to draw on it quickly. Most use ink or charcoal, but some believe blood makes the spell more potent."

"Do you?"

Sarah gave a half-hearted shrug. "It wouldn't work for me anyway, but I guess I can understand the reasoning."

"Miss Garza," came a stern voice from behind them, and Sarah swore under her breath. Elder Thompson glared down at Sarah, his mouth a thin, disapproving line. "Do I need to remind you why you're here?"

The two recruits next to them turned back to their spell books, looking smug.

"I am being punished," Sarah replied.

"You are undergoing remedial classes, Miss Garza, because of your failure to perform in the field."

"It's punishment," she said to Vic. "Cruel and unusual, if you ask me."

"It's mandatory," the old man corrected. "The Chief Sentinel believes you would benefit from a reminder as to the basics of your training."

"I mouthed off," Sarah told Vic. "And I'm stuck here until Xan stops feeling sadistic."

"Miss Garza!" the Elder snapped. "If you are so confident about your abilities, I welcome you to demonstrate." With a wrinkled hand, he gestured to the basket in front of her.

"Do I have to do it with the book?" Sarah asked.

"Yes."

"Suit yourself," Sarah said, sounding resigned.

She stared at the basket of stones, frowning as she concentrated. She held the spell book aloft in one palm, and her eyes flashed to it before returning to the rocks. When she spoke, her voice fell into the strange language, low and lilting and hardly human.

Vic jumped out of her seat when the entire basket went off like a bomb. She coughed against a cloud of misted stone and waved it away from her face. As the scene cleared, Vic stared, agog, at the two-foot-wide hole Sarah had blown through the table.

The entire room went quiet as all the recruits turned to stare at Sarah and, by extension, Vic.

Sarah leaned back in her chair and smiled up at Elder Thompson, who looked furious.

"This is precisely the problem with you Mades," he hissed. "You have no control. You have no appreciation for the art."

Two shrouded servants hurried to the Elder's side to clean up the mess of wood and rock shavings.

"No," he snapped at the pair of them. "Let her do it herself."

Vic thought one of the servants was laughing under her breath.

Though she couldn't be sure, she caught a hint of a repressed smile as they stepped back. Sarah was still beaming at Elder Thompson, though the grin didn't reach her eyes.

"Clean this up," he demanded, and turned to address Vic. "And you . . . you should be wearing a shroud like the rest of them." A wizened finger pointed toward the servants, and Vic felt the muscles in her back tense, preparing her to fight.

"Don't speak to my sister that way," Henry said, on his feet. "Elder Shepherd said she's allowed to be here."

Thompson made a frustrated sound, his hand curling into a fist at his side.

"My tolerance for Shepherd's eccentricity," he replied in a choked voice, "grows thin."

He turned on his heel and swept out of the room.

Vic felt the eyes of the recruits on her back. *Thank you,* she mouthed to Henry, who nodded, looking dazed, and turned away.

"The wise old Elder Thompson," Sarah said, no longer smiling. "Cheery, isn't he?"

Vic sat back down as the female servant she'd caught laughing approached with a brush and a dustpan. This close, Vic realized the veil over her face was slightly sheer, and she caught the woman's eye. She was pretty and young, and Vic had no idea how she had ended up here, with her eyes covered so she could see little more than the floor.

The woman winked. Then she turned and left.

The rest of the recruits returned to their work, their voices carrying on hushed conversations about what had just happened. Henry was grinning at his tablemate, looking sheepish.

Vic and Sarah cleaned up the mess as best they could. With no Elder to supervise, the recruits' voices grew louder and louder, until the room spoke in a dull roar.

"How did you do that?" Vic asked Sarah, eyeing the hole in the table.

"Magic, my friend," Sarah said, eyes wide in mock theatrics. "You should try it."

"I can't."

"Come on, give it a shot." She walked over to the table beside them, with its still-intact basket of stones, and plucked one the size of her fist. Lily/Claire shot her an offended look but said nothing. Evidently, Sarah's demonstration had spooked them out of talking back to her again.

"You're not a recruit, I gather," Vic said.

"Nope," Sarah said. "Graduated from the Order's academy three years ago. I'm a Sentinel."

"You're being punished," Vic said, "with lessons."

"Xan's an asshole," Sarah said. "Sometimes I point this out. He doesn't always take it well."

Vic didn't know who Xan was, but she smiled.

Sarah plopped the rock on the edge of the table in front of Vic. "Try it."

"I literally can't," Vic said. She gestured to herself. "No magic."

"I know that," Sarah said. "Try it anyway."

"How?" Vic asked. She couldn't read the spell book, and she couldn't remember the sounds Sarah had made well enough to repeat them.

"The first witches learned the Universal Language by paying attention to the world around them. It's supposed to be a naturally derived way of communicating the connections between states of matter."

Vic frowned. "You lost me."

"Focus on the stone. Think about how it's formed. What its component parts look like, what the structure is on an atomic level. Stones are the easiest for beginner witches to work with, because they're simple."

Vic leaned forward until her eyes were almost level with the table. She stared at the stone, imagining its parts like Sarah had suggested. It just sat there, staring back at her.

"It's not working," Vic said, feeling stupid.

Sarah made a noncommittal *hmm.*

"What did the Elder call you?" Vic asked.

"Made," Sarah said, and she spread her arms wide like she meant to bow. "I wasn't born a witch like your brother and everyone else in this room. I was Made one."

Vic shook her head, confused.

"It's a different kind of magic," Sarah said. "Born witches commune with the natural world through spells and rituals." She tapped the spell book in front of her. "I don't need any of that."

Before Vic could ask how Sarah knew her brother, or how a witch could be Made, or any of a dozen other questions rattling through her mind, a heavy chime sounded throughout the room, and the students began to stand.

"School's out," Sarah announced as she stood and stretched and headed for the door. After a few steps, Sarah stopped. "Actually." She turned to Vic with a wicked smile, and Vic could almost see an idea forming behind Sarah's eyes. "Come with me."

"I think I'm afraid to," Vic said.

Sarah laughed and sauntered toward the back exit.

Vic cast a look around for her brother. She watched Henry disappear into the hall with the other students. Though many of them looked at Vic as she stood, no one spoke to her, and they filtered out in quick succession, until Vic stood alone in the back of the classroom. She looked at the rock on the table in front of her, frowning, and hurried after Sarah.

VII

As the soldiers of the Order, Sentinels must display extreme command over both magical and non-magical forms of combat. Of the initiates who attempt the Sentinel Exam, only a fraction succeed. The leader of the Sentinels is selected by the Elders, and the Chief Sentinel must be the most capable of the offerings. To further this goal, the Chief Sentinel is reevaluated by the Elders each year, and a new Chief Sentinel will be appointed should any of the Sentinels advance beyond the capabilities of the current leader. Like the Elders, the Chief Sentinel will be deposed should a worthy challenger arise.

—William Ruskin, *A History of the Acheron Order*
(New York, 1935)

"How did you know I'm not a witch?" Vic asked when she caught up to Sarah. They followed a narrow hallway down a flight of stairs.

"The same way I knew your name, and your brother's name, and that you would be in class today confusing the hell out of the other recruits," Sarah said.

"Max told you," Vic guessed.

"Max *warned* me. Right after he ordered all the members and recruits not to hurt you," Sarah said.

"I'm sorry—did they want to?"

"The Order's not used to humans in our business, so he wanted to make sure no one got any ideas."

"Why?" Vic demanded, stuck on the revelation that her presence was so disruptive as to cause violence.

But Sarah wasn't listening. "Did you know the Order had an outright ban on Made witches until about thirty years ago? And women and minorities weren't admitted in any significant numbers until the eighties, and all the Elders are still old white men. Max is the only Made on the Council, and they fought his admission tooth and nail even though he's by far the most powerful among them."

"The recruits looked at me like I had two heads," Vic said.

Sarah scoffed. "The recruits don't know anything."

"So the older members will be more accepting?"

Sarah made a sound halfway between a laugh and a snort. "Fat chance," she said. "Did Max tell you anything about Orcans?"

"About 'organs'?" Vic asked.

"Of course he didn't. I swear, for a genius that man is remarkably forgetful." Sarah looked sideways at Vic. "Orcans are beasts from the Other World. Monsters, creatures of myth and legend, creepy-crawlies, whatever you want to call them."

"'Whatever I want to call them,'" Vic repeated. She wanted to call them nonexistent, but she'd given up on that years ago.

"We hunt them."

"I've heard about this part," Vic said. She remembered the filthy man's words from the night before—before he realized Vic was listening. *I can keep putting them down easy enough.* She recalled the blood dripping from his weapon as he unsheathed it and wondered what, or who, he had been putting down.

"Turn right," Sarah said, and she led Vic down another staircase. Vic realized with a jolt that they had reached the octagonal supply room where she'd been caught last night.

"This is the load-out room," Sarah said. "It's basically your standard mudroom, with a touch of added violence." Sarah gestured vaguely at a rack of weapons with a contrite look on her face. "The Elders don't like us tracking who-knows-what through the front entrance, so we come in the side and drop our gear here."

Vic stopped to examine the weaponry. Torches hung at eye level gave a flickering quality to the light, which danced in the rough metal of the more medieval weapons.

She noted the absence of the blood and muck she'd seen last night and grimaced at the thought of the shrouded servants having to clean this place.

"Why do you need so many types of weapons?" Vic asked.

"Not everything dies the same way."

Vic picked up a dagger and twisted it in the air. It was about the length of her forearm, gleaming metal with a hard rubber handle. She imagined using it against some faceless monster, the blood of something inhuman coating her fingers.

"Your mother was Meredith Wood?" Sarah asked.

The question took Vic by surprise, and she replied, "Yes," with more ice than intended.

But Sarah still looked pensive. "Your mother was a Sentinel, once upon a time. You really didn't know any of this?" Sarah looked at the weapons behind Vic, the dagger in her palm.

"No," Vic lied, replacing the blade in its sheath. She didn't want to share the complexities of her half knowledge about her mother's life. Vic couldn't very well say that she knew only what her mother had seen fit to tell ten-year-old Henry. That Vic knew only enough to be afraid.

Even before Henry's revelation, Vic had picked up enough hints to assume that something strange surrounded her mother. Vic had known from a young age that having a gun and learning how to shoot it would never suffice to keep her safe. The same way she had known not to call the cops when her mom disappeared, and, after she'd been missing for a few days, that Meredith was dead.

Vic thought of the sound she heard the day she disobeyed Meredith. The wet slap of monstrous feet, the way the air curled around the noise. Hadn't Vic known, even then, that something other than a person approached around the corner?

When she'd seen the shadow racing toward the castle last night, her first thought hadn't been surprise. She'd known what it was. She'd known it was something new.

A monster.

"Well, you seem to be taking it in stride." With a last quizzical look at Vic, Sarah strode to the opposite door, through which the giant and Nathaniel had left the night before.

Vic stuffed the dagger into the back of her jeans and jogged to catch up.

"This is the main hallway of the training wing," Sarah was saying as Vic pulled her clothing over the pilfered knife. "And technically Xan's domain." Sarah threw her another roguish look. "He is not going to like me bringing someone new around, I'll tell you that."

"The sadist?" Vic asked, raising an eyebrow.

"The very same," Sarah said with a grin.

"Are you trying to get in more trouble?" Vic asked.

"I'm trying to teach him to lighten up."

"It doesn't seem to be working," Vic pointed out.

Sarah shrugged. "The training wing is actually the largest in the castle, though most of the connecting corridors are underground."

Like the hallway housing their earlier classroom, this one was adorned with elaborate inscriptions on the walls, the stone marred by symbols.

"Recruits work their way down this hallway," Sarah said, pointing to the door labeled with a bronze 8. "Once they've mastered Level Eight, they can apply for full membership in the Order."

Vic noticed a ninth door at the end of the hallway on the left. "How about that one?"

"That's the lift," Sarah said, her tone suddenly stern. "It goes straight down to the cages. You don't want to go in there—it's as good as a death sentence."

Vic pulled back at Sarah's intensity, as if the door would reach out and grab her. It was more heavily inscribed than the other eight, and Vic had the strangest sense that the words were intended to keep her away. An instinct, deep in the back of her brain, warned her to steer clear of those markings. She watched the door out of the corner of her eye as they approached.

"When you're finished with training, you become a Sentinel?" Vic asked.

"Only the dedicated fighters become Sentinels," Sarah said. "There are other positions for those who want to work for the Order. But most members go back to their regular lives afterward."

Vic pictured scores of witches reentering society, newly armed with the ability to wield magic. It lightened her spirits to know that Henry could go through all of this and still have a normal life. She found herself wondering how many witches were out there, masquerading as normal people. She wondered how the power they cultivated here—to destroy, build, manipulate, and who knew what else—got used in the real world.

"How long does training take?"

"It depends. Not all the levels are the same difficulty. Level One, for instance, is relatively simple, and usually only takes a few weeks. People get stuck on the later levels."

Vic nodded along as her eyes caught on two massive wooden doors ahead. Like the doors to the entrance hall, they loomed tall and important.

"Most people take a few years," Sarah said. "It took me four."

Vic's mouth fell open at the thought of four years in this hallway.

"But the record is eight months. That was our Chief Sentinel—he's insane."

Vic was forming a picture of the man Sarah described. She imagined someone middle-aged, trim, and proper, like Max without the whimsy. Overcontrolled, a little ruthless, a drill-sergeant type. Vic couldn't say she was eager to meet him.

Sarah laughed to herself, her eyes dancing with mischief. "He is gonna *hate* this."

Vic didn't know what Sarah meant, but she was distracted from asking when Sarah approached the two stately doors at the hall's end. Her throat felt tight as Sarah placed a palm in the center of one of the massive panels.

The door inched forward with a slow creep, and Vic took a step back.

"Now, this," Sarah announced with a wily grin, "is the Arena."

The gloom was overwhelming. The only light in the massive room came from high windows lining the walls. Though the space might have been well lit on a sunny day, clouds covered the sun and gave the room a muted, shadowy appearance. Symbols similar to those in the hallway covered the walls, deep gouges cut into the stone.

"Only Sentinels and Level Eight recruits are allowed to use the Arena," Sarah said in a low voice.

Vic didn't immediately register why Sarah would call this room an arena. At first glance she spotted only the spanning windows and vaulted ceilings.

Until she looked down—and started back in alarm.

The floor in front of her fell away to a gaping chasm. Beneath her—forty, fifty feet into the ground—lay a sunken circle lined with arched doorways, reminding Vic of the Colosseum, of ancient fighting pits and forced combat. She half expected gladiators to emerge from the narrow gaps in the stone wall, like she'd been swept backward in time to a place more vicious, more primitive.

After a few calming breaths, Vic noticed the stone seating running along the walls of the chasm, and the elevated platform set closest to the edge. It was an amphitheater, hidden under the ground. Fifteen or so witches lingered near the pit's perimeter, chatting idly and uninterested in their surroundings.

Sarah led her to a staircase near the door, and Vic had to pull her eyes from the drop as she climbed down. The stairs had no railing.

Once they reached the base, they stood unnoticed on a platform slightly off the pit floor, which was earthen. Heavy, compacted soil lent the room the heady smell of wild nature.

The witches gathered at the edge of the pit broke apart as a man strode forward.

Vic recognized him immediately.

"Too many of you rely on magic when you could easily do without, and you seem to have forgotten the basics of physical fighting," the man from the night before announced as he turned to face the witches. The energy of the room rearranged as Vic watched him, his hands behind his back and his broad chest forward. "The time may come when you have to fight men, not Orcans, and you need to be prepared."

The crowd grumbled a complaint, and the behemoth pointed a stern finger at them.

"That's exactly what I'm talking about. This is supposed to be the easy part. You've gotten lazy."

Vic couldn't drag her eyes from him. He wore an ensemble of black, which Vic would have guessed was a uniform if the others weren't wearing different outfits. Shoulder-length brown hair was tied back from his face, though more than a few strands hung loose around his ears.

She felt a jolt of vindication that she hadn't exaggerated his size in her memory. But she hadn't expected his appeal. Without all the shit on his face, he was breathtaking. She wanted to call him handsome, though the word didn't quite fit. If he were a sculpture, Vic decided, he would have been carved quickly, harsh lines cut from stone in a fit of rage. Everything about him projected strength—hard brow, thick nose, heavy jaw, muscles bulging at his chest, his shoulders, his thighs.

Vic leaned toward Sarah and hissed, "Who is *that*?"

"Alexandros Galanis," Sarah replied in a masculine bass. "Xan, the Chief Sentinel. He's training Squads One and Two."

So this was the famous Chief Sentinel, who had completed training in record time and who had caught Vic snooping last night. Not an anal-retentive old man but a thirtysomething weapon of war. And Sarah had brought her here to piss him off on purpose.

Vic was in so much trouble.

"Matthews," Xan called. "You and I will start."

A young man with a blond buzz cut stepped out of the group. Vic eyed the breadth of Xan's shoulders with a flash of sympathy for the newcomer, alongside a furious curiosity. She wanted to watch Xan fight, wanted to see if he was as powerful as he looked.

Vic leaned forward.

"We're going to run this quickly, as an exercise," Xan explained.

Now, this made Vic more comfortable than anything else in the castle had. Sparring Vic could work with. The push and pull of flesh across muscle and bone cut the refined edges away from modern society and left only the human drive behind—*survive, keep fighting, try harder.* As Vic watched the men brace themselves, the rows of stone seating and arching windows fell away. These were not witches, this was not a castle, Vic was in no more trouble than usual. She was here to learn, to watch people practicing something she knew better than the inside of her own mind.

One second they stood paces away from each other, arms cocked in fighting stance. The next, the smaller man threw himself forward. Vic heard the smack of flesh as they collided. She cringed when Matthews's fist crashed against Xan's jaw. Hits to the face were rare in disciplined fights. Xan rocked to the side, narrowly avoiding another impact, keeping his hands in a protective posture and swaying to avoid the other man's attacks.

Matthews went for his side in an attempt to get Xan to pull his arms away from his body. Vic would have suggested waiting for Xan to take the offensive, maybe draw him out with more restrained attacks, because there was no way he would fall for such an obvious maneuver. Sure enough, Xan swung an elbow up when Matthews came too close, and Matthews barely pulled his face out of its path. He stumbled, and Xan swayed to the side to knock Matthews further off balance. In an instant, Xan had the smaller man on the ground, one forearm pressed tight across Matthews's chest. Thick cords of muscle, visible through his clothing, tensed in Xan's back and thighs, and Vic's mouth went dry. She marveled at the physicality of it, trying to pretend her interest was purely academic. He was an excellent fighter, the best she'd ever seen. Xan moved faster than he should have been able to, given his size, and each movement demonstrated a complete control of his body. That was why she felt a pit of intrigue in her stomach, Vic told herself. Pure professional awe.

Though he had size on his side, Xan hadn't used it. He hadn't needed to. Vic knew he'd worked incredibly hard to master his craft, and she found herself wishing she could fight him, just once, to see what it would be like. To tangle with someone that skilled, that strong, would be like kissing lightning. Vic would lose, obviously, but it would be fantastic fun.

"Are you okay?" Sarah whispered beside her. "You're flushed."

"What? Yeah, I'm fine."

"Uh-huh," Sarah said, watching Vic with curious suspicion.

Vic shook her head to clear the spell and looked to the other man on the floor.

Matthews smiled good-naturedly as Xan pulled him up, but there was wounded pride on his face, too. Vic knew that look; she'd worn it a thousand times.

"We'll run it again," Xan said. He wasn't even out of breath. "Lin!"

Another witch stepped forward, this time a striking woman with hair so black it was almost blue. She slunk from the crowd with all the grace of a jungle cat about to devour something. Her long ponytail swung back and forth as she walked to the front of the practice area—the cat's tail whipping as it waited to pounce.

"May Lin," Sarah whispered, while her gaze tracked the woman's approach. "Second leader for Squad One."

"Lin will take my place this time," Xan announced. "I want you all to watch how defensive moves change with the size of your opponent."

May Lin faced Matthews with an anticipatory smile. The man winced, which confused Vic. Matthews was considerably larger than May. Though she was tall, she was svelte and couldn't muster as much force as a two-hundred-pound man. Size never guaranteed the advantage, but it made things easier.

"Remember: We're working the basics today," Xan said. "No magic."

Matthews relaxed. He must have been frightened of May's magic, then. Vic wanted to know why. She leaned in closer, gripping the railing.

Again, the fight began without fanfare, though Matthews chose the defensive posture this time, and May leaped forward to meet him. They sparred for longer than Matthews had with Xan, neither of them breaking the protective barrier of arm's length for longer than it took to land a single swift blow. May got Matthews in the ribs once, and they met in the middle, finally close enough for things to get interesting. May swung at his face, but he darted out of the way, and she lost her balance. Then Matthews had his hand across May's shoulders. He pinned her to the earth the same way Xan had pinned him, and cheers broke out.

Xan approached as Matthews pulled May to her feet.

"Now, what did Lin do wrong?" Xan asked the group.

No one answered for a second, then two, then Vic couldn't help herself.

"She tried to counter his momentum, instead of working with it," Vic called. "He's got fifty pounds on her—she doesn't have the power. When he went forward, she should have swung to the side, used his weight against him."

Every head in the room swiveled toward Vic. Xan turned, and his ice-blue eyes locked on to hers. Vic felt her face heat. No one said a word, and Vic worried they could hear her heart racing in the cavernous space.

When no one responded, Vic filled the silence. "Matthews had thrown his weight forward. If she'd shifted to the side, she could have used his own force to push him down." Vic mimed the movements with her body as she spoke, aware that everyone was watching her and no one was speaking. Vic's voice fell away when she noticed the giant approaching them.

Xan crossed the room at an unhurried pace, his eyes pinned on Vic. The silence, broken only by footfalls on dirt, grew heavy, and Vic fought the urge to keep talking. To fill it somehow. Thirty feet crossed in a few seconds, and Xan was at the edge of the pit in front of Vic and Sarah. Vic stared down at him in horror as he wrapped a massive hand around the railing. He couldn't possibly plan to come up here. They were five feet off the ground.

Vic took a step back as he did, indeed, pull himself up to the platform with unnerving ease. He crowded the space as he stared down at her, and her skin prickled with awareness.

"Garza," Xan growled without looking at Sarah. "What is she doing here?"

"I'm showing her around the training area," Sarah replied with deceptive calm.

"You do recall that the Arena is a restricted-access area, do you not?"

He watched Vic as he spoke, as if he needed to keep an eye on her lest she attack. Vic almost laughed at the prospect of causing this man serious trouble in that regard. She was good, but she wasn't that good.

"You said this morning that Vic *couldn't* be a recruit, since she's human," Sarah said. "I assumed you meant different rules apply."

Xan shot Sarah an unimpressed frown, and Vic's gaze slid to the watching crowd, which had shifted ever so slightly closer to the confrontation. May Lin wore a livid expression as she stared at Vic and Sarah.

"Oh, 'Vic,' is it?" Xan said, returning his ire to Vic. Something like anxiety ran up Vic's spine. "You said Victoria last night."

Here was a man accustomed to intimidating people. Vic assumed most people cowered when he looked at them this way, both because of his stature and because of the general aura of threat surrounding him. It rankled her.

"Vic is a fairly obvious abbreviation of my given name," she said.

"And are you enjoying your tour of the training area, Vic? I would have thought you got a decent enough understanding of things sneaking around last night."

"I wasn't sneaking."

"What would you call it? Hiding in the shadows, eavesdropping on private conversations."

"Listen, asshole," Vic said, and someone below her gasped. "What the hell is your problem?"

"My problem," he said, drawing closer and sticking a finger in her face. Vic fought the urge to step back. Or bite it. "Is that you're in my Arena. And before that you were in my load-out room. You're in my castle, which makes you my responsibility. And I don't like liabilities." Each word came out staccato and bracing.

Xan turned to Sarah without giving Vic a chance to respond. "Get her out of here," he demanded, before jumping over the railing and landing silently on the dirt floor.

As he strode back to the group, another voice spoke.

"No."

May Lin had a deep voice, and it hung in the air like a command.

"No?" Xan asked, his voice so low it sent a skitter up Vic's spine.

"No," May repeated. "She wants to be here. Let her try."

The witches shifted behind May. A few muttered sounds between concern and intrigue.

"No way," Sarah said. "May, be serious. She's not a Sentinel."

"She wants to be here, doesn't she?" Turning to Vic, May said, "You want to see how the other half lives?"

Her eyes—a brown darker and deeper than Sarah's—looked mean from this distance. If May assumed she could frighten Vic away, she had miscalculated.

"You want to play. Don't you, Vic?"

Fuck you. "Fine," Vic said.

"No, Vic. You're not trained. You could get—"

"I'm fine, Sarah." Vic patted her hand where it grasped the railing, and the frown on May's face deepened.

Vic crouched under the metal rail and leaped into the pit. Her feet hit the compacted earth and she stood, brushing dust from the tops of her thighs.

"Xan, I was only playing with you when I brought her here," Sarah said. "You can't actually let her do this." But the man in question was watching Vic closely. Assessing her, Vic knew. Judging her, like everyone else here. She set her jaw.

"Lin's right, Garza," he said, gaze stuck on Vic. "She wants to be here."

Vic stopped in front of May and worked out the muscles in her hands. Her outfit wasn't ideal for fighting, but at least she had sneakers on. And her jeans were loose enough that mobility wouldn't be a serious issue. The knife she'd stolen was secure against her back and didn't move when she did. Vic could handle this, she knew. She'd seen May fight already. She had the advantage.

Xan watched her with a vague expression, as if waiting for her to balk. She narrowed her eyes at him before rolling out her shoulders and turning to her opponent.

"Go ahead and call it," she told Xan over her shoulder. "Ready whenever."

After a moment's pause, Xan said, "Standard sparring rules. No faces. No nails. No permanent damage." He directed all this at May, like she was the one hiding a knife. "And no magic," he added, with emphasis on the final word.

"Yes, sir," May said with a serpentine smile.

"Begin."

May was fast—Vic would give her that. She lunged for Vic's midriff. But Vic was faster. She swung out of the way. Vic landed an elbow between May's shoulder blades, and the witch stumbled. Righting herself, May wore an expression of such shocked indignation that Vic had to smile. This made May, if possible, angrier, and her eyes darted to an unguarded spot near Vic's ribs an instant before May struck. Vic deflected the hit with the outside of her forearm.

"You're confined by your sense of proper moves," Vic observed, twisting out of another grab and circling May. "You're not reacting organically."

When May lunged again, Vic grabbed her hand, twisting to the side and pulling her arm behind her back. May tried to pull away, but Vic wrapped her left arm around May's midriff, trapping her other arm.

"I can see what your boss meant," Vic hissed in her ear, and May snarled. "You're lazy."

Vic let her go with a shove, and they circled again.

"You're not used to fighting things that think, are you?"

"Shut up," May ground out, her eyes flashing to different parts of Vic's body in search of a weakness.

The angrier May got, the less rational her moves became. She got faster but dumber, acting out of blind rage. She wasn't used to fighting things that goaded her, either.

Vic didn't want to push her too far, so this time, when May reached for her, Vic let May get ahold of her arm. Then Vic spun and brought the other woman down, using May's forward momentum against her, and they grappled on the floor until Vic locked her knees around May's hips and pressed her to the ground. With Vic's torso low and her elbows cutting into May's arms, the witch couldn't move.

"See, that's what you should have done to Matthews." Vic smiled, and May's gorgeous face twisted in anger. Her mouth moved in fury, which Vic noticed a second too late was not wordless at all. Sounds came from May's lips in senseless syllables, and Vic pulled back from whatever was about to happen too slowly to stop it.

May spat in Vic's face, and a force like a brick wall sent Vic flying backward. She hit the dirt floor and rolled, her head pounding. Blood poured from her nose. Her eyes teared up, and Vic couldn't see through the wet haze. Warm hands wrapped around Vic's shoulders and pulled her to her feet, and she blinked fast, wiping the blood from her face.

"Are you hurt?" a rough voice asked. Xan's face swam in front of her, eyes bright and concerned, and his hands hovered over her face. But her nose wasn't broken, and Vic didn't have time for this.

"Get away from me." She batted his hands away. "What the fuck was that?" Vic twisted toward May, who was propped on her elbows in the dirt.

Though she'd expected May to look pleased, to flash another cruel smile, her eyes weren't even on Vic. They were watching Sarah, who pushed past Xan.

"Are you okay, Vic? I'm so sor—"

"What the fuck is wrong with you?" Vic angled around Sarah to yell at May. "That was a fair and fucking square fight. Work on your grappling and try harder next time, asshole."

"Enough," Xan said, putting a palm on Vic's shoulder. She smacked it away and rounded on him.

"Oh, now it's 'enough'?" Vic spat, poking the middle of his massive chest and ignoring the hard heat of the muscle under her fingertip. "Where were you and your fucking 'enough' thirty seconds ago?" Behind Xan, a Sentinel took a step back.

"Watch it," Xan warned her, fire dancing in his eyes.

"Oh, yeah, I'm the one out of line here. I forgot. What is wrong with you people?"

"You're the one out of place here," he growled. "That"—he pointed at May—"should have scared the shit out of you."

Vic rolled her eyes, and May—now rising—spoke. "I get why your brother insisted on coming early. Most recruits wait until they finish college, but I understand now. He needed to get away from *you.*"

Was that true? Vic's body went cold, and her hands curled into fists.

"Enough!" Xan bellowed, and he moved to block Vic's view of May. "Sentinels—out! Lin, Garza—I'll see you in my office."

Moving slowly like they didn't want to miss anything, the Sentinels broke apart and left the pit. May stared at Vic with a hateful expression before storming after them.

Vic held Xan's gaze as he considered her, blood and tears staining her face. Adrenaline tore through her veins, fierce and wild. She didn't break eye contact, daring him to say something, daring him to look down on her for being here, for not being like him. She had done well, dammit. She had won the fight before May threw magic in her face. But Xan didn't look judgmental. He looked surprised, and a little sad. Something Vic couldn't name passed between them. Anger, maybe, or admiration. Her skin grew hot.

Xan broke their connection first, turning to follow the Sentinels out of the Arena.

"Don't bring her here again," he ordered Sarah as he walked away.

VIII

Orcans have worn many faces throughout the centuries. They have been described as religious phenomena, as demons, as monsters, as the manifestations of mental dysfunction. Cultures the globe round have sought to explain their presence. Some assume that such creatures must belong to the natural world, hitherto undiscovered species, while many dismiss accounts of their existence entirely. Still others view them as a blight upon the world, accursed entities sent by the heavens to punish those who violate a preordained moral code.

The Acheron Order knows that each of these explanations fails to capture the true nature of these beings. Orcans, as the name implies, originate from Orcus—the land of the dead. They are born of that world and to that world they belong.

When Orcans gain access to Earth, they have devastating effects on human populations. They revel in violence toward humans and seek them out as prey. They are ravenous beasts, endlessly roaming in search of meat and pain. When they happen upon our world, they find abundant sources of both.

—William Ruskin, *A History of the Acheron Order*
(New York, 1935)

V ic opened the door to a rush of cold, stagnant air and knew that Henry had not come back yet. Sarah had invited Vic to join her in the dining hall for dinner, but Vic didn't have an appetite. In the dim cast of the living room fire, Vic saw a stack of books alongside another handwritten note from Max. *Recommended reading,* he wrote. Homework.

Since dropping out of school midway through the tenth grade, Vic had relied on reading. Before, when learning was expected and hours of her day carved out for the task, she had taken the glut of information for granted. But as the distance between her and the classroom widened, Vic took to research as a substitute for formal education. Whenever something new came up that she didn't understand, she stayed up late plugging the gaps. Books became a lifeline, a way to pretend she fit in with everyone around her.

She felt a wave of excitement at the prospect of doing the same within the castle, and she pawed through the stack quickly.

The first two books were heavy and clearly the Order's version of textbooks—*A History of the Acheron Order* by William Ruskin and *Theories on Transmogrification* by Terrance Vern. Like everything else in this castle, the leather-bound books looked older than they were. But the details gave the game away. They had the shape and faded pattern of old books, but new stitching and a rigidity in the spine that only accompanied a fresh printing.

This dissonance gnawed at Vic, and she had the odd sense that everything around her was designed, at least in part, to lie.

The other books in the stack were smaller and thinner. They bore identical leather bindings, with gilded names and dates along their spines. Archives of three separate Elders, from three seemingly random years. Vic wondered how Max had picked them.

Vic went over to the sitting area with the books under her arm and curled into the chair nearest the fire while she waited for her brother to return.

After her misadventure in the Arena, Vic had explored the castle. Sarah caught up after a few hours and told Vic more about the Order, including that most recruits joined after college, as May had said. Henry had, it seemed, come early.

Questions ricocheted in Vic's mind as she tried to focus on the words in front of her. Not one week ago she had lived in fear of this place, these people. She and Henry kept their lives private, unobtrusive, for fear of witches coming to drag him away from her. Vic had lived almost ten years worried that this place was real, and it took Henry one day to abandon all that fear in favor of trust—in their mother, in the Order, in the training process. The speed with which his expectations had changed gave Vic a kind of whiplash. She wasn't sure she knew what to believe anymore.

The door to the apartment clicked open in the near darkness, and Henry jumped when he saw Vic sitting by the fire.

"Vic! You scared— What the hell happened to your face?"

"I got in a fight. It's fine."

"Oh my god." Henry paced the living room. "I can't believe you were fighting already. First with the professor, now someone else? We've been here *one day.*"

Vic waved a dismissive hand at him. He really ought to be used to this by now, given how often Vic came home from the gym bearing evidence of sparring.

"This is so embarrassing," Henry was saying. "I'm trying to make a good impression, and my older sister is picking fights."

"How do you know I picked it?" Vic asked.

Henry sent her a flat look, as if to say that if there was ever a conflict, he could be certain his sister sat at the front of it, egging it on.

"Fair enough," Vic said. "But we need to talk."

Henry raised his eyebrows in a question as he sank onto the far side of the couch.

"Apparently it's not normal for Order members to start training at eighteen," Vic said. "Apparently most wait until they finish college."

Henry frowned.

"But that Elder, Nathaniel, made it sound like you were already behind," Vic said. "It's fishy." Vic eyed her brother, watching for some sign that he already knew this. He pursed his lips in concentration but said nothing. "Did you talk to him at any point, other than when he came to the apartment? Or anyone else from the Order?"

Vic wasn't sure what she was asking. If Henry had conspired behind her back to come early? If Henry knew something he wasn't telling her?

"Of course not," Henry said with an offended look. "That guy scared the shit out of me. You heard him, he made it sound like I had no choice."

Vic deflated with a sigh. "I just wish I understood what was going on."

"What if," Henry began, his mouth tight, "it's something to do with Mom?"

It was Vic's turn to look confused.

"Mom told me that I was destined for something great," Henry said. "You heard her. She said that I was *chosen,* that was the word, that I could do what no one else could."

Vic watched him, frowning. A part of Vic had always believed, implicitly, that her mother was telling the truth. Of course Henry was special—Meredith had treated him that way his whole life. And he really was a wonderful kid: kind and funny and sociable. But another part of Vic wondered how much of it was a mother's blind belief that her son *must be* special. Apart from all the little things Vic loved about Henry, she'd never seen any evidence that he was truly exceptional.

"Maybe," Henry went on, the words slow and careful, "I'm needed here."

"Needed for what?"

Henry shifted on the couch. "I ate with some of the older recruits at dinner tonight," he said. "People who've been in the castle longer than a few weeks."

"And?" Vic prompted when his words trailed off.

"And they seem to think the Order is heading for something bad."

"Bad like what, exactly?"

"Like war."

Unease rippled down Vic's spine. They couldn't stay here if the Order was about to become embroiled in something deeper. Henry couldn't be safe in a world on the brink of war.

"I don't know how much of it to believe," Henry said, affecting lightness. "It's just rumors, so far. Innuendo, nobody knows for sure."

"Henry, if something bad is about to happen, we should leave."

He paused for a long moment. "I don't want to leave."

"But you don't *have* to be here," Vic said. "If Nathaniel lied about the urgency, you can wait a few years. You can come back after you've gone to college, like everybody else."

Henry said nothing.

"Don't you see?" Vic said, rising from her chair. "You can come back later, you can still have a normal life. It's not over."

"I don't want to go back," Henry said.

"Why?" Vic asked, desperate. "You haven't finished high school, you haven't gone to college. You know how hard I worked to make sure you had a chance to do all of that. You know how important it is to me that you graduate."

"To *you*, Vic. It's important to you."

Vic had spent years working to ensure Henry's life could be easier than hers—she took extra shifts so he could stay in sports, she missed sleep to help him study for classes she never took—and he was willing to leave it all behind.

"Bullshit," Vic shot back. "It's important in general. Do you want to be stuck working the kind of jobs that hire high school dropouts for the rest of your life?"

Henry shrugged it off, like real-world concerns couldn't touch those blessed enough to be in the Order.

"Coming here," he said, "it's like skipping the line. The Order controls reality—we can do whatever we want! Order members become presidents, senators, important people."

"Yeah, and I bet they all still went to college."

"I would be wasting my time in school, sitting on my hands in math class. Here, I can actually do something. I have a role to play in all of this, I know I do."

Vic stared at him, stunned and frustrated by the turn their conversation had taken. He was resolute. He spoke with the conviction of a teenage boy already convinced of his place in the world, and no one could persuade him otherwise.

"What am I supposed to do," Vic said, "while you're off playing your role? Where will I be?"

If she didn't belong with her brother, where did she belong?

But Henry just looked at her, a mix of pity and uncertainty in his eyes.

"I need to take a walk," Vic said. She stormed away from him, toward the door to the hallway, though it was nighttime and she'd been warned more than once not to wander the halls after dark.

"Vic, wait—"

But the door slammed shut behind her.

Anger and confusion warred in Vic as she raged through the halls, alongside a sickening feeling of helplessness. How had everything gone wrong so quickly? Her brother meant the world to her, and she could feel him pulling away. She couldn't stomach feeling out of place, or out of the loop, or the anxiety that came with Henry insisting everything was fine.

What *was* she doing in the castle? Vic wondered. Was she really here to keep Henry safe? Or was she looking for something else? Maybe she wanted a role of her own, to have her own desires matter for once.

Vic could hardly think through the haze of fractious energy driving her forward. She didn't know where she was going until she arrived.

She crept into the octagonal supply room and eyed the weapons inside.

Vic had left behind the stolen dagger when she fled the apartment, and she regretted it. Her fingers itched to close around something lethal. She wanted to fight, she *needed* to fight—more than she had in years.

She reached for a short sword and cleaved the air in front of her. Vic held it aloft, watched as the blade balanced perfectly before she swung it again, pretending there was someone in front of her fighting back. She turned on her heel and stabbed forward.

At the fringes of Vic's vision, something moved, and she twisted the blade toward it on instinct. Her mind flashed to the shadow she'd seen the night before, the sentient dark writhing toward the castle, and she readied for a real fight.

But Vic lowered the weapon when she recognized the figure half concealed by the darkness.

The Chief Sentinel leaned against the opposite wall, watching her.

"You scared the shit out of me," Vic said. She put the sword back where she'd found it, ignoring the slight tremor in her fingers.

"You know how to use that." It wasn't a question.

"Yeah." Vic crossed her arms in front of her. She could only make out the shape of him, though his eyes seemed to shine in the darkness like a cat's. Human eyes didn't glow without light, she reminded herself, though his seemed to. Little pinpricks of silver-cerulean amid the shadow.

"Why?" Xan asked, his voice almost a whisper. It rumbled in Vic's chest, and her heart drummed in response.

"I'm not entirely sure," Vic said. Her conversation with Henry had left her feeling wild, untamed, and unafraid of this man who should have terrified her. "I learned how to use a lot of weapons after my mom died."

Vic didn't mention her near-constant fear, the footsteps behind her and the wet slap of something closing in.

"Why suffer so much training if you didn't think you were going to use it?"

She shrugged. "I found it satisfying."

Vic couldn't discern his expression through the darkness, but he watched her for a long moment before replying.

"You look upset," Xan said. Vic bristled at the thought of him taking note of her vulnerability. She felt a flush in her cheeks and knew that he saw it.

"I argued with my brother."

"Is that why you're here?" he asked. "To blow off steam?"

"Maybe I just feel at home surrounded by weapons," Vic said, and she was only half kidding.

Xan stepped out of the shadows, still wearing the all-black training outfit. He walked toward her, and she took a step back on instinct.

But she wouldn't let herself cower.

Xan stopped inches in front of her. He reached above her, and Vic inhaled to soothe the hammering of her heart. She was sure, somehow, that he could hear it. She stared at the thick column of his neck, the delicate Adam's apple, the lines of muscle she could see through the fabric of his shirt.

She breathed deeply, his scent wrapping around her throat like a fist. Sweat and soap and something Vic couldn't place. Earthy and primal.

Xan plucked a similar sword from the rack behind her and stepped away.

"Come with me," he said, turning away from her. Vic shook herself. Had she really just smelled him? What was wrong with her? "Bring that with you."

Vic shot him a confused look, and Xan dipped his head toward the row of swords behind her.

Get your head in the game, Vic scolded herself. He was a very powerful, very dangerous man. And he wanted her to bring a weapon.

Sword in hand, Vic followed Xan through a doorway and down a small hallway into an empty room. He didn't turn on any lights, but high windows overhead cast glum moonlight around the space. It was a training room of some kind, with an open padded floor in the center. It reminded Vic of a gym, and some of her anxiety lifted.

"I want something from you," Xan said when Vic faced him.

Her eyes slid down to his waist, tapered and fit in his black uniform pants.

"Not *that*," he growled, and Vic bit back a smile. "I want you to attack me."

Vic opened her mouth in surprise. "But these are actual swords," she pointed out.

Xan lifted an eyebrow as if to say *and?*

"You don't practice with sharp swords," Vic replied, a taste of annoyance in her tone. "It's dangerous."

"I'm not worried that you'll hurt me," Xan replied, and Vic scowled at him.

"You're not the one I'm worried about," Vic said. "Maybe you'll use this as an excuse to slice me into tiny little pieces." But she flipped the sword in her hand and got ready to fight.

One side of Xan's mouth turned up in a smirk. "I don't need a weapon for that."

Vic grumbled *witches* under her breath and lunged forward.

Xan knocked her sword out of the way as she dove and swung his weapon toward her back. But Vic expected as much and twisted out of the way. She struck for his midriff again, and he parried.

Vic knew to watch his eyes as they fought, not his weapon. The sharp, gleaming blade tempted her gaze downward, but Vic knew better. The sword would move only when Xan had already decided where to strike. His eyes would show Vic his plans as he made them.

Clearly, Xan knew this lesson as well as Vic did. Their eyes locked as they danced.

His were pale and sharp, under a hard brow frowning in concentration. The longer Vic kept her eyes trained on his, the more she imagined they glimmered in the light, opalescent like storm clouds shifting behind a windowpane.

As soon as Vic started moving, she felt better, her frustration bleeding out in every thrust, clash, and spin. She moved with instinct, thinking as little as possible, and her mind sang with relief.

Xan was so much bigger than Vic, bigger than anyone she'd ever fought. She had to work to stay focused, to not think about the size of him, the sensuality of their bodies moving in tandem with each other. Fighting was like sex, she thought. All instinct and muscle. And Xan was very good at it.

But so was she.

"Where did you learn to do this?" Xan asked as he narrowly deflected a strike to his shoulder.

"Lots of places," Vic replied distantly, aiming for his lower back. Xan twisted away, and she pursued him. "Why won't you attack me?"

Vic went for his left shoulder again, because she'd noticed he was slower on that side. Still, he deflected the hit and kept moving.

"You did the same thing with Matthews earlier," she pointed out. "I know you're better at this than I am. You don't need to worry about frightening me."

Vic could feel herself relaxing as she moved. She got faster and sharper and found herself not even needing to glance at Xan's body in order to attack it. She kept her eyes on his, watching the blue-gray grow more focused, more agitated.

When he didn't respond, she continued, "Is it a control problem, I wonder?" She smirked. "You keep yourself so tight, so rigid. It's all defense because you don't want to lose control." Vic heard the edge in her voice, the invitation. She knew Xan was unaccustomed to being teased.

She pursued him again, getting faster. Xan knocked her sword away.

"I think I'd like to watch you snap," Vic said, jabbing for his sword hand as Xan slid out of the way.

His lips pulled back in a smile that was half snarl, and he stabbed forward. Vic jumped out of the way and spun.

"Finally!" Pure energy coursed through her veins. "I knew this would be fun."

They met in the middle, again and again. Their weapons hit with the clang of striking metal. Xan gritted his teeth. Now he was breathing hard, his skin slick with sweat. His broad chest rose and fell, its rhythm speeding up to match hers. Vic counted her breaths as she began to feel the exertion, keeping them measured and even. Vic parried with a strike and grinned at him, and he returned it, his teeth flashing white in the dark.

Vic feinted to the left and arced her blade, but where Xan had been standing there was only empty air.

She threw her head back, laughing.

And then the blade was on her throat.

She jerked to a stop as she felt the cold press of metal on her neck. Her sword fell to her side.

Xan was an arm's length from her, his chest still heaving, but the point of his sword was at Vic's jugular. If she moved a fraction of an inch, it would break the tender skin. If he pressed . . .

Vic swallowed, heart pounding. An icy bead of sweat slid down her spine.

She didn't take her eyes from his as Xan considered her. He stood stock-still with the blade at her neck, watching her face with a hard expression, as if weighing the consequences of killing her, splitting her throat and removing the annoying liability that had infiltrated his castle.

He pulled the blade away and threw it to the ground. Vic took a gasping breath.

"You're better at this than I expected," he said, his voice gruff and raw.

Vic stared at him as she felt a change in the air. She didn't know if it came from him or her or if it was only in her head, but she watched the hard set of his body as he watched her, breathing hard. All of a sudden they were no longer a witch and an interloper, fighting in an empty training room. They were a man and a woman, drawn together in the dark. For an instant Vic was certain it was not in her head, she was not the only one who felt the pull. She licked her lips and watched him trace the movement with his eyes.

"I knew your mother," Xan said, and the spell broke. "Not well," he admitted. "But she helped train me when I first got here, a little more than ten years ago. She was a Ranger Sentinel by then and only came around occasionally. She was one of the best."

"What happened to her?" Her voice was almost inaudible.

"The official word is that she was killed on a hunt," Xan said.

"You're skeptical," Vic said. He kept his eyes on hers as he spoke.

"Rumor has it she was working on something before she died. She tried to break into another group, a rival of the Order's."

"I didn't know the Order had rivals," Vic said.

"This other group," he said, "they're a lot worse than the Order."

Vic raised an eyebrow.

"They don't care about human casualties the way the Order does. And they're determined to bring the Order to its knees."

"It's gonna be war," Vic whispered, remembering Henry's warning. The recruits could sense the rising tension in the air.

Xan nodded without taking his eyes from hers.

"What can I do?" Vic asked, and Xan's brow furrowed in confusion.

"I'm not telling you this so that you can help," he said. "I'm telling you to leave."

Vic scoffed. "If you think I'm going anywhere without my brother, think again."

The expression on his face softened for an instant before he frowned at her again.

"Max has it in his head that magic can be learned," he said. "That there's a third option instead of just Born or Made, like we've all been taught."

"What does this have to do with me?" Vic asked, though she had a suspicion she knew where he was going.

"Max thinks that you, and I mean *you*, can pick up enough of the language by being here, by taking classes, that you can become one of us."

As he spoke, Vic felt a horrible sensation behind her breastbone. It felt an awful lot like hope.

"If he proves his theory," Xan said, "if you learn what he wants you to, Max thinks he can hold you out as the reason the Order needs to ease some of its rules. He thinks it could change everything."

"You don't agree?" Vic asked.

"Whether Max is right or wrong doesn't matter," Xan said. "He thinks he can control the outcome, and he can't. He thinks he can keep you safe, and he can't promise that."

"Why?"

"Use your head. When has changing everything ever led to a peaceful outcome?"

"And if I refuse to leave?" Vic asked.

Xan broke eye contact, watching the ground for a long moment. When he spoke, his voice was a deep grumble, almost resigned.

"If you won't leave," Xan said, hesitating, "then I have a job for you."

Vic raised her eyebrows. "That was fast."

"I came with a contingency. You seemed stubborn." Vic smiled at him, and he frowned. "The Sentinels' combat skills need work."

"And you want me to help?" Vic asked, taken aback.

A ghost of a smile touched Xan's face. "They will not like losing to a human. I imagine many of them will find it . . . motivating."

Vic couldn't help herself. She laughed. "You want me to rile them into fighting better?"

"You know your way around, and I could keep an eye on you," Xan said with a shrug. "I've had worse ideas."

Vic watched him through narrowed eyes, but when she spoke, she said, "Fine." She would have agreed no matter what reasoning Xan gave. She would take any opportunity to fight him again, to practice, to have a purpose in this place.

"On one condition," Xan added. "I'm in charge. When I say jump—"

"I jump as high as I can," Vic finished for him.

Xan nodded. The look on his face suggested he already regretted asking Vic for help.

"Tomorrow," he said, backing away from her. "Sarah will bring you." He pointed at the sword on the ground. "Put those away before you go to bed."

"Aye, aye, captain," Vic said with a smile. Xan shook his head as he left Vic alone in the empty classroom.

As Vic plucked Xan's sword from the ground, her chest was warm, and her muscles were alive.

There might be a war on the horizon, and Max might have some harebrained scheme to give Vic magic, and Henry might be determined to stay. But Vic had a job to do.

IX

Nearly all witches are born to long-standing magical families, and the Order gets most of its recruits from members who put forth their own children. The Order occasionally finds children outside of these lineages who are born with magical resonance, which is observable from birth due to their possession of the distinctive ocular Lumen.

The Order does not extend entrance to, nor does it train, those who claim themselves "Made witches." Though these individuals possess certain abilities, and though their eyes display a variation of the Lumen, they are not eligible for admittance to the Acheron Order, owing to the risks associated with uncontrolled expressions of Veil magic. Ruled by their emotions as they are, these humans rarely possess the skill to control their own abilities.

While some Elders have campaigned for the admission of these so-called Made witches, no such attempts have succeeded. These individuals do not rely on ritual or spellwork and are thus unbound by the rules that govern the practice of the ancient arts. Their abilities, while occasionally surpassing those of even powerful Born witches, are fickle, and the expression of Veil magic is equally likely to lead to the death of the practitioner and those around him as it is to further his goal. The risks, in sum, are too great.

—William Ruskin, *A History of the Acheron Order*
(New York, 1935)

T he Sentinels met for training in a small, unoccupied Level Eight classroom. They didn't have a dedicated space of their own, according to Sarah, because they rarely needed one. Extraordinary circumstances, Sarah said, meant they were training now more than ever.

Vic thought of Xan's admission last night that the Order was careening toward war with a rival group intent on destroying them. He'd looked vulnerable as he said it, like he feared the possibility even as he accepted it.

He did not look vulnerable today.

Xan stood at the front of the small classroom with his arms crossed in front of his chest. The posture exaggerated the cords of muscle in his arms, which Vic avoided paying special attention to as she sat down. With his feet shoulder-width apart and planted firm, he looked more prepared to leap into a fight than to lecture at bored-looking Sentinels. Again he wore the all-black ensemble Vic was beginning to suspect were the only clothes he owned, and he glowered at each and every person who entered the room.

Vic had been looking forward to Sentinel training all day, but her face fell when Sarah led her into another classroom. She was tired of class. She wanted to beat someone up—or get beaten up, she wasn't picky. Vic and Sarah had already attended Elder Thompson's presentation about the origins of magic and the way that the "originally learned practice of magic became the genesis of a line of Born witches that could be traced all the way to the modern ranks of the Order." Sarah had fallen asleep. When her snores drew the attention of recruits several rows ahead of them, Vic had kicked her.

After more than two hours of fighting to stay awake, Vic had suffered through another go-round with the rocks. She'd made no progress, other than proving to herself that she could stare for at least two minutes before needing to blink. When Elder Thompson wasn't looking, Sarah had levitated the stones across the room, exploding them behind unsuspecting recruits.

Henry had made a point of walking to class with Vic, though his chipper mood soured throughout the lesson. He struggled to break more than a crack in the stone in front of him, and Vic could tell that he was frustrated. Vic caught him smiling only once—when a dust-covered Elder Thompson yelled at Sarah for performing the lesson's task perfectly, directly over his head.

Vic and Sarah were among the first to arrive for Sentinel training, and they sat near the front. Xan must have warned the Sentinels that Vic would be here, because none of them looked at her with surprise. Most of their eyes slid over Vic as she entered, though a few gazes lingered in curiosity or anger. May Lin glared at Vic when she sauntered into the room and took a seat in the last row. After that Vic felt a hostile gaze boring into the back of her head.

There were far more Sentinels than there were Level Eight recruits, and they crammed into the classroom until they sat shoulder to shoulder, some huddled on the floor.

Xan stood at the front of the room holding a notebook—his hand spanned its entire width, Vic noted with a jolt of interest—and put on a pair of wire-frame glasses that he pulled from his pocket. A delighted huff of laughter escaped her at the sight of this huge man with tiny reading glasses. Sarah shot her a confused look, and Vic pulled herself together.

She was here on a provisional basis—Xan's disapproving glance made that obvious—and Vic was not about to get kicked out for laughing at the Chief Sentinel.

"Three case studies to start the day," Xan announced. "Then we'll break into squads and get to training."

Unlike the recruits, none of the Sentinels brought materials to take notes, and most of them leaned against the backs of their seats, looking resigned. Vic slid her notebook back into her bag.

Glasses perched atop his perfect nose, Xan read aloud. Vic bit back a smile.

"The year is 1807," he began. "Setting is a community on the outskirts of the Canadian wilderness, which the Order suspects has been overrun by Orcans. An Elder"—Xan checked his notes—"John Colton, takes a corps of Sentinels to stamp out the infestation, but they thought the problem was a handful of loose Orcans, not a legion. By the time Colton realizes his mistake, twelve Sentinels are dead. After that, it takes almost two months to get eyes inside the village. What they found was a ghost town 'overrun with the living dead,' according to Colton. When the Order finally cleared the town, Colton noted with surprise that the Orcans seemed to have the forethought and self-control necessary to spare some of the humans, so as to provide fresh meat for later. He called this 'an invaluable gift, dampened only by the needless loss of Sentinels required to extirpate the horde.'"

"Jesus Christ," Vic muttered with a grimace, though no one else in the room reacted.

"Now," Xan said, lowering his notes and eyeing the Sentinels over his glasses. "Can any of you tell me what happened?"

A curly-haired Sentinel in the first row raised her hand. "Was there any evidence of forbidden practice among the villagers before the swarm?"

Forbidden practice?

"Not that we know of," Xan replied, "but we can't rule it out."

"It sounds like draugrs to me," another Sentinel replied, this time a man of about thirty sitting behind Vic. "If corpses were coming back."

"I don't think draugrs would know to save meat for later," the woman replied.

"Ellie's got a point," Xan said. "What else could it be?"

Vic watched the Sentinels consider the question. Morbid the topic might have been, but this was far more interesting than the Level One courses.

"It must have been more than one kind of Orcan," May said from the back row. "Reanimated corpses are a red herring."

"You think corpses were coming back by coincidence?" the man behind Vic asked.

"It could be incidental, yes. If there were witches in the village using forbidden magic, they could be brought back no matter what killed them." Turning to Xan, May said, "It sounds like a Gosk of some kind. Maybe a fugosk or a norgosk."

"And how would you kill them?" Xan asked.

"Carefully."

A few of the Sentinels huffed laughs, but Xan shot May a look and she continued. "They're weak between the plates of armor on their backs. You'd have to stab them. As I said, carefully."

Xan nodded. "The record on this case isn't great, but I think you're correct."

"Give someone else a shot next time, May," one of the men called, and May put a hand up in an appeasing gesture. She leaned back in her seat as if welcoming the others to go ahead.

"Next case," Xan said. "Colonial America. Witnesses report that a young man arrived barefoot and bleeding after walking from the nearest settlement, some fifty miles up the Connecticut coast. The teenager had a strange mark burned into his chest and a series of deep gouges in his abdomen. According to the kid, he was part of an exclusively male settlement, mostly indentured servants or workhouse occupants from London. A brutal winter, exacerbated by the settlers' poor preparedness, left more than half their number dead. Among the survivors was a self-proclaimed witch doctor, who began using rituals with the participation of the other colonists. Despite initial success summoning fire and killing game, something started to hunt the settlers during the night. The teenager called them 'men who were not men.'"

Xan lowered the notebook and looked at the class.

This time Sarah volunteered an answer. "Demons," she said. "Plain and dry."

"How do you know?"

Sarah counted the reasons on her fingers. "They look like people, they hunt at night, and the burn on the kid's chest would be consistent with a demon attack."

"Demons?" Vic whispered to Sarah. "Like Bible demons?"

"Same name, different idea," Sarah whispered back. "The Christians named a lot of Orcans in the early days."

Vic's head spun.

"What would you do?" Xan asked, looking annoyed at Vic's interruption as Sarah refocused on him.

"Assuming I'm the colonial-era Order?" Sarah said. "Nothing."

"Nothing?" Xan asked, eyebrows raised.

"Demons probably killed all the settlers and went back to Orcus." She turned to Vic and added, "Unlike most Orcans, demons don't like to stick around after they hunt."

"Very good. Final case: 1989. Rural Pennsylvania. Farmers have been complaining to the local authorities for months about cattle mutilations, animals wasting away, refusing to eat. No one pays attention until two teenagers go missing in a cornfield. No bodies are found, and the cattle mutilations stop. What gives?"

"Alien abduction," the male Sentinel behind Vic announced.

Vic shot a look of shock at Sarah, who shook her head tightly. No.

"Any serious suggestions?" Xan asked.

A muscular woman to the left of Vic raised her hand. "Goat-sucker," she said in a deep voice. "El Chupacabra."

"Bryce, you know we don't call it that," Xan said without looking up from his notebook.

"It won't hunt again for a few weeks after a feed," Bryce went on. "The goat-sucker makes a nest in cave systems, where it drags prey to eat slowly. So you can either lure it out or wait for it to get hungry again."

"And how do you kill it?" Xan said.

"Stabbing ought to do it," Bryce said. "Dip the knife in goat's blood if you want to be extra sure it's dead."

"Correct." Xan snapped the notebook in his palm shut. "Is everybody ready to get to work?"

A resounding confirmation came from the Sentinels. Evidently, Vic was not alone in preferring fighting to classroom instruction.

"Split up by squad," Xan said. "Two squads per training room and One and Two in the Arena. You know the drill. We're working hand-to-hand again today."

Vic tried to follow Sarah when she left the room, but Xan pulled her aside. He put Vic with Squads Six and Seven, while Sarah was on Squad Three. He tasked Vic with running them through the basics and said he would check back in an hour.

Together, Squads Six and Seven comprised a dozen witches, all of whom watched Vic with confused furrows between their brows, like adults astounded to find themselves under the supervision of a kindergartner. None of them had been there to witness her fight with May yesterday, and Vic had no idea what, if anything, they expected from her.

So much for easing her in gently, Vic thought.

She threw a nervous smile at the Sentinels and wiped her palms on her thighs. Though she'd been fighting for years, Vic had never taught before.

"I figured we could run some practice fights," Vic said. Her voice tilted up at the end as if it were a question, and she scolded herself for her timidity. "See what y'all need to work on, and then maybe come up with some drills."

No one spoke.

"Who wants to go first?" Vic asked, pasting on a smile.

The Sentinels stood silent, staring at her.

"You," Vic said, and she pointed at the largest man among them. "Come here."

More than an hour passed, and Xan made no reappearance. Vic went over some of the basic defense maneuvers with the group, who had obviously learned all of it before and forgotten. But the rust wore off the more they practiced, and Vic worked up a sweat.

Though none of the twelve Sentinels showed hostility toward Vic, she wondered if they worked harder than they otherwise would have to avoid being outshone by an outsider, like Xan had predicted. But if the witches fought hard to avoid losing to a human, Vic fought even harder. She was not about to be proved weak in front of the Sentinels.

Vic threw another witch to the ground and turned to discuss the move with the group when she noticed someone in the doorway, watching her.

A sinewy blond woman whom Vic recognized from training yesterday leaned against the doorjamb.

"That'll be all for today, guys," the woman said, and Vic frowned as the witches she'd been training ambled out of the room without a backward glance her way. Vic turned and began stacking the mats she'd pulled out for practice.

"Sorry to interrupt," the woman said.

When Vic did not reply, she added, "My name is Em. Sarah asked me to bring you to the Sentinels' lounge. She said she found something you'll want to see."

"What did she find?"

Em shrugged, looking impatient, and Vic pushed the last mat into place and followed her out of the room.

Down a hallway, up one staircase, then another hall, and they came upon a set of double doors, which Em pushed open. Along one side of an expansive room, shelves held ancient-looking books. Windows on the adjoining wall showed a bleak day, casting the room in shadow. As she stepped forward, Vic noticed the rug in the center of the room had been moved. There was a faint outline of dust on the floor where it had lain until recently, about a foot away. The image made the hair on Vic's neck stand up. She took a step back.

Behind her, the doors swung shut, and a rush of air hit Vic's back. Em turned to stand in front of the doors with a determined frown.

"This isn't the Sentinels' lounge, is it?"

"No." May Lin walked forward from the shadows on the other side of the room, toying with a narrow silver dagger. Another figure moved in Vic's periphery—a reedy Black man Vic recognized from this afternoon's session. There were three Sentinels in the room, and one Vic.

"Sarah didn't send for me, did she?"

May's lovely face twisted. "She did not."

"Do you mind?" Vic asked as she crouched to pull back the worn carpet. Underneath it, the stone floor was marked in a pointed pattern—not quite a star, more the way a child would draw the sun. Spikes around a circle. The image had been burned into the floor.

"What is it?" Vic said, keeping her voice casual.

"Step inside and find out," May told her with a smile. She spun the knifepoint against the pad of her finger as she spoke. May was comfortable with the blade, and she wanted Vic to know that.

"Thank you, but no." Vic glanced around her. There was only one way out of the room, and Em stood in front of it.

"Don't look so apprehensive," May said. "We only wanted to talk."

"Oh, yeah?" Vic asked, raising her eyebrows.

"You proved yesterday you can fight," May said. "But you're out of your league."

If Vic could lure Em forward a few feet and distract the others somehow, she could make a run for it. But the others had magic. Vic didn't know how much damage they could do in the seconds it would take her to flee.

"We've discussed it among ourselves, and we believe it's best if you leave," May said.

"What do you expect me to do wrong, exactly? Burn the castle down? I'm only trying to—"

"To what? Poke and prod and shove your nose where it doesn't belong?"

"You don't know what I want," Vic said. "Maybe I have a thing for flying buttresses and murderous women." She shifted until she was in the right position to move fast, her feet hips' width apart and poised to run.

"Your stupidity will get someone killed. If we're lucky, it'll be you."

"Are you always this dramatic?" Vic asked.

"You're a fool," May spat. "You're thinking about fighting us, aren't you? You're trying to game a way out of here, but it won't work. There are three of us here, and we kill things for a living."

"Yeah, you're highly trained, I heard about that. That's why it took me two whole minutes to get you on the ground yesterday."

"Grab her," May told the man at her side, and Vic moved.

Vic pretended to lunge for May, and Em rushed forward. Vic spun back to the door, aiming for the thin gap between Em's back and the wall. Her fingers closed around the brass handle, but a heavy hand wrapped around Vic's arm as the third Sentinel grabbed her from behind. On instinct, Vic flung her elbow into his face. He jerked away with a wet shout, blood pouring from his nose. Vic twisted out of his grip and wrenched the door handle. It opened an inch before an unseen force slammed it shut, a gust of wind ruffling Vic's hair. May.

Vic threw a look over her shoulder before pulling harder on the door. May stood with her arms crossed, watching Vic.

"You're not going anywhere until we're finished here." Beside May, the man Vic had hit held his sleeve over his nose, tilting his head back to stem the flow.

"You're supposed to lean forward," Vic told him, breathing hard. "Otherwise blood runs down your throat and you can choke."

"That's enough!" May snapped.

"Just a piece of advice," Vic added under her breath.

"I said that's enough! Do you ever shut up?" May took a step toward Vic.

From the far side of the room came the tinkling of broken glass, and all three witches turned toward the window. They paused, identical expressions of horror dawning on their faces, before a brilliant white light filled the room. Vic threw a hand in front of her face.

When the light dimmed, a lone black bird sat atop the high back of a chair behind them. It stood still as a statue, its beady eyes gazing impassively at the scene.

Vic angled her head as she watched it, confused. But the others were already moving.

"Fuck! Fuck!" May shouted, pushing Vic aside and hurrying to the door. "You said he was out of the castle!"

"That's what Xan told me!" Em shot back. "We have to get out of here before—"

"Bit late for that, ladies."

Max was standing against the bookcase with his hands in his suit pockets, once again the old movie star caught between takes. When he saw the male witch's bloody face, Max gave a sympathetic wince. "Hello, Michael. Best not to lean your head back when your nose is bleeding, I'm afraid."

"Yes, sir," the witch named Michael replied, and Max handed him a handkerchief, which he appeared to conjure out of thin air. Michael pressed it to his face and leaned forward.

"Now, what are the three of you up to?" Max asked May and Em, the latter of whom stopped tugging on the now locked door.

May stared defiantly at Max, while Em kept her eyes on the floor, and neither of them replied. Max wore a pleasant expression as he waited, eyebrows half raised, for any of the three witches to speak. The silence dragged on until it became oppressive.

"We were only trying to scare her," Em blurted out.

"Why would you do a thing like that?" Max asked.

Another pregnant pause. The raven followed Vic's gaze as she looked between Max and the Sentinels.

"She doesn't belong here," May said, her voice harsh.

"And is it up to you to decide who belongs in the castle and who does not?"

"It's against the rules."

"I know the rules quite well, May. I wrote many of them."

"This one is a rule for a reason. People will get hurt."

"It wasn't too long ago that the same argument was used to keep Mades out of the castle."

May looked away, and Vic wondered whether she was a Born witch or a Made like Sarah. "It's not the same."

"Yet the comparison stands, doesn't it?" Max faced the window, and the raven flew to perch on the shelf nearest him. "You may go," he told the three witches. "I will inform the Chief Sentinel about what's happened here, and he will address your insubordination as he sees fit."

"Yes, sir," Em and Michael intoned, while May seethed.

The three Sentinels left Max and Vic alone for the first time since her arrival at the castle.

"Are you all right?" he asked, watching her face, and she nodded. "I heard what happened in the Arena. And I heard you're helping the Sentinels train. You've been busy."

"What's with the bird?" Vic asked, unable to hold the question in. The raven sat on the shelf behind Max's shoulder, staring blankly at the two of them.

"My familiar," Max said. He stroked the underside of the bird's beak, as if free-roaming ravens were as normal a sight as house cats. "Do you like him?"

"It's a bit creepy, to be honest. His movements almost track yours."

"Don't listen to her, Augustus," Max told the raven. "You're not creepy at all."

"You say 'familiar' like I should know what it means."

"You should," Max said, still stroking the bird, while the animal's eyes remained locked on Vic. "You should learn whatever you'd like to know. Familiars are a relic of a bygone time. Powerful witches used to imbue creatures with their souls and their power, making them functionally immortal. They bind with living witches and multiply their power."

"You're saying there's a dude in there?" Vic asked before she could stop herself. She stared at the bird's black eyes like she expected to see humanity hiding inside them.

"There are several dudes in there," Max replied with a smile. "Augustus holds the collective memories and abilities of a line of witches dating back even further than the Acheron Order. I am the Ninth Raven—there were eight before me."

"And you'll join them," Vic guessed.

"Someday," Max replied.

And he would spend eternity trapped inside a bird. What a horrible thought.

"How are you enjoying Avalon Castle?" Max asked as he returned his attention to Vic. "Putting aside the events of the last hour, of course."

"Putting aside the events of the last hour, I still find it unsettling."

"Some of that can't be helped," Max said. "Drafty hallways, too many empty apartments."

"Witches learning how to kill each other in the basement."

"Exactly. It's unavoidable." Max raised a curious eyebrow. "How are your lessons coming along?"

"I'm becoming very adept at staring at rocks."

He watched her like he expected her to say more. But there was nothing to report. Vic had no magic and could do nothing more than stare.

"It's making people angry," Vic said instead. "My being in the classes, helping with the Sentinels. They don't like it."

Max turned back to the raven and petted it with a finger. "Growing pains," he said. "They'll get over it eventually."

"And hopefully no one kills me in the meantime," Vic said.

"No one will kill you," Max said. "I told them not to."

"Thanks."

"It was no trouble," Max said, having failed to detect Vic's sarcasm. "Although seeing you reminds me." He stood straight and patted the pockets of his suit. "I have something for you."

He pulled an empty hand from his vest pocket, and Vic watched in confusion until an object formed atop his palm. The hair on Vic's arms stood alert as a key knit itself together. Heavy and brass and identical to the one to her and Henry's apartment.

"Meredith kept rooms in the castle for more than two decades," Max said, and her stomach dipped. "I thought you might want to visit."

Vic took the key from Max's palm. Electricity ran through her fingers when she touched it, like static from a rug in winter. She measured the weight of it in her fist, imagined it in her mother's hands.

"If you'd like to learn more about her life here, it's number 481, in the Northwest Wing. We closed that wing about five years ago. You'll have privacy."

Vic slipped it into her pocket. It sat cold against her fingers.

"You can stay, you know," Max said. "As long as you need to."

"I can't stay," Vic said. "I'm not a witch, I can't do any of this. I'm only here to . . ." Vic stopped.

"Why are you here?" he asked.

Because she wanted to keep Henry safe? Because she wanted to prove herself to a woman who had been dead almost a decade? Or because she was desperate for a purpose, for a place where her actions had more weight than they did in the real world, where Vic shuffled aimlessly from day to day? She remembered what Xan had told her last night. Max wanted Vic to prove the Order wrong—to learn magic, and in doing so show them all a new world was possible.

"I'm curious," she said.

Max looked at her with pale, incisive eyes and seemed to hear the sentiments she held back. He smiled when he spoke.

"Unanswered questions; I understand. But I urge you to consider what happens when you've answered them. When you peel away the final curtain, will you feel satisfied returning to the world outside?"

Vic wasn't sure.

X

The eight levels of training proceed as follows:

Level One. The transport and structure of inanimate objects.
Level Two. The manipulation of waves carrying both light and sound.
Level Three. The use of complex conduits.
Level Four. The creation of original spells.
Level Five. The creation and disassembly of protective and defensive wards.
Level Six. The transport and structure of complex forms.
Level Seven. Mental defense.
Level Eight. Combat.

After the successful mastery of each of the levels (as determined by the Elder responsible for such level) recruits proceed to the final step: an induction trial overseen by the Elder Council. Only then can they become members of the Acheron Order.

—William Ruskin, *A History of the Acheron Order*
(New York, 1935)

Vic kicked the door to apartment 481. Then, for good measure, she kicked it again.

It looked just like all the other doors in the castle. Hardwood, carved to perfection, and adorned with a knob of blood-red glass.

In the three days since her conversation with Max, Vic had visited Meredith's apartment no fewer than seven times. Each visit followed the same structure: Vic found the door, exasperated at the end of countless meandering hallways. She put the key Max had given her into the lock and twisted, her heart beating loud in her ears. Each time Vic felt the click of the inner mechanism as the lock disengaged. Each time Vic pushed hard against the door, and each time it rebuffed her.

She'd taken to sitting in front of it, staring at the wooden face of her mother's secrets.

Vic's patience wore thin. She'd stopped by the locked door for the third consecutive morning on the way to class. She was running exceptionally late, but she couldn't resist the thought that this time the door would change its mind and admit her.

It did not.

And so she kicked it.

Vic made no attempt to quiet her swearing as she stormed away from the door. She marched toward the training wing, trying not to obsess over what might lie inside Meredith's apartment.

Halfway down the empty hall, Vic stopped.

She could feel someone watching her. A gaze stuck on her spine like the push of a finger. She turned.

But the abandoned hall was as empty as it always had been. The doors to long-vacant apartments stood still and silent around her, and the hallway stretched too far for anyone to be watching around a corner.

There was nothing in the hall but a few haggard portraits and long shadows between windows.

Vic kept walking, though she couldn't shake the sense that she was not alone.

Breathing hard from the walk and the frustration, Vic flung open the door to the lecture hall where she'd spent the last week listening to Elder Thompson drone on and stopped dead in her tracks.

"Shit," Vic said aloud, and heads spun toward her.

"Ms. Wood," Nathaniel said from the podium Elder Thompson typically occupied, looking as dull and proper as always, his expression punctuated by a slight frown. "How nice of you to join us."

His face made clear that he found nothing about Vic's arrival *nice*.

"And I see you've brought your manners."

Vic slid into the open seat beside Sarah without replying. She could see Henry, sitting in the front, slump down in his seat as if fearful of being associated with his tardy, swearing sister.

Things had been frosty between the siblings. When Henry found out Vic was training with the Sentinels, he disapproved. He told her to back out; he worried that she would get hurt. When she insisted on doing it anyway, he opted for the silent treatment, and had been pointedly avoiding Vic for three days. She'd considered telling him about the key Max had given her, but the thought of Henry being able to open the door that denied her made Vic inexplicably sad. Still, she wished he would grow up and have a conversation with her. She stared at the back of his head and contemplated throwing something at it. That would force him to talk to her.

"As I was saying before Ms. Wood's interruption," Nathaniel went on, "your lesson today will deviate from the traditional Level One curriculum. I believe, and several of my fellow Elders agree with me, that you are owed a special lesson on consequences."

Vic turned to Sarah and whispered, "Why is *he* teaching?"

Sarah shrugged. "Maybe Thompson's got the flu."

"Today we shall focus on the Acheron Order's role in society," Nathaniel was saying, "and what shall befall us if the Order can no longer perform its duties."

"I hope he dies," Sarah added.

Vic choked on a shocked laugh, and Nathaniel stopped talking.

"Did I say something amusing, Ms. Wood?" Nathaniel asked.

Vic shook her head. The first time she'd seen Nathaniel, he had frightened her, casting his magic over her with questions and scorning her answers. Now she was expected to sit in respectful silence and listen to his wisdom. It chafed.

"The risk of Orcans overtaking the human world—is that funny to you?"

"No," Vic said.

Nathaniel cocked an eyebrow.

"No, sir," Vic said. She stared at the wrinkles on his neck as if she could will them to wind tighter and choke him. Mean eyes met hers, and Vic looked down, remembering the cold sweat of his mind invading her own.

"It would behoove you to pay attention," he said with a malignant smile. "You need to learn, after all." He said it with a hint of mockery, like there was nothing he could teach that Vic deserved to know.

He returned his focus to the room at large.

"We shall begin our demonstration earlier today than usual. Convene in fifteen minutes in Limbo."

He shut his notebook with a slap and marched out of the room.

"Limbo?" Vic asked Sarah, who stared at the spot Nathaniel had vacated with her mouth ajar. Sounds of surprised curiosity and excitement filled the space as the recruits gathered their belongings.

"What is he thinking?" Sarah said under her breath.

Vic waved a hand in front of Sarah's face. "What's Limbo?"

"Another training room," Sarah said absentmindedly. "Level Eight."

"We're skipping ahead?"

"I have no idea." Sarah shook her head, eyes wide.

Vic could not complain about spending the day doing anything other than staring at stones, but nerves swirled in her stomach as she followed the crowd of recruits into the hallway and down a staircase, spiraling deep under the castle. Each time Vic thought they must have met the bottom, they kept going, until the group finally peeled away into a windowless landing lit by two flaring torches.

Through a doorway they found a classroom, and Sarah pulled Vic to the side to watch the other students file in and gather behind them. The confused concern on Sarah's face made Vic's palms slick with anxiety. She wiped them on her jeans.

The other recruits had grown accustomed to Vic's presence, though some still threw antagonistic glances over their shoulders at her, and the group as a whole settled a few feet away from Sarah and Vic. There were no Mades in this class of recruits, Sarah had told her with a meaningful look.

A male recruit sneered at Vic and Sarah as he passed, but Vic was too distracted by the space around her to respond.

If she hadn't known it was a classroom, Vic might have called it a dungeon. The room was lit by torches, and condensation coated the

WE WHO HAVE NO GODS ✳ 103

rough stone walls, every inch covered in scratch marks. Stone ceilings loomed high overhead. On one side of the room was an immense metal doorframe, beyond which the ground fell away, revealing a pit like an old mining shaft. Vic couldn't see the bottom of the chute, and the hair on her arms rose.

"Today's task is to observe," Nathaniel said. He stood beside the yawning doorway and faced the students. "You won't see this room again until you've proved your ability to face what lies beneath us. Many of you will never see it again."

"No way," Sarah breathed.

"There are those among our community who have lost faith in the mission that has been the Order's central focus for centuries. These individuals would jeopardize our Order's ability to maintain control, all because of some lofty ideas about the treatment of those beneath us."

Vic felt Sarah grab hold of her arm.

"Though some of my fellow Elders disagree with me, I believe all of us—especially those new to our ranks—ought to be reminded of why we are here, and what is at stake." His eyes met Vic's. "We must *understand* what we risk when we disrupt the established order."

He faced an inscription beside the door and spoke to it in the Universal Language Vic did not speak. The hand around Vic's arm tightened.

The marks on the walls flared red, and the noise began.

Metal moved beneath the floor. The whirring of a machine far past its prime was loud and low in Vic's ears. It clanked along, growing louder as it grew closer, until Vic saw movement from the pit beside Nathaniel. A massive cage reared out of the earth and slammed into stillness when it met the opening. The crowd took a step back.

Everything went quiet.

It was an Orcan.

It stood on bony knuckles, foot-long claws curled out from humanoid hands, its front two legs longer and more muscular than the back pair. Its skin was a bloodless white, covered in rigid spikes along its spine.

The creature watched the students through milky, unblinking eyes. It was taller than any of them, almost as tall as the doorway itself.

"This specimen is a laetite," Nathaniel said. "The Sentinels captured it in Greenland last year."

He picked up a thin metal stick.

"The laetite, like most Orcans, is carnivorous and feeds on the flesh of humans. The Sentinels were alerted to the existence of this particular creature by the disappearance of a number of hunters. The laetite is most content in less populated areas and travels long distances to acquire prey."

Nathaniel struck the bars of the cage with the rod he held, and electricity sparked through the metal. The creature stumbled in pain. Its face opened like a blooming flower, four sides of its mouth lined with rows of pointed teeth. The sound it made was unnatural and far too loud. Many of the students clapped their hands over their ears.

"See that?" Shouting over the sound, Nathaniel struck the cage again, and the creature shrieked in pain once more. The inside of its mouth was a brilliant black. "The laetite has more than two hundred teeth, each as sharp as a razor."

The creature lifted onto its back legs and grabbed the bars, snapping its jaws at Nathaniel.

Vic saw what happened next in stunning detail.

The front panel of the cage wasn't closed properly. It rattled for an instant, and it snapped.

In a heartbeat, the creature ripped away the cage door and hurled it across the room. Students screamed as the jagged metal hit the back wall.

The creature leaped from the cage with disturbing grace and lunged right for Nathaniel.

With a shout, he sent another jet of electricity at the creature's chest, and it reared back on its hind legs before lashing out, swiping Nathaniel to the side. He fell backward, hitting his head with a loud smack, and lay still on the floor. The room erupted into pandemonium as the creature advanced on the figure closest to it.

Vic's heart stopped.

No.

Henry.

The creature lunged toward her brother, who stared up at it with wordless terror.

Vic did not think. She didn't give herself even a moment to consider what she was doing.

Throwing herself forward, Vic sprinted toward Henry and hit him with her outstretched hands, sending him splaying onto the floor beside her.

But she'd done what she needed to do.

The creature turned on Vic without a pause. Its face split wide, countless blackened teeth like daggers, and it roared down at her, the sound blocking out everything else in the room. Vic stared at the black hole of its throat and wondered if it would be the last thing she'd see. If this was her life, Vic thought, she hadn't done a half-bad job. She'd saved her brother, like her mother had told her to, and that should be enough for Vic—shouldn't it?

As the laetite reared up, Vic caught its eye. A thin membrane under its eyelid swept up to cover the opaque white, as endless as snow blanketing an ocean.

And then a flash of iron and a sound like a bedsheet being torn in half, and black fluid sprayed from the creature's throat as it fell forward, its neck opened like a spout. Dark blood pooled on the stone in front of Vic.

Sarah stood over the dying creature with a weapon she must have conjured from thin air. A sword the length of her arm glowed ghostly silver as she lowered it, and Vic was entranced.

She thought of her mother, imagined Meredith in Sarah's place, wielding a weapon against a creature inhumanly strong and vital, and Vic felt something new thrumming through her veins.

Jealousy.

Want.

Vic *wanted* to do that. She wanted to learn how.

She caught Sarah's eye and returned the Sentinel's cautious smile, which grew wider and wider until she and Sarah were beaming at each other.

Vic looked away when Henry called for her and saw he'd pulled himself to his knees a few feet away. When he saw the smile on Vic's face, he frowned.

"Are you okay?" he asked.

"Never better," Vic replied.

Part II

LIMBO

XI

Extending admission to those who claim power over Veil magic marks the end of the Acheron Order as we know it. By happenstance, these humans have stolen the power of the Veil, which they wield without ritual or structure, which kills them as often as it aids them, and which they are wholly unable to control. The Acheron Order exists on a foundation of rules and order. Structure, ritual, the rigidity of our practices, all provide the essential supports upon which we operate. These humans have none of this. They respect none of this. This edict marks the end of our way of life, a way of life we have sworn with our blood to protect. This will be the death of us. I wholeheartedly dissent.

—From a letter circulated by E. Martin Key in response to
the Thirty-Second Council of Elders' decision to admit
Made witches to the Acheron Order (1992)

A lonely car cut the slice of road visible through the treetops. From her vantage point hundreds of feet above the ground, Vic saw everything. The mountains, tipped in white, the sloping hills guarding them on either side. And that car was the only sign of life. Vic raised her palm to the window and leaped back in alarm.

Though the frame was the same arched shape as those throughout the castle, the window had no panes. No glass. Nothing to stop Vic falling to her death. She clung to the stone window frame and pushed her body away from it, claws of panic scaling her throat.

Her heart pounded as she scanned the circular room. Rugged stone walls were broken by eight windows and an altar set with miscellaneous artifacts. The floors were bare save a grate at the center.

Vic saw the man the second time she searched the room, as if he had appeared once he decided to be discovered.

She was not surprised to see him here.

He was tall but not oppressively so. He was neither muscled nor gaunt. He wasn't old or young. He was handsome but only slightly— his was an attainable sort of perfection. The dark suit he wore had been tailored to his exact measurements. Blond hair was combed away from his face, and he wore a curious expression as he examined Vic.

"Have we met?"

The stranger smiled when Vic spoke. Not a brilliant smile, like Max's would have been, but more practiced.

"My name is Aren Mann," he told her in a smooth voice. "It's a pleasure to make your acquaintance, Victoria."

She did not wonder how he knew her name. Of course he knew her name.

"Are you a member of the Order?"

He smiled again, displaying a row of perfect—though not dazzling—white teeth.

"Alas, I am not," he replied. "I have not been welcome at the castle for some time."

He didn't look menacing, and Vic did not feel fear. Deep in the back of her mind Vic realized that her reactions did not make sense. She should be frightened. She should be confused and scared and this man should not be trying to have a pleasant conversation with her.

"Have you visited the North Tower?" Aren Mann asked in a casual tone.

"No."

"It's the only room in the castle with a view of the river. Although, after that display, I doubt you would appreciate it. You're afraid of heights?"

Obviously she was afraid of heights. If Vic fell from up here, they'd have to hose her off the cobblestones.

"What is this place?" Vic asked. She ran a finger along the altar's edge.

"My old workroom. I doubt anyone comes up here these days."

"You brought me here." Suspicion crept into Vic's tone as reality dawned. She wasn't in control of this interaction—he was.

"In a manner of speaking, I suppose I did."

Vic stretched the muscles in her hands as she scanned the room for exits. She could hit him. She could incapacitate him, and she could run. But where would she run if she didn't know where she was?

Aren continued to study her, his eyes dropping to her hands before lingering on her face. A smile played about his eyes as he watched Vic weigh her options.

"Why?" she asked.

He shrugged, but it was an affected nonchalance. Vic caught the tension in his shoulders.

"Curiosity, mostly. I wanted to meet you." He raked his gaze once more over her face. "Well, meet you again. It's been years and years. I doubt you remember."

She did not.

"That's the third time you've done that," Vic said. "Mention something assuming I'll ask for more detail. You drop a breadcrumb and expect me to pick it up. You're not welcome at the castle, you 'suppose' you brought me here, we've met before, though I don't remember." She ticked them off on her fingers. "It's an annoying habit."

His smile broadened.

"I'm dreaming," Vic guessed.

"You tell me."

The intensity of his stare was unsettling. It wasn't degrading, like Nathaniel's. It wasn't concerned, like Max's had been when last they spoke. It was, quite simply, strong. He paid full attention to her, every firing synapse in his blond head focused on a singular point: Vic.

"How are you enjoying Avalon Castle?" Aren asked, and Vic decided that none of this was actually happening.

"I feel out of place," she said. "Like I woke up one day in someone else's body. Everything around me is unrecognizable, and I'm running in circles trying to understand."

"Some of that is simple observation," Aren said. "Little of your life before will serve you here."

"I understand the rules are different. Everyone tells me every chance they get that I don't belong here and that I shouldn't bother shutting the door on my way out."

"You don't belong." Aren said it without judgment. It was a fact, plain and simple.

He pushed away from the wall as Vic inspected the altar. A basin, a bundle of black sticks, a wood-handled knife the size of her palm, and an empty chalice. Vic bent to examine the underside of the slab, but the bottom was flat and unremarkable.

Aren wore a curious expression when Vic looked back at him.

"Does anyone ever tell you you look quite a bit like your mother?" Another breadcrumb.

"No one ever tells me that." Because she didn't. Vic was a little taller, a little thicker, darker and meaner. Instead of blue, Vic's eyes were brown, and she frowned more than she ought to. It had annoyed Meredith, when she'd been alive to notice. But their fundamental difference ran deeper than their looks or temperaments. It was something that sat at the center of them, keeping them apart.

"Are people at the castle being unkind to you?"

"Do you care?"

"I told you. I'm curious."

"Some of them are," Vic said. "They look at me like I'm dangerous, which is ridiculous considering I have no power here."

"The Order is weaker than they would like to admit," he replied, pacing half-moons around her. "You represent a compromise—one human allowed into the inner sanctum could mean more are coming. No one outside the Order's control knows what the Order does. They like it that way."

Vic remembered Xan's warning. If Max was right and Vic *could* learn magic, she would be responsible for disproving one of the Order's fundamental principles. They believed, without reserve, in their exceptionalism. Proving them wrong would change everything. *When has changing everything ever led to a peaceful outcome?*

"On a more practical note," he went on, "with your allegiance uncertain, they fear you could pass information to any of the Order's many enemies."

"'The Order's many enemies,'" Vic repeated. "Am I to assume that includes you?"

"It certainly does," Aren said with a smile. "The Order and I possess incompatible views about how magic should function in a society."

"You are not concerned with secrecy," Vic guessed.

Aren picked up one of the blackened sticks from the altar and began twirling it between his fingers.

"The Order's obsession with secrecy is a position born out of fear. Some of which is valid, and most of which is not." The stem danced through his fingers as he spoke. Measured, like it followed the pace of his breathing. "I am not a man prone to fear."

Vic wasn't sure how much of this to believe. If her subconscious had created this scene, this man shouldn't have any more information than she did.

"Do you know how a witch is Made?" he asked.

The stem froze in the air.

Vic shook her head. "No one talks about it."

She'd asked Sarah at dinner a few nights ago, and Sarah, looking wary, said it happened by accident and changed the subject. It never came up in class. Even when Elder Thompson discussed the history of the Order, even in the books she'd been assigned, the idea of Made witches was referred to only in passing, in a tone of rebuke. But Vic could admit—here in her own mind—a furious curiosity about it. The question had run unimpeded under her thoughts ever since she'd learned about the possibility. It was tantalizing, the idea that someone could *become* the kind of person who belonged here. Even if it was a shadow of belonging, that of the second-class, it was better than being an outsider.

"Because no one knows," Aren said. "We understand the me-

chanics of it. We have watched it happen a thousand times, cata-
loged each of the steps, memorized the contours of the process. We
know that, to all observation, the human dies. Their hearts stop,
blood stills in their veins. And seconds or minutes or hours later,
they rise. We know what it looks like from the outside, but no one
knows how it works. Even those who have survived it never recall
the experience. No one knows what lies in the space between the
living and the dead. No witch, in all the many centuries of practice,
has ever determined the secret to who gets Made and who does not.
Despite thousands of attempts, no one has ever succeeded in manu-
facturing Made witches. Only a handful of witches throughout history have ever been Made on purpose, and only one of them is still
alive."

"Max." Vic didn't know why she said it, why she thought of Max
in that moment. His power, the fear he inspired in the other Order
members. It made sense.

Something flashed across Aren's face. Anger flared in his bright
blue eyes, and Vic was certain that this was the first honest emotion
he'd shown her. A glimpse, as brief as a lightning strike, of the man
behind the curtain.

"You wound me," Aren said. The mask slipped back into place. "I
did all that work, and you think of Shepherd. Tsk-tsk."

Vic stared at him. "You?"

Aren nodded, his eyes on the stem in his hands as its dance re-
started. "I was a Mage with the Order for years. I was Born, you see,
to an ancient line. But it was my job to push the boundaries of my
abilities, to find out what the Order didn't already know. It was the
natural thing to do."

"How did you do it?"

"It took a very long time," he said. "Years of work and practice.
Though in the end the only thing that mattered was the willingness
to try. It's a gamble, and it could just as easily have gone the other
way."

"You were willing to die for the chance to become more powerful?"

Aren smiled. "For the chance to *learn,* Victoria. And yes, of course."

"You don't remember anything?" Vic asked.

He watched her carefully before speaking, and Vic had the unpleasant sensation of being understood by someone she did not know. "I do not," he said at last. "But that's not the path for you, little dove. You have more exciting things in store."

Vic frowned. She hoped that none of this was real. The alternative was too invasive, too alien. But if this was all in her head, she could at least sort her thoughts.

"Max believes that I can learn magic," Vic said. "Without having to be Made, I mean."

Aren nodded, like the news was unsurprising. "Shepherd has nurtured this theory for a long time. I'm sure he's delighted at the chance to test it."

"How is that different than being Made?" Vic asked.

"Made magic is Veil magic," he said. "It comes from a different place; it behaves differently. It's the Order's most sacred belief that Born witches alone are blessed with the magic of the natural world. The suggestion that this could be learned, acquired, undermines their entire philosophy." Aren shrugged. "Shepherd is an iconoclast."

"Do you think he's right?" Vic didn't know why she should trust this man, if he was a man.

"Suffice it to say I am one of many who are eager to see the outcome."

When Vic said nothing, he leaned closer to her.

"Would you like to find out?" he said.

Vic looked up at him, wary.

"What do you know of Orcan magic?" Aren said, leaning away from her and straightening the items on the altar.

Vic shook her head, considering. "It's forbidden," she guessed, recalling mentions of dangerous magic.

Aren gave a derisive smile. "Ah, yes, that's what they call it. But it's a kind of magic like all the others, available to witches who need it."

"Why is it forbidden, then?"

"The Order would have you believe that using magic of the realm of the dead threatens the integrity of the Veil. But there's nothing inherently wrong with Orcan magic," he said. "The Elders practice it, after all."

No one had told Vic that.

"Despite this hypocrisy, the Order is deathly afraid of Orcan magic," Aren said.

"Why?" Vic asked.

"It can lead to unexpected . . . outcomes," Aren said, and he met her eyes with a shrug. "It eats."

Vic wanted to step away from him then. She wanted to run. But something held her to the spot. Some desire within her overwhelmed any concept of consequences.

"Orcan magic is easier to manipulate than its earthly alternative," Aren went on. "So even witches with little or no training can become dangerous if they start playing with the dead."

Vic remembered Nathaniel's warning when he came to collect Henry. He said that witches without training were dangerous. He said people like her mother hunted them. Could this be what he meant?

Aren beckoned with an outstretched palm.

"Your hand," he said.

"What do you want me to do?"

"Test Max's theory for me," he said. "If you're learning the Language, if you're picking up on things the Order doesn't want you to understand, the spell will work. If it doesn't work . . . then you have your answer."

With significant unease, Vic held out her left hand.

"Your dominant hand, please."

Vic reminded herself that she was dreaming, that nothing that happened to her here would follow her into reality, and stretched her right hand forward. His palm was warm under hers and strong fingers held her steady. When Aren reached for the knife, Vic jerked backward. Aren's fingers closed around her hand and kept her from pulling away.

"Be brave, Victoria. You will like it."

Biting down a rush of anxiety, Vic forced herself to stay still. She stared at his hand as he pressed the sharp tip of the knife into the pad of her index finger. She hissed when the point broke the skin, and a drop of blood welled up. Crimson slid down to her palm.

"One more," Aren murmured, then did the same thing to her middle finger.

Vic held her breath as the blade dug in and exhaled when it pierced the thin barrier of skin. Another trail of blood dripped from the new slice in her hand.

"Follow me," Aren said, directing Vic's attention to the altar in front of him. He held the reed in his hands like a pencil and drew on the stone surface of the altar. The reed crumbled and left black dust behind. "Use your two fingers and repeat what I'm showing you."

He couldn't hurt her here, Vic reminded herself, because none of this was real. She was dreaming, and the pain in her hand would be gone when she woke.

Vic mimicked his movements on the stone, beginning with a straight line about the length of her hand. Two V's, crossing in the air, three shapes like X's with longer tails. Then, Aren watching Vic's face, they pressed their palms flat in the center of the symbol at the same time.

It was a rush Vic had never felt before. Blood burned in her cheeks as all her senses flew open. She could hear the trees whistling in the wind below. She could hear Aren's heartbeat like a drum in her own chest. She tasted the room as she inhaled, notes of blood and charcoal and the crisp mountain breeze. The sensation lasted an instant and was gone, and Vic was left laughing breathlessly over the table.

"I knew you had it in you," Aren said, and Vic smiled up at him, and his mouth twisted in a crooked, unconscious grin. It made his face look almost boyish, and Vic couldn't help imagining this imposing and controlled man at her age, eager, as she was, to make a name for himself.

"Magic," he said. "Just a taste."

"Forbidden magic," Vic said, and her smile faded as it dawned on her that she might have made a mistake.

Aren waved a disinterested hand, and practiced calm took over his face again. "Nothing to worry about. More a parlor trick than anything."

"Why . . ." Vic struggled for words. "Why are you helping me?"

"I've been exiled for years," Aren said. "And you're interesting, even if you know almost nothing about what's happening to you. Perhaps *because* you know almost nothing about what's happening to you. And I could not disagree more with the Order's stance on secrecy."

Aren leaned in until their faces were inches apart.

"Spread my secrets far and wide, Victoria. Knowledge cannot hurt me."

Vic bristled at his proximity. Before she knew what he was doing, his hands were on her.

"What are you—"

"Shhhh," he whispered in her ear.

Aren spun her around. One of his hands held one of hers, the wounded one, while the other grasped tight around Vic's waist. He led her forward with his chest at her back. Held captive in his embrace, Vic saw the snow-capped mountains and a streak of winding blue she knew must be the river, and it was a stunning scene. She was too distracted by the feel of warm hands on her body to realize what he was about to do until it was too late.

"You must face your fears, Victoria." His lips brushed the shell of her ear as he spoke, his breath hot on her neck. "It is the only way to grow."

And he pushed her.

Vic woke gasping. Her body pulled into itself like she really had fallen from the North Tower. She lay there panting and clutching at her chest before the truth settled in her mind. At her back were rough, unfamiliar sheets and a hard mattress and none of it had been real.

It had felt real, though. The wind biting her skin. Colors of the sky and the ground swirling around her. The terror as she fell.

What a horrible dream.

And what had the man said before he pushed her? Something about facing her fears.

Already, the finer points slipped through her mind like oil through her fingers. Vic forced herself to remember as much as she could before she lost it all. Made witches, secrecy, something about Max.

That man had shown her a spell. A parlor trick, he'd called it.

Vic wondered how her subconscious had come up with such nonsense. Was she really so desperate to fit in that she was dreaming about strange men helping her practice magic?

She banged her head back against the mattress. Her skin was covered in a thin layer of sweat, and she felt bitterly cold. She'd kicked the sheets away in her sleep, leaving her legs tangled in a mess of russet fabric.

Vic groaned and pulled herself up to sit. She'd slept, as she always did, in a pair of underwear and a T-shirt, but it was freezing in the castle in the middle of the night, and the sheets were too wet to warm her. She felt disgusting. She needed a robe and a hot shower and a break from all this madness.

Vic rubbed her eyes in the darkness and froze at a flash of pain.

Her breath came hard and shallow as she squinted at the hand in front of her face.

On the tips of her first two fingers were bloody holes like snake-bites.

Vic scuttled back against the headboard with a shriek. She swallowed and tried to breathe, but she was panicking. She couldn't wade past the abject terror that everything had gone very, very wrong.

Something moved in the darkness.

She was not alone—there was someone in the room with her.

The curtains were pulled shut and it was black as pitch on the far side of the room, but she could feel someone, or something, crouched in the darkness. Watching her.

Vic thought instantly of the man from her dream, the blond man who must exist in reality. Had he followed her here? She thought of the shadowed Orcan, the laetite, any number of unspeakable things that might lurk in the darkness.

"Who's there?" Vic called.

She climbed out of bed and kept her back to the wall.

"I know you're here," she said, trying not to sound scared. "Who are you?"

Vic strained her ears for any sound of movement, but her eyes wouldn't adjust fast enough and she couldn't see a damn thing.

But the presence of another hung heavy in the room like a hot breath, and she could feel eyes tracking her movements. A watchful gaze scraped her skin like a needle's tip.

"I can feel you," she said, but only silence replied.

Vic edged along the wall until her fingers closed around heavy velvet. She took a gasping breath and wrenched the curtains open, drenching the room in moonlight.

It was empty.

There was no one there.

XII

Familiars are created when a witch elects to transfer their soul, and with it their power, into a vessel that will outlive them. This vessel, often in the form of an animal, then binds to a living witch, combining the power of the former with that of the latter. This power can grow over the centuries, as the familiar continues to select bond-partners from among living witches.

The practice of soul transfer—the art of creating a familiar—had fallen into decline even before the Order banned it. The process kills the witch's mortal body, and creating a familiar capable of passing on their essence is not guaranteed. Rooted as it is in forbidden practice, the creation of familiars was prohibited by mandate during the Second Council of Elders. Soul transfer has been all but eradicated in recent centuries, and only a rare few familiars remain.

—Terrance Vern, *Theories on Transmogrification*
(New York, 1999)

"Rural Virginia, 2005. Two hikers go missing in the woods east of the Appalachians. Local police find their packs, alongside what they assume to be animal markings in the nearby trees—"

"Wendigo."

Xan turned his spectacled gaze on Vic, frowning.

"Am I right?" she asked.

"Let me finish," he grumbled. "Their bodies were found a week later, completely devoid of fluid."

"So I *was* right," Vic said.

Xan raised an eyebrow in silent invitation for Vic to explain.

She sighed.

Nothing had happened in the week since her encounter with the laetite in Limbo. Not a single goddamn thing. Vic hadn't gotten any better at any of the tasks Max thought she could figure out how to do. Training with the Sentinels was going fine, but Vic was as magicless as ever. Plus, she was exhausted. She hadn't slept the night before, and she was bone-tired. Tired of being useless, tired of being surrounded by people who could do what she couldn't. Tired of doors closing in her face.

The whole thing made her fractious and angry, and Vic sank back in her seat with her arms crossed over her chest. She waved a grumpy hand. Someone else could explain.

A Sentinel named Ellie raised her hand. Xan nodded for her to speak.

Class that morning had been shit, too, just like always. Elder Thompson droned like he always did, and the rest of the class ignored the two shrouded figures guarding the back of the lecture hall. The young woman was missing today.

Vic played with the twin cuts on her fingers. She hadn't said a word to anyone about the cuts or last night's dream or the man who was definitely real. Aren Mann. Vic didn't know anything for sure, and she was not so desperate for answers that she'd jeopardize her place in the castle to find out about him.

It might be nothing, she told herself.

"I have a case study," Vic said, raising her hand. Xan faced her, lowering his notebook. When he said nothing, Vic began.

"Baton Rouge, 2006," Vic said in a low, supercilious voice that only halfway mocked Xan's. "A Sentinel is dispatched to an abandoned building by the water. No reports of missing persons or any injuries, but there's an Orcan inside." Vic reached deep into her memory to find the right words. "She doesn't see the creature, but she hears it. It sounds like . . . wet footsteps, and it's large. It growls. What is it?"

Xan frowned at Vic as she spoke, his face pensive, but Sarah spoke beside her.

"Parlangua," she said. "I can't be sure without a visual or more behavioral evidence, but it sounds right. Parlangua used to stick around the bayou banks, but in the last few decades they've been roaming into more populated areas."

Xan took off his reading glasses and folded them in his hands.

"How would you kill it?" Vic asked, facing Sarah.

"Wooden stake to the liver."

"Only the liver?" Vic asked.

Sarah nodded. "And it's gotta be wood. Preferably from a local gum tree."

Xan was watching Vic when she turned to face him. She raised her eyebrows at him to carry on.

"Get out," he said. Vic stared at him in surprise. "I'll speak to you in the hallway."

"What the fuck?" Vic demanded.

Xan pointed to the door at the back of the room. "Hallway," he repeated, an edge to his tone.

Vic glared at Xan as she shouldered her bag in a huff and stormed out of the room. Sarah shot her an apologetic look. From the back row, May waved with her fingers as Vic passed. Vic flipped her off.

In the hallway, Vic paced, fuming. She heard Xan dismiss the Sentinels, followed by dozens of chairs scraping the floor as they stood. The crowd shuffled out through the front doors, into the training area, with their assignments, and Vic was alone in the opposite hallway. Keeping her away from training was just cruel. Had Vic ever wanted to hit something so badly in her life? When Xan closed the classroom door behind him and stood facing her, she rounded on him.

"Are you sending me to the principal's office?" Vic sneered. "We were discussing Orcans—I brought up an Orcan. Tell me how that's inappropriate."

Xan watched her without speaking, his arms folded in front of his chest. He looked huge and imposing and, honestly, hot as hell, and it made Vic even angrier.

"Is your ego really so fragile you can't take a little bit of back talk?" Vic spat. "Is that what's going on here? I sassed you in front of the class, and now you have to remind me who's boss."

Xan watched her like an adult waiting for a screaming child to run out of steam.

"You don't get to—"

"You need rest," he said.

Vic stopped short. Her anger fell out of her in a rush.

"You look like you haven't slept in a week," Xan said.

"It's rude to tell a woman she looks tired," Vic said, confused at the direction the conversation had taken.

"You look like shit," Xan said, and Vic knew he was right. Her hair was messy and the lines under her eyes had grown dark and thick. "You're going to hurt yourself if you go into training like this. I won't let that happen."

Vic stared at him, sure that a combination of wonder and plain old shock covered her face. Was he worried about her?

"If a Sentinel kills you by accident, Max will blame me."

Ah. Vic sighed.

"Take the day off," Xan said. With a massive hand, he gestured at Vic's face with an expression of disquiet. "Deal with *this*. That's an order."

Vic hadn't shut her mouth by the time Xan left her alone in the hallway. She should be offended, but Vic knew he was right. She *was* tired. That dream had woken her in the middle of the night, and then she had been convinced there was someone in her room, and after all of that she knew better than to try to sleep. Sleepless nights were nothing new to her, but this was something different. Vic was well and truly drained, like all the life had been sapped from her.

Vic wandered back to the apartment in a daze.

She needed rest. She needed sleep.

But the castle was empty. The Sentinels were all in training, and most of the recruits were likely practicing on their own in the training wing. It was Vic's best chance to do what she had known she needed to since she saw the wounds on her fingers this morning.

Research.

She needed to find the man from her dream, and she needed no one to see her doing it.

If Aren Mann was real, and if he really was exiled for some crime against the Order, perhaps some of the living Elders mentioned him in their archives.

Vic found the castle's main library opposite the dining hall. She'd visited a few times in an abortive attempt to find out what kind of magic held Meredith's door shut, although she'd spent the last few visits obsessing over Orcans. After the encounter in Limbo, Vic was determined to learn everything she could about the creatures, and that meant studying on her own. Some evenings a few recruits worked in the library, and Sarah told her the Order employed Historians, though Vic hadn't seen any of them in the massive space.

Inscriptions above the door either warned her to flee or welcomed her inside. They were runes, she knew, spells borrowed from people long dead. More magic she didn't understand.

High, segmented windows peeked through the maze of book-shelves. The room was packed with rows of books huddled so tight she had to squeeze between the stacks. An unimaginable amount of knowledge hid here in the mountains.

Vic's fingers danced along leather spines as she wound into the thicket, pulling books at random. They screeched protests at her opening them, speaking for the first time in years, if not decades.

She found Max's archives atop a high shelf. His were more orga-nized than the other Elders'. He structured them like journals, with each volume corresponding to a month of the year. But the collection was incomplete. Dark spaces sat where months should have been, and no new entries had been added for nearly two years.

The volume belonging to the month Meredith died was missing. Vic thought about the key Max had given her last week, and the apartment door that would not admit her. Vic swallowed against a tide of emotion, frustration first and foremost, and resolved to try again with the apartment as soon as she'd had a good night's sleep.

She found what she was looking for at the end of January 2016.

A full page had been dedicated to Aren Mann. Beneath a photo, it read:

> Aren Mann was born January 2, 1973, to Samuel and Rebecca Mann, outside Laurel, Mississippi. He began his training with the Order in 1993 and worked as a Mage from 1995 until his appointment to the Elder Council in 2010. Following Mann's departure from the Order in 2014, he formed the Brotherhood of Mann, an extremist organization headquartered west of Mount Katahdin in northern Maine. Since the Brotherhood's creation in 2014, nearly a third of the Order's active members have defected.

Vic had to read the text twice to make sure she understood. He was real, she realized, though Vic had suspected as much since she saw the twin marks he left. The man in her dream was real, and he had been an Elder. He left the Order and took a huge chunk of its ranks with him. A mass exodus explained the castle's present emptiness. Why had no one told her?

No one had mentioned him at all.

Except Xan had told her about a rival faction threatening the Order. A rival faction that didn't care about casualties or harm, that didn't care about keeping witches a secret from the rest of the world. He was talking about Mann, wasn't he?

A trembling panic in her fingers, Vic tore through the shelves around her in search of archives bearing Aren's name. If he'd been an Elder for four years, he must have written archives. Vic knew it was one of their core responsibilities.

She scanned every row in the vicinity but found nothing. A mark of his exile, perhaps, erasing his memories from the collective history.

Returning to Max's writing, Vic couldn't find another mention of Aren's Brotherhood. She skimmed as many of the archives as she could, but the Elders seemed to ignore the organization, even as it ate away at the Order's membership.

It seemed only a short time later that Vic noticed the shadows had grown long and the torches flared to life. Soon it grew frigid in the expansive space. When Vic saw condensation in her breath, she took it as a less than subtle sign to stop. She did need rest, after all. She could keep looking tomorrow.

When Vic turned to leave, she noticed a book on the floor in front of her. She found the empty space on the shelf and replaced the book where it belonged.

Vic saw more books on the floor as she turned the corner. Someone had knocked over a stack on a nearby table. Books lay scattered on the scarlet rug.

The library took on an eerie quality as Vic studied the silence for signs of life. Inert shelves loomed overhead, shadows stretching from dim torches between them. Vic held her breath and listened for the quiet hints of something lurking nearby.

But the library was dead silent. Her mind flashed to the shadowed creature she'd seen darting toward the castle. Vic doubted it made any sound when it moved, and all the shadows around her came alive with potential threat.

It was time to go. If she stayed any longer, her mind would force the shadows to shift. She would see movement on the edge of her vision and convince herself that, whatever that thing was, it was closing in on her.

But she noticed another pile of books strewn on the side of the alcove, some face down, their pages bent and torn. Searching the shelves, Vic saw a dark section high above her head. An entire shelf's worth had fallen onto the floor, as if someone had hooked their arm behind a row of books and swept them down in a fit of rage. But it was much too high to reach.

More books had been wrenched down the deeper Vic went, until they crowded the floor, and she took pains to avoid crunching their spines underfoot. Hardly any books remained on the shelves, and messy heaps filled the aisles.

As she approached another narrow aisle, Vic heard a faint buzz.

It was almost unnoticeable, but she was listening hard.

Vic knew then, in a dim, almost subconscious corner of her mind, what she would see around the bend.

Flies.

Hundreds of them.

Crawling over the face and exposed innards of a corpse.

It lay across the middle of the aisle, its head propped up on the shelf. The head and torso were surrounded by books, knocked down by the body as it fell. The abdomen was torn open, split wide in a tangled seam. A mass of red and purple and black blood and viscera spilled onto the library floor. Ribs stuck out at odd angles, flashes of white jutting from the mess like broken piano keys. Patches of burgundy, shiny skin mottled the neck and arms in dark blisters where the blood had settled. A length of black cloth, torn and bloodied, blended with the gore.

Almost in a trance, Vic stepped forward to look into the corpse's face. At her approach, the flies scattered. They lifted off the curdled skin like a sheet wriggling in the wind. Clouded eyes sat in the sockets, staring resolute into the void. Vic's stomach lurched when she recognized the face staring beyond her.

It was the female servant. Still shrouded, now dead.

For the second time since arriving at Avalon Castle, Vic turned and ran.

XIII

There are, to the knowledge of this writer, four remaining familiars. The fox, the viper, the willow, and the raven. Owing to the rarity of these creatures and their discernment in selecting bond-pairs, a connection with one of these ancients earns one a revered position in magical society. The viper and the willow have not bonded with living witches in centuries, and their current whereabouts are unknown. The fox bonds consistently with the strongest son of the Ramour family. The raven, renowned as the oldest and most powerful of these beings, has not taken a bond-pair since the death of the Eighth Raven, Elder Christopher Matheus, in 1965. A Ninth Raven has yet to be chosen.

—Terrance Vern, *Theories on Transmogrification*
(New York, 1999)

V ic's heart pounded in her ears as she wrenched open the apartment door and locked it behind her. Henry looked up from where he was studying on the couch as she bolted past into her bedroom. Kneeling, Vic pulled her duffel from under the bed and started throwing her belongings into it. She grabbed an armful of clothes off the floor and shoved them into the bag.

"We're leaving!" she shouted in a shaking voice. "Now."

Henry followed Vic into her room. The crease between his brows deepened when he saw her packing. "What's going on?"

"We have to go." Vic pulled the drawer out of her bedside table and shook the contents into her bag. "Get your stuff together."

"Did something happen?"

"We'll talk about it in the car." Vic tossed the empty drawer aside.

"Vic, what happened?"

"We don't have time for this. Where is it? Where is it?" She hoisted the edge of the mattress up and rooted around until she found the knife she'd stashed there.

"Whoa, Vic! You brought a dagger?"

She ignored him, tucking the sheathed knife into the back of her jeans and marching into the living room. Henry needed to hurry. He needed to get his things so they could leave.

"We need to find the car," Vic said. "It should have enough gas to get us back to the town we passed on the way in. We can get a room there, too. I saw a hotel—"

"Vic."

"Driving in this weather isn't ideal, but we'll be fine if we leave now. The snow—"

"Vic, talk to me."

Vic spun to face him. "Get your stuff, Henry. Now!"

Her phone was charging in the kitchen. She turned toward it, and—

Henry grabbed Vic by the shoulders and brought her face in line with his. Vic saw confusion in his eyes. Confusion and no small amount of fear.

"You need to tell me what's happened."

"Someone is dead," Vic choked out.

"Who?" Henry asked.

Vic shook her head. "I don't know her name. She wasn't there today."

"I don't know what that means."

Vic knew she wasn't communicating clearly. It was a minor miracle she could communicate at all, when she couldn't think. Her mind was a blank wall of panic. They had to get out of here.

Henry shook her. "You need to calm down."

She couldn't breathe. She couldn't get enough air.

She saw Henry's face crawling with flies, mouth agape in a perpetual scream, and he was the one lying prostrate on the library floor, torn open by something bigger and meaner than he was. Ribs. Blood. Organs. Clouded eyes staring into nothing.

She couldn't stop it. She couldn't calm down.

Henry tugged Vic to the sitting area and pushed her toward the couch. She sank into the cushions and fought the urge to flee. Henry took the seat beside her and grabbed her shoulders again, forcing her to look at him.

No bugs there. No blood, no gore. Just Henry.

He was intact. He was okay.

But he looked scared. Scared and small, like he had when Meredith left. Looking at Vic like she might know what to do. Same as the last time, Vic had no idea.

"You need to tell me what's going on," he said.

"She works in the castle." Vic could hardly pull air into her lungs. "She's dead."

"How do you know?"

"I found her," Vic gasped. "In the library. There was blood everywhere. In the books, the carpet, everything was covered in it." Heaving breaths failed to soothe the tightness behind her breastbone. "We have to leave, Henry."

"We can't leave," he replied, frowning. "We should find someone, though. We need to report this."

"No." Vic squeezed his wrists. "Something's killed her, Henry. It could still be here. We have to leave."

"Whatever it is, the Order can deal with it. But we have to tell someone."

Vic shook her head. "I can't go back there. Whatever it is could come back."

"Putting aside the facts that it's pitch-black outside and that we don't know where the car is and that neither of us knows how to drive in snow, we can't just leave."

"We'll figure it out."

"Do you think we're better off stranded on the side of the road in a snowstorm?"

They *were* better off on the side of the road. Anywhere but here.

Henry must have seen her resolution, because he squared his shoulders. "I'm not leaving," he said gently.

Vic's hands fell into her lap. "You're not safe here," she told him. "No one is."

"The Order can take care of it, Vic."

"The Order can't take care of anything," she cried. "Don't you see? It's all falling apart around them."

But Henry was shaking his head. He put his face level with hers. "Vic, if you don't feel safe here, you can leave. You don't need to protect me anymore."

Vic opened her mouth. Closed it. Of course she needed to protect him. She'd been protecting him her whole life.

"I can't leave you." Vic's voice sounded frail, distant. When Meredith left, Henry was ten years old. He'd just lost his mother, and he was frightened. Vic was, too, but there was never any room for her to show it. She had to protect him, had to manage his fear, make him feel safe. She hid her own weakness from him, determined to deal with it in private. But eight years later, now it spilled out of her like blood. She couldn't hold it in anymore. She was terrified, and she felt weaker than she ever had.

"Maybe you should leave me, Vic," Henry said. "If things are falling apart, have you considered that maybe you're making it worse?"

"How can you say that to me?" Vic whispered. "I'm trying to protect you."

Henry squinted in disbelief. "Are you?" he asked, his voice gentle and low. "I worry about you, Vic, and it's distracting me. I'm too busy focusing on you—on the shitty things the other recruits say, on whether or not you're safe—and I'm falling behind. I'm missing things in training."

Vic was shaking her head.

"I know this has been hard for you," Henry said, and she shook his hand off her shoulder. Vic hugged her arms around her chest like they were the only things keeping her organs inside. "I know you don't want to let me go. But maybe . . . maybe it's time."

This wasn't happening. Vic couldn't leave him here, not after what she'd seen, not after everything she'd learned. The Order was on the brink of war—the castle was not a safe place. Not for Henry, not for anybody. Vic had sworn to Meredith that she would protect Henry, that she would keep him safe no matter what.

"I belong *here*," Henry said, "with people like me."

"I'm like you," Vic said. "I'm your family."

"And I love you too much to let you get yourself hurt," Henry said. "You won't go with me. Will you?"

Vic was going to cry. She felt the choked sensation at the top of her throat, and the muscles in her cheeks grew tight. Henry reached for her again, but she slapped his hand away. Vic vaulted to her feet.

"No," Henry whispered. "I won't."

Tears ran down Vic's face as she watched him. She couldn't do this. She couldn't leave him.

Vic walked to the door of the apartment and pulled it open. She had to go somewhere, she had to do something. Every instinct in her wanted to fight, break things, hurt herself or someone else. Her hands shook, and she clenched them.

Fleeing down the hallway, Vic had no idea where to go. If she could find Sarah, Vic could ask her, but all Vic knew was that Sarah lived on the fourth floor. Vic needed to find a staircase.

But as she watched, the hallway curled to the left, cutting off access to the stairwell with a loud groan.

Vic swore.

She ran forward in the new direction. There had to be a staircase along here somewhere. She searched the walls for something she recognized.

Of course the castle would confuse her tonight of all nights, when it had left her alone for days. Of course it would send her skittering through dark hallways the one night she knew something prowled nearby.

It didn't even surprise Vic when the hallway cut itself off short. Dead end. She threw up her hands with a frustrated shriek. But when she turned, she saw a staircase she had missed. Vic didn't know where she was going but up, or what part of the castle it would spit her out in.

As Vic barreled around the landing, she ran headlong into a familiar figure.

Max grabbed Vic around her upper arms to stop her falling backward. He grew somber as he took in Vic's teary, panic-stricken expression.

"What is it?"

She stared at his face, watched it twist with concern.

"Someone's dead. Murdered," she said. "In the library."

Max's eyes betrayed a grim acceptance, like he'd been waiting for something like this to happen.

"Come with me."

Max—why hadn't she thought of Max? He could help her. Max would know what to do.

Vic wound through the halls behind Max, fighting to pull her breathing under control. She reminded herself that she was allowed to feel afraid. She had seen something few people would ever see. It would be alarming if she saw that body and felt nothing, wouldn't it?

The woman had suffered, that much was obvious. Vic imagined what her last moments must have been like—the pain and fear and cold. Vic wanted to rip the image from her mind but it stuck there, nestled deep like some kind of rot.

Max gestured with his right hand, and Vic thought for an instant that she saw some kind of marking, a dark and shimmery tattoo. But the instant she registered it, the mark disappeared, leaving only clean, unblemished skin.

Vic jerked down when a bird flew by above her. She flung her hands over her head, and her mind jumped to the body in the library. Max caught her arm and pulled her up with a comforting smile. His raven, she remembered, his familiar. Nothing to fear. She caught a streak of black as it disappeared around the next corner. Vic tried to slow her breathing.

They came upon a set of double doors, which swung forward to admit them. Lights flared to life, and a fire sprang up in the hearth. Crowded shelves stretched to the ceiling on all sides. Vic felt suffocated at the thought of being back in the library. But they were on another floor, several flights above the library, and this room was warm.

Max led her to a tufted sofa, and Vic's legs shook as she sat. Max crouched in front of her, gray eyes boring into hers.

"You need to breathe, Victoria. You're panicking. Which, while understandable, is not, at present, abundantly helpful."

To her astonishment, Vic laughed. A reedy laugh that came more from surprise than mirth, but it disrupted the panicked rhythm of her breathing enough that she could speak.

"What—"

A pounding at the door made Vic jump. Her face swung toward the sound as Max called for someone to enter.

The doors parted before the words left Max's mouth, and the Chief Sentinel swept into the room. Xan wore the same black training clothes he always did. In fact, he looked like he must have come from the training yard, despite the lateness of the hour. His long hair was loose around his face, and stubble obscured his jawline. The room shrank a degree as Xan crowded the space. Vic was surprised he could enter the doorframe without ducking. Max's raven flew over his head to perch on the shelf behind Max's desk.

Xan's pale gaze swept over her body, anger taking root in his brow.

Vic rubbed a furious hand over her cheeks. Just this afternoon Xan had told her she looked worn out, that she needed rest. She wondered what he thought of her now, crying and half-hysterical. Vic hated that Xan bore witness to her weakness, that he could look at her and see and hear and feel how scared she was. The evidence was all over her face.

"What happened?" Xan asked, his voice low and serious.

His eyes looked like glass shards, sharp and unforgiving. Xan held Vic's gaze as Max spoke.

"Thank you for coming so quickly. Victoria found a body in the library."

That got his attention, and Xan's expression grew dark. He took a long breath, still watching Vic's face.

"Something has gotten inside the castle," Max explained.

Xan nodded, as tense as a coiled spring.

He looked like a god of war, Vic thought. Solemn and silent and fearless. She bet he wasn't afraid of whatever he might find lurking in the stacks downstairs. She should be scared of him, she knew. Anyone with that degree of power and control was worth fearing, but Vic found it strangely comforting. Xan could find whatever killed the woman downstairs, and he could fight it, and kill it, and Vic could feel safe again.

"Search the castle. Secure the exits."

But Xan hesitated. His frown grew more pronounced as he stood in the doorway, watching Vic.

"Yes?" Max asked.

Xan shook his head, then swept out of the room. The door sighed shut behind him.

Max returned his attention to Vic for a moment before he stood. He collected a glass of water from a bar on the side wall and handed it to Vic, who took it with shaking hands.

"You were about to speak when Alexandros came in," Max reminded her.

Vic stared at the water in her palms. "I was going to ask what happened."

"You tell me. What do you remember?"

"I went to the library this evening. I wanted to find out more about—" Vic cut herself off and looked into Max's eyes. He nodded for her to continue, and Vic hoped he wouldn't be angry with her when she did. "I had a dream last night that I was in the North Tower. Only I've never been to the North Tower. A man there told me his name was Aren Mann."

A shadow fell over Max's face. But he didn't seem surprised to hear that either.

"He said that he was exiled from the Order. I can't remember much else, but I remember that." Vic shook her head. "I didn't even know if he was real."

She toyed with the cuts on her fingertips, rubbing them against her thumb as she kept them hidden in her lap.

"Where did you start?"

"I went to your archives."

"A wise idea. What did you find?"

"You wrote that an Elder named Aren Mann left the Order and formed a competing faction. You called it an extremist group."

"I did."

Vic's voice shook as she described the rest of her evening in the library.

"I've never seen a dead body before," she said. "Not even at a funeral."

"Nothing can get into my office, I promise," Max said. "Even Alexandros can't get inside unless I admit him."

Vic wished Xan were there still.

It was a wild thought that came out of nowhere. Xan drove Vic nuts, ignored her most days and fought with her when he didn't, and yet, when her hands shook with fear and exhaustion, Vic wanted him nearby. She would feel safe standing next to him, she knew. Vic almost laughed at the absurdity of it.

"What can you remember about the body?" Max asked.

"It was ripped open. Like something ate her from the inside out."

Max frowned again. Vic waited for him to ask more questions, but he stayed quiet, mulling over her words.

After a long pause, Vic broke the silence. "What do you think did it?"

"You already know what did it."

"No, I—"

"You do. Think about it."

"I don't know anything about monsters. I work in a restaurant." She *worked* in a restaurant, Vic reminded herself. Now she spent her days learning magic she couldn't practice.

"You've been working with the Sentinels; you've studied Orcans. Try to remember. Do any of the creatures you've learned about attack like this?"

Vic ran through her memory, trying to match details. It was hard to mesh the horrible reality she'd seen with the dry descriptions of ink on paper. Some creatures mauled their prey, but this was no ordinary mauling. One variety of Orcan parasite made its home in victims' stomachs and chewed its way out of their chests. But this was too big to be a parasite.

"Strix."

"How do you know?"

"They're giant birds, which explains why so many of the books fell from higher shelves. It would have to have been either very tall or flying. Flying makes more sense."

"That's not all," Max prodded.

"Strixes disembowel their prey and eat their innards," Vic said in a flat voice. In an odd way, sorting through the details helped calm her down, forced her to think rather than feel. "But how did it get into the castle?"

According to the account the Sentinels had gone over, strixes' wingspans stretched as far as five meters. Vic couldn't imagine one flying through the library door unnoticed.

"You know the answer to that one, too."

Vic sifted through her memories again. "Window," she decided. That was why it had been so cold in the library. One of the massive windows must have been left open or broken.

Max nodded again.

"But why?" Vic asked.

Max leaned back and watched Vic carefully before he spoke. His gaze was so intense, Vic couldn't stand it. She focused on the wall behind him. Max had a library's worth of books in his office, alongside the bar with its dazzling medley of liquids in cut crystal decanters, and Vic wished he'd offered her something stronger than water. She could use a drink.

"In your dream," Max said, "did Aren Mann say anything to you about the Order?"

"Something about secrecy, and secrecy not making sense." Vic shook her head. "He called the Elders hypocrites for practicing Orcan magic."

Oh, god, Vic thought. She had done a spell with him, and the next day an Orcan got loose in the castle. Had Vic brought this about by practicing forbidden magic? How badly had she broken the rules?

"Orcan magic can be deployed to disastrous consequences," Max said. "But there's nothing inherently wrong with it. Good and evil are human concepts, and they give us no insight here."

"Could someone accidentally summon an Orcan?" Vic asked. She edged her thumbnail into the cut on her index finger and pushed. Had her own foolish insistence on belonging here led to the death of an innocent woman?

"This was no accident," Max said, his voice full of force. "Not only would the person responsible have to summon the creature, they would also have to break through dozens of very strong wards protecting the castle. No, this was premeditated. Likely planned months in advance."

"Why?" Vic said. "Why would someone want her dead? What could she have done to them?"

Max sent Vic a pitying look and shrugged. "It's not about her. It's not about anyone in particular, I'm sure. This is our home," he said, a sad sigh in his voice. "The castle is the Order's stronghold, our fortress, a symbol of our power and history. What better way to undermine the Order than to set a monster loose within our own halls?"

"She didn't do anything wrong," Vic said. "She was just there." Vic remembered Xan's warning—*they don't care about human casualties.*

Max shook his head, looking older than ever. "She didn't do anything wrong," he repeated.

"So you think it was Aren Mann," Vic whispered.

"I know that it was."

The man in her dream. Charming and cavalier and wearing a mask of calm. Max thought he'd killed someone, an innocent woman just doing her job.

"Is this what the Brotherhood of Mann wants, then?" Vic asked. "To tear down the Order?"

Max ran a hand through his patchwork of black and gray hair. "The Brotherhood has no interest in preserving the Veil. They believe the Order has limited itself by focusing on balance. They use Orcan magic freely."

If the Elders were to be believed, the free use of Orcan magic could lead to the unleashing of Orcan creatures upon the world en masse. It would be apocalyptic. Vic couldn't imagine why anyone would advocate for that. Aren didn't seem like someone who would burn the world to a crisp on a lark.

"What is the Order doing to stop them?"

"So far? Very little."

A massive fist rammed against the door to Max's office, and Vic jumped to her feet, her heart in her throat.

Max stood and sighed. "Come in, Alexandros."

The door swung inward with a bang, and Xan charged back into the room. If she thought she'd seen Xan angry before, she'd been wrong. Hostility flooded the room when he entered, choking the air. His dark hair was swept back from his forehead like he'd run there, though he bore no signs of exertion. His eyes landed on Vic immediately, then Max. The instant she saw him, Vic knew Xan had not found the strix.

How he had searched the castle so quickly, Vic had no idea.

"Nothing?" Max asked.

He shook his head and crossed the room to stand beside Vic, his anger palpable.

"Victoria suspects the creature is a strix," Max said.

Xan nodded, looking at Vic from the corner of his eye. "The wounds are consistent with a strix attack, and there was an open window on the western side of the library."

"The Brotherhood has finally attacked," Max said.

"Yes."

"The Elders will want to investigate," Max said. "And we should inform the rest of the Order before they find out elsewhere." Max looked apologetically at Vic. "Allow me to beg your pardon in advance. This will not be pleasant for you."

Before Vic could ask what he meant, Xan stepped forward, and held his arm out in front of her for an instant before he pulled it back. When she looked up, Vic noticed Max had caught the gesture as well.

"You cannot seriously be thinking about bringing her," Xan said.

"She's in training," Max said, meeting Xan's eyes. "All the other recruits will be there."

Xan gave an exasperated shake of his head. "You're still going to push this?" Xan's voice fell low. "Someone's dead, Max. We should get her out of the castle while everyone is distracted."

"What are you talking about?" Vic asked.

"I will need to convene the Order," Max replied, watching Xan's face. "Tonight."

"She will not be safe down there," Xan said. "Max, you need to think this through."

But Max turned to Vic. "What do you think?" he asked. "It's your decision—you can come to the meeting with Alexandros and the rest of the Order present, or you can leave the castle."

Vic swallowed and looked up at Xan. He wasn't looking at her, but she could see his anger in the tautness of his face and neck. He was furious at Max. At Vic, too, probably.

Not twenty minutes ago Vic had wanted out of this castle. She'd wanted to take Henry and run as far as she could. That had been fear talking, the old voice in the back of her mind telling her to run. Already, it began to quiet. She couldn't abandon Henry—leaving her brother behind was unthinkable. But Vic had another reason to stay, one that became more present in her mind each time she wondered why she was still here: She wanted to know what they wanted to keep from her. Vic wanted to see the other side of the door.

"I'll go," she said.

Beside her, Vic thought she felt Xan sigh.

Max nodded, all business, and moved toward a narrow table in front of his desk. The raven, which had sat so silently that Vic hadn't noticed its presence, took flight and perched on the edge of the table.

"Where is it?" Max mumbled to himself as he scanned a row of jars beside the desk. "Where is—there."

He plucked an ancient-looking glass jar and set it on the spell table, then pulled a flat stone basin forward and eased the jar open. It was full of something dark and viscous. It might have been mud once. Vic moved for a better view and caught Xan watching her through narrowed eyes.

She shot him a look, and he turned away from her, frowning.

Max scooped a glob of the stuff out with two fingers and drew a series of inscriptions on the base of the bowl. He worked with the swift ease of an artist sketching a scene he'd witnessed a thousand times. The pigment stuck like dried paint, but Max's lines were smooth. After a few seconds, he straightened.

He rubbed his hands together, and all traces of the paste disappeared as if he'd washed them. He reached across the table and drew a black match from another jar. It flared to life without being struck, and Max dropped it into the basin.

Vic jumped when it exploded, and Xan put a hand on her back to steady her. A puff of fire filled the basin and was gone. Max's drawing burned bright as dying embers, then faded.

Xan elbowed Vic gently and put his hands over his ears, encouraging her to follow suit. She did, though she didn't see why it was necessary, and turned back to Max.

Vic had less than a second to consider the strangeness of the display before pillars of fire flared from the candles lining the walls. Another instant, and she understood the need to cover her ears. An angry shriek resounded from the walls, as if the castle were screaming. It came from everywhere, all at once, as every atom of the walls wailed.

"Follow Alexandros," Max mouthed to her, then strode swiftly out of the room.

"Where is he going?" Vic shouted.

But Xan watched her without speaking, his face grim. Then he moved toward her, and Vic fought the urge to step back. What had gotten into Xan? He kept touching her, like small contact was typical between the two of them, like he had a right to put his hands on her skin. On another night, Vic might have welcomed the change. Not today, not when she felt raw—exposed, like a gaping wound.

Xan put his hands on Vic's shoulders and leaned in. Vic held her breath.

"No matter what happens," Xan said. His voice was low, and loud enough to hear over the alarm. It rumbled through Vic's chest. "Do not try to run, and do not let them know that you're afraid."

And he turned and pulled her out of the room. And Vic felt the edges of fear creep across her mind like a shadow.

XIV

The Acheron Order rarely meets. Members live across the globe, and bringing them together creates logistical problems even the most patient among the Order struggle to tolerate. Most disputes are resolved by committee. The Elders act as the go-betweens for different groups within the Order, and much of an Elder's day is spent conversing with members and addressing their concerns. For the Order to be drawn together, all at once, something truly great or truly terrible must be under way.

—From the archives of E. Scott Crew (1973)

Vic struggled to keep pace with Xan as he swept down the hallway. On all sides, billowing candles and torches lit the castle like a house engulfed in flame.

For the first time since Vic had arrived at Avalon Castle, it came alive. All around them, doorways flew open and rooms' occupants poured into the halls. Witches pressed against one another in the typically desolate corridors. All of them headed in the same direction—down.

People crowded against Vic and Xan as they reached a stone staircase. The steps were compressed in the center from use and the walls echoed the lamplight in shades of orange and red. *Descending into hell,* Vic thought as she pushed through the crowd.

Xan didn't have to fight through this mess, she realized. No one shoved against *him.* After losing her footing in the torrent, Vic grabbed a fistful of Xan's T-shirt to steady herself. The skin under her knuckles was hot and hard, and Vic couldn't help noticing how muscular he was under all the clothing. As if reading her thoughts, Xan shot an offended look over his shoulder, clearly fighting the urge to throw her off him. If he wanted her to keep up, then they should hold hands, she nearly snapped back. Perhaps that would pacify him.

Then again, after his behavior in Max's office, maybe he would welcome it. Vic swallowed.

Down the stairs they went, flight after flight, until Vic was sure they were beneath the Arena, deeper even than Limbo. Vic wondered dimly if the Order's fixation on re-creating a medieval castle extended to the maintenance of a dungeon. It smelled like it did. The air reeked of dirt and moisture and something old. And the deeper they descended, the stronger the smell became.

The staircase bottomed out into a tunnel. Surrounded by wet stone, the passage angled down and dragged them into the earth.

And there were even more people than before. The crowd thickened, and Vic turned toward an influx of witches. They were coming out of the walls, she realized with a jolt. Along the sides of the tunnel, narrow gaps opened where stone had been an instant before, and people hurried through. Some looked confused, a handful excited, but none of them marveled at the fact that they had popped out of solid rock.

While Vic goggled, a rough hand closed around her waist, and she gasped. Her eyes shot up to find Xan's glowering face only inches from hers. She started backward, but the hand on her waist held her still and her breath hitched. She caught a look of something in his eyes, a flash at the contact like he felt a shock, too. But it was gone in an instant and he was glaring at her.

"Keep up," Xan said. "And stop stretching out my shirt." His mouth came up against her hair for an instant, ruffling the air around her ear. A shiver ran down her spine. But then Xan was moving, and the hand around her waist left a buzzing cold when it fell away and encircled her wrist. He pulled her forward into an enormous space.

A cave, Vic realized. A vast cave full of people.

A massive fire at the front threw the space into dappled light, and Vic was struck once again by the sense of moving backward in time to a place deep and ancient. Vic gaped in horror, not realizing she had stopped again.

The room had been carved into a pit. Steps led in a semicircle to a stage at the bottom. A dais, she supposed, was the proper word, though she had never before had an occasion to use it. The platform was elevated above the lowest steps and arranged with rough-hewn wooden thrones. But Vic's gaze stuck on the crude sculpture behind them.

It might have been a tree once, with a trunk nearly as wide as the dais around it. Carved by man or nature or some force belonging to neither, Vic could not tell. At least thirty feet tall, the statue curled up toward the rock ceiling, roots and branches spiking out from its center. In the middle of the wide trunk was a face from a nightmare. Hollow eyes slit sideways and opened to nothing. Its open maw held the flames that lit the room. It screamed fire, and witches swarmed around it like moths.

A blurry form pulled Vic back to reality. Sarah lunged toward her in a swirl of messy hair and a flash of pink pajama top.

"Are you okay?" Sarah shouted, and Vic nodded.

The rough hand slipped from her arm, and Vic reached for it without thinking. But over Sarah's shoulder, Vic watched Xan's dark head disappear through the crowd. She felt exposed without him, as if he'd thrown her to the wolves. Sarah pulled Vic to the steps, which the rest of the witches began to use as seats throughout the massive space.

They found an opening at the far edge and sat against the stone wall. This must be the entire Order, Vic thought as the space grew cramped. Most of them looked ruffled at the rude awakening. Plenty had their hands over their ears, and they faced the front of the room, waiting.

Men in black gathered on the dais. They wore heavy sleeveless hooded tunics, which split at the center and ran down their fronts in two thick bars. Of everyone in the room, these men looked the most at ease. A few of them lounged on the ugly wooden chairs placed in a crescent around the platform—there were twelve thrones, one for each Elder.

Max stood beside Elder Thompson, looking strained as he surveyed the crowd.

One of the older men moved to the front. He pulled his hood up, and it fell in front of his eyes and nose, leaving only his mouth exposed. Vic frowned at the reminder of the human servants, and scanned the room to find that none of them had followed the Order into the earth. Meetings must be for witches' eyes only, Vic realized, and she shifted in her seat.

The Elder's lips were thin and cracked with age. He held both hands up with palms facing the room, and his mouth moved. Something in the palm of each hand flared red. The roar around them was snuffed out like a candle.

Silence fell thick and heavy on the expectant crowd. Vic's ears rang at the sudden absence of deafening noise.

When the Elder spoke again, his voice sliced the air. Vic felt the words hit her chest like a hammer and knew that he spoke magic more powerful than anything she had heard before. As he finished, a pulse ran through the room. Vic's heart beat faster. The meeting had begun.

"Elder Shepherd has called an emergency assembly," the old man announced, his voice dry as sandpaper. Vic heard him as clearly as if he had spoken directly into her ear. A murmur rippled through the crowd.

Max stepped to the front of the dais and bowed to the other Elder. He did not raise his hood before addressing the room.

"I'm sorry to interrupt your evening, and to force so many of you to return to the castle on such short notice." Max nodded to a group of older witches. "Rest assured I would not have bid you come if it was not necessary."

He spoke in a clear voice that seemed to resonate within the earthen walls.

"A member of our community was killed last night. Her body was discovered in the library this evening."

Vic saw confusion, fear, concern on the faces of the nearby witches. Some searched the crowd as if looking for a missing member.

"The deceased was Rachel Ogden."

Rachel Ogden, Vic repeated to herself. How had she forgotten to ask her name?

"Ms. Ogden worked as a servant for the Order for nearly a decade."

The Elder beside Max still had his hood up when he spoke. "You summoned us here because a human was killed?"

"We believe she was killed by a strix," Max said. "An Orcan has entered the premises."

A shock ran through the crowd, and the shouts began.

Chaos built on itself as voices echoed through the room. People turned and talked to their neighbors, speculating about what could have led to this, if it had been an accident, how this could have happened within the castle.

"The creature has not been found," Max continued over the noise. "Obviously, this is a matter of grave importance, and we need to—"

"Who found the body?"

Nathaniel lounged on one of the thrones behind Max. He leaned forward when he spoke, as if to relish the answer when it came.

"I did," Max said without hesitation. "During my nightly rounds. It was clear she was attacked by something that should never have been able to access the castle."

Nathaniel sat back, his eyes narrowing.

"Our stronghold has been breached," Max continued, returning his attention to the room. "As such, we must enact additional protocols to protect the castle. The Sentinels will resume constant patrols, and a team will be sent to—"

"Perhaps additional protections are necessary," Nathaniel interrupted. Max faced him with his hands behind his back. "But it's no secret we've fallen behind on respecting existing protocols."

"Elder Carver," another Elder cut in beside him. "This is not the venue for this discussion."

"But this is the perfect time to discuss a matter that affects us all,"

Nathaniel said. "How often do we get the chance to resolve disputes with the whole of the Order present?"

Max watched Nathaniel but made no effort to stop him.

"As many of you are, I'm sure, aware," Nathaniel continued, "a human was recently permitted to enter the castle without escort or, as far as I can tell, any protective measures in place at all."

Ice flooded Vic's veins.

"Not only has this human been given an apartment in our castle, she has been caught spying on the Chief Sentinel on at least one occasion."

Vic couldn't hear the crowd's response over the blood rushing in her ears.

"What's more, this human has been invited to participate in training, and has accompanied Level One recruits for almost two weeks."

Some of the bystanders gasped. Vic was too stunned to think through what Nathaniel was saying, or the others' reactions to it, as the room fell into outraged conversations again. Anger radiated from the crowd as its energy grew.

Each word hit Vic like a drumbeat.

"The mandates of the Acheron Order are clear as to how we must respond to such a breach."

Max's face was an expressionless mask as he watched Nathaniel.

"Given the severity of the offense, the only appropriate punishment for the Order member responsible is expulsion."

The gravity of Nathaniel's words sank home. He'd condemned another Elder. He'd called for Max to be cast out. Because of Vic.

"And . . ." Nathaniel was still talking. Why the fuck was he still talking? "As for the human in question, the rules are clear. She must be silenced."

Vic caught several eyes watching her. A few people pointed, some shouted. The crowd realized where she was, and who she was. Nathaniel followed the room's attention until his gaze found Vic's.

Lit from behind by the fire, Nathaniel looked at Vic like he had the night they met. As though she were vermin, a particularly repellent insect he wanted nothing more than to crush under his shoe. Vic was less than him, less than anyone here.

How dare he look at her like that.

"Can I respond?" Vic called into the silence, no magic amplifying her voice.

"No," Nathaniel said.

"You're talking about me. I will respond."

"This is not a court of law, Ms. Wood," Nathaniel replied, giving every appearance of boredom. "You have no rights here."

"My mother was Meredith Wood," Vic said. "For her sake, at least, don't look at me like a piece of pond scum—any of you," she directed at the crowd.

Members made sounds of disagreement.

"You wish to contest the rules?" Nathaniel asked. A sickening smile twisted his face. He shrugged with one shoulder. "Fine."

Vic shot a look at Sarah, whose eyes were wide with fear.

"I invoke the Rite of Trial," Nathaniel said, and the crowd went silent.

"Absolutely not," Sarah said under her breath. "No way."

"If you wish to defend your place here, Ms. Wood," Nathaniel said, "this is the way to do it."

"Max won't let him do this," Sarah said.

Vic searched the crowd as if she would find clarity on the shocked faces surrounding her. At the back of the room, Xan stood alert, poised like he was about to jump. He was staring at Max, his eyes set under a furious frown.

But when Vic cast a questioning glance at Max, his eyes were on her. Slowly, almost imperceptibly, he nodded.

"This could kill her, Max," Sarah shouted, her voice pleading. Max shot her a stern look, and Sarah fell quiet.

Nathaniel was smiling. "Come here, Ms. Wood."

Vic wanted to ask what it was, what Nathaniel was talking about, what she needed to do, but her mind went blank as she stared at the men on the dais. Max, whom she trusted, whose fate was on the line as much as hers, had nodded for her to go ahead.

She pulled herself away from Sarah, who stared at her with horror as Vic found a narrow aisle through the crowd and began to descend.

Vic recalled Xan's words—*do not try to run, and do not let them know that you're afraid.* Had he and Max known this was going to happen? Had they expected this? Vic set her jaw. She would not run. She would not show fear. Vic hardly noticed the crowd's attention. She was too focused on the robed men in front of her as she approached like a condemned woman walking to the gallows.

"Stand here, Ms. Wood." Nathaniel indicated the center of the step leading up to the dais, several feet wide and a foot beneath the raised platform.

Vic breathed hard through her nose, counting each breath to hold panic at bay. Her heart pounded. She stopped at the center of the step and glared at Nathaniel.

"Elder Key, if you don't mind," Nathaniel said, addressing the old man who had opened the meeting.

The old man nodded and turned toward the sculpture behind the Elders. With bare hands he reached into the fiery mouth, and Vic suppressed a gasp. A second later, he extracted a metal box, weather-beaten and ancient, still glowing red from the flames.

He approached Vic with the box in both hands. His skin, wrinkled and thin, bore no sign of burns.

Vic shot a questioning look at Max, who was watching her with stone-cold severity, a furrow in his brow and an expectant gleam in his gaze. Whatever was in that box, Max thought Vic could handle it.

She stood straight and pushed her panic aside. She would not give Nathaniel the satisfaction of seeing her scared.

"The Rite of Trial," Nathaniel began, addressing the crowd as if he were lecturing recruits, "has existed since before the Acheron Order and is the best-known means of testing an individual's aptitude for magical practice."

He opened the box without reacting to the heat.

Within lay a pair of shackles.

Thick and warped with time like they hadn't been used for a thousand years.

The cuffs were several inches wide, and instead of chains they were connected by a band of solid metal. The wearer's forearms would be bound together, rendering them unable to move.

The metal glowed red, and the air over the box shimmered with heat.

"The mechanism is quite simple," Nathaniel said. He picked up the gnarled pieces of metal. "The shackles are composed of a potent energy that even an untrained witch—given the proper, shall we say, motivation—will be able to untangle."

Nathaniel opened the shackles on both sides and faced Vic.

"There are two possible outcomes of the Trial," Nathaniel said, muddy eyes on her. "If the person undergoing the Trial possesses any magical ability whatsoever, they will succeed in the Unthreading and free themselves of their restraints. If they do not . . ." One side of his lip tilted up in a cruel smile. "Well, the traditional alternative was death. But rest assured we will intervene before it comes to that."

Vic couldn't think through the rage and fear hounding her mind. She couldn't focus on Nathaniel's words through the disdain in his eyes. The possibility of death at the hands of these . . . whatever they were . . . hardly pierced the haze of Vic's anger.

"Your arms, Ms. Wood," Nathaniel said, standing in front of Vic. He wanted her to do this herself, to make clear she chose this. He was the worst kind of bully, Vic thought, one who made his victim feel responsible for the torment.

Slowly, Vic stuck her arms out in front of her.

Her hands balled into fists, and she held the muscles taut to avoid shaking.

She expected burning pain as the red-hot metal neared her skin.

She expected heat and fire. Branding marks and the smell of singed flesh.

But when the shackles closed over Vic's wrists, they were ice-cold.

Vic's kneecaps hit the stone floor with a smack.

She didn't feel the impact.

She couldn't feel anything beyond the pain.

Pain, everywhere. Every part of her body exploded in electric, white-hot anguish.

It was a sensation completely foreign to Vic. Broken bones, turned ankles, a punch to the face—nothing had prepared her for this.

She twisted on the ground as each cell in her body was strangled by magic she couldn't see.

Something came off the shackles like smoke, pouring across her skin and leaking into her mouth and nose, and everywhere it went it brought blinding pain.

Every nerve ending in her body felt flayed alive.

Vic couldn't see, couldn't think, couldn't sense anything but pain.

But after a minute, or an hour, or an endless day, she noticed—an errant thought dancing across a feral mind—that she hadn't breathed since the gasp she took as she fell.

Vic focused every inch of her body on taking a single breath, and she found that one sip of oxygen made the pain a little less prominent.

And so she kept on breathing until she was inhaling slow and steady, and the pain began to recede.

Vic could almost see the magic winding around her body like a snake intent on constricting her to death. But what was she supposed to do with it? *The Unthreading*, Nathaniel called it, but Vic couldn't see any threads. Couldn't see anything but the illusion of smoke pouring into her.

She breathed hard and heavy and solid until eventually she could pull herself back to her knees, and she could feel her own body enough to register that her knees *hurt*. Kneeling *hurt*.

But this was a different kind of pain, one Vic knew well. When she fell while training, this was what it felt like. When her hand slipped while sharpening a knife, and the skin split open at the slice, this was what it felt like. This kind of pain was predictable. It sent a message; it had a purpose. Pain meant her body was alive enough to fight.

Vic focused on the pain in her knees, on the realness of the ache, and felt herself shoving the shackles' artificial hurt away from her. It wasn't real, she realized. It couldn't rip her apart the way broken bones and torn skin could. It was pain for pain's sake, and that was useless to her.

Her eyes flared open, and they were wet like she'd been crying. The world was fogged with blood-red clouds, and Vic blinked until she could see Nathaniel through the mess. He looked down at her with pure hatred.

"Enough!" Vic growled.

Max leaped forward and pulled the shackles from her arms in an instant. The second they left her skin, the pain fell away like it had never existed. No hurt, no damage, just a dull ache across every part of her.

Vic fell back to a seat, stunned.

She felt burned, exhausted, wrung dry by the magic that had coursed through her skin, bringing nothing but agony. But she had almost done it, hadn't she? She hadn't died, she hadn't lost. A fragile hope took root behind her sternum.

She was so close.

Max threw the shackles aside and grabbed Vic's shoulder. He smiled, weakly, though his eyes were wild.

But no one said a word.

The room was dead silent, and everyone stared at Vic.

One of the Elders behind Nathaniel moved forward.

"How are we to interpret . . ." He stared at Vic like she'd grown a third eye.

"Obviously, there has been a mistake," Nathaniel spat, facing the Elders.

"I've never seen this before," another Elder said, and the Elders talked over one another, arguing.

"She cheated!" someone called from the crowd.

"Now, hold on," the first Elder began as the noise within the room grew.

Max leaned toward Vic and whispered, "Get ready to run. This is about to turn bad."

"It hasn't already?" Vic hissed in disbelief, her voice hoarse and low.

Max pulled Vic to her feet with a wry smile and turned to mouth something at someone in the crowd.

The Elders were screaming at one another now. One of them was in Nathaniel's face, a finger ramming his chest, and the crowd met their energy. They were angry; they were confused. No one knew what it meant, and no one wanted to listen to explanations.

The crowd burst to their feet. Shouts surrounded her, and Vic spun in confusion, catching a haze of faces watching her. One of them stood out—Henry. He looked upset, angry or hurt or some combination. He must be worried about her. Vic called out to him.

Hands grasped Vic's arm and she swung around to defend herself. But it was Sarah behind her, looking horrified and slightly awestruck.

"Now, Vic. Come with me."

A body in front of her cut off Vic's view of her brother, and she backed away from the shape. A hand grabbed her arm, and she slithered out of the grip. Someone reached for her, and Vic kicked them. The witch fell backward with a grunt of pain. Vic bumped into a body behind her as she wrenched backward. There were people on all sides of her now, closing in.

Sarah pulled her to a narrow split in the cavern wall. Vic would never have noticed it on her own. Sarah pulled the stone away like a curtain to reveal a passageway.

While Sarah slipped into the passage, Vic cast a look at the chaos behind her. In the back of the room, leaning against the wall and watching as if he had not a care in the world, stood Xan Galanis, his arms over his chest and one foot propped up behind him. Even in stillness, the power he held was obvious. Physicality and violence peeled off him in waves Vic felt from across the cavernous space.

And he was staring right at her.

She felt his gaze on her like a physical touch, and it sent a shiver down Vic's spine. She found herself hoping that Xan would not be the one tasked with silencing her, if it came to that. He would destroy her.

Vic forced herself to turn, to follow Sarah through the gap and into the cramped passageway. She couldn't stand without hitting the ceiling, and she lost Sarah's face in the darkness. Shadows clung to Vic as she stumbled behind the vague outline of the Sentinel.

Voices at their backs grew louder as the others realized where they had gone.

Other people had entered the passage. They were close behind and getting closer.

Vic didn't need Sarah's one-word warning. She was already running.

XV

From its earliest days in the colonial era, the Order used a deep network of ancient caves as a meeting place. Their location was too remote for outsiders to easily access, and the rough geography provided ample security for the burgeoning organization. The Elders met in the deepest parts of these caves for gatherings of grave importance.

When the time came to construct the Order's fortress, the land over the ancient catacombs proved the obvious choice.

—William Ruskin, *A History of the Acheron Order*
(New York, 1935)

Vic ran headlong into the darkness. Noise ahead gave her Sarah's location, and she followed blindly through the narrow corridor. She didn't know what would happen if they were caught, but she had no desire to find out. Vic threw a pointless look over her shoulder and didn't notice that Sarah had stopped in the middle of the tunnel until Vic barreled into her back.

Grunting, Vic struggled to right herself. She cut off her apology when she realized why Sarah had stopped.

The passage ended abruptly a few feet in front of them. Bounded by the rough stone and barely visible through the darkness lay a wooden door with a gleaming red handle, identical to those lining the hallways hundreds of feet above them. Vic stepped forward and tested the cut-glass knob. The door swung open. Sarah wore an expression of amazement as they peered into an apartment similar to the one Vic shared with Henry.

Sarah stepped through the opening with a dazed look on her face. Vic followed with more reluctance, closing the door behind her.

"Holy shit," Sarah breathed, looking awestruck at the door. "I know Max is powerful, but sometimes I'm still surprised."

Vic stared at the door as realization dawned. *Max* made that passage in the side of the cave? "How do we get back to the main castle?"

"We don't need to," Sarah replied in a dazed voice. "This is my apartment."

Vic examined the space with new interest. Posters hung on the walls and a healthy amount of clutter littered the room. Sarah walked to the kitchen and withdrew a bottle of whiskey from a cabinet above the refrigerator. She plucked two coffee mugs from a rack by the sink and poured a generous helping into each, then offered one to Vic.

She drank it one gulp. The liquor burned a path down her throat, and welcome heat radiated through her limbs. She plopped the empty mug on the coffee table.

Vic rubbed her face, and her hands came away bloody. She shot a panicked look at Sarah, who tossed her a wet rag from the kitchen. In the hallway mirror Vic saw that the blood had come from her eyes, pouring out of her like tears. She scrubbed her face clean, though red smears stuck in the thin skin around her eyes like day-old eyeliner. Vic looked like rolled-over shit and felt even worse.

Sarah sighed as she slumped onto the couch. The rag hit the floor with a splat as Vic fell into the armchair opposite Sarah. They sat in silence, both staring into the middle distance until Sarah spoke.

"Holy shit."

"Holy shit."

"I never thought Nathaniel would be that bold." Sarah's face turned angry at the memory. "Calling for Max's expulsion is just stupid."

"He said I should be silenced," Vic said, hung up on the phrasing.

"With all the alums and professionals present, he was trying to rile people up. You saw how angry some of them got. And to invoke the Rite of Trial . . ." Sarah shook her head, her eyes full of shock and anger.

"That sucked." Vic rubbed her knees over her jeans. Her kneecaps weren't broken, but she'd have nasty bruises in the morning. "I didn't pass, did I?"

"You didn't fail."

Vic shook her head. She had no idea how to process what had happened.

"That was—"

Someone pounded on the door, and Vic twisted to face it in alarm.

"Garza," came the unmistakable growl of the Chief Sentinel. "Open up."

Vic wondered how he had gotten there so fast. "Tell him I'm not here," she whispered, and Sarah's face cracked into a grin.

"Who is it?" Sarah sang.

"I know she's in there."

"If you're here to kill me, you'll have to take a number," Vic called.

Vic heard a muffled thump she was pretty sure was Xan's forehead hitting the door.

"Let me in."

Sarah opened the door a sliver. "What's the password?"

"I'm your boss."

Sarah imitated a buzzer. "Try again."

"Have you been drinking? It hasn't even been fifteen minutes. Were you doing shots?"

Buzzer again. Sarah started to close the door in his face. Xan shoved his forearm against it and pushed until he stood in her living room. Vic took a step away from him, remembering his hand on her waist and wishing she had another whiskey.

"That defeats the entire purpose of the password system," Sarah grumbled, and Xan scowled at her before turning on Vic.

"I am not going to kill you. Are you seriously that melodramatic?"

Vic put a hand on her hip. "Someone suggested that I be 'silenced' in front of a cave full of people tonight. Who's melodramatic?"

Xan rolled his eyes. "I came to *check* on you. Sometimes the castle eats people."

"We're fine," Sarah said.

"Keep your heads down tonight," he said. "Things should cool off by morning, but you know how the Order can be."

"Wait, go back to the thing about the castle eating people," Vic demanded, raising a finger to get his attention.

Xan snatched her hand out of the air.

"What the fuck!" Vic tried to tug her arm away, but Xan held her wrist with both hands and she couldn't pull away. He lifted the fingers of her right hand up to his face, eyeing the cuts there.

"What is this?" Xan said, tugging the sleeve of her sweater up her forearm and turning her hand in the air.

"What is what?" Vic asked. She wanted him to get his hands off her. They made her warmer than the whiskey had, and fractious, even as she registered a sinking suspicion that he knew what those marks meant. Her secret was out, and she didn't even know what it was.

Xan rounded on Sarah. "Did you know about this?"

"No," she replied, angling for a peek at Vic's arm. But there was nothing there, only the wounds on her fingers.

"Stop manhandling me," Vic insisted. She tried to twist out of Xan's grip. But he held tight to her hand, and all she managed to do was tangle herself in his arms. Vic fought not to dwell on the hard, warm chest against her back, until Xan turned her to the side and reached for the bottom of her sweater. He pulled it up to expose her back, and Vic shrieked when she felt a rough hand at the top of her jeans.

"You brought a weapon down there?" Xan demanded, pulling the knife from Vic's waistband.

"Sick," Sarah breathed behind her.

Keeping hold of Vic's wrists in one hand, Xan tossed the knife to Sarah.

Vic pushed against Xan in a pointless attempt to free herself, and Xan pulled his arm tighter across her chest. She shot an angry look at him, but the effect was diminished by the way she was crushed against his front.

"Why the fuck do you have that?" Xan spat.

"Bold of you to ask, considering I'm halfway to a half nelson," Vic said, her voice muffled by Xan's forearm across her throat. "Seems like a weapon was a wise idea."

"Wait a second," Sarah said, examining the side of the blade. She looked up with a smile. "This is one of ours."

"You stole it," Xan said. "That's nice."

"Get off me," Vic growled, and she threw her weight against the hands trapping her. Xan let her go this time when she twisted out of his grip, and Vic stumbled away from him. She put her hands on her hips and glared at him, panting.

Xan glowered at her. "Do you know what that is on your arm?"

"On my arm?" Vic asked, looking at her wrist. "There's nothing on my arm."

"She can't see it, Xan."

"She can't see it, of course!" Xan said, and he looked livid. He grabbed Vic's hand and held it in front of her face. He poked a spot at the top of her wrist, right below where a watch would have sat. There was nothing there but skin. "That," Xan said, prodding it once more. "You can't see that?"

"I have no idea what you're talking about." Vic wrenched her arm away. Xan paced a furious circle before turning back to Vic.

"Of course you don't. Who did you do that with?" Xan demanded.

"Do what with?" Vic cried.

"It's a bind," Xan said. "Whose is it?"

"Nobody's!"

Nobody's, Xan mouthed, and he looked like he wanted to throttle Vic. "It has to be *somebody's.* Tell me who you did that with."

"It wasn't supposed to be real," Vic said, losing steam.

"It must have been real. I'm looking at it."

"I was dreaming. I was in my bed the entire time," Vic said, and Xan's frown deepened. "There was no way it was real."

"Who told you that?"

"No one had to tell me that," Vic said. She had no idea what Xan meant by "bind" and wasn't sure she wanted to find out. "It's like a baseline fact of reality. Things that happen when you're dreaming aren't real."

Xan ran both his hands through his hair and stormed across the room. He turned and marched back to Vic.

"Whose is it?" he demanded, looking wild, incensed.

"I won't tell you." What would Xan do if she told him the truth? It would get her kicked out of the castle. Perhaps worse. *She must be silenced.*

"If someone in this castle is using you for Orcan magic, you have to tell me."

"I don't have to tell you shit." Vic crossed her arms and looked for the whiskey.

"Was it Max?" Xan demanded.

Shooting a glance at Sarah's stunned expression, Vic stammered, "Of course it wasn't Max!" But Xan looked like he didn't believe her.

He paced the entryway, looking half-crazed.

"You never, ever do magic you don't understand!" Xan yelled. "You idiot!"

As Vic was about to shout back, a slim figure slipped into the room, and Vic stepped away from Xan. She pulled the sleeve of her sweater down to cover the mark she couldn't see.

The three of them stood silently as May Lin walked in. Vic's eyes darted to Sarah, who didn't look the least bit surprised.

"This is a weird energy," May noted in a velvet voice. "What did I miss?"

"Play nice, May," Sarah said. "Vic's had a hard night."

"I'll say," May said. "You barely made it out of there, by the look of it."

Xan shot Vic a scalding look. "I'm not done with you." He pointed at her arm before storming out of the apartment—leaving Vic and Sarah alone with a witch who, last Vic checked, wanted her dead.

"Vic, you've met May Lin," Sarah said with forced congeniality. "She's going to behave."

May shot Vic a smile that looked more like baring her teeth.

Vic was still shaken by her conversation with Xan. Concerns ran through her mind at double speed, not least that May might attack her again. Her eyes jumped to the dagger, sheathed on the side table and a hair out of reach.

Sarah, seemingly unaware of the tension filling the room, went into the kitchen to grab another drink. Vic watched May with her arms crossed. Sarah hummed under her breath as she opened and closed cabinet doors. When Sarah flounced back with the whiskey bottle and another mug, she barely registered the two women staring each other down.

"Sit, sit," she said to Vic, patting the couch beside her. "We have lots to discuss."

Vic walked over to her, stopping to pick up the knife on her way. Once she had the weapon in hand, she cast a deliberate look at May, who raised an eyebrow. Vic took the armchair across from Sarah again and held out her mug for a refill. May leaned against the wall on the other side of the room and accepted a cup from Sarah.

"How did you do it?" May asked, suspicion thick in her voice. "The test is supposed to kill you if you don't have magic. You shouldn't have been able to last as long as you did, let alone get up on your own."

Vic looked at Sarah. "Why is she here?"

May kicked off of the wall like she wanted to fight Vic again, but Sarah stopped her with a wave. "May's a Sentinel. She probably just wanted to make sure I was okay."

"*You* were okay?" Vic asked. "Nobody tried to kill *you* tonight."

"Look, you—" May began, but Sarah threw her hands up.

"Cool it, May, or I'm kicking you out of my apartment," she said with a sharp look at the Sentinel, who fell back into silence against the wall with a furious look on her face. "Back to business," Sarah said. "During the Rite, did you . . . see anything?"

"Like threads?" Vic remembered Nathaniel calling success *the Unthreading.*

"Yes!"

"No."

Sarah's face fell into a confused frown. "So you didn't use magic to pull yourself out of it?"

Vic shrugged again. "What could you see?"

"The magic is old as hell," Sarah said. "It looked like a big knotted cloud. I've never actually seen them perform the Rite before."

"And when I got up?" Vic asked, wondering if the threads had gotten more organized. Maybe she'd done something subconsciously, used magic without knowing it.

"It looked the same," Sarah said, "except you were kneeling, and you had blood coming out of your eyes."

Vic slumped back in her seat. She cast a wary glance at May, who was watching Vic and Sarah through narrowed eyes.

"Nathaniel wants me silenced. Is there any chance I'm wrong about what that means?"

"Unfortunately, no," Sarah said. "He could go the humane route and try to get the Elders on board with changing your memory of the castle. Convince you it was a dream or something. But spells like that are hard to execute and faulty. More likely, he'd opt to kill you and have done with it."

"Lovely." Vic emptied her mug. The whiskey burned less now that her murder was up for discussion.

"Nathaniel knows that the Elders wouldn't agree to that, even if you failed the Rite. That's why he insisted on doing it with the alums and professionals there. None of the Elders would stand against Max, unless there was pressure from the members."

"Would Max do anything to the others if they opposed him?" Vic asked. She couldn't imagine him vengeful.

"They're not worried he'll retaliate," Sarah said. "They're worried he'll leave. The Order is too fragile to risk losing Max's support."

Vic struggled to pair the reality of the Order's vulnerability with the front they put forward—stone and antiquity, a sacred institution too powerful to fail.

"Enough about Max," Sarah said. "Tell us what happened before the meeting."

Vic shot a questioning look at May, but Sarah nodded for her to go on.

It didn't take long for Vic to recount the evening's events, though she left out the details that felt most pressing to her. The thick white of Rachel's eyes, how the flies made her entrails look like they wriggled of their own accord.

Sarah shivered.

"You're a Sentinel," May said behind Sarah, her face scrunched in a concerned frown. "How does *that* gross you out?"

Sarah rolled her eyes and waved for Vic to continue.

"Max lied about finding the body himself," Vic said.

"You saw how the members reacted to you," Sarah said. "He probably wanted to make sure their attention stayed where it should—we've been attacked."

"Max thinks the Brotherhood of Mann is responsible."

Sarah made a face as though she were considering something unpleasant. "The Brotherhood couldn't have broken the wards from the outside. If the Brotherhood was behind it, they've infiltrated the castle."

Of course they had infiltrated the castle. Aren had come to Vic in her dream—surely he could do the same to others here.

"Could it have been Nathaniel?" Vic asked. "Maybe he's working with the Brotherhood."

"Nathaniel is a piece of shit," Sarah said. "But he's loyal to the Order. I don't think he'd do something so against the mission unless he was desperate."

But Vic knew he was willing to break the rules. He'd brought the Level One recruits to Limbo, after all, to prove a point. He'd lied to

Henry to get him here as quickly as possible. How much of a reach was it to think he'd set an Orcan loose in the castle?

"Besides, the Elders have been postponing war with the Brotherhood for years," Sarah said. "They've even made concessions, offering the Brotherhood their places back in the Order if they abandon their more radical positions."

Sarah's tone made her disapproval of this strategy obvious.

"If I remember right, Nathaniel was in charge of that effort. He acted as the Order's emissary with Aren Mann until negotiations fell apart."

So Nathaniel had a means of contacting Aren? And he'd asked Max about who found the body, so he likely knew it had been Vic. It seemed clear to her that he was worth suspecting, at the very least.

"All of this has left the Brotherhood and the Order in a kind of stalemate. Members of the two groups rarely interact, but we kill the Orcans they spawn whenever we get the chance."

I can keep putting them down easy enough. But this is only going to get worse if we don't address the source of the problem.

"The main ideological disagreement between the Order and the Brotherhood is whether or not to use Orcan magic?" Vic asked.

"Not exactly," Sarah said. "You might have noticed the Order doesn't care much for us Mades. We're hard to find, harder to train, and almost impossible to control." Sarah paused to down the rest of her drink. "The Brotherhood takes it a step further. They think of Mades as . . . like they're diseased. Like it's something wrong, a mutant kind of magic."

"But Aren Mann is Made," Vic said. She remembered that part of her dream. He'd done it to himself while working as a Mage for the Order.

Sarah made a disdainful sound. "Like prejudice needs to make sense," she grumbled.

"But I don't understand," Vic said. "Can't they see he's a hypocrite?"

"He's both Born and Made," Sarah said, sounding tired. "Which he says gives him credibility to speak on Mades. He says most of us are cosmic accidents, missteps in evolution. He would know best, since he pursued it on purpose."

Vic had a hard time squaring this worldview with the man she'd met. "So he wants to cast Mades out of the Order?" she asked.

This time, it was May who replied, and her voice was ice-cold.

"He wants to kill them."

XVI

Magic pulled from the land of the dead provides the most assured way of acquiring power, for it is the only known means of collecting and transferring the abilities of others. Familiars are the most potent form of this transition, as they allow transfer of a witch's full powers to another. Lesser-known means include soul binds, by which two living witches share ability, and the creation of blood stones, by which a practitioner can distill the essence of a being into a conduit for later use. Blood stones can be created using either man or animal essence, and the souls of the long dead and of the recently deceased are both accessible, though with varying degrees of potency. The creation of blood stones remains, however, strictly prohibited by the Acheron Order.

—Terrance Vern, *Theories on Transmogrification*
(New York, 1999)

The sun had crept up from the horizon by the time Vic left Sarah's apartment. They'd stayed up late, arguing about the future, until May slipped out to return to her own bed and Sarah fell asleep on the couch.

Vic stayed awake. Her skin felt cold and weak from the lack of sleep, and she couldn't force her thoughts to clear. Aren Mann had set an Orcan loose in the castle, Vic had survived a test designed to kill her, and a woman had been eviscerated by a strix. It was too much for her to ponder on a full day without sleep.

But everything caught up with her as she wandered through the empty morning halls.

Vic hadn't known the murdered woman, Rachel, though she had seen her shrouded figure every day in the back of the lecture hall. But Vic felt a deep hollow when she realized that a person had stopped existing. Vic would go back to the lecture hall in the next few days, and class would plod along as it always did, and an entire human being had left the world behind. Rachel probably had a family, people who loved her, going through horrible pain. Vic knew she would never forget the sight of the dead woman on the library floor. Brown eyes clouded over and staring into a world Vic couldn't see.

She couldn't let the rest of the night overshadow that image, though it threatened to.

The rough glow of the catacomb walls, the cruel look on Nathaniel's face. The pain when the shackles clamped shut.

Aren Mann wanted to kill Mades, though he'd become one himself in a bid for power. He would do anything to gain it, including place his life on the line. A gamble, he'd called it. But as she walked alone, Vic could understand his motivations. She would do the same, wouldn't she? If she could guarantee the outcome.

If not for power, then for purpose, Vic would take the plunge. She remembered the shock and horror on the faces of the Order after she emerged from the Rite not triumphant but not beaten either. And she wished they hadn't looked so hateful. It would be nice, wouldn't it, to fit in?

She had fallen in over her head, but she still felt she could learn how to swim. Vic could get what she wanted out of this place, if she tried hard enough. If she fought with everything she had, she could gain some semblance of a role in a world that wanted nothing to do with her. Vic could prove her mother wrong—she could prove herself worthy of the love Meredith always denied her.

Light too sickly to be called sunlight snuck through the windows at an angle and cast the world in strange proportions. Small things threw large shadows as the castle contorted itself in the early morning, and Vic walked as fast as she could without running.

The strix was still loose, after all. Though Sarah was confident it had left the castle, the creature had not been found.

On the landing of the staircase leading to her and Henry's floor, Vic sensed movement above her.

Her head jolted upward.

Her heart sped up, and the muscles in her arms and legs readied to run.

Most of the landing lay concealed in shadow, and Vic stared into the spiral of the stairs overhead, waiting for the darkness to shift.

After a long pause, Vic shook her thoughts away and continued on. Her fear was making her see things that weren't there.

Vic hurried down another flight of stairs and into the corridor housing her apartment. There were no windows in that stretch of hallway, and darkness obscured the final part of her path. With a deep breath, Vic reminded herself that she was a grown woman who was not, as a matter of fact, afraid of the dark, and she plunged toward the door.

By the time her hand grasped the doorknob, Vic's pulse pounded in her ears, reminding her that she might be, slightly, afraid of the dark. She fumbled through unlocking the door and pulled the key from the lock.

As she twisted the knob, Vic felt something brush across her neck.

It was faint. It might have been nothing at all.

But goosebumps rippled across her flesh. She had felt something. A brush of wind in a draftless hallway. Someone breathing on her neck.

Almost against her will, Vic turned to face behind her.

Her key fell to the floor with a clatter.

A figure coalesced in the precise spot Vic had left a moment before. It had form and no form at the same time, as if it had a center of mass but no edges. Nothing but darkness, shifting into and out of a monstrous, shapeless thing. It was much larger than a man and seemed to fill the space as it moved away from her.

As if the creature noticed Vic's gaze on its back, it stopped.

It turned without turning.

It had no eyes, no face, no shape at all. But Vic knew, with horrifying certainty, that it was looking at her.

Her breath caught in her throat.

For an endless moment, they stared at each other.

She couldn't tell what it was thinking. If it was thinking.

Her chest rose and fell as the creature watched her. Vic had seen the laetite, and she had seen the shadowed thing, *this* shadowed thing, at a great distance. But watching it up close was uncanny. She was in another world. One constructed in the corners of the world she knew, its passageways and turrets built along the fringes while no one noticed. Knowing that such a thing could exist, in some abstract way, could never compare to seeing it firsthand. Magic must be addictive, Vic realized. To stare at the bare face of another reality was invigorating. Vic could only imagine how thrilling it must be to master it.

As she stared, the creature shifted. The shadows that had formed its body a moment prior settled back into their natural places as darkness sped away from her.

Vic wanted to shout at it to come back. She had no idea why.

She remembered being a child and hearing an Orcan around the corner, moments before Meredith had ripped Vic from her frightened trance. Vic remembered standing immobilized as the sound grew closer, and she had spent two decades wondering what made that noise.

Vic sprinted after the creature.

She bolted into the stairwell in the wake of the formless dark. The thing was fast. Vic almost lost her footing on the stairs, but she stumbled to a stand and caught a hint of a shadow turning the corner in front of her. If she lost it, even for a second, she knew there was no getting it back. She darted after it, though she had no idea what she would do if she caught up.

Her pursuit led her down one endless hall and into another, until she saw a touch of darkness streaking toward the front entrance.

She tore after it and skidded to a stop in the dining hall.

Vic had been here many times, every evening for a quiet dinner with Sarah. The other witches typically avoided Vic, and she ate quickly. But in the early morning it was stone-cold and quiet. She scanned for the creature, looking for any movement in the dark corners of the room and the long shadows cast by empty tables and chairs.

She was breathing hard as she stared around the space—far too large for a castle so poorly inhabited. Without thinking, Vic pulled the knife from her back and unsheathed it. Its leather holster fell to the floor as Vic spun, knife in hand, looking for a living shadow.

First, she felt the air move. Barely a breath, but she felt it ruffle her hair.

Then, she heard it.

A whoosh as enormous wings cleaved the air, and Vic hit the ground on instinct.

She twisted onto her back and stared up as the shadow loomed over her, blocking out the light.

But it wasn't the shadow this time.

It was the broad, open wings of the strix.

Vic rolled away as the massive beast reached toward her with talons as long as her hand. She couldn't think about anything other than those talons, which Vic knew could tear her skin as easily as paper.

The strix couldn't fly close to the ground. Chairs and tables littered the space. The creature flew back to hover about a dozen feet overhead, and the movement of its wings sent her curls dancing around her face.

Vic's heart hammered as she army-crawled toward the closest table.

She still had the knife in her fist. Vic crouched under a heavy wooden table and prepared herself to strike.

But she realized that she'd lost sight of the creature, and she couldn't feel the wind from its flight anymore. A horrible sinking feeling hit her right before she realized where it was.

The strix tore the table away from above Vic with a clawed foot, flinging it across the room, where it shattered against the wall.

"Get down!" someone shouted behind Vic.

Vic ducked.

And just in time.

Vic felt something streak over her hair and land, with a thunk, in the strix's chest. A volucrine shriek filled the hall as the creature bellowed in pain, the wood-handled end of a knife jutting from its torso.

But it wasn't dead yet, and now it was angry.

It leaped at Vic again, teeth gnashing the air in front of her face as she skittered to the side. Out of the corner of her eye, Vic watched Xan run up behind her, still clad in his black training outfit and furious.

Xan rounded on the creature, but he didn't have any weapons. The knife he'd thrown was probably the only one he had on him. Vic watched in shock as Xan ran toward the strix unarmed.

The creature attacked him claws first, its sharp talons heading for Xan's chest. Xan grabbed the strix by the jaw. Vic stared in mindless horror as she heard a ripping noise, and she knew Xan was about to be torn to shreds.

Vic had no idea what Xan was doing, but she had to help him.

She ran up behind the strix and thrust her blade into the creature's neck at the exact moment she heard a wet wrenching sound. A crack as loud as a whip split the air, and Vic had no idea what it was until the creature crumpled in front of her like a doll.

Xan had broken its neck.

Vic stepped back from the strix as it fell. A heavy wing hit the floor with a slap, but Xan was already stepping over it.

Rough hands landed on either side of Vic's face. She started, but Xan held her in place as he turned her head from side to side. Vic was struck for an instant by the similarity of the action to what he had just done to the strix, but the hands holding her were gentle and warm.

"Are you hurt?" Xan asked.

Eyes of vivid gray-blue swam in front of Vic's, and she couldn't think of anything but the odd look of concern on Xan's face, so close to hers.

She opened and closed her mouth for a second before her words returned to her.

"Am *I* hurt?" Vic shot back. "I'm not the one that attacked a strix with my bare hands." She pushed Xan's hands aside and examined his body.

But he had not been disemboweled. He had not, apparently, even been scratched.

The whole front of his shirt was destroyed, though. There were massive tears in the black fabric, and Vic stared at the unmarred skin underneath. Vic had anticipated muscles, but he was a real athlete. These were not the vanity muscles of a bodybuilder. No, here was solid, well-fed strength, honed through countless hours of fighting. And he had chest hair. A perfect amount of chest hair.

Without thinking, Vic reached for him. She felt a jolt of electricity when her fingertips met the skin of his abdomen and lowered her hand until her palm lay flat against his stomach, smooth and warm and hard. Under her touch, a muscle twitched, tensing for an instant and then stilling. How was it possible that he hadn't been hurt? What kind of sense did that make?

When she looked up at Xan, Vic froze. He was watching her through dark eyes, and the look on his face was unmistakable. Hunger.

Vic pulled her hand away and stepped back. Her heart was loud in her ears as she remembered that they were alone in the early-morning castle, and he was looking at her like he was starving.

"How are you not hurt?" Vic asked, avoiding his eyes.

"You forget where we are," Xan replied, his voice low.

"Magic," Vic whispered. She shook her head.

"What were you thinking," Xan asked, "running after a strix all by yourself?"

Vic lifted a shoulder. "I thought I saw something."

"So naturally you gave chase," Xan said, sounding resigned. "Goddamn it, Vic. Do you have any regard whatsoever for your own safety?"

Vic crossed her arms in front of her as she realized she was suddenly very cold.

Xan caught the movement and his frown deepened. He watched her for a moment before he spoke. "I'll walk you back."

Vic looked at the corpse of the Orcan beside them. She remembered the last time she'd seen Xan. He'd seen the bind, and he'd screamed at her for doing magic she didn't understand. If he learned the truth, that the bind was with Aren Mann, surely he would kick her out. Or worse.

"I'm fine."

"I insist."

Before she could object, he had an arm around Vic's shoulders. She noted the warmth of his skin, the hard muscles of his inner arm, before he began to shove her forward.

"I don't need an escort," Vic said, jerking her head toward the strix. "The thing's dead."

"Maybe I'm worried you'll get lost."

Vic scowled up at Xan as he tugged her along. "Aren't you going to tell anybody about the corpse in the dining hall? It would be a nasty surprise if they found it at breakfast."

"They already know," Xan said, pushing her to the exit. "And you don't want to be here when the others arrive."

"Aww, are you worried about me?" Vic asked in a sickly sweet voice.

Xan shot her a flat look. "You're a little chaos bomb," he said. "After what happened last night, I would rather not test the Order's capacity to handle you today."

Last night? Vic thought, before she realized that it was a new day. The Rite, the catacombs, the fiery mouth behind the dais, they had left all of that behind with the rising sun.

"Did you sleep?" Vic asked him. It couldn't be later than seven, maybe eight A.M.

"No."

"Me neither."

They walked through the halls for several minutes without speaking. Xan kept his arm around Vic even after it was clear she wasn't going anywhere, and she found herself enjoying the warmth. And the pressure. It was nice to be held. Vic wondered what it said about her that she was so starved for this man's affection that even being herded felt good.

"You did well last night," he said in a quiet voice as they entered the hallway to her and Henry's place.

Vic looked up at him in surprise. He wasn't mocking her or yelling at her or grumbling under his breath about her unpredictability, like he usually did when they interacted. He was complimenting her. For some reason, that affected Vic more than anything else had since the meeting. She blinked against an unwelcome swell of emotion.

"That's never happened before, with the Rite," he added.

"Never?" Vic asked. Sarah had said the same thing.

"Not in the Order's history, at least."

Vic chewed on the inside of her cheek.

"What do you think that means?" Did Xan think Max's plan was working? Did he have his own theories about why, or how, Vic was able to do what no one else could?

He turned to face her, and Vic realized they had come upon her apartment door. He dipped to pick up her key where it lay unmoved from where she'd dropped it earlier. He held it out for her, and she clenched her fist around it.

Xan met her eyes, and the ice-blue depths of his alarmed her. Vic took a half step away from the intensity of his stare, but he was reaching for her again.

His palm cupped the side of her face, so soft she could barely feel it, and his thumb ran gently up from Vic's chin until it landed on her bottom lip. He pulled her lip down, exposing the wet inside.

"I think it means you're very strong," Xan said, meeting her eyes. His hand fell away, and Vic licked her bottom lip without thinking. His gaze flashed to the movement and then back. "And I think that's all it means."

Xan turned away from Vic and walked back in the direction of the dining hall.

His shirt, Vic had failed to notice, had completely repaired itself.

XVII

The Elders met tonight to discuss a startling development. A Mage by the name of Aren Mann, who has been a member of the Acheron Order since his trials and induction in 1995, sought a hearing with the Elder Council. He revealed to the gathered Elders that he had succeeded in having himself "Made" after a yearslong study of the process. He disclosed this information to the Council alongside a request for leniency, as he kept this goal secret from the Elders and pursued it to the detriment of his Mage duties.

The Elders decided, by a vote of 7 to 5, to absolve Mr. Mann of consequences for his misconduct because of his forthrightness in communicating his misdeed and the significance of his contributions to the Order.

~~To speak candidly, I worry about what this means for the future. Rare few witches have succeeded in accomplishing what Mann has. Even before this transformation, he held power rivaled by few in the Order. I fear now that he has surpassed even the Elders. I worry who, if any of us, would be able to control him.~~*

—From the archives of E. Thomas Stanley (2007)

*Indicates a section of the original text removed prior to archiving.

"This seems like a terrible idea," Vic announced. Again.

Sarah didn't turn around at the comment—she'd grown weary of Vic's pessimism a quarter mile back. May rolled her eyes and tromped deeper into the forest. Vic hurried after them, well aware that following two highly trained, albeit irritable, witches through the woods was preferable to being abandoned there.

As much to frighten away the wildlife as to protest Sarah's grueling pace, Vic made as much noise as possible while stomping through the underbrush. She stepped on every fallen branch and crunchy patch of ice she saw through the lumpy blanket of snow.

It had been a week since the Brotherhood attacked, and tensions within the castle had reached a fever pitch. While some members of the Order seemed to care about Rachel's death, most focused their energy on the most obvious sign of change: Vic. She drew hostile eyes every time she left the apartment and sat in training like a bug under a magnifying glass, her skin crawling. But the Order must have heeded Max's instructions, because no one tried to harm her.

For his part, Henry had reacted to the meeting the way he reacted to any unpleasantness—with undeterred optimism and a general sense of detachment. It drove Vic nuts. The day after the meeting, she cornered him at the kitchen table and insisted they hash it out. Vic thought he must be suppressing his emotions. The situation was precarious; surely he was frightened. But Henry insisted everything was fine and left for training.

Vic had not revisited the conversation they'd had after she found Rachel's body, though a sick feeling of guilt twisted her stomach. Henry had begged her to leave the castle, and for the first time in her memory, Vic had ignored his wishes in favor of her own.

Xan let Vic return to working with the Sentinels once he deemed her adequately rested, and she'd spent most of the last week in the training wing. The Sentinels' combat skills had improved, and Vic reveled in the chance to fight people who knew what they were doing. It was exhausting, and Vic fell into bed every night too tired to dwell on any of the many questions looming over her.

After the meeting, May Lin hung around Vic and Sarah more often than not, though Vic shot sidelong glances May's way and never turned her back on the Sentinel.

"Tonight," Sarah had announced at breakfast, "we are going out."

May, sitting on the far side of the table from Vic, sighed into her coffee.

"Y'all have an 'out' here?" Vic asked.

"No," May replied in an acerbic tone. "We do not."

"It's the closest thing we have," Sarah said. "And you'll enjoy it. Both of you."

But Sarah refused to divulge any details about what they would find on the other side of their walk into the forest. She claimed it would ruin the surprise.

And so Vic found herself hiking through icy woods with two witches after sundown.

"To be clear: no human sacrifice, right?" Vic asked.

"Nope!" Sarah sang.

"No ritual slaughter of any kind?"

"Not tonight," May said.

"No dancing naked under the moonlight?"

"Of course not," Sarah replied. "It's cold out."

"We could light a fire," May suggested.

Sarah told her to hush.

It was colder than Vic could remember experiencing before. She didn't own anything bordering on a winter coat, but Sarah had been eager to supply her with one before they left the castle. Sarah pulled a thick white puffer from the bowels of her overflowing closet and tossed it in the general direction of Vic's seat on her bed. A few seconds later, a pair of pink gloves landed beside it. Sarah wore nothing near Vic's shoe size, so she trudged through the woods in sneakers.

Vic realized the instant the frigid wind hit her face that she had not left Avalon's doors since entering them. The castle had an odd ability to distance its occupants from the world beyond it. Her life, her past, even time itself couldn't find Vic there.

Reality came into sharp focus as Vic struggled to wrest oxygen from the icy air. She rubbed her gloved hands against the sides of her face to warm it and sniffled back a drip of liquid insistent on exiting her left nostril. While the winter looked serene from the comfort of the castle confines, it was absolutely god-awful to be outside in it.

Vic cursed herself for coming. She cursed Sarah for having the wretched idea, and she cursed May for lacking the good sense to put a stop to the whole thing. And if some of that cursing made its way out of her mouth, that was hardly Vic's fault.

May chuckled beside her.

"Laugh it up. I bet you're comfortable," Vic said, pointing at May's knee-length black down jacket. "You look like a tire."

"It's not my fault you packed like an idiot."

Vic had no idea how Sarah navigated the dense forest without the sun's help. To Vic's eyes, they wandered into vague darkness, and May grabbed Vic's arm to stop her from walking into a tree.

"Don't touch me," Vic grumbled, pulling her arm away, and May rolled her eyes.

"Fine. Next time I'll let you run into it."

Vic kept looking over her shoulder for signs of people nearby, but there was no one. No houses, no roads, no evidence of civilization at all. Avalon Castle really did exist in its own separate world.

"Are you going to murder me, is that it?" Vic asked. "All this time you've pretended to be normal so I would go into the forest with you. But really you're woodsy cannibal witches who lure unsuspecting women to their deaths so you can stay beautiful forever."

"If that was our goal, we would have picked someone younger," May said.

"Gross!" Sarah intoned from the front.

"So you admit that you want to eat children?"

"Or someone with more flesh to offer, at least," May said, ignoring Vic's question.

"Hey, I'm plenty fleshy," Vic said. "You would be lucky to eat me." May scoffed.

"Or maybe this is a virgin-blood thing. 'Cause if so, you are horribly mistaken. I know I'm grumpy, but I can promise that I'm not—"

"We're here!"

Vic pulled up short. Ahead of them, a small clearing appeared, lit by thin moonlight bouncing off the snow.

At the center, a dilapidated structure huddled in what meager light reflected from the sky. Gray stone and wood fell in upon each other in the loose shape of a house. Vic saw a single dirtied windowpane still intact in each of the two frames on either side of the door. Or the doorway, she should say, as no door hung there. Whatever this once was, it had seen better days.

Sarah and May moved forward without hesitation. Vic stepped over several rows of large, misshapen stones, which formed a series of interconnected circles spanning the length of the clearing.

"Okay, now I'm actually worried."

"For the last time, we are not going to murder you," Sarah chirped. "Come on."

The steps creaked a death rattle as Vic climbed onto the porch. She marveled that the place remained upright and cast a wary eye at the condition of the exterior walls before following Sarah through the open space where a door ought to be. Vic couldn't see anything on the other side, but she didn't immediately understand that there must be a reason for that.

Vic gasped when she crossed the threshold.

Dozens of people mingled around a large firepit at the center of an open space. The interior of the hut must have borne witness to some serious magic, Vic realized, because the walls were immaculate. The ceiling provided the only internal sign of the building's decay. Desiccated rafters had collapsed in some places, and the grim sky peeked through patches the roof once covered. Despite the gaping holes overhead, the room was warm and cozy. Light from the fire tangled with rows of candles set along the walls, dripping with wax and adding to the well-loved atmosphere. It reminded Vic of a dive bar. If they had dive bars in the Paleolithic era.

Vic recognized a few of the people scattered throughout the room as the Sentinels and full-time members who lived in the castle. Some waved at Sarah and May, and Vic caught a handful of curious glances. But no one looked angry that she had come. After a week of suspicious eyes trailing her movements, Vic appreciated the lack of interest more than she would have expected.

Sarah leaned toward Vic like she meant to tell a secret.

"We call this Lethe Castle," she said. "And there's only one rule when you enter."

"Forget everything," May said from Sarah's other side.

"Clever."

"It's very high school," Sarah said with an apologetic smile.

Vic shrugged, her eyes on the witches lingering throughout the space. She didn't have enough high school memories to be offended by the similarity.

"It can be strange for people coming to the Order for the first time," Sarah said, turning to hang Vic's coat beside her own. "It's like we regress when we get to the castle. Out in the real world, we're a bunch of taxpayers, but you stick us in the wilderness and summer camp rules apply again."

As she spoke, Sarah found a crate along the wall and pulled out a bottle of wine. She unscrewed the metal cap with a click.

"See?" Sarah asked, eyeing the bottle's label. "I think high schoolers and members of the Acheron Order are the only people in the world who drink this stuff voluntarily."

Vic accepted a glass with a laugh.

"What is this place?"

"Some of the full-timers come here to relax when we're off duty," Sarah told her. "It's the only spot we've found that's far enough away from the castle we can actually feel at ease, but not so far that we can't make it back in time if there's an emergency."

"No one lives around here?" Vic asked.

May shook her head. "The Order owns most of the land on this side of the mountains."

"So we're free to do our business without fear of prying eyes," Sarah added, brows high with drama.

"Except mine," Vic pointed out.

"Except yours," Sarah agreed.

Vic drank in the scene with the wine in her hand, leaning against the wooden railing running the length of the wall. The drink was gross, which she expected, but the ambience was pleasant. A steady thrum of noise filled the room as people spoke in low, relaxed voices. It reminded Vic of nights in the restaurant right before closing. With almost everyone gone, the evening slowed to a crawl. Those still unwilling to part ways with their company hung around the edges, and the staff started to clean up despite them.

She smiled to herself, feeling more relaxed than she had in weeks. She felt bold, in her element among the Sentinels and the professionals who just wanted to forget the castle for an hour or two.

"So, May," Vic said, handing her glass to Sarah for a refill. "What's your deal?"

May arched an eyebrow. "My deal," she repeated in a tone as sharp as the knife Vic suspected she had hidden somewhere on her person.

"Yeah," Vic said, nodding thanks when Sarah returned her drink. "You've been hanging around me and Sarah, and you haven't tried to kill me in two weeks. What gives?"

"For the record: I never tried to kill you."

"Killing, grievous bodily harm," Vic said with a shrug. "To-may-to, to-mah-to, am I right?"

"If I *had* tried to kill you, you would be dead," May said.

"Okay, that's enough of that," Sarah said, putting a placating hand on May's arm. "Nobody's killing anybody."

"My deal," May replied with a touch of distaste, "is that I'm a Sentinel. I'm a Born witch from an oldish line, though I'm the first of my family to join the Order. I've been here for eight years."

"I thought all witches joined the Order," Vic said.

"American witches," Sarah added, with a face like the words tasted bad. "Otherwise you have to earn a spot."

"My parents have middling power," May said, still not looking at Vic. "But they're obsessed with gaining more. They moved to the U.S. because of the Order. Their marriage was a deliberate attempt to build a stronger bloodline. When I was born with more power than either of them—"

Vic started. "Wait, they got married because they wanted to—"

"Half the people in this room were conceived under similar circumstances," May said, and she finally met Vic's eyes, though hers were cynical and cold. "Old bloodlines, new bloodlines, it's exhausting trying to keep up with who wants to fuck whom for which political advantage. Never mind that it doesn't even work most of the time."

"That's unbelievable," Vic breathed.

"My parents got what they wanted. The Lins have joined the Acheron Order," she finished in a tone of pronouncement.

Behind Vic came the pop of a speaker turning on, and May groaned. Vic watched as witches drifted toward an open area, and then loud music poured into the room.

Excitement fluttered in Vic's chest. Sarah and May were talking, low under their breath, heads nearly touching. Sarah caught Vic's eye and smiled.

"Dancing!" Vic cried above the music. May folded her hands over her chest. "Oh, come on, Sarah, you have to come with me. I don't want to dance by myself."

Sarah smiled at Vic with a look of bemusement. "*You* want to dance?" Sarah asked. "I would not have expected that."

"I *love* dancing," Vic said. "It's like a built-in excuse to let loose, to stop thinking and let the music take over. How rare is that?"

Vic stilled when she felt the energy of the room shift. It was subtle, almost imperceptible, as something like a breeze tilted the air. It reminded Vic of what happened at the meeting, when the Elder's words spread a chill through the crowd. The fire in the center of the room fell low for an instant before flaring again. Vic scanned the witches for signs of alarm. Sarah and May had gone on talking, unaware of Vic's distraction.

A shape passed in front of the window, and for half an instant Vic expected the shadowed Orcan to enter. But a familiar figure walked inside. Xan's hair fell into his face as he bent, but he made no attempt to pull it back. He stood almost as tall and wide as the doorframe he entered, the angel of death come to call on mortals. Maybe that was the pulse she'd felt—he'd sucked all the air out of the room, and the rest of them hadn't noticed they were suffocating yet. He wore the same all-black outfit as always, and Vic found herself imagining his closet lined with identical rows of black pants and shirts, each hanger a standard-issue inch from the ones beside it. Xan hung his chore coat on a hook by the door and ran a hand through his hair before approaching a trio of witches. A short woman with dirty-blond hair handed him a beer from a cooler. The bottle looked small in his hand.

Sarah's fingers snapped in front of Vic's face, and she blinked. She hadn't heard Sarah talking to her.

"What are you looking at?" Sarah demanded as her eyes followed Vic's. "Oh."

She looked at May with wide eyes.

"Xan is here," Sarah added in a stage whisper. "Xan and Vic had words the last time they spoke." Vic hadn't told Sarah about their encounter after the strix, about Xan touching her face with an expectant look in his eyes. The memory felt hot to the touch, unexplainable.

"I think she's a tiny bit scared of him," Sarah said.

"She'd be stupid not to be," May replied. "Xan's a scary motherfucker."

"And maybe a teeny, tiny bit of something else," Sarah added.

Vic shot Sarah a look. Had she been that obvious?

"Is that right?" May asked, her eyebrows higher than Vic had ever seen them.

"No, of course not," Vic whispered. "I don't even know why you would suggest that."

"Are you sure?" Sarah asked in an innocent tone. "Are you *positive* there's nothing going on there?"

"Of course I'm sure." Vic leaned in, dropping her voice. "I mean, he's hot. I'd have to be blind not to notice that he's hot. But no, absolutely not. He's tried to kick me out of the castle like a dozen times. He called me a liability."

"Heterosexual mating habits are a mystery to me," May said.

"That's not what's happening here," Vic snapped. "There is no . . . mating. Stop talking about that, immediately."

"He's coming over here," May observed.

Of course he was fucking coming over here.

Vic reached for Sarah's arm. "Come dance with me. Now."

But a mischievous smile bloomed on Sarah's face.

Vic didn't have to turn around to know that Xan was behind her. She felt the air move out of the way to accommodate him—before a deep voice announced his arrival.

"I'll dance with you."

The hair on the back of Vic's neck stood at attention. She was as ready to follow that voice as any of his Sentinels would be.

Vic tugged on Sarah's arm in a silent plea. Sarah did not budge.

A heavy hand landed on Vic's waist and pulled her to the side. Vic followed, aware that she should object to the manhandling. But his hold was firm and gentle, and Vic looked up at Xan with a wrinkle in her brow. Again with the proprietary touches, just like the night of the Rite. What had gotten into Xan? Still, Vic's heart began to pound in rhythm with the music.

He led her toward the open space some witches were using as a dance floor, his hand like a brand against her side. Vic wanted to squirm away from the touch. She wanted to lean into it. Again she breathed in the smell of him, like earth and sweat-slicked skin mixed together.

"It'll be fun, I promise," he said, dropping his head close to hers. His breath teased the right side of her face. He was only inches away. "I've always thought dancing is like . . ." Xan paused like he wanted Vic to draw the wrong conclusion. "Fighting. Don't you agree?"

Vic nodded, still staring up in confusion. Was he flirting with her?

"Since we're both very good at fighting, I assume our skills will transfer," he added with a knowing look.

He was definitely flirting. Vic's stomach flipped.

She stuck her hand up and brushed his forehead with the tips of her fingers. "Are you sick?" she asked. "You don't feel feverish." But he did feel hot, like a furnace burned beneath the surface of his skin. Vic put her hand in her pocket, her skin buzzing.

Xan chuckled and pulled her to a stop beside another small table along the way. Vic looked behind her at Sarah and May, expecting them to be watching her with poorly repressed glee. But they were oblivious to the strange scene unfolding between Vic and Xan. Sarah was explaining something, complete with sharp hand gestures, and May's face broke out in the first real smile Vic had ever seen on her.

"What were you talking about when I came in?" Xan asked, pulling Vic's attention back to him.

Vic found another bottle of wine and poured herself a glass. "You know, I don't remember."

He leaned in toward Vic. "Did I distract you?"

"Don't play dumb," Vic told him. "Of course you distracted me. You came in here looking like you rode in on a hellhound. All doom and gloom." Vic imitated his constant frown. The music wasn't so loud they had to shout to be heard, but they stood closer than they normally would. The proximity ran like electricity over Vic's skin.

"You're in a room full of witches and my 'doom and gloom' stands out to you?"

"You're a foot taller than anyone else in here. And they"—she spun her glass toward a nearby gaggle of witches—"all seem relatively normal." Vic swung the cup in his direction. "You do not."

"Many in this world would take that as the highest compliment."

"Of course they would. God forbid anyone in this castle behave like a normal human being."

"People in this castle have no interest in normal human beings. I thought you realized that by now."

"Yes, because it's so much better to be aloof and sanctimonious all the time."

"Look at you with the five-dollar words."

"Big shocker: I'm literate."

At that, Xan laughed, deep and real, with an edge that pulled at Vic's nerves like a piano wire. Strong and casual, as if it belonged to someone else. A man who didn't loom around like the prince of darkness all the time, who didn't live in a castle and spend his days hunting monsters. Vic wanted to stop, wanted to make him do that again, wanted to figure out what made his laugh resonate in her chest.

She swallowed.

"And what kind of name is Xan, anyway?" Vic demanded, trying to pull the conversation back onto a track that didn't involve staring at his throat. "I've never met anyone named Xan."

"It's short for Alexandros, which is Greek."

"And Alex was taken?"

When he laughed this time, it was harsh and humorless, and Vic had no urge to make him repeat it.

"Alex was far too common a moniker for my parents."

Vic scoffed.

"Victoria is not such a common name either," he pointed out.

"Sure it is. It's one of the most common names in the country."

"Victoria, Henry," Xan mused. "It seems your mother had a penchant for royalty. Is your middle name Elizabeth?"

It was.

Instead of replying, Vic turned to the dance floor when a loud electronic song made a discordant shift to nineties R&B. No DJ, she noticed, just someone with a playlist. She smiled to herself and looked back at Xan.

"I thought we came over here to dance," she said, sending him a defiant look. "What are you in the mood for? We could two-step, we could waltz, we could grind against each other like middle schoolers.

I assume they taught you everything in whatever rich witch finishing school you all popped out of."

"I think they call that college," Xan said with a smile.

Vic rolled her eyes and pulled her sweater over her head. It was getting hotter in here by the second, and she needed to shed a layer. She didn't even think about the movement until she lowered her arms and caught Xan watching her chest, now half covered by a tank top.

He found her eyes a moment too late, and Vic smiled at him, feeling like a cat watching a mouse.

Oh, yeah. How had she forgotten? Xan could pretend all he wanted that he was controlled, composed, perfectly at ease in a situation that would never surprise him. But Vic had seen the desire in his eyes, and she knew at least one way to unbalance *him* for once.

Vic pulled away from him to approach the dance floor, looking back over her shoulder.

"Will you let me lead?" Xan asked, his voice low and dark and his eyes locked on Vic.

"If you can keep up."

And then she was dancing. And, oh, how Vic loved dancing. Xan was right: It was like fighting, like fucking, like any good kind of instinctive movement, and she had almost forgotten how free it felt to be in a place like this, moving her body in time with something outside of herself, surrounded by others doing the same. Vic pulled her hands through her hair as her muscles grew loose and happy, and she didn't even jump when a large man slid behind her.

Xan took her hands and spun her around, and Vic twirled in some combination of a more formal dance with whatever reflexive movement lived inside this music.

She laughed mid-spin, and she thought she caught a smile on the perpetually serious man watching her move through heavy-lidded eyes.

Xan pulled her back against his front, and Vic went happily. He put one hand on her waist and held her close. His body was hard behind her, his hips rocking hers, and she breathed heavily against the music and the heady smell of him. His other hand came in front of her, loosely grasping her shirt above her stomach like he wanted to pull it off. In that moment, Vic would have let him.

It felt good. Felt right, like they were always supposed to end up there, two bodies twining in a crowd full of people who weren't paying attention.

Vic led, and he didn't try to stop her. Xan followed every movement, and Vic reveled in the touch, the heat, the fact that this man of all men was under her spell. She felt drunk on power and shitty wine.

Emboldened, she pressed her ass against him. His head fell into the crook of her neck, and Xan breathed against her, and Vic felt the brush of his beard against the sensitive bare skin. A wave of pleasure radiated out from the spot, and she shivered.

"That tickles," Vic said, not sure if he could hear her over the music. Not sure she wanted him to stop.

Xan rubbed his jaw over the skin of her neck again, slow and deliberate, and Vic threw her head back with laughter.

When the song ended, she watched Xan out of the corner of her eye. A smoldering cast fell over his expression, dominated by the hunger she'd seen there once before. And then he was moving her. Fast, he pulled her across the room, away from the crowd, until he pushed Vic against the rough wall opposite the dance floor.

Vic's chest rose and fell as she stared at him. The witches behind them were milling about, but some were definitely keeping an eye on the Chief Sentinel, who had Vic pinned.

"You need to leave," Xan said, his voice almost a growl, and Vic knew he meant the castle, he meant forever. "You *need* to."

"You don't want me to go," Vic replied, surprised by the breathiness of her own voice.

"Yes, I do," Xan said, meeting her eyes. His were serious, set, and Vic knew he meant every word. "I know you think you can find a place here, but you're wrong."

The words fell on Vic like a bucket of ice water, and she needed to get away from him. She tried to pull back, but he held her tight.

"I'm not going anywhere," Vic said, pulling harder against him. Between the stone wall behind her and Xan in front of her, Vic thought the wall was more likely to give way.

"Whatever you're looking for here, I can help you. You want to find out more about your mom—I can help you. But you need to leave when you're done. Once you've got closure."

Vic thought of the locked door she couldn't open, the window into her mother's world she couldn't see through.

"Meredith had an apartment in the castle," Xan said. Not for the first time, Vic felt as though he'd read her mind. She knew of no magic that would let him do that, and the fact that he understood her so well made her skin feel itchy and unsettled.

"I know that," Vic ground out. She got more frustrated with this man by the second. Had she really felt powerful only moments before? "I can't get inside."

Xan's eyes fell from hers, and he looked as though an unpleasant thought had occurred to him. When he looked up, his gaze locked on her wrist. On the mark Vic couldn't see. She'd forgotten it was there.

"You might try again," Xan said. "The outcome might be different this time."

"What are you—"

"I've been thinking about it," Xan said. "About the Rite and what it means. You might have had help."

He must have still thought Max was responsible, Vic reasoned. He must think she had pulled on Max's power somehow. Of course, if he knew that Aren was behind this, Xan would never suggest what he was suggesting.

Vic didn't answer, but the horror she felt must have been clear on her face, because Xan's expression softened.

"I know you think you can find something here, some purpose in all this madness. But you can't. You'll die trying to belong."

"You don't know anything about me."

"I know a lot about you," Xan said. "I know you learned to fight because somewhere, deep down, you knew that you were vulnerable. You knew you were born different from your brother, and you thought you could fix it by getting stronger. I know it's killing you that all that work won't matter in the end. You could be the best fighter in the world, and May Lin could set you on fire in the time it took you to throw a punch."

His eyes, pale and icy, grew closer to Vic's.

"I know you like it when I touch you," he said. "I know you've been wanting me to do this since the night we met," and Xan drew close enough for his breath to fan across Vic's face, and the skin on the back of her neck grew hot. His eyes dropped to her lips, and he was going to kiss her. And damn her, Vic was going to enjoy it, even when she was furious and humiliated and vibrating with the urge to flee.

Her eyes fell closed as his palm slid up the inside of her right forearm, still trapped between Xan and the wall. His skin was rough as calloused fingertips teased the soft skin of her arm. His palm came to rest over Vic's, like they were holding hands, and he ran the pad of his thumb over the spot on Vic's wrist where the mark was.

"And I know you have no idea what you've gotten yourself into," he said, his lips brushing hers for an instant, so faint it might have been his breath.

Vic's eyes snapped open. His face hovered an inch above hers, and Vic seethed.

"I'm going to bite you."

"Don't," Xan said. He dropped her hand and it fell to Vic's side. "I might like it."

"Get away from me," Vic said, and she pushed him.

He took a step back with his hands in front of his chest.

Sarah, sensing the storm, appeared behind him and asked Vic in an unconvincingly chipper voice if everything was okay.

"Xan was just leaving."

"I was just leaving," Xan repeated.

But when Xan turned to walk away, Vic saw a darkness had fallen over his face. Eyebrows hard over his eyes, and full lips in a tight line.

He looked miserable.

XVIII

Most practitioners employ conduits in some form. They ease the manipulation of magic and allow the witch to focus their energy on more complex tasks. Most common among them are the raw elements, which borrow the organizational structure of the natural world. Innovative Mages have succeeded in creating conduits in the form of most weapons, and some may even be inked into the skin.

—William Ruskin, *A History of the Acheron Order*
(New York, 1935)

Vic woke up angry. The second her eyes peeled open, she picked up where she'd left off the night before. Only now her head hurt.

She'd stumbled back from Lethe with Sarah and May, although they found their drunken amble out of the forest far more pleasant than their sober walk into it. Vic's interaction with Xan stuck in her brain like a rock in her shoe. She wanted to kick him. She wanted to shoot him.

Vic couldn't believe his audacity. Playing with her feelings, mocking her attraction to him. Insisting that he knew her feelings better than she did, that he knew what she ought to do better than she did.

Xan was a perfect example of everything wrong with the Order. They held power over a group of people they had no desire to understand, whose lives they knew nothing of and cared little to learn about. Though the Order pretended their obsession with balance originated in altruism, they didn't use this power to improve the world around them. No, it was all about rules and structure and what everyone else could and could not do. You'd have to be obsessed with control, Vic reasoned, to hide in a castle in the middle of nowhere and think you understood the world better than those who lived in it.

He thought all Vic needed was closure. That learning more about her mom would be enough to send Vic on her merry way.

Was he right?

Vic remembered the Meredith she knew. Honey-haired and bursting with energy, Meredith would have been out of place roaming the cold stone halls of Avalon. Her laughter bounced off the walls of each apartment they lived in, earthy and infectious and slightly louder than it ought to be. Meredith put her whole body into projecting joy, and the sound made sense in their home. Vic tried to picture that laugh cutting through Avalon's emptiness, bringing life to a desolate place.

The two images could not coexist, and the inconsistency made Vic's teeth hurt. The divergent threads gnawed at her. One, she reasoned, must lead somewhere.

When Vic met Sarah and May at breakfast, Sarah looked as hungover as Vic felt. Sarah had pulled her hair up, badly, and her eyes, usually a rich brown, were dim, and Vic knew she looked about the same. May, by contrast, was as neat as ever. She sat with her back dancer-straight like she held court at the table, and Vic scowled at her.

"Good morning to you, too," May said.

Vic groaned as she burned her tongue on her coffee. Behind her, Henry walked by on the way to his usual table, tousling Vic's hair as he passed. She shot him a grouchy look and patted her hair back into place.

"You jinxed us, Vic," Sarah said. "This doesn't usually happen."

"I think it may have been the shots' fault," May said as she buttered a piece of toast from Sarah's plate.

"Vic's the one who suggested shots."

Had she? "I forgot we did shots," Vic said.

Lethe Castle indeed provided an excellent venue for losing memories.

Now that Vic thought about it, she *had* suggested shots. After Xan left, she wanted something to pick her mood up off the floor. If the flashes she retained from the rest of the evening were any indication, tequila had done the trick.

Sarah put her head atop her stacked forearms with a pitiful moan. May patted her shoulder and nudged the toast toward her face.

"You wanna beat the shit out of each other?" Vic asked.

"I'm not sure that's a healthy way to deal with our emotions," Sarah said, looking to May for backup.

But May said, "Sure," at the same time, and Sarah sighed.

After a breakfast of fat and protein soaked up the worst of their headaches, the trio entered the training area and stepped into a room Vic had used before with the Sentinels. In the middle were the routine elements of training: mats and weights and the like. A series of laden shelves spanned the side wall, each lined with a sprawling collection of items. Vic assumed most of them were conduits—objects that allowed a witch to manipulate the shape of energy in the air. Others, she had no clue. Vic stared into the empty eye sockets of a large animal skull and came up with exactly zero guesses as to what purpose it served.

"As far as I know," May said, "no one's made use of the elk skull yet."

Vic approached the mat, pulling off layers until she wore only a sports bra and athletic pants. She'd put a bandage over the mark on her wrist, though Xan's words played in her mind whenever it caught the corner of her eye.

Sarah climbed atop a stack of mats and sat cross-legged with her chin in her hands, still visibly ruffled.

"What are we doing here on a Saturday, you guys?" Sarah asked. "It's not right. We're supposed to be relaxing."

"Relaxing?" May asked. "What's 'relaxing'?"

Sarah just shook her head.

Vic was, she thought, coming to understand the prickly Sentinel. What if May's hostility toward Vic had nothing to do with her? What if it was about Sarah instead? May seemed protective of the other woman, and Vic knew from experience that people could do wild things to protect those they cared about. She was here, wasn't she?

"I haven't had a chance to fight Vic since the first day," May said. "I've been feeling excluded."

"I think Xan keeps you two apart for a reason," Sarah said, her voice muffled by the hand holding up her head.

"The groups you've been working with have gotten a lot better," May told Vic. "I'm curious what the fuss is about."

Vic stifled the urge to preen at the compliment, putting her hands on her hips.

"How's about we make a deal?" she said to May, who looked at her with eyebrows raised. "You need to work on your grappling," Vic said, and May frowned. "As I'm sure you remember, I just so happen to be great at grappling. I can help you out."

"In exchange for?"

"I've got a magic problem," Vic said, and both witches shot her shrewd looks. "There's a door I can't figure out how to open."

May nodded with her eyes narrowed. When Sarah began to ask for more information, May cut her off. "Let's do it."

Two minutes later, Vic had May flat on the floor. "How did you do that?" May groaned as she rolled over and pushed herself up.

Vic hadn't broken a sweat. "You use too much power on high-energy moves. It doesn't matter how fast you are, spinning for a kick is a waste of resources. You're slowing yourself down, leaving yourself open to attack."

"Where did you learn all this, anyway?" May grumbled, looking peeved but evidently not with Vic.

"Lots of places," Vic said. "I used to switch gyms every few months, so I learned a little of everything."

"Why would you do that?" May asked, and Vic wondered if May realized they were having an actual conversation for the first time, almost like friends.

"When my mom disappeared, my brother was convinced people were coming to get him. So we lay low. I thought getting well known in any one spot was a bad idea."

"Didn't you have the same job for that whole time?" Sarah asked.

"Most of it, yeah. But I worked in food service," Vic said with an ironic smile. "Who's the last waitress you remember?"

"Do you have people back home who miss you being gone for so long?" Sarah asked. "Friends, family? A boyfriend?"

Vic paused, then said, "No. It's just me and Henry."

And it was true. She had always kept her romantic entanglements strictly casual, never knowing when she might need to pick up her life with Henry and flee. Her co-workers had tried inviting her out over the years, but she always declined. Henry was her best friend and her only family. The only person she had ever allowed herself to need.

Sarah and May looked at her like they saw too much, and Vic's throat tightened.

"Let's go again," Vic said.

May and Vic went at each other, and out of the corner of her eye Vic saw Sarah climb on tiptoe atop the stack of mats and pluck a glittering stone the size of her palm from an upper shelf. A blue light emanated from the rock and took the shape of a dove in front of Sarah like the inverse of a shadow puppet. It flapped its wings and hovered until—with a grunt—Vic flipped May onto the floor.

Sarah peered down at her. "You heard Vic. Stop trying to round-house her."

"What is that?" Vic asked, staring as the bird took flight and arced overhead.

"I'm trying to hold up May's end of the bargain," Sarah said, shooting a pointed look at May, who stood hunched with her hands on her knees, breathing hard. "You can think of magic as a bunch of threads hanging in the air. When you want to make something happen, you weave the threads into the shape you want them to take."

"Elder Thompson explained all of this," Vic said, impatient. "But I've been staring at rocks the whole time I've been here, and I haven't seen shit."

"I've been thinking about that," Sarah said, plopping back to a seat. "Maybe the stones are too simple. They don't have magic already formed, just energy waiting to be made into something."

"I don't understand."

"The Rite," Sarah said. "Maybe you could withstand it because the magic was already there."

Hadn't Xan suggested Vic could have had help? That the mark on her wrist, the bind she'd entered unwittingly, had given her abilities she didn't understand?

"Let's test it—make something," Vic said.

Still breathing hard, May reached to a lower shelf and tugged a thin wooden box about the length of her arm from behind a medley of objects. A layer of dust coated the surface, and May withdrew a dagger, patinated with age. Holding it in one hand and resting the blade atop her other forearm, May fell into a fighting stance.

She pulled it back like a bowstring and twisted, shooting forward and cleaving the air with the grace of an expert. The blade whistled as it swung. When May brought it down in front of her hips, Vic stared, awestruck, at a pattern suspended in the light. A rune, like those carved along the castle walls, glittered in front of May.

Vic reached for it.

"Don't," May warned as Sarah lifted a foot to nudge away Vic's hand.

"It's a defensive mark," Sarah said. "It would burn you."

"Try to untangle it," May said, watching Vic closely.

Vic stared at the rune. She could almost see the threads they were talking about, but she couldn't pick one apart from the rest. She couldn't see a pattern to the shape's construction, not yet.

The rune dissolved into the air.

"I didn't do that," Vic said, her eyes wide. "Where did it go?"

"Back where it came from," May said as she replaced the dagger in its box and on the shelf. "Let's go again."

May did better this time, and Vic started to get winded.

"What did Xan say to you last night?" Sarah asked, peering at Vic where she lay on the floor. May had gotten her down, but she'd rolled herself in the process, lost control, and Vic threw her off. They lay panting beside each other.

"What? Nothing."

"He said something that upset you," Sarah said.

"Do we have to do this now?" May asked.

"We're not doing anything," Sarah said. "I'm just asking."

"He didn't say anything," Vic said. "Again," she told May.

May and Vic were mid-throttle, their arms locked around each other's shoulders, when Sarah spoke again.

"You know he's single."

Vic's head whipped toward Sarah, and May tackled her.

"Thirty-three. Never married. Unattached." Sarah looked at her nails as she spoke. Vic rolled until she was on top of May, her knees locked around May's waist. May groaned with frustration.

"Why are you bringing this up?"

"I thought you might be interested to know that."

"I'm not," Vic said. May tapped out.

"You are into men, aren't you?" Sarah asked.

Vic stood to grab water from the fountain nearby. "Sure, but I never really date. I dabble."

"Is that what the kids are calling it these days?" May asked.

"You have problems with intimacy," Sarah said.

"I'm a liberated woman," Vic replied, thinking of all the one-night stands that never made it to midnight. "I'm not afraid of sex."

"I didn't say sex—I said intimacy. You can't let yourself be vulnerable enough to form a connection with anyone."

Vic stared at her. "What is with you today?"

Sarah shrugged. "I'm bored. And my head hurts." Turning to May, she added, "You know Vic stole a dagger from the load-out room? She took it to the assembly and everything."

May raised an eyebrow at Vic. "We should go to the shooting range next. We've got some weapons down there that would blow your mind."

"Fuck yes," Vic replied, pointing at May. "But first, I am not leaving this room until one of you tries something with that elk skull."

"I told you," Sarah said in a wistful tone as she lay on the stack of mats with her head lolling off the edge. "Problems with intimacy. Can't even have a conversation with her."

May tried a few spells with the skull, none of which resulted in any reaction, until her final attempt caused it to emit a dull clacking noise, like a death rattle, and May replaced it on the shelf with clumsy fingers. Facing backward this time.

After a particularly hard round, May and Vic lay on the floor opposite each other while Sarah hopped down from the stack of mats and began sifting through the shelf near the floor.

"Where's the door you want to open?" Sarah asked as she began sorting a row of brilliant gemstones by color.

Vic pursed her lips and considered avoiding the question. The thought of explaining her relationship with her mother made her stomach hurt.

"My mom's old apartment is in the Northwest Wing," she said. "But there's some kind of ward on the door."

The sympathy on Sarah's face made Vic look away. She couldn't stand when people looked at her like that.

"Is that why you're still here?" May asked.

"I thought I was training," Vic said, pulling her legs to her chest and wrapping an arm around her knees.

"You said you've just been staring at rocks."

Vic sighed. "It's not like there's a place for me here. It's a medieval castle, for fuck's sake."

"Cathedral," May said. "You mean a cathedral."

Vic shot a confused look at Sarah, and May added, "Everyone says 'castle,' but this place is actually designed like a cathedral. Medieval castles didn't look anything like this."

"So your plan was to find out what happened to your mother?" Sarah asked. "That's why you're here."

"I wouldn't say I had a plan." *Though, yes,* Vic thought, with discomfiting awareness that Sarah had been paying more attention to her than she'd realized.

"How old were you when your mom died?" Sarah asked.

"Sixteen."

"You're stuck," Sarah guessed. "You can't move on, can't love anybody, can't do anything *real,* until you find out what happened."

Sarah was watching Vic with an intensity she didn't like, as if she could see right through her. Vic avoided her gaze. "I *can't* do anything real," she agreed in a half-sarcastic tone. "That's how I wound up here, hiding from the real world with a bunch of witches."

"This is the real world," May protested.

"The real world has more people in it," Vic said. "And waiting in lines and using public bathrooms and cooking for yourself."

"Your real world sounds bad," May said.

"It is, a lot of the time," Vic said. "Let's go again."

When they finished, Sarah sat cross-legged on the mat beside them.

"Let's talk about opening this door," she said.

XIX

The Acheron Order is the final remnant of what was once a global network of witches working in collaboration against the problem of Orcans and Orcan magic. The Order, having outlived all its brethren, is forced to make difficult choices about how to expend finite resources. As a result, the Order focuses almost entirely on the United States, only occasionally venturing out into Western Europe and other parts of North America. For the time being, the rest of the world is, however unfortunately, on its own.

—William Ruskin, *A History of the Acheron Order*
(New York, 1935)

Vic nearly lost her nerve in the corridor. She'd found a murdered woman last week. She was attacked by the creature that did it the next morning. Why it seemed a good idea to do this alone, at night, Vic couldn't explain.

All she knew was that she *needed* to try. Sarah and May had walked her through the process of removing a ward, and—though she felt a guilty twinge at the prospect of pulling on the bind, of intentionally using Aren Mann's abilities—she had no choice. It was her mother's apartment, her mother's life, her mother's secrets, and she needed to get inside.

The strix was dead, anyway. She'd seen Xan break its neck with his bare hands, watched the creature fall as he stood over it, staring impassively at the corpse. It was gone, the castle was on high alert, and the Order was loath to be taken by surprise again.

Yet she still listened hard as she crept through the darkness. The shadowed creature she'd last seen outside her and Henry's door was probably still in the castle. She'd encountered it so many times she'd become almost desensitized to its presence. Vic even found herself wondering if it was an Orcan at all. Perhaps it was another mark of the castle's magic, rather than a being of its own. Maybe someone was messing with her.

It hardly mattered. Tonight, she was willing to take the chance.

If Vic was stuck, as Sarah had said, suspended in time by the death of her mother, by the secrets that swirled in Meredith's wake, upending Vic's world—then tonight she would become unstuck. She would face whatever lay inside Meredith's sordid second life and emerge free from the past. If Vic knew what had happened, she could move on. She had to.

Though Vic thought she'd grown used to the eerie atmosphere of the castle at night, the portraits threw sinister smiles down at her as she passed, and she began to feel the familiar fear inching up the small of her back.

She knew Sarah had wanted to come along. Vic saw the eagerness in the Sentinel's eyes and the disappointment when she left Sarah and May without asking them to accompany her. But Sarah should have known Vic was never going to ask. She would not invite anyone else into the messy business of her memories. Not when she couldn't untangle the knot of her feelings about her mother. To pluck one out and explain it to a stranger was impossible when she couldn't understand it herself.

As Vic climbed a staircase in the Northwest Wing, the air around her shifted. A familiar and not entirely unpleasant sensation—a brush of breath against the crook where her neck met her shoulder, as if a lover sighed against her skin. Her head fell back without thinking and she exhaled.

Catching herself, Vic scanned the hallway for movement. It had felt like someone was next to her, breathing her in, as gentle as a kiss. Her mind flashed to the shadow, and Vic wondered if it stood eye to eye with her right now. There was no shape, no change in the darkness, but Vic told herself she saw it in front of her face, staring.

Her heart raced. Vic considered returning to her room, but she cast the idea aside out of hand. The shadow didn't feel menacing. She perceived no threat hidden in the darkness.

And she'd prepared for this. The strix was dead, the shadow had never tried to hurt her, and she'd pilfered another dagger before leaving the training area that evening. Sarah had watched her do it with a half-amused, half-exasperated expression, and Vic had smiled, bashful, and tucked the new dagger into her pants.

She kept moving.

She was ready. She would do it this time, whatever it took.

Vic made one more turn before she started to notice apartment numbers.

There: 481.

Vic took a deep breath and shot a nervous glance in either direction. Nothing in the hallway save moonlight and shadow.

She pulled the brass key from her pocket, and it stuck as she turned it in the ancient lock. Vic pushed against the heavy door and felt the unseen hand holding it shut. As expected. She sighed.

Vic knelt in front of the door. She ignored the sting in her knees from the bruises she'd given herself during the Rite.

Her eyes locked on the air around the knob, as Sarah had told her. She slowed her breathing and relaxed the muscles in her shoulders. In her mind's eye, she tugged on a string hidden within her arm, under the bind-mark, where the magic lay dormant, and ignored the flash of shame at where—or whom—the magic came from. No time for regret right now; Vic had to focus.

It might have been minutes, or an hour, before the air began to move.

Something like a web wrapped around the handle, knotted and old like thick tree roots had grown one over the other. It was a tangled mess, and Vic fought to keep her breathing under control. If she got too excited, she could lose focus, and she'd have to start over.

But there it was, magic hanging in the air, just like Sarah said.

Vic suppressed the urge to rip it away, to force the tendrils aside and wrench the door open. Instead she imagined, in vivid detail, what it would look like if she could reach a hand forward and brush away a strand.

As she did, a single limp thread of dull silver fell from the mass and dissolved in the air.

Vic gasped.

She could do it. She might not be able to make magic of her own, but she could pull it apart. Vic didn't even care if Aren Mann was helping her open the door as long as she got to see the other side of it.

It took ages.

When Vic finally cleared the last strand, she stood with shaking hands.

She grasped the knob again and twisted.

The door creaked open on aged hinges, beckoning Vic inside.

Meredith's apartment had the same floor plan as the one her children shared on the opposite side of the castle, only flipped. Vic imagined that she crossed the threshold into a parallel dimension— a mirror that mimicked her movements an instant too late.

Vic jumped when the door swung shut behind her, and she felt a force like a whisper cover the handle. Like a cold zipper crunching closed up her spine, and Vic knew the ward had resealed itself.

It was dark inside, lit by nothing but a strip of moonlight from a window across the room.

Vic flicked the switch in the entry hall, but no lights came on.

Stacks of books lay scattered over every flat surface in the room, each covered by a coat of dust. The spines were worn like they'd been read slowly, held aloft in the palm of Meredith's hand. The walls were crowded with framed artwork Meredith must have selected and hung. Even years after its owner abandoned it, the apartment had a lived-in, well-loved atmosphere that Vic could not remember in any of the temporary homes she'd had as a child. Max had said that Meredith had this apartment for decades, and it stood to reason that this—more than anywhere Vic remembered—was her home.

Vic didn't believe in ghosts, and she hadn't seen anything at Avalon

Castle to convince her otherwise. But this place felt haunted the way real places felt haunted. There was life here, once, and now there wasn't. Meredith's absence hung in the air like a specter. Vic saw it in the dust atop her beloved books, in the way one chair sat slightly farther from the table, as if Meredith would return and sit at any moment. She saw it in the bottle of wine half-drunk on the counter, the same varietal Vic favored now.

The open door on the left led to a bedroom, with a wooden bed frame just like Vic's on the other side of the castle, and floral sheets under a layer of dust. Whoever last made the bed had been sloppy.

On the bedside table sat a photograph within a wooden frame, and Vic reached for it. She cleared the dust with her sleeve, expecting to see her own or her brother's face.

Not the three people smiling up at her.

Her mother beamed from the center of the frame, seated on the floor in front of the red couch on the other side of the wall. Meredith, her hair light and smooth, smiled a big, toothy grin at the camera like she'd been caught mid-laugh when the flash went off. She was young, maybe Vic's age, maybe a little older, but it was hard to tell with Meredith, who never lost her youthful glow.

Behind her sat two men, flanking her in relaxed poses on the couch.

To Meredith's left, Max Shepherd. His hair was solid black, without a hint of the white he would develop, and he wore large wire-rimmed glasses as he smiled a sardonic half grin at the camera. His legs were crossed in front of him, and Meredith had one hand wrapped around his calf.

But Vic was stricken, staring at the man on Meredith's opposite side. A man who barely seemed to have aged at all.

Aren Mann was the only one not looking at the camera. He had both legs up on the couch and he was looking at the other two with unabashed joy on his face.

Dread clogged Vic's throat.

The three of them had been friends.

Close friends, by the look of it. Close enough for Meredith to keep a photo on her bedside table, when Vic hadn't seen another photograph of anyone else in the apartment. And now Max and Aren led opposite sides of what was about to become a war, and Meredith had been dead for almost a decade.

Vic stared at Aren's face as apprehension crept into her mind. He couldn't be that bad, could he? Not this smiling man sitting beside her mother, looking at his two friends like they meant the world to him. If he was as the Order described him—cruel, calculating, power-hungry, intent on eradicating an entire population of witches—how was it that he looked so normal?

And if Aren was what they told Vic he was, and Meredith was friends with the monster, what did that make her? Where had Meredith landed in the fight between Aren and Max?

Her pulse sped as the past reasserted itself. There were secrets in this apartment. Vic could feel them like a physical presence.

She'd come here for closure. She'd wanted to understand the world her mother lived in, find out how she died. She had never considered that she might not want to know.

With trembling hands Vic pulled the photo from its frame. She folded the picture in half and slid it into her pocket, but she dropped the frame, and it fell to the floor and shattered.

"Shit."

Vic looked around like someone would see her, like Meredith would materialize to scold Vic for breaking her things. But the apartment was dead silent and empty.

She backed out of her mother's bedroom and approached the closed door across the hall.

The first thing Vic saw when she pushed it open was more books. Loose papers rustled in the breeze of an open window. The air was frigid.

Thick stacks of papers cluttered an antique desk, but when Vic stepped into the room, she froze.

There was someone sitting behind the desk.

For a brief moment—an instant, a heartbeat, the time it took a single synapse to fire—Vic thought it was her mother sitting across from her.

But it couldn't be. And it wasn't.

The moonlight from the window filtered in behind the woman and cast her in shadow. But the stranger had dark hair. It fell down her back in a solid sheet of black and turned pewter where the light glanced off it.

The woman sat stock-still with her back to Vic. The desk, piled high with papers and books, obscured most of her figure.

Vic's first instinct, still rooted in the realities of the world outside the castle, was to apologize for intruding.

"I'm sorry, I—"

But her voice died in her throat when the woman turned. Her head and shoulders shifted slowly, and Vic had the distinct awareness, deep in her gut, that she was not surprised to see Vic.

The woman had high cheekbones, and a broad jaw hung low on her face. Her skin, paler than pale, the skin of a corpse, glowed in the moonlight, and shadows hid her features. Her eyes, Vic saw, were dark and piercing.

Vic noticed with a jolt that the stranger was naked. Her collarbones stuck out from her chest, skin taut and translucent, and Vic saw the contours of her exposed breasts as the woman turned. Vic should look away, she should leave, she should never have come.

The woman's mouth opened, and her jaw—so much wider than it ought to be—fell almost to her sternum. She breathed hard through her gaping mouth, pulling drafts like she meant to taste the air. It whistled through her throat with a low rattle.

Vic backed toward the door, her body preparing to escape while her mind was too stunned to leave the strange woman behind.

Vic heard her own voice in her head like a hit drum.

Get out.

Get out.

Something moved in the corner of her vision, and Vic flinched as she searched for the source. A dark shape crawled across the floor and up, near the side wall. The moonlight hit it just right, and Vic saw. It was a wing—a dark, leathery wing—and Vic's mouth fell ajar as she followed its bony advance across the room, where she saw that it sprouted from the woman's shoulder blade.

The thing's mouth fell open wider, and Vic understood why it couldn't close all the way. Long canines like a wildcat's sat on either side of its mandible, too large—much too large—for a human. Vic couldn't move. She couldn't breathe. The wing made a wet sound as it scraped across the floor. Papers fell from the desk with a muffled thump.

Get out.

The thing in front of her began to rise. Two wings narrowly avoided the walls on either side of the room as it drew itself into the air. At first Vic thought it was standing up. Until its torso cleared the desk and Vic saw what lay beneath it.

The creature's body ended at the rib cage, and it ended messy. The skin at the base of its ribs was torn, gaping, dark and rotted on the edges. Organs hung loose below the creature's half body as it rose, and Vic finally took the gasping breath she needed. Intestines swung under the shredded rib cage like wet ropes, trailing across the desk as the creature moved toward Vic.

GET OUT.

In a flash, it lunged at her.

Vic's back hit the wall with a smack. One of the creature's pale hands reached for Vic as it dove. Long claws at the end of each bony finger narrowly missed her throat.

The beast hovered in the air in front of her face, and Vic shoved it backward and vaulted toward the hall. Her foot caught on the lip of the office door, and she fell forward while rounding the corner. Her hands hit the rug as she stumbled, the raw skin on her palms searing. She pushed herself up and into the hallway.

The beast's claws snagged her hip. Vic twisted out of its grasp and tried to run again.

But a spiny hand caught Vic's arm around the elbow and spun her around. Now facing the monstrosity, she felt her head snap backward as the creature wrenched her toward it.

A horrible smell hit her. Rancid milk and vinegar. Vic gagged and tried to pull herself back, away from the thing, away from that hideous reek.

But its hold on her arm was too strong, claws stabbing her skin through her sweater, pain flaring hot and red. Vic thrashed and pulled away, but its grip only tightened. Vic tried to kick it, but her feet swung loose in the air. There was nothing beneath the beast's rib cage to kick.

With one arm pinned in place, Vic snaked her other hand behind her back, reaching for the handle of the knife she'd hidden there. Her heart beat panic in her throat as the backs of her nails scraped her skin from the awkward angle, but Vic finally had it. She gripped the rubber handle of the dagger she'd stolen and spun it around in her hand.

As fast as she could, Vic slid the blade into the creature's side, and it screamed with rage, but it did not falter.

Vic reached for the weapon again, thinking she had to hit the creature in a precise spot, the neck or the heart, to kill it. Vic couldn't remember what she was supposed to do, if she'd ever known. She grasped at the blade in the creature's side, the blood-coated handle slipping in her fingers. But the thing's claws lifted and flicked Vic's hand away. With a roar it pulled the knife from its side and threw it across the room.

The creature pulled in a slow breath through its mouth again. Lower in the throat and louder. A swirling sound came from inside it, like a snake uncoiling, and Vic watched in horror as a length of spindly dark rope fell from the monster's open jaws.

When the coil began to move of its own accord, Vic realized what it was. The thing's tongue fell heavy in front of her face. Black in the dim light and about the width of a finger, it was at least a foot long. At the end, a bulb perched like a putrid flower on a vine. Vic stared as the bulb opened and closed, its petals gasping for air.

Vic realized what it planned to do an instant before the slimy tongue hit her face with a slap. She clenched her lips together as hard as she could. Barbs on the end of the tongue moved, and Vic felt their searching bite on her cheek as it crawled. She let out a muffled whimper when the thing's tongue slithered toward her mouth. It tried to pry open her lips, and Vic writhed away from it. Vic threw her head from shoulder to shoulder to shake the tongue off, but it stuck, latched on her mouth as it fought to wriggle inside.

Desperate, Vic pushed her body weight backward, straining into the beast's hold on her arm. She used the momentum to kick both of her feet out this time, and she aimed her legs as high as she could. Forcing her weight into the thing's hand, Vic felt white-hot pain as its claws tore deep into her arm, but her right foot hit its mark. It connected with one of the wings. A loud crunch, and the creature's tongue whipped away from Vic's face as it bellowed in pain. The tongue swung madly in the air as it opened its mouth wide and snarled.

But it loosened its hold enough that Vic tore herself free and fled down the hallway.

With a damaged wing and without Vic to hold it up, the creature fell to the floor with a smack and a growl. Throwing a glance over her shoulder, Vic watched the beast pull itself up onto its hands. It began to pull its body forward, its claws clinging to the hallway carpet for purchase. It wriggled toward her like a viper.

Vic barreled into the door to the outside—to safety—and ripped at the knob. But it was locked, pulled shut by the same magic that had kept her out. Panic roared in Vic's head as she tried to focus on the ward again, focus on getting out. She needed to think, needed to—

A clawed hand wrapped around Vic's ankle and yanked.

Vic twisted toward her attacker as she fell. Her shoulder hit the stone floor first; the back of her head a split second later. The blow stunned her. Her head pounded. A fog crept across the sides of her vision. She couldn't see.

Claws sliced the flesh of Vic's calf as the creature wrenched her toward it. Vic's hand shot out to grab the wall, grab the bookcase, grab anything. But her fingers closed around empty air, and the beast started to drag itself upward along her body, toward her face.

Vic screamed.

Two lungfuls of air tore their way out of her body with force.

It was a sound Vic had never heard before. Primal, trapped deep inside on the off chance it might one day become necessary. In the back of her muddled brain, Vic realized she had never needed that scream before.

Behind her, something hit the outside of the door like a battering ram.

Vic thrashed around, trying to push the thing off her, trying to pull herself out from under it. She kicked out blindly, hitting nothing.

Writhing on the floor, Vic looked around her mother's home in a desperate hunt for something that could save her. She thought of the bind, tried to pull on it, tried to force magic out of it and into the monster, but no relief came.

She pushed both her hands into the creature's face. Keep its mouth away from hers, that was the last defense, the animal impulse. *Don't let it get its tongue inside.*

But it was stronger than Vic, and her arms wobbled against the pressure of its body bearing down on her. Vic locked her elbows, but it would break her arms before it gave up. It gnashed thick teeth at her, and Vic held tight to the bottom of its jaw. Saliva, slimy and putrescent, fell onto her hand as she shoved its face away from hers.

Behind her, BANG BANG, as something heavy hit the door.

Someone was trying to get inside. Someone who could help her.

If only she could open the door.

Keeping her arms locked tight, Vic twisted her head back until she could see the door, and she was begging her mind to focus, to clear enough for her to see the threads again. And by some miracle she made them out, first thin in the darkness, then clear as day. And with her mind she reached out and pulled one away, just as the creature managed to shove one of her arms to the side.

Her eyes were on the monster again as it bent toward her face.

Vic almost didn't notice the change in the air.

But she heard the door slam open behind her.

On the edge of her vision, a shadow shot into the apartment. It pitched forward in a blink, gathering energy as it hurtled across the room on a silent wind.

The beast noticed the movement an instant after Vic did. It reared back, but not fast enough.

The shadow was upon it.

Vic pulled her legs away as the darkness landed in front of her and began to change.

First, the shadows coalesced into the form it wore last time she'd seen it, brutal and menacing, a predator carved out of darkness. But once there, it continued to clarify and combine. The shape re-formed and refined until it resembled something vaguely human. Except it was much too large to be human.

Shadows danced around a core of solid flesh that took the rigid shape of a man in black, darkness clinging to his body like clouds around an angry planet.

The shadows took the unmistakable form of the Chief Sentinel.

Xan did not look back at Vic as he advanced on the legless creature. The beast on the floor scanned the room the way Vic had, frantic for an escape. But it, too, found no refuge in the long-abandoned apartment.

As Xan stalked toward it, the creature decided to go on the offensive.

With strong hands on the floor, it propelled itself toward Xan's face, and Vic gasped. It was going to do to Xan what it had tried to do to her.

But Xan murmured in the Universal Language, and a wooden staff materialized in his hands. Not a staff, Vic realized. A stake the length of a spear. And Vic remembered what she had forgotten in her panic. The only way to kill this creature: an ash-dipped stake crafted from the wood of a casket.

As the Orcan leaped at him, Xan thrust forward with practiced precision. The spear pierced the creature's body, entering the base of its sternum and tearing through the exposed innards there. The beast shrieked. The sound, high and loud, drilled into Vic's brain. Her head throbbed. The thing's flesh withered. The gray skin pulled in on itself and convulsed. For a moment, the body twitched, until it collapsed. It hung limp from the spear still clutched in Xan's hands.

He threw it aside with a grunt of disgust. The body smacked the wall and slid to the floor.

With his back to Vic, Xan lowered his head as if in prayer, and his shoulders rose with long, slow breaths. His hands compressed into fists before splaying out, like he was fighting the urge to hit something.

Finally, he faced Vic. He crouched in front of her, and their eyes locked.

Pale blue eyes like shards of broken glass, Vic remembered. Though now she imagined them as mirrors. She could see herself as Xan saw her. Bloody, broken, and scared. Curled on the floor like a frightened kid.

Xan had saved her life.

Her pulse beat fast beneath her ragged breathing, and Vic gave up hope of controlling it. She didn't want Xan to see her panicked and taken apart. But she couldn't tell him to leave, or send for someone else to help her, or get up of her own power. She was paralyzed by fear and still breathing heavily. Vic couldn't fix any of it, so she stared into those cold blue mirrors and hoped he didn't see how frightened she was—of him, of this world, of the corpse a hair's breadth from her feet.

Vic realized that the face around those eyes was angry. His brows met firm around a frown. His skin was speckled with the creature's blood. Fitting that he should be covered in gore again, when Vic had first met him in the same state. Same as he had that first night, Xan watched Vic like he wanted to kill her himself. At the end of an evening such as this, Vic would not have been terribly shocked if he tried.

It rattled Vic that he could be angry with her for getting attacked. She was a liability, after all. He'd said so himself. A bomb set off inside the careful walls of his castle. Any disruption, especially a disruption involving Vic, must be her fault. The thought angered her, and anger pulled her through fear. The adrenaline faded from her limbs and left a chill behind.

In its absence came pain. Her arm hurt, her head hurt, her ass hurt, her shoulder, her calf—everything hurt.

"It's not my fault," Vic said in a shaking voice. "You can't be mad at me for this. It's not fair."

A muscle in his jaw jumped, but Xan said nothing.

"You don't get to be angry."

"Oh, I'm angry," Xan said. He shot a hostile look at the dead Orcan on the floor, and its lifeless body twitched like he'd smacked it. "I'm fucking furious."

"You're the Chief goddamn Sentinel," Vic said, biting out her words. "It's your job to guard the castle, to stop shit like this from happening."

"You think I don't know that?" Shadows jumped around him like cast-off candlelight. Vic wondered if he did it on purpose, or if the shadows danced in an unconscious display of agitation.

Vic leaned away from him.

"Why *the fuck* would you—" Xan cut himself off and rubbed his temple. "Where are you hurt?"

Vic narrowed her eyes at him. Xan was so far beyond losing his cool; she wasn't sure what to make of it.

The shadows roamed over Vic like they were looking for injuries.

She couldn't feel them as they grazed her skin, but it felt intimate all the same. Vic assumed, after what she'd seen tonight, that they were a part of him. Xan's gaze lingered on the wounds on her upper arm, the worst of her injuries.

"Let me see." He reached for her arm, and Vic forced herself to relax as he held her left arm aloft and peeled her sweater back. Xan inhaled through his teeth as he examined the torn flesh there.

Four claw marks were deep, almost to the bone and bleeding heavily. Her muscles and nerves must have been torn, too, because Vic couldn't make a fist with her left hand. That was bad.

Vic looked away as she caught a glimpse of yellow she knew was fat. She refused to pass out.

Xan pulled a short knife from his waist and, fast as a flash, sliced the outside of his right forearm. Vic gasped. She stared in horror at the swell of bright blood that flowed from Xan's arm into the carpet below, droplets loud enough to hear.

But he wasn't paying attention to her. His eyes were on Vic's arm with such intense focus that Vic couldn't help following his gaze, though she didn't want to see the wounds again. But the flesh was knitting itself together, an unseen force pulling skin and muscle back into place like invisible stitches. Vic stared, agog, as she realized what Xan was doing.

It took only a few seconds, and it wasn't perfect, healed skin that replaced the deep cuts. Rather, it looked as though she'd suffered a much less severe wound, more a scratch than a gouge.

"What the—"

Xan plucked her off the floor, and she groaned as the room swirled around her. He carried her to the exit.

It took a second for Vic to register her irritation at being jostled and at just how easy it seemed for him to lift her. Vic was by no means a small woman, and she had never before had this particular experience.

She made a weak attempt to free herself, and Xan clutched her tighter against his body.

Vic adjusted herself so the wound on her hip wasn't bouncing off of Xan's stomach. She thought she heard him grunt.

The door slammed behind them with enough force to knock a painting off the wall. The clamor of the aged frame breaking against the floor echoed through the empty hallway as Xan stalked away from it and up a staircase. Vic bobbed with each step, but she did not put her arms around his neck to steady herself. She crossed them in front of her chest and ignored how this irritated the partially healed lacerations on her arm.

Vic stared at the hard set of Xan's face as he marched down another hallway. Deep purple hollows had bloomed under his eyes. He looked exhausted, more worn out than she would have thought possible.

"It was you this whole time," Vic said. "I saw you. In the hallways at night, on the grounds coming toward the castle." She ran through all her memories of the shadowed thing she now knew was a human man. She'd seen Xan, again and again, beginning her first night here.

Her mouth fell open at an appalling realization.

"You were in my room!" Vic cried. The night she'd dreamed of Aren Mann, she'd known there was someone in her room. Someone in the corner, hidden in the shadows. "Were you *watching me sleep?*"

Vic would have sworn he looked sheepish, but it was gone in a flash, and he returned his gaze forward. Xan said nothing, and Vic stewed.

"I can't believe it," she whispered, her anger coming to the fore. "You were spying on me. You've been watching me for weeks."

Then Vic recognized a set of double doors right as Xan hammered a kick against them, jostling her. The doors swung inward of their own volition, and Max stood up from behind his desk at Xan's unceremonious entrance to his office. Surprise turned to concern when Max saw Vic bloodied and clutching her arm.

Without a word, Xan dropped Vic onto the couch in a pile. Vic shot Xan an indignant look as she righted herself, but he had already turned away from her.

Xan marched back out the doors, and they slammed behind him.

XX

While magic for transportation purposes is possible, the expense of such all-encompassing practice precludes its use in all but the most urgent circumstances. With this in mind, some practitioners excel at giving the illusion of transport by means of disguising their form, elaborate camouflage, or outright manipulation of another's senses. But this is, like much magic, deception.

—Terrance Vern, *Theories on Transmogrification*
(New York, 1999)

Max didn't spare a look for Xan as he left the room. The older man's eyes ran the length of Vic as he faced her. Vic's will to fight fled the room with the Chief Sentinel.

"I went to Meredith's apartment."

Max's eyes widened.

"Something was in her office." Vic shuddered at the memory. "An Orcan. I thought it was a woman at first. I thought it was . . ." Vic shook her head.

Max's voice was low when he asked, "What was it?"

"Manananggal."

Vic had recognized the Orcan once it rose from behind the desk, though she hadn't recalled the name in her panicked state. Of all the creatures she'd learned about at Avalon, the manananggal left a distinct impression.

"It attacked me."

The words did little to convey the depth of Vic's terror. They fell far short of how it felt when the monster's claws sank into her skin, or the way its tongue crawled toward her lips. Vic suppressed a gag and wiped her sleeve across her face.

"I tried to fight it off," Vic said around a building lump in her throat. "But it was too strong, and when I tried to run away, it caught me." She closed her eyes to the sight of Max's sympathetic face. She hated the way these words sounded coming out of her mouth—a dry description of a most vivid memory. Boiled down to its component parts, the story sounded almost boring. Vic couldn't stop her hands from shaking. "That's when Xan showed up. Or materialized, is more accurate."

"You've finally witnessed his abilities in action, I see."

She supposed she'd witnessed them a number of times.

"What is he?"

"Some of the strongest Born witches show a special aptitude for certain kinds of magic," Max said. "That form comes naturally to him."

"He came out of nowhere, killed the thing that attacked me, and brought me here."

"He was able to enter the apartment?"

Vic remembered the sound of banging against the door from the outside.

"No," she said. "I had to let him in." She hadn't undone the entire ward, but she'd started on it, and Xan must have been able to do the rest.

They fell silent as Max considered this, and Vic's head throbbed. She put a hand to her forehead and waited for the pulsing to abate. Max seemed to remember something and crossed the room quickly.

"A doctor will be here soon," he assured Vic when he returned to the seat in front of her.

She nodded. Her head still hurt, but the worst of the pounding receded.

"Max?" Vic asked in a small voice. "Is someone trying to kill me?"

Max thought hard before replying.

"I do not think so," he said.

"First the strix and then the Rite and now this," Vic said. "I can admit a fair amount of coincidence, but this is past the point of plausibility."

"I'm not sure that it is," he said quietly.

"Nathaniel wants me dead," Vic said. "I can see it in his eyes—he's got to be behind this, Max."

But Max looked like he was at a crossroads, a deep frown etching his face as he considered how much to tell her. Trying to decide whether to be honest or to deflect. Finally, he sighed.

"Victoria, I must confess something to you."

Apprehension wound down Vic's spine. Max was the reason she was here, the reason she could stay. He had been the first to welcome her inside, and he had treated Vic with more respect than anyone here. She thought of the photograph—of Max sitting alongside her mother and Aren Mann—and Vic wasn't sure she wanted to hear whatever Max thought he ought to confess.

"I had an ulterior motive in giving you the key to Meredith's apartment," he said, and Vic waited for the other shoe to drop.

"Your mother was a highly capable witch and a beloved friend of mine. But she was distrustful. She barred entrance to her apartment whenever she left the castle. When she died, whatever wards she had in place locked shut. No one had been inside that apartment in eight years."

Max swallowed, and Vic had the sense he was nervous about how she would react. He didn't want to tell her, but he plunged on.

"When you arrived at Avalon, I thought you might be able to bypass the protections. Spells react differently when they recognize their maker, and sometimes they recognize aspects of their maker that might be present in a close relation. Being made of Meredith's own flesh and blood, you might have been able to get inside. So I gave you the key."

"You didn't give Henry a key."

"I did not."

"But I'm not—" Vic shook her head.

"Because I *knew* you could do it. And you did, didn't you?" Max asked.

But she hadn't, not on her own. It wasn't her power that opened the door. She'd leaned on someone else, someone that would horrify Max. Vic should tell him—Max deserved to know that his theory was wrong. Vic bit her lip.

"I would never have sent you there if I thought it might put you in danger," Max said, his eyes beseeching. "I even convinced myself that I did you a favor, that you would appreciate a glimpse into your mother's life here."

But Vic hadn't gone to Meredith's apartment because of Max. It wasn't Max who'd pushed her to go. It wasn't Max who'd planted the idea of pulling on the bind. All Max had done was give her the key.

"It seems I was foolish to think the wards were the only protection guarding Meredith's sanctuary."

"You're suggesting the manananggal was there to deter intruders," Vic said.

"The way I see it, there are two people who could have brought that Orcan into Meredith's study," Max said. "Meredith, for one. I wouldn't be surprised if she invoked something of that nature in the event that her privacy was invaded. She had the talent to pull it off." A ghost of a smile tinged Max's face. "And the requisite disregard for the rules."

"And the second one?" Vic asked. The photograph sat against her hip like a shard of ice. Meredith, Max, Aren. Friends, now enemies. One dead, two left to continue fighting.

When Max replied, he spoke slowly. "We should discuss the circumstances of your mother's death."

Vic stopped breathing. Blood rushed in her ears. She had to know, though the idea sent a wave of panic through her mind. She *had* to know, but she wasn't sure she wanted to.

"The official conclusion was that she died on a hunt. It's what the reports say and what most people in this castle believe. It is not, however, the truth."

"She was murdered," Vic said. She'd known already, hadn't she?

She had to. She knew what Max was going to say next before he said it. She'd known the second she saw that photograph.

"Yes."

"Henry doesn't know."

"Few do."

"You know who did it." Vic did, too, though the thought landed like a punch in the gut.

"Aren Mann."

The man in the tower. The only one in the photograph not looking at the camera. The one who'd opened the door.

"Why?"

Knowing eyes locked on Vic's. "Meredith's role in the Order changed as she got older. She didn't want to hunt Orcans anymore. When the Brotherhood defected, and the tectonics of our world shifted, she began to focus on Mann. She was concerned about his growing influence and power, and she foresaw where he would take his followers years before the bulk of the Order caught on. In the period leading up to her death, Meredith infiltrated the organization with the aim of taking Mann down from the inside."

"You think he killed her because he found out she betrayed him?"

"The last thing I ever heard from Meredith was that she'd found something. I never knew what."

Vic reached into her front pocket and pulled out the folded photograph. Her fingers, she noticed, were covered in blood. She handed it to Max.

When he pulled it open, his eyes widened.

Then, to Vic's surprise, he smiled.

"She would have kept this, wouldn't she?" Max said under his breath. "Sentimental Meredith."

He tried to hand it back to Vic, but she shook her head. She didn't want it anywhere near her. "What happened between the three of you?" Vic asked, her voice a whisper. Her head spun. Where was the doctor?

Max's eyes were sad. "I could never predict Meredith," he said. "Aren Mann and I were at each other's throats from the day we met, but Meredith kept us civil. Even when things fell apart, she kept us connected. She played both sides, made both of us think she understood us, made us believe we could come back together. I never knew what she actually believed until she died for it."

A knock at the door interrupted Max.

"Come in," he called, and the doors to the office swung inward to reveal a short, balding man carrying a leather bag. "Thank you for coming so quickly, Marcus. Victoria here has been injured."

Marcus approached her with studied detachment while Max sank back and sifted through papers on his desk. The doctor plied Vic with questions about her medical history, her injuries, and she told him what she remembered.

"I don't suppose you have some kind of magical remedy for any of these?" Vic asked, hoping that his bag contained something more potent than Western medicine. She remembered Xan stitching up the cuts on her elbow, thinking the doctor must be even better at it than Xan was.

"I'm afraid not. Medicine and magic rarely mingle."

Vic frowned.

Max took a seat on the chair nearest Vic. His raven—which Vic had not noticed until that moment—flew to rest at his back.

"Innate healing ability is rare enough to be nearly mythical," Max said. "Some powerful witches can heal wounds, but it's incredibly draining. Most would prefer to suffer physical ailments than incur the cost of attempting to heal them."

Vic stared as the doctor brandished a regular old stethoscope. That explained the circles under Xan's eyes. Why had he done that?

"Although witches do tend to heal at a slightly faster rate than non-magic humans," Max added, as though they were discussing the concept as a theoretical matter and not the injuries to Vic's real-life, non-magical body.

"Made witches, no matter how dire the injuries that lead to their rebirths, almost always return fully or nearly fully healed. If you believe, as I do, that Made witches actually enter the Veil when they nearly pass, then it becomes more about a connection to the physical plane than about anything the body does."

Vic sighed.

"I haven't had the time to write this theory down or disseminate it, and it is a bit radical, but I suspect many in the Order would agree with my proposition over the more determinist points of view available."

Max kept on like this while Marcus worked, which Vic found extremely annoying until she realized that being annoyed with Max kept her mind from the shining implements Marcus pulled from his bag.

When Marcus extracted a long silver syringe, Max opted to say the most distracting thing he could think of.

"Will you help me take down the Brotherhood?"

Vic's head whipped toward him, and Marcus grabbed her arm to hold it still. Max leaned forward and rested his elbows on his knees.

"I can't do anything," Vic said.

"You discount yourself. You can do many things."

"Yeah, I know that. If you need your restaurant managed or your makeup done or your oil changed, I'm your girl. But magic, Max? I opened a door this evening, and it took me two weeks." And she hadn't even done it alone. In fact, she'd done it with the aid of the person Max wanted her to help him destroy.

"I told you I never understood your mother. Two decades into our friendship, Meredith remained a mystery to me. Being around her was exciting. She drove me wild a lot of the time. But Meredith was like a force of nature. She did and said exactly as she pleased, and no one ever knew what that was going to be until it was."

As he spoke, sadness etched into the lines of his face. He looked his age, worn down by years of conflict and loss.

"That fire she had—it's in you. Don't argue with me. The mere fact that you could open that door means you're more like her than you think."

Vic was shaking her head. It was a nice thought, but Max was wrong. She couldn't put her finger on why, exactly, she was nothing like her mother. It was deep under the surface. The sound of laughter in their apartment that Vic could never replicate.

"Meredith might be key to this whole thing. The Order, the Brotherhood, whatever comes next. You can help me unlock it."

"She didn't tell me shit about the Order," Vic said, "let alone that she spent two decades in it. If this whole story boils down to my knowledge of my mother, then I'm afraid you're screwed."

Whatever the doctor had given Vic spread through her limbs like a pleasant fire.

"The Brotherhood is the reason your life has been so difficult," Max said. "The reason you had to drop out of school, the reason your mom is gone, all of it."

Vic let out a quiet, bitter laugh. "My life has always been hard. Long before Meredith disappeared for good, I picked up all the slack she dropped while fighting for the Order. She'd leave for days, weeks sometimes, and I carried everything she left behind. Even when she was around, she missed so much she couldn't remember the simple things, and all the responsibility for fixing it fell to me. Now you tell me I need to pick up where she left off? Again?"

"Something is happening to you," Max said. The doctor's hands stilled where they were bandaging Vic's calf. "You can feel the change, I know you can. Something inside of you is waking up."

But Max was wrong. Nothing was happening to her. She hadn't done any of it on her own.

"You were supposed to be powerful, you know?" Max said. "Meredith meant you to be the most powerful of all of us. She might have given up on that idea, but I never have."

Vic rested her head against the couch. Everything hurt. All she wanted was to curl up somewhere warm and hope she didn't remember any of this tomorrow.

"I think you'll do it, you know," Max said. "Meredith used to do the same thing. She would hem and haw and complain all day long, but she would wake up the next morning and do the hard thing that needed to be done."

Her senses started to fade, like lights flickering out down a hallway.

"I'm not like her," Vic said.

"You are just like her," Max said.

"I think you're full of shit."

"I know." And he sounded genuinely sorry.

Vic's vision went last. Her head fell sideways on the sofa as she passed out.

XXI

Places have a magic of their own, built and grown over the centuries. As such, feats that are impossible for a single witch become possible through the borrowed power of an ancient place. For instance, the Order's fortress at Avalon Castle remains one of the only places in the world where witches can travel freely through the ether, relying as they do on the castle's assistance.

—Terrance Vern, *Theories on Transmogrification*
(New York, 1999)

Vic woke up when her face hit the floor. She groaned and shut her eyes. The air was cold, but she was warm. She pulled her knees toward her chest and tried to go back to sleep.

"Nice of you to drop in." Aren's voice came from somewhere north of her pounding head.

Vic moaned. Not again.

"Oh, it's not so bad. You only fell a few feet."

Hands gripped Vic's shoulders and pulled her from the floor, and she was too disoriented to protest. Aren propped her up against something ridged and bumpy.

"Where am I?" Vic mumbled, but she didn't need to ask. She remembered the space as soon as she drew the energy to open her eyes. The assembly room, under the castle. Cave walls and carved stone steps. They were on the dais where the Elders sat. Aren was mocking them. Vic groped behind her and found that she leaned against the sculpture at the back of the stage. To her immediate left, its gaping mouth hung ajar. Without the crowd of witches in black robes and the blazing fire and the animal tension, it became an entirely different—though no more welcoming—space.

"You'll have to forgive me for your ungraceful entrance," Aren said. "It appears they've given you a strong sedative. Normally, I assume, you would have the reaction time to land on your feet."

Vic resented the implication that it was her fault he dropped her. She scowled at him as she rested her head on the sculpture behind her. Her neck did not possess the strength to hold itself up.

"What do you want?"

"Such attitude. I merely wanted to make sure you were okay. I heard about some funny business at the castle. Something about a human facing off with a manananggal." He gave Vic's bruised and bloody appearance a once-over. "And losing."

"Who told you that? It's been like an hour."

"I can't believe it—the Order can't even keep the beasts out of the castle now."

Vic narrowed her eyes at him as her conversation with Max came back to her. Leave it to Max to reveal critical information when she was in pain and slipping out of consciousness. Sarah swore he was a genius, but he seemed to lack core interpersonal skills.

With great effort, Vic hoisted herself up to a standing position, keeping one hand on the statue for balance, and turned her back on Aren.

"I don't want to talk to you," she said.

"Whyever not?" Aren bounded around her until they were face-to-face again.

"I'm in pain."

"Oh, that's not why."

"I don't like you."

"That's better. Are you still upset that I pushed you? Because you know that wasn't real."

"Max told me you murdered my mother."

Surprise flashed in Aren's bright blue eyes, and he took a step back. "Is that all he said?"

"He said you killed her when you found out she'd been spying on you for the Order."

Again, his eyes flared. "Meredith never did anything *for* anyone, I can guarantee you that."

"You're avoiding the subject."

He leaned in and locked eyes with Vic.

"And how would you react?" he said, voice low. "If I told you I caught Meredith spying and killed her out of spite, what would you do?"

"Did you?"

"Answer the question first. Then I'll tell you."

Something dangerous lay in his flinty eyes, so close to Vic's. She couldn't focus. She couldn't think. Whatever that doctor had given her swam through her thoughts like syrup, slowing everything down.

"I don't know," she finally said. "I can't even stop you from grabbing me in my dreams and forcing me to talk to you. I don't know how you would react if I accused you of murder."

"You already did, Victoria."

"I only told you what Max said."

Aren leaned against the statue, his arms crossed as he scrutinized Vic.

"It hurts my feelings that you would suggest I *force* you to talk to me," he said after a long pause. "I'm a delightful conversationalist. Ask anyone. And for the record, I did not murder Meredith Wood."

"Why does Max think you did?"

"Because he hates me? Because he envies me? Because he's cast me as the villain in the great melodrama of his life? I don't know—you'll have to ask him."

Vic shook her head. She couldn't talk to Aren right now, not when she struggled to stand and her legs shook underneath her. Vic leaned against the vile sculpture as she fought to wade through the fury and exhaustion clouding her mind.

"And what about this?" Vic said, shoving her arm forward. His eyes trailed to the spot on her wrist, and for an instant Vic thought she saw something there. Something dark against her skin and complex, but it was gone, and only bare flesh stared back at her.

"What about it?" Aren asked with an affected shrug.

"It's Orcan magic," Vic said.

"I'm fairly certain you knew that when you agreed to participate," he pointed out.

"Because I didn't think it was real," Vic said.

Aren raised an eyebrow. "Did I tell you that?"

Vic breathed hard as her anger took control over more rational emotions. He was a monster, a murderer. He wanted to tear the Order down, kill people like Sarah—she should not egg him on. She should not make him angry. And yet . . .

She found herself asking, "Someone said it was a bind. What for?"

"Normally this curiosity comes before you perform magic together."

"Tell me."

Aren watched her with false kindness. "I'm only trying to help you."

"And yet you keep doing *this*," Vic snapped. "You bring me here. You won't let me out. You hold me captive in my own head. You bat me around like a toy."

"You're just like your mother, aren't you? What are you going to do about it?"

"Stop fucking comparing me to my mom," Vic spat, and she shoved him in the chest, hard, with both hands. And they fell. Together, they toppled over, through the floor and down, too far down. Vic hit the ground again, and rolled away.

When she came back to herself, Aren stood over her, watching her face through a frown. They were in a different room, one Vic did not recognize.

Vic scampered to her feet and spun. They weren't in the castle, Vic was sure of that. In place of gothic curves were modernist lines— sharp angles and brutal edges. The wall at her back was made of glass. Windows overlooked a black forest, lit only by an abundance of stars. In front of Vic hung a gilded mirror as tall as she was, the only thing in the room save an altar and a wall of shelves glittering red.

"How did you do that?" Aren asked. He watched Vic with an odd expression. Awe, maybe, or horror. "You took control. I've never seen anyone do that."

"Where the fuck is this place?"

"This is my home." Aren spread his arms in a gesture of welcome, the dazed look still on his face. "You'll have to forgive the mess. I wasn't expecting visitors."

Vic strode away from him, sick of him, and approached the wall of shelves. From the floor to the ceiling, square compartments the size of a hand each contained a single red stone. They glittered with internal light, and below each sat an inscription in tiny, careful print. Vic reached for an oblong stone at eye level.

"I wouldn't—" Aren began, reaching to stop her.

But her fingers closed around the rough stone.

The steering wheel was leather, white and clean and polished smooth, and it was a perfect day. He held the wheel with a single hand laid softly over the top of it, and he stretched his right arm sideways over the bench seat, where he could brush the pads of his fingers over Anne's shoulders whenever he felt like it. They couldn't have picked a better day to visit the coast. They'd beaten tourist season, and they didn't mind the chill. Neither of them was a born swimmer, and they relished the opportunity to sit by the sea without the distraction of other beachgoers.

He was pleased enough to get the car out of the garage. His friends at the club had teased him for buying the convertible, typical midlife-crisis mobile, but he loved it. It was a beautiful day, and Anne smiled up at him with the wind in her hair, and how could he regret a single choice that had led him here?

"Look out!" Anne shouted, and he twisted forward.

A man in a suit stood in the center of the road, his arms at either side of his hips and palms facing forward. He stared at the car with a determined glare as they careened toward him. What the fuck was he doing, standing in the middle of the road? They were going to hit him.

He slammed on the brakes, and they cried out as they fought—and failed—to stop. The car slid sideways, to the edge of the road overlooking the cliff, and he didn't feel the guardrail give way, but the final impact—when the car collided with the surf—he felt. He felt every moment.

Vic jerked back. The stone fell from her shaking fingers, and Aren caught it before it hit the ground. He replaced it in its nook and adjusted it to face forward.

"I warned you not to do that."

"That was . . . that was . . ." Vic gagged around the urge to vomit, to expel remembered pain. Hot blood and icy water, the crunch of bone and metal, and the sound of a drowning scream.

"A blood stone, yes. Are you familiar?"

They held the essence of the dead. Of the people Aren had killed.

"They were strangers. They were having a nice day, and you . . ."

"Yes, yes. It's unfortunate, but things are often unfortunate in war."

Vic looked behind him at the rows and rows of identical stones. There were so many of them—hundreds, thousands. Bile crept up her throat.

"Why?" she breathed.

"Power, my dear." He shrugged as he said it, but his eyes held a sorrowful heaviness. Was he ashamed of his actions? Or was he ashamed that Vic bore witness to them?

Vic backed away from him. In her mind's eye, Aren's features changed. Sharper, meaner, harsher. She couldn't get away from him fast enough. Her back hit the cold glass of the window, and she stilled.

"You are who they say you are," Vic said, realizing the truth of her words as she spoke them. "You set the Orcan loose in the castle, you kill people, you . . . you killed my mom."

"You know nothing about the world you were born into," Aren said as he approached her. He shook his head, a pitying look on his face. "You think you've stumbled upon a morality play—good and evil, clearly delineated, an obvious choice. But there are no heroes in this story, Victoria. You think Meredith didn't know what I was up to? You think Max didn't? None of us are innocent here."

He closed the distance between them. Aren looked down at her, his face inches from her own. Vic shook her head.

"I did *not* kill Meredith. I didn't need to. She was on my side, in the end. She would have brought you to me, if she'd lived. You and Henry."

Vic swallowed around rising panic. Her brother, oh god, he knew about her brother.

"I may be a murderer," Aren said. "But murderers are hardly in short supply in the world you've stumbled into. Condemn me all you want, but I'm right in the end. And I, for one, haven't actually hurt you. Not once."

He rested a hand against Vic's cheek, his palm warm and dry and heavy on her face.

"Remember that."

Vic ripped her head back, away from him, not caring if she smacked into the glass. She didn't want his hands on her.

She woke alone, gasping. She was back in her bedroom in the castle, with no idea how she'd gotten there and no energy to find out. She imagined the shadows shifting around her as she fell back into a fitful sleep.

XXII

Magical factions rarely war with one another. During periods of rapid upheaval, such as plague, famine, war, or technological advancement, new groups have emerged to challenge existing attitudes about the role of magic in society. Most often these conflicts revolve around the proper means by which those equipped to use magic should approach the non-inclined public.

The heavy toll of taking these disagreements to the battlefield has, for the most part, discouraged rival factions from seeking drastic solutions through violence. Such conflicts have been resolved through diplomatic means (see the Council at Oxford and the Tunisian Agreement for two examples). As of the date of writing, there has not been a war between magical groups in a millennium.

—William Ruskin, *A History of the Acheron Order*
(New York, 1935)

"Sepsis from superficial wounds is incredibly unlikely but not impossible."

"Jesus Christ, May. Lighten up. She's not going to die."

"I agree. I said it's incredibly unlikely."

Vic opened her eyes to Sarah and May at loggerheads on the other side of her bedroom. Beside her, Henry had pulled an armchair up to the bed. He sat with his head on his fist, propped up on the armrest, watching the two women bicker with an expression of extreme annoyance.

When he noticed Vic was awake and watching, he smiled before looking back at the other two and mouthing *Kill me*.

Vic's laugh stuck in her throat, which was dry and sore from shouting. The rough sound stopped Sarah and May squabbling as they turned around and flew toward the bed.

"They've been arguing since they got here," Henry told Vic, not bothering to hide the edge in his voice. "Around six this morning."

"How are you feeling? Are you okay? Are you in pain?" Sarah volleyed questions at Vic like she was shouting answers to a quiz. Vic's head spun.

"I am decidedly among the living," Vic said with a pointed look at May, who didn't even have the decency to look sheepish.

"As I said," May replied, "it was always unlikely that your injuries would kill you. I don't know why everyone got mad at me."

Sarah rolled her eyes and leaned over Vic, scanning her face. Vic suspected Sarah would have peeled back an eyelid or opened her mouth for a more thorough inspection if she thought she could get away with it.

"I feel fine," Vic assured an unconvinced Sarah. "Whatever that doctor gave me is working wonders."

"Demerol," May said with an appreciative nod.

Sarah swatted May aside with a flit of her hand. May moved to the foot of the bed and began inspecting the wooden bedpost.

"A manananggal!" Sarah cried. "Can you believe it! I can't believe it. We're never going to let you go anywhere alone now. I hope you know that. May and I are moving in. We'll take turns escorting you to the bathroom."

Vic and May shared a look of horror. Henry laughed, the bastard.

"It is remarkable that you survived," May said.

"Not this again," Henry muttered.

"I don't mean her injuries. A few stitches and a mild concussion are nothing compared to what the Sentinels deal with on a regular basis." Vic did not feel the need to point out that her injuries would have been worse, much worse, if Xan hadn't healed her. Addressing Vic, May added, "You were alone with a manananggal for, what, five minutes? Maybe more? They usually take humans down in seconds."

"Isn't their quarry usually sleeping?" Vic asked.

"That's true," May said, not detecting the sarcasm. "I would be curious to see how likely it is for a human to survive when they're conscious. Maybe everyone who's awake gets away."

"Come on, May," Sarah said. "Vic did very well."

"I'm paying her a compliment. She might be one of the only survivors out there."

"Even if they start out sleeping," Vic said, "I imagine most people wake up when the . . ." She stuck out her tongue and pointed to her throat, remembering the Orcan's barbed tongue trying to wriggle inside.

"Excellent point," May said. "Something else to consider."

Henry interrupted, "Why don't the two of you go see about getting Vic some food?" Vic smiled at the obvious ploy to get Sarah and May to leave. They must have been bothering him for hours before Vic woke up.

But at that moment a silver-domed tray materialized on the bedside table, and Henry sighed. Vic pulled the cover away to find toast, eggs, a cup of coffee. Max's doing, no doubt.

"Speaking of," Sarah said. "What did the tongue taste like? I've always been curious."

"I don't know, like something rotten," Vic said. She chewed as she tried to find a fitting description. Oddly enough, discussing her ordeal like this eased her spirits. Henry stared at Vic like she had an arm growing out of her head.

"I would imagine it tastes like spoiled meat," Sarah said, turning to May. "Like when you're fighting and you accidentally get a little bit of Orcan blood in your mouth."

May looked askance at her. "That doesn't happen to me."

"Really? It happens to me all the time."

"That's because you're not careful."

"Isn't the legend that manananggals sleep in graves during the day?" Vic asked, and the two Sentinels nodded. "It tasted like something that came out of a grave."

Henry lost his patience.

"That's it," he announced. "Get out."

Vic burst into laughter at the shocked look on Sarah's face.

"I want to talk to my sister." Henry pointed at the door.

May looked affronted at the abrupt dismissal, but Sarah took it in stride. She pulled May from the room, shouting over her shoulder that they would be back soon to move their things in. Vic heard May object as the apartment door shut behind them.

Henry faced his sister. "They're so fucking weird, Vic."

"I like them," she said, picking up another piece of toast.

As he watched her, Henry seemed to deflate. He looked exhausted. "What happened to you?"

"I went to Mom's old apartment," Vic said, and a look of realization crossed his face. She told Henry about the manananggal in Meredith's office, the attack, and Xan saving her. When she remembered what had happened afterward, Vic stopped. She set her food aside and put a hand on Henry's arm. "Have you ever heard the name Aren Mann?" she asked him.

Henry frowned. Slowly, he shook his head.

"He's the leader of another organization, that one the other recruits told you about. He calls it the Brotherhood. He and Max knew Mom when they all worked in the Order together."

"What does this have to do with us?" Henry asked, still looking confused.

"Mom, Max, Aren, they're all connected. What happened to Mom was *because* of all of this. She warned you about bad men coming to find you. She told you to run. What if she was talking about the Brotherhood? What if *they're* the ones we've been hiding from all this time?" As she said it, Vic knew it was true. She heard the conviction in her own voice and realized that Meredith must have been worried Aren would come for Henry.

"Are you sure you haven't heard about the Brotherhood?" Vic asked him, sitting up. "Nothing about Aren or another organization like that?"

Henry was shaking his head. "Maybe Mom was wrong, maybe I misremembered. I don't know, but she's been dead for a long time, Vic. We need to move on."

Vic stared at him. "I can't move on," she said quietly. She couldn't.

"Max said this guy, Aren Mann, killed her. He says she was murdered for investigating the Brotherhood, that she was—"

"Look, Vic. All you're doing is convincing me that you're not safe here."

Vic sat back, stunned. "I'm not—"

"Let me tell you what happened to *me* last night," Henry said. "Max brought you here around two in the morning. I woke up to him pounding on the door. I thought someone was breaking in. Turns out, you were unconscious, and Max had you sort of levitating beside him."

Vic found the mental image of her limp body hanging unsupported extremely unpleasant and tried to shake it off.

"I've never been so scared in my life," he said. "I thought he'd killed you. I thought you were dead."

Vic reached for his arm and squeezed it.

"I don't know what I would do if something happened to you," Henry whispered. "Probably burn the whole place down."

"I'm sorry," Vic said in a quiet voice.

"*You're* sorry?" Henry said. "*I'm* sorry! I should never have let you come here. This place is too dangerous. I don't know what I was thinking."

"It's okay."

"No, it is not okay!" Henry bolted out of his chair and paced the worn rug. "It is not okay," he repeated, softer now. "You were supposed to be safe in the castle. The Order was supposed to keep you safe. At least keep the Orcans from getting inside the fucking walls. You know, the thing they've done for centuries? But the Order can't even do that these days."

The sudden reversal of their roles unsettled Vic. She played the protector, the older sibling reacting with righteous indignation to the treatment of the younger. She was the one who got angry; she was the one who shouted. She paced back and forth while Henry sat nearby, smiling bemusedly and waiting for his high-strung sister to calm down.

He spun to face her, looking manic. Vic had never seen him like this.

"You have to go," he said. "Leave Avalon. Every day that you're here, I'm scared that something's going to happen to you. I can't let you stay."

"But I'm fine, I promise. I have it under control." But Vic knew, even as she swore, that she couldn't promise anything, that she had nothing under control.

"You're the only family I have," Henry said. "I could never live with myself if something happened to you and I knew that you were here because of me."

"But I need to be here. I just learned that Mom was murdered. I still need to—"

"I don't care if Mom was murdered," Henry said. He huffed a laugh like he'd surprised himself. "I don't care," he repeated with a shrug.

He sighed and fell back into the chair beside her. Vic watched in silent shock.

"Mom's been dead since I was ten, Vic, and even before then, she was gone all the time. I don't remember her the way you do. I don't *grieve* her the way you do. I'm not going to let you kill yourself trying to avenge someone who didn't even care enough to stick around."

Vic swallowed. "I can't leave you—"

"I know you think you can help me here, but you can't. I'm more prepared for this sort of thing than you are."

Vic wondered if that was true. They'd been in training together for weeks. She'd seen Henry break rocks, maybe even move them once or twice. But he wasn't excelling the way some of the others were. She watched him growing more frustrated with every day that he fell behind. Did he blame her for that? Vic wondered. If he thought she was distracting him, did Henry think Vic was responsible for his failure to meet his own lofty expectations?

Some of her thoughts must have shown on her face.

"Are you serious?" Henry demanded. "You *still* don't think I can take care of myself." He vaulted back to standing. "I'm a witch! I belong here. You're not. You don't. It's that simple."

"You don't get to talk to me that way."

"It's the truth, Vic. This delusion has gone on long enough. You're tough as nails and you can fight—you don't need to prove that to me. And I know that some people have tried to convince you that what happened in the catacombs matters. But the only way that the Rite matters to me is that they *could have killed you.* And I would have had to watch. Do you really not see where I'm coming from?"

Vic sank into the pillow behind her and said in a small voice, "It's been my job to take care of you my whole life. Do you expect me to walk away the second it gets harder?"

Henry fell into the chair beside her again and put his head on the bed.

"I'm sorry for being mean," he murmured into the comforter. "Last night scared me. This whole thing scares me, and I . . . don't know what I would do if anything happened to you."

Henry looked so much like a child in that moment. Doe-like eyes turned up at Vic like he was ten years old and she was the only person who could help him. God, she loved the little guy so much it hurt. That was the problem, wasn't it? Vic hadn't figured out what to do with the adult he'd grown into yet. It would hurt to leave him—it would hurt to stay.

"It's okay," she said, touching his curls. "I'm sorry, too."

For some reason, she didn't tell him about Max's request to help him take down the Brotherhood.

A shadow rose in her mind, the memory of Xan pinning her to the wall in Lethe, telling her to leave.

I know you think you can find something here, some purpose in all this madness. But you can't. You'll die trying to belong.

Realization dawned on her, the pieces clicking into place. Ice crept into her veins.

She had unfinished business with the Chief Sentinel.

XXIII

For the middling practitioner, ritual is a necessary hindrance. Only exceptional witches are able to draw power without the aid of ritual and spellwork. And a rare few among the strong are able to do so reliably, without fail, and without endangering themselves.

—William Ruskin, *A History of the Acheron Order*
(New York, 1935)

Vic knew the castle well enough to know she stood directly above the training wing. She crossed her arms over her chest, ignoring how the movement tugged at the cuts.

After an afternoon spent waiting and brooding and kicking the events of the last few days around in her mind, Vic had slipped out of the apartment and wandered until she found herself staring at the stained-glass window she'd discovered her first night there.

She'd since learned the legend it depicted, having heard it in the slow monotone of Elder Thompson's lectures on the history of the Order. A woman clutching an open jar, unleashing chaos upon the world. Pandora and her box, or the Order's malformed version of it. The Order had no tolerance for mythology, but they couldn't resist the symbolism of the tale. They believed in no god, or gods, or any righteous path whatsoever, but they believed in mistake. Human failure, above all else, had the power to shape the world. Someone slipped, at some point, somewhere, and the Order arose to pick up the pieces.

Now Vic wondered if Pandora had enjoyed what she'd done. When she cracked open the lid to humanity's sins, did it feel like freedom? Did she feel a rush of pleasure at the knowledge that she had confounded every expectation anyone dared have of her? Did she look back on her choice with pride or self-loathing?

As she studied the glass, Vic half expected to see a shadow wrench itself toward the castle, as she had the last time she stood in this spot.

Though she knew now it wasn't a shadow at all—not a monster, just a man.

"What are you doing?"

Speak of the devil, and he shall appear. Right on time.

"I was just thinking about you," Vic said without turning around. Though she didn't jump at Xan's sudden appearance, her heart raced behind her breastbone. Vic felt untethered from herself. All the strangeness of the castle had crept in around her corners—the wildness gripped her insides, twisting her into a state of transcendent fury she hardly recognized. She felt wild in a far-off way, like all her strings had been cut.

"What are you doing out this late?"

"I saw you the first time I came here." Vic pointed out the window. "Right there. Streaking through the grounds."

"Are you listening to me?" An edge cut his voice.

"Scared the shit out of me. I thought you were an Orcan." Vic huffed an angry laugh. "Until last night, I thought you were an Orcan."

"You thought there was an Orcan loose in the castle, and you . . . didn't mention that to anyone?" Xan asked, his voice low and vexed.

Vic shrugged and cast an apathetic glance over her shoulder. Xan stood with his arms crossed, scowling. "Shows how little I know, I guess."

Xan made an impatient sound and once again demanded to know what she was doing.

"I was looking for you, actually," Vic said. "I had the sneakiest suspicion you would show up here."

She turned away from the window and walked down the hallway. Heavy footfalls followed.

"Can you tell me why, after what happened to you last night, you decided to wander around the castle after dark? Alone?"

"I'm not alone," she said as she found a staircase and began to descend. "My little shadow is following me."

"Where are you going?"

"You are, aren't you?" Vic asked. "Following me, I mean. You have been for quite a while. I wonder—was your goal to keep me safe, or to keep others safe from me? Do you even know the answer to that question?"

Behind her, Xan said nothing. Even to her own ears, Vic sounded distant, flat. Rage circled her spine like a spinning coin just about to topple. Anger filled the void inside of her, the empty space where her mind usually sat.

"Surely you noticed I sleep in my underwear," Vic said. "Were you in my room on business or pleasure?"

A hanging candle on the wall nearby flicked out, and Vic ignored it. She turned toward the training hallway and into a Level Eight room the Sentinels sometimes used.

She stopped when Xan followed her into the empty classroom and the door slammed shut behind him. High, arching windows cast the room in dim moonlight, and Vic squared her shoulders as she faced him.

Xan had the oddest expression on his face. Wary, worried almost, with his fists at his sides. But he was not angry with her. Not yet.

"Talk to me," he said, taking a cautious step toward Vic. "What's going on?"

She stepped away from him.

"Hit me," she said.

He shook his head. "I don't want to hit you. I want to talk."

"Please," Vic said with a saccharine smile.

"You're upset," he said. He held his hands palms-out toward her, but he didn't try to approach her again.

"Am I?" Vic asked. "I can't tell."

"You are," Xan said, and he had a hideously understanding look on his face. Vic hated it. "I think you get angry when you're scared."

"Hit. Me."

"Vic, please calm down. You're angry, and you're hurt, and—"

"Not as badly as I should have been," she pointed out, challenge in her tone. "I've thought about it all day. Before the monster, before Max, before anything, the one thing I can't stop thinking about is you. The shadow that's been following me since I got here. The way you healed the cuts on my arms, and the bags under your eyes so heavy they look like bruises."

They were still there now, gleaming evidence of his expenditure. Xan had done serious magic to mend her.

He said nothing, but his eyes were searching, open.

"Max told me healing wounds was almost impossible," Vic said. "Even the doctor only gave me medicine. Why did you do that?"

Still nothing but those kind, piercing eyes, like she wasn't staring back at him with rage.

"We're playing the quiet game, I see," Vic said. "I was never any good at that." She rolled out the muscles in her arms. Vic wore a sweatshirt and sweatpants, which allowed for movement even if the extra fabric was a risk. "Then *I'll* hit *you*."

And she jumped.

Vic went for his face, thinking *that* would entice him to fight back, but Xan edged out of the way, and Vic stumbled to the side.

"Let's discuss this," he said. It was so condescending that he wasn't even afraid she might hurt him. And, Vic figured, he had no reason to fear her. Not when he had all the odds on his side. Size, magic, skill. She could bounce off him like a fly.

"Fight back," Vic said, swinging at him. "This is boring."

This time, he caught Vic by the wrist and pulled her against his chest to hold her still.

With her free hand, Vic reached to smooth the line between his brows with the pad of a finger. "You shouldn't frown so hard," she told him. "You'll get wrinkles."

Xan caught her other hand and held her wrists together in his fist. Vic smiled up at him before ripping out of his hold. As his balance shifted, Vic kicked him in the sternum.

He grunted and rounded on her.

Unlike the last time they fought, they had no weapons, and they were much closer to each other. The rush of proximity warmed Vic's blood. She wanted to fight, to hurt, to vent some of her frustration on the world.

Xan tried to grab her again, and Vic spun away.

She lunged for his midsection, expecting him to fall. But he was solid as a rock, and she barely darted away as his hands closed over her arms.

Vic faced him again, breathing hard.

"Use your magic," she said, and confusion flickered on his face. "I want to see it."

His voice was gentle, like he spoke to a frightened animal. "Come on, sweetheart. Let's talk about this."

She saw red. "What did you call me?"

Vic kicked at him again, and he dodged it. Xan wasn't fighting her, not really, not as well as he could. She could feel his energy mounting, but he wasn't angry enough to go for it.

She could fix that.

"Fight me," Vic growled.

She jerked to the side to unbalance him, and he took the bait. She tackled him.

They hit the ground hard, though he took the worst of it. Vic landed on a muscular chest and shoved away from him. Xan made an exasperated sound.

He still wasn't taking her seriously.

Vic reached under the back of her hoodie and grasped the rubber handle of another hunting knife she'd stolen from his load-out room. With the blade in hand, she twisted toward him, aiming the point of the dagger at Xan's throat.

His eyes flared with surprise in the instant it took Vic to send the blade home.

But right as the knife should have split his skin, Xan was gone, dissolved into darkness like ink in water, and Vic fell forward as the weight supporting her disappeared.

She would have sliced her chest as she fell—she should have—but a shadow-dipped hand grabbed her wrist from behind. Tendrils of dark pulled her fingers from the handle, and the blade flew across the room.

Vic twisted toward the form but it was gone again. She stood on shaking legs, looking for a patch of darkness she had just provoked to violence.

"There it is," she said, half laughing, crazed with rage and frustration.

The shadow materialized in front of her in the massive form Vic had chased the other night. Xan's anger was rough in the air like a shout.

She reached for him, and her fingers closed around empty air.

But then Xan was Xan again, solid and human and glowering at her.

"What the fuck were you thinking?" Darkness twitched in her periphery, and Vic watched in wonder. "Are you *trying* to get hurt?"

"I wanted to see."

Xan was shaking his head in disbelief. "You are the most insane, infuriating person I have ever met. No wonder you're so hard to keep alive." He threw his hands up. "You keep wandering around, attacking things that can kill you in a heartbeat."

"Is that what you've been doing," Vic said, "trying to keep me alive?"

"Of course, you demon," he growled. "And you're not exactly making it easy."

"'Demon,' 'sweetheart'—we're all over the map today." Vic rolled her eyes and stalked away from him. "Let's go again."

"We will absolutely not 'go again,'" he said, following her across the room.

"I won't try to stab you this time," she said. "Promise."

"No way in hell, Vic. I saved your life last night—I'm not going to kill you today."

"Oh, don't pretend to care about my well-being," Vic spat, rounding on him. "You just feel guilty."

"Guilty? I saved your life!"

"And you did such a gallant job of it, too," Vic said, her face so close to him she could feel him breathing, harder and harder as she spoke. "*After* you sent me into that apartment in the first place."

Surprise twisted his face for an instant before a serious expression took its place. Regret, maybe, or anger.

"That's how you got there so quickly, isn't it?" Vic asked. "You were in the hallway. I felt you there before I went in. You were right outside, waiting for that thing to attack me."

"Vic, I wasn't—"

"Tell me, Xan. How long did you have to wait to be sure it hurt me badly enough I'd want to leave?"

"You have it wrong, I—"

"Max told me he needed access to Meredith's apartment, and he thought I would be able to do it. You're close with Max, aren't you?"

Harsh eyes bored into Vic's as she spoke, but Xan stopped trying to argue.

"It had been weeks since Max gave me that key. I'd given up trying to get inside. Which you knew, because you've been following me since I got here. So when I went to Lethe, my little shadow came behind me. You suggested that I use the bind to open the door. I know you did it on purpose. At least Max had the decency to own up to his part in the whole thing."

A shadow fell over Xan's face, and Vic wondered if that meant he was losing control. She decided she didn't care. He'd manipulated her. He'd gone to Lethe, made her think—for a minute or two—that she had power over him, that she mattered to him. But he was playing with her, using her obvious attraction to him to get what he wanted, what his boss needed.

"You've made it clear you don't want me here. But Max won't make me leave. Quite the opposite. It must have seemed like a great opportunity. A two-for-one deal: Max gets into the apartment, and you get to scare me away."

Shadows curled around his hands like twitching fingers, eager to lash out at something, and Vic half hoped he would. If Xan snapped at her right now, she would snap back. He could overpower her, but she'd take her pound of flesh on the way down.

"That's why you healed me, isn't it? You went too far; I got hurt worse than you expected, and you felt bad."

Vic wanted to laugh. She wanted to scream.

"Do you have any idea whose magic opened that door?" she asked, her voice falling to a dangerous whisper. "Whose bind I have on my arm?"

Vic thought she saw his eyebrows pinch forward in confusion.

"You thought it was Max," she said. "Even though I told you it wasn't. But why would you believe me? Little old me? Surely I was lying. I'd say just about anything, and you'd believe none of it."

She ran a hand through her hair, growling when it caught a tangle in her curls.

"It was Aren *fucking* Mann," she snarled at Xan. And *there* was the root of her fury. At him? At herself? She didn't know. She didn't care. Inside her sat a ball of fire, twisting and breaking and demanding that she do *something*, anything.

A rough hand closed around her wrist and wrenched her forward.

"What did you say?" he whispered.

The air around her went cold, like Xan was really losing control now. Vic ripped her arm out of his grip and strode away.

"This fucking place," she said. "You fucking people. You think you can control me because I'm weak. Because I came here without the power that you have, or the knowledge, I must be pliable. Here's poor, powerless Vic, ready to be used. I can be pulled in every direction. I can be dragged out of bed in the middle of the night. I can be cowed, frightened, hurt, manipulated. Whatever the almighty Order wants, heap it on top of me. I'll deal with it."

She threw her hands up. There was rot at the center of this castle. Strength and weakness, in a narrow sense, were all that mattered. And the weak? Well, the strong could do with them as they pleased.

Not Vic, though. Magic or no, she was done being used.

"I'm not sure it's wise to trust Max with your life." Xan's voice was quiet, but she heard the fury in it, the warning.

Vic stopped. Xan could not be suggesting what she thought he was. Max was the progressive Elder, the one who carved the path forward. Xan's closest ally.

"You don't trust Max?" Vic asked, cautious.

"I understand Max," Xan corrected her. "We've worked together for a decade. I know how he operates. I would trust him with my life—I would not trust him with yours."

Xan approached Vic as he spoke, his voice low and urgent.

"Max is so powerful, sometimes he forgets he has limits. He might say he can guarantee your safety here, but he can't."

"And you know better than Max does?"

Xan was right next to her now, and Vic looked up at him. She saw the dark lines under his eyes, the mark of many sleepless nights and the lengths he'd gone to to save her. He watched her face for a long moment before responding.

"I know my limits," he said.

Ice-blue eyes bored into hers. Vic was acutely aware of him as he loomed over her, overwhelming as always, blocking out the moonlight. It would be easy to get lost in a man like this, to get dragged under by the anger and fear and power until all she knew was those eyes watching her.

The words he'd whispered at Lethe haunted her.

I know you like it when I touch you.

And she had. She probably still would, and she hated herself for it.

Xan leaned down until they were eye to eye, and Vic hated him even more.

"Come with me," he said softly. "I want a chance to explain myself."

She should run, Vic thought. She'd told him about the bind, she'd screamed in his face, even tried to stab him. She should run and hide and not follow him down darkened corridors. But she wanted Xan to have a reason for all of this. She wanted her anger to be misplaced, she wanted him to have meant some of what she'd sensed the other night.

Vic nodded.

Her heart battered in her chest as she followed him down a hallway off the back of the classroom. They entered a large, unfamiliar room full of couches and tables and lined with wood-paneled shelves, and Xan led her through a door into a small office tucked in the corner.

On one side of the room sat a faded leather couch across from a heavy wooden desk. One wall was occupied by a large black screen, and Vic stumbled at the sight. She'd become so accustomed to the analog ways of the castle that she'd almost forgotten about the everpresence of technology in the real world. Xan moved behind the desk, and Vic crossed her arms over her chest as he bent to open one of the drawers and withdrew a framed photograph. Vic turned in surprise when the lamp behind her flicked on without him touching it.

When she looked back, Xan stood in front of her with a focused expression, his hand reaching to offer her the photo. She took it slowly.

It was an old picture. Two teenage boys posing for the camera with their backs together, laughing.

"Who is this?"

"Sit down." Xan gestured to the couch behind her.

Vic sat on his desk instead, and he chuckled under his breath.

One of the boys was clearly a young Xan, short-haired and beardless. He must have been Henry's age, maybe younger. On his chin he had a little dimple, a line down the center that Vic supposed was still there now. Vic had the urge to run her finger over his jaw to find it.

She didn't recognize the boy beside him, though they looked alike. The other boy was a little taller and had curly hair around his ears. But he had the same blue eyes and a matching dimple in his chin.

"My older brother." Xan leaned against the desk beside Vic. His hip bumped and settled against hers, but Vic didn't scoot away from the contact. "Dimitri. Another pompous Greek name," he added with a knowing raise of his eyebrows. He squinted at the photo. "Here we were sixteen and eighteen, I think."

"You look alike," Vic said, handing the frame back to him.

"Dimitri was born without magic," Xan said. "The first Galanis in five generations without power."

Vic looked at the image with renewed interest. Dimitri looked young and fit, happy and at ease beside his magical brother.

"He was older," Xan said, "but I was always the favorite. I was the one who would carry on my parents' legacy with the Order, and that was all that mattered. You'd think he would have resented me, but Dimitri was always protective of me. He thought I needed all the help he could give me."

The situation sounded familiar to Vic, and she felt a knot in her throat. "Are you saying I remind you of him?"

"Not really," Xan said, looking at her with a crooked smile. "He was nice to me."

Was, Vic noted. The smile fell from his face.

"But with Henry, yeah, the resemblance is hard for me to shake. Maybe I'm seeing what I want to see, I don't know, but you look at Henry the way he looked at me."

Again Vic noted the past tense. Xan looked tired, and all her anger had left Vic behind. She felt raw and sad and she had an awful sense she knew what Xan was about to say.

"He was killed by an Orcan the summer I turned seventeen. About six months after we took this photo."

"I'm sorry," Vic whispered.

"It's been a long time," Xan said, his eyes on his brother, forever frozen at eighteen. "This year makes seventeen that he's been gone. I've lived with his absence for as long as I lived with him."

Vic watched his face, so carefully composed and contemplative. Even now, Xan was the picture of control.

"Dimitri was about to go to college, and I think he was nervous about leaving me alone with my parents. We fought a lot. I didn't always behave the way the golden child ought to. It was big news that summer that there were a handful of disappearances in a nearby town. It was all anybody could talk about, and I overheard my dad on the phone one day with another Order member. Orcans, he said. Something in the woods. But they couldn't get the Sentinels out for a few weeks—they didn't have the manpower."

A humorless smile tilted his mouth.

"I was seventeen and thought I was invincible, so, of course, I tried to find it. I was a witch, after all, and if the Order wasn't going to help, then I would do it for them. I'd be lying if I said I didn't want to be a hero, that some part of me wasn't in it for the glory." Xan shook his head. "He followed me into the woods. I didn't notice until it was too late. The Orcan was a leshy, a forest demon. The first Orcan I ever saw in person. Dimitri never had a chance."

"Did you kill it?" Vic breathed.

"Not fast enough."

Her eyes stung. "It wasn't your fault."

"I know that," he said, looking at her. "But I know better now than to think I can control who lives and who dies."

Xan set the photo on his desk and trained his eyes on Vic's face. His stare was so intense, and he was so close to her.

"I am not, by nature, a protective man," he said. "People think I am. They think that I'm here, doing this job, because I want to keep people safe. But it's rare I get the chance to save anyone. What I do is clean up afterward."

Vic hated that image. She hated the idea of himself Xan put forward, like he did nothing more than show up late and throw away the trash.

"When you came here, it caught me unexpectedly. I felt protective." He looked surprised even now, and he shook his head. "That's why I followed you around, although for a while I told myself I was keeping an eye on you. I wanted to save you from this place. I wanted to get you out of here."

Vic swallowed, a tight, painful emotion in her chest. "I don't need saving."

But he *had* saved her, at least once. She'd be dead if not for him.

"I knew you would say that," Xan said, almost smiling. "As it happens, you're wrong."

He punctuated his words with a tap on the top of her knee with his index finger. The motion sent a ripple of energy up her thigh.

"Ever since the night you got here, I've begged Max to send you home," Xan said. "I hate this plan he has for you. It's risky, it's not going to end well. Even if it works, it's not going to end well."

" 'When has changing everything ever led to a peaceful outcome?' " Vic said, repeating his words from weeks ago. He'd been telling her that since the beginning, hadn't he?

"Max is so set on this path. Maybe he thinks the risk to you is worth it; maybe he doesn't even see the risk. But I do, and I refuse to accept it."

Xan rubbed a hand over his jaw, looking older than he was.

"Yes, I did whatever I could to get you into that apartment. I thought if Max got *that*, at least, he might give up on keeping you here. And I thought maybe that was what you needed. If you had a glimpse of your mom's world, it would help you let go."

He stood, almost vibrating with nervous energy, and faced the black screen. Vic watched the hard set of his shoulders as her head spun.

"I never would have done it if I'd known Mann was behind the bind," he said, sounding almost choked with anger. He met her eyes again, with the desperate, wild look she'd seen there earlier. "And I had no idea there was an Orcan inside. None. I was waiting outside, yes, but just in case something went wrong—I had no idea what."

Xan looked at his hands, folded in front of his waist, and when he spoke his voice was tight and restrained. "When I heard you scream . . . all I could think about was being seventeen and losing the one person who really mattered because I thought I could control what no one can control."

He stood in front of her, and Vic stared up into eyes like storm clouds. His gaze was like a weight pressing against her mind, making it hazy and hard to think.

The one person who really mattered.

Vic shook her head, heart in her throat. "I'm not that person for you," she whispered. "I'm an outsider, a liability. I don't belong here. That's what you said."

He brushed her hair aside and cupped the side of her face. Vic leaned into the touch. The searching look was back in his eyes, like he wanted something badly.

Wanted *her.*

"You're exceptionally strong," he said. "You're vibrant, even here, where there has never been any life."

His other hand went to the opposite side of her face.

"I know this, Vic: You *deserve* to survive this place."

"What do you want from me?" Vic whispered.

"I never want to see you again," he said, and it sounded like a caress.

Sitting on his desk as she was, they were the same height for what might have been the first time, and Vic's whole world narrowed to the face in front of her. The palms on her cheeks were hot and rough, the only warmth in a cold room in a cold castle, and when Xan breathed his exhalations danced across her face. The force of the look in his eyes, the intensity of Xan's confession and request, overwhelmed her—a tidal wave dragging Vic under. She couldn't focus with him looking at her like that, couldn't think of anything except jumping out of her skin. She wanted to run from the room like a frightened animal. She wanted to hide, burrow inside him and stay there forever.

Vic started it.

Before she knew what she was doing, she had a hand behind his head, her fingers weaving into his hair, pulling him toward her. Xan went willingly, as if commanded, closing the distance between them.

There was no moment of timidity, no coaxing before they opened for each other. There was nothing sweet or soft about the two of them. They met in a tangle of tongues and teeth, two starving lovers meeting for a final meal.

Xan slipped a hand behind her waist, encircling her, and Vic pulled him closer until their chests were pressed together. She wanted to seal herself to him, to suffocate any distance that dared separate them. Her nipples were hard, and she knew he noticed that when Xan grunted a pleased kind of sound, and his other hand wrapped around her hips to squeeze her ass.

Vic ran her fingers along the hair on the back of his neck, marveling at the silken smoothness of the strands as his head drifted down. His mouth left a chill trail on the side of her face. His lips closed against the side of her neck, and Vic sighed.

With his hair between her fingers, Vic made a fist. She forced his head back and smiled at the open-mouthed surprise on his face. His lips were shining, red, and his eyes clung to hers in a daze. Vic pulled his lips back to hers, and Xan hummed a happy moan against her mouth.

When had his smell become so familiar to her? Sweat-slicked skin and dirt and something distinctly Xan that she would recognize anywhere. She thought of fighting as she pressed herself against him, and she wasn't sitting on his desk anymore. Xan held her up with one arm behind her back and the other under her, and Vic was vaguely aware that she was moving against him in an instinctive rhythm they both knew. But she had no space to be embarrassed at her eagerness—not when Xan mirrored it, not when it was all she could think of. All she was at that moment.

"Yes," she said against his mouth without thinking. "Yes."

Her mind was overrun with a single-word chant: more, more, more. She needed *more*. She needed everything.

The force of that feeling overpowered her, turning her inside out. Only dimly did she realize, in the far back corner of her mind, that this had never happened before. None of her late-night liaisons had felt like this. Never before had she come undone so quickly. Not once, before tonight, had Vic thought that to stop what she was doing would be to die.

The realization hit her with a slap.

"Stop," she said.

Xan froze. Slowly, he set her on her feet and pulled his hands away from her body.

Vic avoided his eyes as she tugged her clothes back where they ought to be. She breathed hard, trying to collect herself. She wanted him with a ferocity so intense, so foreign, it was almost need. Maybe it was. She couldn't handle it—she couldn't hold it inside. It was like staring at a flame while every cell in her body screamed for her to reach out and grab it.

When she looked up at Xan, gray-blue eyes, half out of focus, watched her with a mixture of hunger and apprehension that she understood all too well. Did he feel the same kind of desperate need that she did? Did it scare him the way it scared her?

"Did you mean it?" Vic said. "Do you want me to leave?"

Very slowly, he nodded. And Vic understood.

For the first time in Vic's life, someone had put her first. Someone had prioritized her well-being, her safety, at the price of anything else. Xan would disappoint his friend, would thwart Max's plans for the Order, would deny himself what he clearly wanted—to keep Vic safe. And that, before anything else, Vic understood.

She backed away from him, breathing hard. She stopped at the doorway, reaching for the frame to steady herself. Her knees were shaking.

"I will," Vic said.

Xan looked so alone, standing in his office, his shoulders hunched forward, surrounded by an empty room. But his voice was resolute when he replied. "And don't look back."

Vic nodded, and she fled.

Part III

THE CAGES

XXIV

While the Sentinels are based at Avalon Castle, where they train and prepare, their work often takes them elsewhere. However, the hyperconcentration of magical usage in the area around the castle does generate greater frequency of Orcan activity in the surrounding environs.

—William Ruskin, *A History of the Acheron Order*
(New York, 1935)

In a town off the coast of Lake Champlain, night came early. The town was dying anyway, and small. A bit too small, if Aren was being honest. He would have preferred to make his debut somewhere grander. Somewhere more memorable.

He stood on the corner of the closest thing the hamlet had to a town square. A few blocks of too-long grass hemmed in by a post office, a chapel, and a handful of homes clad in crumbling shiplap. Here was a part of the world left behind by industry, without an economy to stand on and too few tourists.

Though he'd fallen out of familiarity with it, Aren was accustomed to the unrefined underbelly of the world. Unlike his friends in the Order, Aren had not come from one of the old lines. He had not inherited property or wealth, much less had he spurned them. His parents had known they had a family history of magical resonance, but they did not celebrate it. Magic passed through his bloodline like a cancer. It appeared at random in a few unlucky souls, and it was never welcome.

Some recent ancestors had fallen in one of the great conflicts, and their deaths had frightened the family off the concept of magic in its entirety. Or so said Aren's mother. Round about the 1820s, the Mann family fled to the United States to escape a revival of religious fervor in the homeland. But in the New World they met oppression at the hands of magical practitioners much crueler than European zealots. Rebuked by the preternatural, the Manns turned to God. The men in his family became preachers, of all things. They stood before crowds and decried witchcraft, Satan, and all of his counterfeits. But Aren saw the tendrils of the occult in their liturgy once he knew to look for them. For all they reviled their past, the Manns never quite learned to forsake it.

When Aren was born with the ability to wield light, his parents did their best to exorcise it from him. When that failed, the family resolved to ignore the boy's abilities. Anxiety remained that he would stumble upon a way to use his talents, so his parents impressed upon Aren the utmost importance of never giving in to the baser urges. He grew up in an unspoken panic that one day his control would snap and he would fall prey to the evils his parents predicted. He said his prayers every night. He went to college—a small one, pious, and unknown to the likes of the Order—and listened to his family when they said that to exercise his abilities was to risk eternal damnation.

But one night his steps on the righteous path faltered. After a bit too much to drink and too many months away from his parents' influence, he found himself kneeling on the cement floor of his dorm's basement with a paring knife in his hand.

He turned the night to day and waited for his retribution to arrive.

It never did. No lightning crashed down from the heavens to smite him. No pox fell on his house. No, nothing happened at all except that Aren felt an overwhelming sense of purpose for the first time in his life.

He packed his bags that night and left for Avalon Castle the next morning.

Everything that happened from that point—with Meredith, with Max, with the Order and the Brotherhood and the countless smarmy shits lining the halls of that hateful castle—happened as a result of that overwhelming sense of purpose. Aren had chased that feeling ever since. He had chased it to Avalon, to Max and Meredith, to the voice that called from the dark.

He still chased it. It woke him in the middle of the night and kept him crawling back to the world that had scorned him. It would be his again, he knew. He needed only to fight for it.

Some of the past could never be reconstructed. Aren would never again sit under cover of an elm tree with Max and Meredith, envisioning a better world they would create together. Lightning never struck the same spot twice. But remnants of the past lingered, and would continue to linger, until Aren claimed them.

And so he stood, back straight and strong, on the corner of a too-small street in a too-small town, tearing a knife through his palm and tossing blood to the ground.

It used to require more effort from Aren to block out the sun.

The trick was simple enough, and he'd been doing it for decades. He hardly felt the skin stitch itself shut over the wound. He spilled no blood on his suit.

Two children, playing alone in a snowy yard beside him, began to wail when the sun was snuffed out.

Lights flicked on in the homes nearby.

Humans stepped onto their porches and peered at the darkened sky, calling for others to come look. The midday sun still perched overhead, but none of its rays reached the villagers. The ether seeped the sun's light from the air before it hit their eyes, and they stood in front of rotting homes staring up at the mystery.

On a cloudless afternoon, the scene must have looked distinctly alarming to someone who had never seen it before.

Aren remembered his first time. He hadn't trusted his own eyes then, so strange was it to see the source of light but no light itself. All these years later, Aren could recall with perfect clarity the horror he felt when first he looked upon the blackened star.

It was darker than night. There were no stars, no moon to reflect the sun's rays. Darkness fell, heavy and suffocating.

Aren watched the townsfolk discover this as they bumbled about. Steadying hands held railings and shoulders in search of stability. Flashlights followed, then headlights, high beams, exterior lighting, anything to let them see. None of it worked, of course. That was the brilliance of Aren's spell, after all. They pointed phones at the sky to capture something they couldn't explain.

Aren wondered why so few of them looked scared.

Neighbors gathered at the ends of driveways, communing in confusion. Children clung to their ankles, more frightened than their parents but unwilling to miss the excitement. Over their heads, adults tossed questions at one another. Some of them knew exactly what was going on, and they were eager to explain. It was a new kind of fog, you see. Something had floated in from the lake and settled over the area. Everyone knew the factory upwind dumped all sorts of shit they weren't supposed to in the water. Pollution, that was responsible. But not from the lake, no, some kind of chemical spill. A weather event, actually, was more likely. The planet was changing. Freak weather happened all the time.

They were curious, unsettled, but not truly frightened. Not yet.

A portly man in a dirty gray uniform approached Aren's place on the corner. The man stood unsteadily on his feet as he squinted. No doubt the man saw little more than the outline of Aren's body as he peered into the darkness.

"You lost?" the man called from a few feet away.

"Just passing through."

The man nodded, still intent on observing the demands of polite society even when he could barely see his hand in front of his face.

"You're a ways off track if you're headed to the lake. You wanna get back on the main road and—"

"I'm headed west, actually."

"Something wrong with your car?" The man scanned the dark road for a vehicle that was not there.

"No."

He'd stopped in front of an auto shop, Aren realized. Tires littered the icy lawn. Equipment long since eaten by rust lay alongside them, and a dingy sign advertising the business hung at eye level. He'd assumed it was abandoned, but its sole employee had disabused him of that notion when he came out to investigate the strange man on the corner.

"You ever seen anything like this?" The man gestured at the sky. The cursive name on his uniform was *Jack*.

"Never like this," Aren replied.

"Me neither, man," Jack told the darkness. "More and more of the time, it feels like the world is ending. Crazy shit keeps on happening."

"It certainly seems that way sometimes."

"Aw, well, I gotta head home and check on the family. You get where you're going safe, now."

Aren watched him stumble toward a beat-up truck in the next drive over. Rust bubbled up from the wheel wells like mold, and the man fumbled for the door handle and clambered in. The truck spewed a cloud of smoke as it roared onto the road in front of Aren. It did little to advertise the man's professional prowess that he drove such a husk around town. If he had lived in this helpless place, Aren would have trusted a different mechanic.

He walked the opposite way down the narrow lane. A few cars passed as the residents of the town sped home.

On the corner across from the post office, some of his Brothers had already gathered at the town burying ground. This would be their first foray into the world Aren had built for them, and they looked nervous. Aren felt only the cool kind of calm he felt before every crisis—though there would be no crisis today. This day was an opportunity, pure and simple, ready to be seized.

The Brothers' muted conversations fell silent when Aren approached, and they drew back to watch him as best they could in the nonexistent light. But they didn't need to see him to play their parts. They had practiced this.

Aren nodded, and they hurried into a circle on one of the walking paths among the graves. Macabre it may have been, but a cemetery was the most efficient place for what they were about to do. Even humans understood that places held memories, and some magic was best aided by the memories of the dead. Especially the old dead.

That was why Aren had chosen this place, after all. This town, with its too few inhabitants and too little connection to the outside world, had one of the oldest cemeteries in the nation. Not only was it old, it was more fruitfully populated than average, owing to an outbreak of influenza that had ravaged this village unusually hard at the turn of the last century, back when it had been an emergent industrial hub. Lots of dead lay here, far more than one would expect.

No one needed to speak. This day had been months in the making, years. The time for discussion had passed—all that remained was the doing.

One of the older Brothers began to carve symbols into the cold ground. It must have been difficult, Aren noted, to slice the icy dirt with such precision. But the Brother gave no sign of struggle. He had prepared for his part well.

The symbols were beautiful, in their own way. Aren had designed them himself. Trial and error over many years led him to the perfect combination of forms and figures.

Aren had performed this ritual so many times—in so many places and iterations over the years—that it came as easily to him as breathing. Only the magnitude was foreign, and he felt his heart race as they began their ministrations.

Nothing happened at first. The dead rarely conformed to one's schedule. Something of this scale would take time. Despite his years of waiting, Aren marveled at his own impatience. His eagerness did not show on his face, but he heard the blood crush through his thoughts.

Aren left the other men in the graveyard and walked away with measured steps. A row of black SUVs lined the walkway into the cemetery. One of the rear doors of the frontmost car swung open as Aren approached, and he took his time getting in, casting a final glance toward the dark sun hanging high above him.

The car turned onto the icy road and peeled away from the cemetery gates. Trees sped by the windows in the darkness, but Aren paid no attention. It was on to the next. The die had been cast.

They had hit the highway by the time the screaming started.

XXV

It has long been theorized that Made witches pull their magic directly from the Veil, making the magic itself fundamentally distinct from that of Born witches. Made witches, unlike their more distinguished counterparts, need not rely on spellwork or ritual to connect them to the natural world. Their abilities are more innate, driven by a poorly understood connection to death more than by anything rooted in the world around them.

—Terrance Vern, *Theories on Transmogrification*
(New York, 1999)

"Today will be the last day most of you spend in this classroom."

Vic didn't lift her eyes from the notebook in front of her when Nathaniel spoke. He'd taken over classes today, as—he said—he was most equipped to prepare them for what was to come. Vic was surprised the Order let him teach again, after the incident in Limbo. Then again, Nathaniel was an Elder, and likely did as he pleased.

Most of the recruits were advancing to Level Two, having demonstrated adequate ability to manipulate objects. Most of the recruits, in this context, meant everyone but Vic. She hadn't done a damn thing.

Whatever ability she'd demonstrated when she opened Meredith's door, whether borrowed or her own, had not reappeared in her lesson this morning.

"For your final task as Level One initiates, you will destroy the item in front of you," Nathaniel was saying, in a voice as snotty and boring as a textbook. "These are more complex than the stones most of you have already mastered. Dissolution of an intricate structure will enable you to advance."

Vic was only half listening. In a spiral notebook she scribbled everything she could remember about her time at Avalon. She'd taken diligent notes since her first day of training, but she wanted to fill in the gaps. She'd take nothing but her memories when she left the castle for good, and Vic didn't want to forget anything.

She did not attempt to transcribe her conversation with Xan the night before, which she could barely stand to replay in her mind. The memory sat like an exposed wire in the back of her brain, begging her to touch it, begging her to get burned. He'd tasted like sweat, and she'd liked it. His brother had been killed by a leshy. He'd asked Vic to leave, and she'd agreed. She'd woken up with a tightness in her chest—her own Pandora's box of crushing feelings, which she tried, in vain, to force back inside.

"You may begin."

On Vic's table, a block of knotty petrified wood shattered in front of Sarah. Vic covered her face with her palm without looking up, and splinters bounced off her knuckles. Sarah sighed.

"Are you giving up, is that what's happening?" Sarah asked.

"I'm not giving up."

"You're not even trying," Sarah pointed out, picking up the ancient hunk of twisted volcanic rock in front of Vic and setting it on top of her notebook. "You're doodling."

Vic moved the jagged stone aside and eyed a crudely drawn manananggal. "I thought it looked pretty good."

"Come on, Vic. What's going on with you today?"

The classroom was noisy, full of students fumbling through spells aimed at breaking things. Bangs and crashes rattled in Vic's ears and made her head hurt.

"Are you worried about your safety? Because May and I can—"

"I'm not scared," Vic said. "I'm just thinking."

"You can talk to me, you know," Sarah said.

"Ms. Wood" came an obnoxious voice behind her, and Vic rolled her eyes as Nathaniel approached their table. He looked between the mottled form Vic was supposed to destroy and her drawing. "Still failing, I see."

"Yep." Vic smiled up at him.

"Elder Shepherd will be so disappointed. It seems he was wrong about you after all." Nathaniel leaned in until he rested a hand on the table in front of Vic, his body hovering over her.

"Looks that way," Vic said.

Sarah threw her a worried look, but Vic ignored it.

"Have your plans to stay in the castle changed at all?" Nathaniel's voice dropped low, as if to avoid the recruits overhearing. Like they were discussing something private, soft and amicable, and not like he had tried, only days ago, to have her murdered.

"Does that bother you?" Vic asked. "That they're *my* plans. That I leave your castle when *I* decide, and you can't do a damn thing to make me?"

Anger twitched in his muddy eyes. "You have no claim to the secrets of this place," he hissed.

Vic knew she shouldn't provoke him, not when she believed he was the tie between Aren Mann's Brotherhood and the Order. She shouldn't lean into the skid when he was so close to her and she was so overpowered here. But she couldn't stand the look in his eyes, and she refused to sit quietly while he insulted her.

"The mission of the Order has been to keep the realities of the world away from humans for centuries. Centuries, Ms. Wood. Do you have any idea how long that is? My family has been a part of that mission since the Order's founding, and we have never, not once, allowed a human to enter our world the way you have."

"Some would call that progress," Vic replied, though she wasn't sure she believed it.

Dimly, she registered that the sounds of the classroom had quieted. The other recruits were listening.

"I've tried to puzzle it out," he said. "But I can't find rhyme or reason for why Elder Shepherd has taken a liking to your particular strain of human mediocrity."

Nathaniel assessed Vic down the length of his nose, his eyes lingering on her chest.

"I can't even imagine the allure he sees in you."

Something awful lay beneath that stare. A virus meant to make her feel small. Nathaniel saw Vic as less than, worth only a small number of uses, and he assumed others saw her the same way.

"It sounds like your problem lies with other members of the Order," Vic said. "You should take it up with them and leave me out of it."

"How dare you—"

Vic looked away from him and focused on the shape in front of her. Cold and hard now, though once the stone had been molten and wild. Once, a long time ago, it ran red and hot and ruined everything it touched. Vic could see the form of it now, layered and twisted, black and brittle where heat and gas had warped the shape of it. She wondered if it missed running fast and dangerous.

Sarah jumped back from the table with a shout when the stone began to melt.

Not exploding, or shattering, or making any noisy display of power, the edges of the thing began to dissolve. It shone red and Vic blinked against the heat as the rock transformed back into the magma it used to be and melted through the table.

It made a searing sound as it hit the stone floor, and then that, too, began to melt.

Vic looked up at Nathaniel, who'd backed away from her.

"Does that count?" she asked.

Sarah grabbed Vic's arm and pulled her away from the growing hole in the floor. Nathaniel stalked away from Vic without a word. The class erupted into chaos around them.

"How did you do that?" Sarah said.

Vic shrugged, staring at the burned black hole under the table. All she'd done was look at the stone. She was angry with Nathaniel, and she was staring at the stone, and was that all it took? Was she imagining it, or was the skin on her wrist beginning to burn?

Sarah tugged Vic into the hallway, and Vic caught the frightened eyes of several other students as they passed.

"We have a couple of hours until Sentinel training. We should talk to Max, see what's going on."

"I'm not going to Sentinel training," Vic said.

"What?"

Vic hadn't told Sarah about her exchange with Xan, and she wasn't going to. She couldn't begin to explain the way it had pulled her apart, left her open and raw. The feeling was new and frightening, and Vic imagined once again trying to shove a jar shut after its contents had fled.

"I have to go," Vic said, pulling away. She marched down the hallway, leaving Sarah alone, staring after her.

A sprinkling of snowflakes landed on her eyelashes and she blinked. Vic sat on a carved marble bench beside a spanning elm. All its leaves had fallen, its branches crawling toward the ground like they sought comfort from the cold.

Vic tucked her hands under her knees and eyed the castle's desolate courtyard. Frosted windows stared down at her on all sides, and gossamer sunlight filtered through the clouds. Vic's footprints were the only mark upon the snow.

She'd come outside in search of solace, pulling on her borrowed coat and gloves before throwing open the castle doors and wandering out. She'd expected to find clarity outside, if the castle's influence would wane enough to let her think.

But she'd sat on that bench, playing and replaying the questions in her mind, and she hadn't found any fucking peace.

Though she hated to admit it, Vic wanted to belong here. She wanted to sit down to a meal with Sarah and May and not feel hostile glances bouncing off her back. She wanted Xan to look at her with something more than fear for her safety, and she wanted to be the kind of woman who could see her desires through without fear wrapping around her ankles, dragging her down. Vic wanted to be powerful, the way the others were. She wanted to feel at home, like she had finally arrived where she was always supposed to be.

But every time whatever power she might have reared its head, Vic flinched from it. It wasn't hers, and she had long since lost control.

She hadn't found closure in the castle. She hadn't done anything but open doors she couldn't walk through, find new questions she couldn't answer.

"It's freezing out here."

Vic turned to see Max descending the steps into the courtyard, in a gray suit with a darker overcoat and his hands buried in his pockets. Snow fell on his hair. Though the dappling of white aged him, it made him look whimsical, less austere.

"How's the arm?" he asked.

Vic stretched her left arm in front of her and twisted it side to side. Did Max know what Xan had done for her? Did anyone?

"Nothing to complain about," she said.

Max swept ice from the seat beside her and sat.

"I can't imagine my mother here," Vic said, watching the leafless branches of the elm tree shudder in the wind.

"I can't imagine her anywhere else," Max said. "We sat under that tree for an afternoon one spring. Meredith kept catching people watching us, which made her all kinds of angry."

"Why?"

"It was 1993, and we were the first class of recruits to include Mades. Myself and three others came that year, though I was the only one who made it to initiation." He shook his head at the memory. "It was a period of adjustment for everyone."

"They were unkind to you," Vic guessed. She knew her own treatment in the Order likely paled in comparison to that of the first

Mades, especially when *she* had the express support of an Elder. She doubted Max had had the benefit of someone like himself.

He frowned, like the memories were distant and unpleasant, but his answer was diplomatic. "Change can be difficult."

"I can't imagine my mom took kindly to feeling slighted," Vic said, smiling. "She used to get so fired up whenever she thought someone was disrespecting her."

"Exactly," Max said. "She caught one too many glares and accidentally gave an Elder the finger." He pointed to an arched window three stories up. "The three of us were called in to be disciplined."

Aren Mann was with them, then. Vic tried to imagine him alongside her mother and Max in the courtyard surrounded by melting snow, and she couldn't do it.

"How did the three of you meet?" Vic asked.

Max sighed. "We were in the same class, but Mann and I were always . . . unusual."

"Powerful?"

"Outcasts," he said. "Aren came from the South, from a poor family with no influence, and he had this awful accent." Max laughed under his breath. "Like a hillbilly wandered into the castle by mistake."

That sounded nothing like the refined man who ripped Vic from her dreams. Who killed innocent people to advance a bloody cause.

"But everyone loved Meredith," Max said, his face lost to the memory. "She was old money, old manners, with a wild side. The magic, like everything else, came naturally to her. I never understood it."

"She never talked about her life before me and Henry," Vic said. All she'd known before she showed up here was that Meredith was an only child, that her parents were dead, and that she didn't like to talk about the past. "But I always wondered if she grew up rich, especially as I got older. It was something in the way she carried herself. . . ."

"Like royalty?" Max asked.

Vic nodded. "Like she would do what she pleased, and everyone else would fall in line. And we did."

"I loved that about her," Max said. "We became friends because she decided that we would be. I don't think it ever occurred to either me or Aren to question it. Meredith's word was law."

Max shook his head in wonder and seemed to pull himself back to the present.

"Back then the Order was stronger than it is now, but it was brittle. We didn't see the cracks in the foundation until they broke open, and Aren fled, and everything went to shit."

He smiled, almost embarrassed.

Vic wanted to ask how. How did everything come apart in the end? How could he have been friends with someone like Aren and not noticed the rot at his core? How could any of this happen to the three smiling people in that photograph? *How how how, Max?* she wanted to demand. She wanted to scream.

"Why are you still here?" Vic asked. "Your friends are gone and everyone treats you like some kind of freak."

Max laughed. "It would be a tremendous waste to have experienced everything I have and not use it to improve the lives of those who come after me."

"And you believe the Order is capable of improving," Vic said. He would force it to, if it came to that. That was what he was doing with Vic, wasn't it? Proving the Order wrong, showing them a better way.

"Walking away is easy. Washing your hands of the whole sordid business and finding peace somewhere else, that's easy. Like it or not, the Order has power, and power is the only thing you need to make things better."

He bumped his shoulder against Vic's.

"Congratulations, by the way," he said. "I heard about what happened this morning. Welcome to Level Two."

"I didn't do it right," Vic said.

"But you did it. You're doing fantastically, just as I knew you would."

Half a day had passed since she'd told Xan who was behind the bind on her wrist—if he'd wanted to go complaining to Max about the security risk waltzing about the castle, he could have. The fact that Xan kept quiet only underscored for Vic the significance of her promise last night. Xan was scared for her, and he was willing to keep secrets from Max to keep her safe. She owed it to Xan to keep her word.

Here was Vic's chance to tell Max for herself that he was wrong. She could show him the mark on her wrist, the evidence of her failure to belong. The imprint of magic she could neither see nor understand. Vic had let the enemy behind the gates, and Max deserved to know. He deserved to hear from her that she was not the success he imagined.

But Vic couldn't bring herself to disappoint him. She couldn't break the illusion that she somehow deserved to be here.

"Why did Meredith leave the castle?" she asked, hiding her eyes. "If this was everything to her, why did I grow up a thousand miles away?"

"Isn't it obvious? She did it for you. Meredith worried you wouldn't be safe nearby."

Vic thought of Xan's brother, who'd been unlucky enough to live in the Order's orbit, and wondered if he would have survived if he hadn't been sucked into this.

"You were born in the castle," Max said, and her eyes snapped up. "You lived here for a few months before Meredith took you away."

"I didn't know that," Vic whispered.

"Meredith cared about the Order more than anything. Until you came along."

Vic shook her head. "But she came back. She set me aside and came back."

Max's palm landed on Vic's shoulder, and she faced him with tears in her eyes.

"Now she's dead, and Henry's here, and I'm alone. And all of this because she couldn't leave the castle behind. She couldn't pick me over Avalon."

"I don't understand much about Meredith, but I know that she loved you," Max said. "I know it like I know my own name. She loved you."

"Not enough," Vic said, and she was crying. "She didn't love me enough to stay."

Max pulled Vic forward and wrapped his arms around her. Vic went eagerly, crushing her cheek against his wool-covered chest and letting him hold her as she sobbed. Her throat burned and her chest heaved, and she felt two decades of confusion and grief fall out of her. They stayed that way for a long moment, silent but for the wind and Vic's sobs, which eased at the relief of releasing her most deeply held secret.

Vic sat back up, wiping the tears from her face. "I wish you were right, Max," she said. "More than anything, I wish I could learn how to do this. If she left me for this place, this power, maybe if I could learn how to use magic, I could . . . become someone she would have come back for."

"Of course you do," Max said. "How could you not?"

"I thought I could find something here. Some connection to my mom, maybe. Or a sense of belonging I've been missing since she left."

Max squeezed her shoulder.

"But it's not working," Vic said. She recalled Xan's words the night before, the open fear on his face. His request had been so simple. Save herself. Leave. "And I'm scared."

Vic squared her shoulders and sniffed, pushing the emotion aside.

"Whatever you think you need me for, Henry can do it," she said.

"He's strong, and he's dedicated. And he and Mom always had a special connection—he can help you."

Max watched her with a somber expression.

"It was always supposed to be him, anyway," Vic said. He was *chosen,* according to Meredith. He would do what needed doing.

Max nodded, and he must have understood that Vic had already decided.

"You will have a place at Avalon as long as I am here," he said. He paused a moment and then stood, sweeping snow from his front. "You know where to find me."

Vic didn't trust herself to speak. She nodded thanks.

He touched her shoulder a final time before turning and leaving the courtyard.

Vic wouldn't come back here. She knew that. When she left, it would be permanent.

Lightning never strikes the same spot twice.

The thought appeared unbidden in her mind, as though set there by someone else. Vic shook it off, along with the strange feeling that accompanied it. The sense of being stared at, though no one was around.

XXVI

The strix's wings span three to five meters, and the strix can fly for extended periods of time without needing to land. The strix is vulnerable to both magic and non-magic flame, and can also be killed by severing the spinal column.

—From the archives of E. Matthew Stephens (1947)

V ic had not returned to the library since the night she found Rachel's body. She wasn't sure why she walked there now. After leaving the courtyard, she wandered aimlessly through the castle, meandering until she stared at the imposing face of the archives.

She couldn't shake the similarity between Rachel's murder and the attack in Meredith's study. She knew the strix was Aren's doing, that Rachel's death came down to nothing beyond coincidence. Rachel had been the unfortunate victim of forces outside her control, collateral damage in a war that hadn't started yet. Whether it was Meredith or Aren who orchestrated the manananggal in Meredith's apartment, Vic had no idea, and she wasn't sure she cared. She dwelled instead on the outcomes of the two attacks, how easily one could have become the other.

Vic felt none of the library's mystique today. The books did not call to her with the promise of forbidden knowledge. She felt no compulsion to pull them down at random and explore. She just felt tired.

She carved the same path she'd taken the last time she'd come, all the way to its fateful conclusion. When she reached the spot where she'd found Rachel torn apart, Vic stared at the empty floor. There were no bloodstains marring the carpet. The nearby books had been wiped clean and returned to their proper places as if nothing had happened. She wondered what they'd done with the body. Why hadn't Vic asked?

She would never have the chance now.

Her questions would become as lost to Vic as the books in this room, as her friends and her brother would be. Her part in the story had come to an end, and she would never get to repeat it.

Lightning never strikes the same spot twice.

This time, the voice that spoke in Vic's mind was not her own. She spun and searched the stacks. *Not there,* it taunted. Vic rushed to the end of the shelf and scanned the aisle. *Not there either.*

But there was no one around her, and no one had spoken aloud. The voice had come from inside of her.

Come on, Victoria. You know what's happening.

Vic recognized that voice. She'd heard it before, though she couldn't place it.

I thought I was more memorable than that.

The faded Southern accent, the hint of mockery. That was Aren's voice. Panic bolted up Vic's spine.

In the dim recesses of her mind, Vic thought she heard a man's laugh.

"This is the bind," Vic said. This was what Xan had warned her about. Of course it didn't exist only for her to pull power through. They were both bound.

The trap swung shut.

What do you think? Aren asked, and Vic stared at the shadowed edge of the bookshelf. She couldn't wrap her mind around the thought of Aren speaking without appearing. She scanned the room for signs of movement, wanting him to materialize around the corner and prove this was all an illusion. He wasn't inside her mind; he couldn't be. She heard laughter again near the root of her brain.

"How long have you been in there?" Vic asked aloud.

How much have I seen, you mean? Before I decided to speak up? Her conversation with Max, her interaction with Xan. Kissing Xan. He could have been there for all of it, lurking in the corner, laughing at her. The enemy was behind the gates.

I'm not your enemy.

"Is this all it does? Give you a fucking walkie-talkie route to my brain?"

Did you really think you could use my magic without consequences? he asked. *Magic* is *consequences, Victoria.*

She thought of the door to Meredith's apartment, the stone in the training room, all the little times she tried to pull on magic that wasn't her own. It had never occurred to her that she might be tugging herself closer to the man on the other end of the line.

You opened the door, Aren said, sounding like a shrug. *I walked through it.*

Vic knew what he meant, the subtle reference to Meredith's apartment and the door he'd helped open. He'd been in her mind for some time now. She backed away from the books. She had to get out of here.

She saw the library's exit, the high arch visible over the stacks, and hurried toward it.

You can't run from me, he warned. *I'll be here no matter where you go.*

Vic tried to ignore Aren's voice as it echoed through her mind. She tried to shove him down, away from her, to where she could pretend none of this was happening.

Your mother wanted you to be powerful. She wanted it very much. I can make that happen.

Max had said something similar, hadn't he? Meredith might have given up that dream, but Max said he never had.

Aren chuckled, and Vic broke into a run.

I haven't given up either. Even Shepherd gets something right occasionally. Blind pigs and acorns and all that.

Vic could get out of here. Vic could outrun him. She could leave the castle and this awful man would stop following her. He would realize she had no more use to him away from here, and that would be the end of this. It had to be. She could get away. She could—back to the real world, back to the restaurant, if they'd take her, and forget all of this happened.

"I'm leaving," she yelled, as if he couldn't hear the thoughts screaming through her panic.

You can try, he said, a smile in his voice.

But the oddest sensation left her spine, like unseen eyes turning from her, and Vic knew that Aren had gone. Where, she had no idea, but she was alone in her mind once again. She threw open the library door and bolted into the cold hall.

She barreled up to their apartment like a woman possessed, and only dimly did she realize that the castle had not impeded her progress at all. The halls were quiet and still and no one interrupted her as she rushed inside.

"Henry!"

No answer.

A few feet inside the door, she slipped. Vic righted herself and looked down to find a piece of paper between her foot and the stone floor. She picked it up.

Scribbled in a half-assed hand was a note from Sarah.

Something big happened in Vermont. They've called the Sentinels away and are evacuating the recruits. They'll take you to a secure location. Stay safe. —S.

Vic's heart hammered in her chest. It was the Brotherhood, she knew it was. Why else would Aren choose this moment to reveal himself? The Brotherhood had done something, and the Sentinels had left to pick up the pieces. Vic had been training with them for weeks, and she wanted, more than anything, to help somehow. The realization that she couldn't left a knot in her throat.

And where was Henry? Vic hurried into his room, calling for him.

The door was open and the bed was unmade and the drawers of his dresser were half-open and empty.

Henry's suitcase no longer sat at the foot of the bed.

He was gone.

He'd gone on ahead and left Vic behind.

Had he left with the Sentinels? Surely not. He wasn't trained—he wasn't ready. He must have evacuated with the recruits. Why hadn't he waited for Vic?

Vic knew they'd been drifting apart. Ever since they'd gotten to Avalon, their relationship had changed. A fissure between them, however minor at first, had grown and grown until Vic couldn't see Henry on the other side.

But how could he leave without her?

She'd asked that question before. Again and again every time Meredith walked out their apartment door.

Vic's chest felt tight.

She was going to leave anyway. She'd promised Xan last night. But here it was, plain as day. As sure a sign as any of Vic's inadequacies.

Another door slammed in her face, another person leaving because she didn't have magic. Another loss, all because she couldn't belong here.

Vic threw her stuff into her duffel, blinking back tears.

On the threshold of the apartment, Vic remembered that she didn't own a winter coat. She shrugged out of Sarah's borrowed puffer and shivered at the sudden temperature change. She folded the coat and gloves and stacked them on the kitchen table. She pulled on the leather jacket she'd brought with her and wanted to scream at the fact that a few weeks ago she'd thought it would be warm enough. Showed how little she knew, like everything else did. She put her fourth, and final, stolen dagger on top of the stack and left.

Her walk through the castle was silent, and Vic tried not to look around corners for shadows moving of their own accord. Whenever she caught her eyes drifting to the darkened edges of the hall, Vic forced herself to keep walking. She shoved all her feelings—about Xan, about leaving, about the heaviness dragging her into the ground—deep inside of her, like she could will her emotions back where they came from.

It had been only an hour or so since Max left her in the courtyard, but so much had changed. Some emergency had pulled the Sentinels away, and Vic knew they mobilized fast. The recruits were gone, too, and maybe the Elders, and god knew who, if anyone, had stayed behind.

She saw no one else in the hallways, and she felt as though she was the only living creature in the castle.

Until she found the entrance hall and saw a lone black bird watching her.

Max's raven sat perched on the upper railing, exactly where Max had been waiting for her and Henry when they first arrived.

Vic couldn't shake the creepiness of the animal's watchful gaze, or the knowledge that the creature was closer to a god than an actual bird. The souls of eight men lived behind those animal eyes, and Max would join them eventually.

Vic shuddered at the thought and walked on.

When Vic shouldered open the massive front door, her car sat in its original spot at the base of the stairs like no time had passed. She clambered in, back rigid, and fought the urge to run back inside. She couldn't look back at the castle, couldn't say goodbye, couldn't force herself to stare at the bald face of her own failure.

Vic knew she would look at the empty passenger seat every few minutes on the drive south, expecting to find someone sitting there. She would scan rooms as she entered and see Henry out of the corner of her eye in the apartment they had shared for so long. But it would be a trick of the light, because he was a thousand miles away and her memory was playing tricks on her.

She sped into the darkening forest without slowing.

Vic did not watch Avalon Castle disappear behind the trees. She did not look back to see the branches knit themselves together to conceal it.

When the driveway yielded to the rural road they'd come in on, Vic pulled the car over and wrenched up the hand brake. Pressure in her throat warned her she was about to start crying, and she regretted leaving more than she had ever regretted anything. She looked back the way she'd come, but Vic saw no break in the line of trees. She could not distinguish one patch of forest from another. There was no going back.

She did not belong there, Vic reminded herself. She didn't belong with Xan, or Sarah, or her brother. Here was another piece of incontrovertible proof.

The sky above her windshield didn't care that Vic was falling apart. Crimson and ocher and the pale pink of fresh-dipped cotton candy taunted her with a display more vibrant than any sunset Vic had seen since arriving at Avalon. Even the heavens celebrated her departure.

When Meredith had left, the life Vic had known vanished. Beyond the next hour, or the next twelve, Vic saw only empty space. She didn't know how she would get the bills paid, or how she would stop anyone from separating her and Henry, or how she would hold herself together on her own. But she had. She'd done it all, and now she would do it again. Vic could survive hard things—the worst day of her life had already happened. She could do it again. She had to.

She could break down later. In about three hours, Vic would hit the town she'd picked as her stop for the night. She would raid the minibar and cry until her eyes puffed up. She'd curl up under the sheets of another new and unfamiliar bed and let all of this overwhelm her.

But for now she would drive.

The sun dipped below the hills in front of her, and Vic flicked on her headlights, though the sky still held the glowing aftermath of the sun's dramatic exit. It started to snow. Wisps fell on the windshield, and Vic clicked on the wipers with a frown. Her time in the Northeast had given her a burgeoning hatred of snow.

A black shape streaked in front of the car.

Vic slammed on the brakes.

She realized her mistake an instant after she made it.

The tires locked on the icy road. The car slid as the rubber failed to find purchase. Vic clutched the steering wheel in panic. Should she turn in to the spin? Turn away? Let it spin itself out without fighting it? Vic remembered hearing that she should do one and absolutely, under no circumstances, any other, but she couldn't remember which was which.

The car swung into a snowbank, and the bumper jammed against a thick mound of ice. Vic's chest constricted against the seatbelt with the impact.

It lasted only a couple of seconds.

Vic stared at the snow in front of her. Her hands gripped the wheel as her breath came and went in shallow heaves.

She was fine.

The air was knocked out of her, and she was scared half to death, but she was fine.

The car? Vic was less sure.

She didn't think she'd hit anything except the snowbank. She hadn't felt any impact before the crunch. The front of the hood and the bumper were consumed under a tall heap of snow. The headlights, her only source of light aside from the dying sky, peeked out of the ice. With shaking hands, Vic put the car in reverse and tried to pull it free. Tires spun with a grind, but the car didn't budge. She was stuck.

Vic didn't know what that animal had been. A dog, most likely. Or a wolf. Vic bet they had wolves in this part of the world.

It might have been something else.

The thought came uninvited from the part of Vic that had spent weeks holed up in a castle studying monsters. She wasn't far from Avalon, thirty miles at most. How far-fetched was it to wonder if an Orcan had found a home in the forest nearby?

She flicked on the overhead light and reached across the front seat for her bag. Her phone had service—not much, but she could make a call.

But Vic didn't know who to call.

No one in the castle could answer, and they were gone anyway. She could get a tow truck, but she didn't know if there was anything wrong with the car. For all she knew, it was stuck on a patch of ice and she could free it. People who lived around here probably knew how to get out of a situation like this. They probably kept something in the trunk to fix it, dry up the ice until the tires got traction, but Vic had nothing. She didn't even have a proper flashlight, for fuck's sake.

Maybe she could wait. This was a public road. Eventually someone would pass, and she could wave them down. Get help unsticking the car. But in the time that Vic had been driving, she hadn't seen another person.

A tow truck, she decided. But they would ask if she could drive it away under its own steam. They would tell her to check.

If the car was busted, she needed to know. And that meant getting out.

Vic gave herself exactly three seconds to feel fear before steeling herself and cracking open the door. The chill plunged into the warmth of the cabin and slapped Vic in the face. She wanted to slam the door shut.

Her sneakers crunched on the ice as she climbed out, and all her layers did little against the frigid wind.

She resolved to make her inspection as quick as possible.

Vic turned on her phone's flashlight and trod carefully on the slick ground to the front of the car. With one hand on the hot hood for balance, she bunched her sweater over her fist and knocked away the ice near the left headlight.

The bumper had dented when she hit the snowbank, but Vic couldn't see any signs of serious damage. She cast the phone's light under the car and saw nothing except ice and asphalt.

No smoke. Nothing leaking. No evidence of an emergency.

On either side of the road, the black forest loomed. The sun had gone, and night fell like a stone on the wilderness. An aching darkness full of awful possibility grabbed Vic's attention before she could pull her gaze away.

This was good, Vic reasoned. She would get back in the car and wait for the engine to melt the ice. She had most of a tank of gas.

Vic turned back toward the car. Her fingers closed around the top of the door to steady herself when she heard—"Vic!"

She froze. The shout came from the woods behind her.

"Vic!" It came again, more desperate now. Torn from the throat in panic.

Vic recognized the voice. She would know it anywhere. She knew that voice better than any other.

It was Henry. Calling to her from the woods.

"Vic!" Henry called again. "Please!"

Vic stood frozen at the side of the car, her heart in her ears as she stared into the forest.

Henry was in there.

Or was he?

He wasn't. He couldn't be. He had gone to a secure location with the Order, like Sarah said. They had taken him somewhere safe, and that's why he hadn't been in the apartment.

But what if they hadn't? What if he hadn't abandoned her at all—what if something had taken him?

Vic knew some Orcans could borrow human voices. Many cultures had myths of monsters echoing human speech, using the cries of loved ones or children to lure victims.

"*Vic!*"

He sounded like he was in pain. Vic took a step forward.

She stopped, paralyzed by fear and indecision and the terrible weight of what was happening.

It couldn't be Henry in the woods. It couldn't be. Vic knew it was probably a trick—she wanted it to be a trick. There was something in the woods, and that thing was trying to draw her into their depths. But these creatures couldn't conjure human voices from nothing. They needed a source. They needed to have heard it before. This thing, if it wasn't Henry, had heard Henry speak. How? Was he here? He couldn't be.

But what if he was?

"Vic, help!"

His voice had moved farther away.

Vic stood motionless, and decision dawned hard and heavy, as it always did.

It might be a trick. It probably was. But it hardly mattered in the end.

If there was even the smallest chance that it was Henry in there, Vic was going to chase after it. If there was even a remote possibility that Henry was in trouble, that he needed help, Vic was never going to leave him. She was never going to get back in the car and ignore the sounds of her brother screaming while she waited until she could drive away.

It didn't matter that she didn't have any magic and that whatever that thing was would probably kill her. If Henry was in there, she was going to help him. She was going to try.

Vic gritted her teeth and ran into the forest.

XXVII

The nuckelavee belongs to the Mirror class, which imitate human form without occupying a human vessel. Though they are weak in their equine neck, nuckelavees possess dual brain function, and removal of both heads is required to ensure the cessation of movement.

—From the archives of E. Matthew Stephens (1947)

Xan knew he'd missed something when he saw the sun. An unnatural darkness blanketed the town, and he might have been frightened if he hadn't seen the blackened sun before. He knew precisely how the spell worked. He'd studied its mechanics, knew the face of its maker.

Mann had been here.

The town lay scattered across a winter landscape, battered homes cast about like discarded dice. The Order marched into town with an organized approach. Theirs was not a traditional fighting style, because theirs was not a traditional opponent. There would be no front lines, no bases of operation, little structure at all. It would be chaos from the moment they entered the territory until they killed the final Orcan. For now, the Sentinels would band together. If they were lucky, they would march in formation until the leads got a sense of the threat, otherwise until the swarm pulled them apart. If they were able, the Sentinels would split into their squads. They would fan out from the center and roam the town until they cleared it or died trying.

Most of the damage was already done. The Order had mobilized quickly—less than two hours passed between the first detection of an Orcan mass and the Order's arrival on the scene—but the Orcans had made quick work of the village. Most of the townsfolk were already dead.

The Sentinels struggled to see through the murk. The horrific brilliance of Mann's spell cut light out of the space between things by breaking apart light waves as they traveled. It not only shut out the sunlight but diminished any human light source, making magical light the sole option. The air around Xan hung thick with Mann's magic, as if he'd left an unseen cloud behind him, which added to the complexity of the Sentinels' task. Casting magic through an existing field was tricky and took more effort than a spell otherwise would. It was genius, really, if the goal was devastation.

Xan called to the others to stay together while he strayed off the road. He was among a select few fighters who had no squad. He and a few of the Elders fought alone so as to move more decisively through the thicket. Other people would just slow him down.

And Xan did not need light to see. Living in shadow occasionally had its advantages.

The town, what remained of it, was in chaos. Orcans had arrived en masse, hundreds of them. They swept over the land like locusts and attacked anything that moved. Like Xan, they found comfort in darkness.

Distant screams echoed through the artificial night, though most of the noise came from predators rather than prey. Xan ran to the yard of a nearby house when he saw movement. An Orcan with red skin crouched on the grass. The creature huddled over its conquest as a starving man would his meal and chewed with blunt, almost human teeth on a long bone stripped of flesh. A femur. The shape of the puddled mass lying prostrate across the Orcan's legs suggested human. The Orcan did not look up as Xan approached. It had no eyes, only an unbroken expanse of crisp red skin pulled so tight white bone glowed through.

Creatures of bone and skin had no organs, nothing to pierce, nothing to slow them down. Sometimes these Orcans were reanimated corpses, bound in the filaments of the dead. But this one brought its Otherworldly body with it, crawling through the Veil in cheap imitation of human form.

Orcans could overwhelm a witch simply by virtue of their quarry's ignorance. Get distracted, misidentify the Orcan, use the wrong tool or the wrong incantation, and you were dead. Approach a creature without having studied it, without prior knowledge of its weaknesses, and you were as good as dead.

One method usually worked, though.

Xan swung hard with the ax in his left hand and turned back to the road before the thing's head hit the grass.

In the quiet of his quarters before he slept, Xan sometimes wondered what it was about him that found a sick sense of peace in what to others must be at best a horrifying necessity. To face an Orcan must be the worst part of many people's lives, and often it was the last, but to Xan it gave clarity. Fighting was simple; fighting Orcans, extremely so. Xan sank into the base of his mind, where panic and fear could not reach him. A form of detachment, he knew, where training and muscle memory took over and the body brought the mind along as an afterthought.

Even the strongest witches were useless in battle if they couldn't control their output. Xan strived not to use magic if he could help it. Especially for a fight like this one, the scale of which remained unknown, Xan preferred to play it safe. He'd conjure his weapons and use his earthly gifts for the fighting as long as he could.

Healing Vic had drained him. Xan hadn't lost that much power all at once since he was a fresh recruit. There was good reason no one messed around with healing magic. It was unthinkably stupid—all his better knowledge warned against it. Xan knew it was a bad idea, knew it was faulty and foolish and reckless. But he hadn't been able to stop himself. She'd looked up at him with her too-big eyes full of hurt, and he'd known he was responsible for it. It was the only thing Xan could think to do to ease the awful tightness in his chest, and it hadn't even worked. He'd carried her to Max's office feeling like shit every step of the way.

He would just have to be more careful today, more cautious than even he was used to. Xan was dangerously close to running on empty, and he couldn't afford to drain himself again.

But where had all that come from? He needed to focus. Not think about Vic—focus. There were dead all around him, and Vic was safe, she'd promised to leave, and he needed to *think*.

Corpses hung out of vehicle windows, caught in a final attempt to flee. A smashed sedan lay crumpled around a streetlight, its windshield torn inward and bloodied at the edges. Human remains littered a nearby lawn, tinting the snow pink. Xan saw no sign of movement aside from the Orcans.

A few people might have found safety in basements, if any of them had had the foresight to get underground. It must have happened quickly. The sun gone, and the Orcans descending a few minutes later. Xan could not imagine there were many survivors. It was a small town, and Xan had never seen this many Orcans unleashed on one place.

But the town was also decentralized. It would have taken the Orcans time to move through the network of homes on the outer boundaries of the area. If people on the outskirts had weathered the initial attack, they could hunker down there and endure the rest. But there was little point in attempting rescues while the Orcans still swarmed. Thankfully, the Sentinels, with their lights and their numbers, offered a more appetizing meal than humans huddled in their basements. If these were summoned Orcans, only recently wrenched through the Veil, as Xan suspected, they would seek out the light source, determined to kill whatever hurt their eyes. Light was new to them, after all, and they hated it. Few would have the sense to flee.

Xan hurried toward the outer range of the occupied area, where a row of houses sat well away from one another in front of a forest. He wanted to get behind the main swath of Orcans, and sent a signal to nearby squads to do the same. If he and the others could get to the back of the mass, they could split the Orcans' attention and trap most of the beasts between the two lines.

He jumped over a chain-link fence to cut across an unoccupied yard. The fence shuddered and creaked under his weight.

A shape in the darkness moved toward him at the sound. A draugr. Far from Xan's favorite creature to fight. The thing reeked. He should have smelled it before it began to approach. Before he even stepped across the street, to be honest. If Xan had been downwind of the creature, it never would have surprised him.

Upon being pulled through the Veil, draugrs reanimated decomposing human corpses. As with many Orcans, no one knew what form draugrs took on the Other Side, if they had form at all, but this draugr's earthly appearance was nasty even by Orcan standards. In the absence of reflected light, its skin lacked the waxy sheen that typically gave the draugr a soapy, mottled complexion. But Xan saw the beady eyes staring toward him from rotted sockets. The draugr looked at him the way an animal looks at its meal, single-minded and mean. The flesh around its mouth and ears had gone first and exposed teeth like rotten cherry pits. Gums had shriveled and pulled back, which gave the otherwise normal human teeth the appearance of sharpness and length. The corpse's head had split like a melon above the right temple in an angry and fatal gash. A car wreck, if Xan had to guess. They were common. For whatever reason, draugrs preferred to occupy the corpses of those who had died violently.

Its arms swung dumbly at its sides, as if the creature had not yet learned to control them. The smell hit Xan with force, and he would have gagged if he hadn't known to expect it.

Xan met the draugr when it lunged for him and levered the stake in his right hand up through the place where the corpse's chin met its neck. The flesh was soft there, and it provided excellent access to the brain. Draugrs would reanimate until the brain stem was severed from the body, forcing whatever remained of the corpse to continue hunting. Xan had once seen a draugr pull itself along with only half an arm attached by a shoulder to the bottom of a head, still searching for food. Burning the remains served as a final prohibition on reanimation.

The thing fell with a great shudder as the sharpened wood skewered its brain, and Xan wasted no time in snapping a thin glass vial between his forefinger and thumb and muttering the spell as he sprinkled the contents on the corpse. It caught fire, and Xan kept moving.

Another fence hopped, and Xan drew close to the town square. He had nearly completed a circuit of the crowd of Orcans. Though plenty had been drawn by the Sentinels' light, many likely remained scattered throughout the homes on the outskirts of town. The Sentinels needed to draw the rest out. The quicker they could extinguish the beasts, the greater the likelihood that some of the civilians would survive.

"Max!" Xan called, knowing the other man would hear him even at a distance. When he narrowed his eyes toward the mass of Sentinels, he found the Elder at the front, fighting off two wraiths. Max hadn't changed from the suit and dark overcoat he usually wore when they left the castle, and he fought with a blunt cane of his own design rather than any of the Order's weapons. Max did not share Xan's reservations about overusing magic during combat and relied on it entirely. Xan wasn't sure Max had ever found the bottom of his abilities. "We need light," Xan called. "We need to get the rest of them here."

Max nodded, knowing in turn that Xan would see it from afar. A wraith swung toward Xan and he ducked, cursing the inevitable spellwork the beast would require. Wraiths lacked physical form and wreaked havoc through condensed magical manipulation. They were impossible to kill without magic.

As Xan phased one arm into shadow and reached for the thing, Max blasted a beam of light from the front of the Sentinel group, nearly blinding in the darkness. It shot upward before expanding, dropping open like a flower and bathing everything in white. Max kept the beacon lit for a few seconds, long enough for any nearby beasts to notice. And they would; it must have spanned miles. The Orcans would see it for what it was—a summons to swarm. They would flock to the light and die like the insects they were.

Xan clenched his shadowed fist around the wraith's neck hard enough to weaken its hold on its magic. He could injure it this way, even enough that it lost hold of its spectral form, but there was only one way to kill a wraith, and it was costly. Bælfyr. Xan had had the sigil inked into his skin years ago, as did many who wanted to summon it quickly. To the outside observer, it was an easy process. A minor prick with knife or fingernail, a dot of blood breaking the inked sigil's line, and the fire appeared. But the simplicity of the summons belied the grueling effort it required, and Xan gritted his teeth even as it created only a small flame. He didn't bother putting it out either, as the fire quickly overtook the wraith and spread to the grass nearby. Light was light, and the Sentinels at least would be smart enough to stay away from it.

Sure enough, a handful of Orcans dove directly into the blaze, trying to fight the fire as they would its wielders. Their shrieks hit the night as they burned.

Only a few houses stood between Xan and the thick of the brawl, and he advanced quickly.

He didn't understand why Mann would choose this place to make his move. It was too small, too unimportant. The Order would have no trouble explaining the destruction of this community. The public's attention would hover over the ruins of this place for a time, but it would pass in a week or two.

As far as Xan could tell, there was nothing significant about this town. He knew Mann had been planning an attack for months. The Brotherhood had collected Orcans, drawing their power in preparation for a mass unleashing. Xan would have expected Mann to choose somewhere strategic. He'd mapped out defense plans for major cities, critical infrastructure, culturally significant landmarks. Xan wondered why Mann would spend all that energy on a place so secluded. What was he missing?

XXVIII

The Acheron Order is named for one of the five rivers in the ancient Greek underworld. Acheron, or Ἀχέρων in the original Greek, flowed from the mortal world into Hades, the world of the dead.

—William Ruskin, *A History of the Acheron Order*
(New York, 1935)

The forest swallowed Vic. The trees, thick and close in the deepening darkness, pushed in on all sides.

"Henry!" Vic called as she moved.

"Vic!"

He was right next to her.

Vic spun, trying to find the source of the sound. The woods were too thick, too dark.

"Where are you?" she shouted.

But there was no response.

Vic weaved through the forest as fast as she could, but it was slow going. She'd never been in a forest like this. The trees, though thin, were densely packed. Too tight, too wild, untouched by human hands. Snow and ice and jagged rock blanketed the ground, and Vic slipped. She couldn't move in a straight line. She couldn't see anything. The forest became a maze of black and gray. Snow and shadow.

She prayed it wasn't actually him. She prayed it was.

Vic twisted through a thick patch of trees. The road behind her had fallen out of view.

The winter air bit the inside of her lungs when she panted for breath. Her exhalations stretched in front of her like smoke.

Vic held her breath, listening for signs of movement, signs of Henry. She couldn't hear anything but her own haggard breathing.

"VIC! HELP ME!"

Behind her this time.

She whirled around, squinting through the darkness. All she could see were the trees, gaunt in the muted moonlight peeking through narrow gaps where leaves once hung.

Vic held her breath as she scanned the stalks in front of her.

The forest went silent.

All the small sounds Vic never gave any thought to stopped. No birds, no bugs, not even the whistle of the wind sounded in the empty forest.

Some long-buried part of Vic screamed in recognition of that silence. She knew what that meant, prey to predator. Something other than Henry called out for her from the forest. Something much worse.

Vic ran.

She sprinted through the thin gaps between the trees. Vic slipped on a patch of ice and grabbed a tree to keep herself upright, and the skin on her hands tore against the sharp bark.

And Vic soon realized she didn't know where she was going. She couldn't remember where the car was. She tried to retrace her path, but fear clouded her thinking. Had she come from that direction? No, the other. She couldn't tell the difference. God, she was such an idiot. She hadn't bothered to lay a trail. She'd been too panicked at the prospect of Henry being in danger. For all Vic knew, she could be running farther into the forest.

But she could not stop.

Perpetual motion was the plight of the hunted. She had to keep going.

A dark shape appeared alongside her. Vic felt a rush of hope. Xan had found her, somehow, as he had last time. She wasn't alone in the forest with an Orcan—Xan had come for her. He would kill this thing, whatever it was, with the same ease he had the manananggal, and he would get her out of here. She knew he would. He would save her.

Vic stumbled, and her hands hit the icy ground. She hauled herself up and twisted toward Xan again. But it wasn't him.

A dark figure stood stock-still between the trees. So still, in fact, that it almost blended in among the motionless pines.

It was tall. Taller even than Xan.

Vic had been right to guess a wolf. That was the closest comparison she could draw. But it was much too large. The size of a bear. It stood on its hind legs and watched Vic without moving. At the end of long arms, claws hung at its sides. But Vic paid little heed to its claws or its shape or even the ghastly size of it. Vic was too shocked by its face.

Or rather what should have been a face, because the beast had none.

Its skull was exposed. The bleached white bone stood out against the black fur coating the rest of it. As if someone had ripped the skin from its face, but only its face, and left it to sit in the sun for a hundred years.

It had no eyes.

A gaping mouth split like a seam, and the thing's bare jaws moved. Open and shut, lipless. Vic stared in horror as her brother's voice fell from the creature's mouth.

"Please come here, Vic."

Vic backed away from it. Even without eyes, it watched her move. She felt its gaze on her skin.

"Don't run away from me, Vic," Henry's voice told her.

It wasn't Henry. It wasn't. It was an Orcan, one Vic had never studied, never heard of, and she had no idea how to fight it.

How had it gotten Henry's voice?

The creature fell onto all fours and prowled toward her.

Vic broke into a run again, though it hurt to pull her eyes from the thing following her. She sprinted forward, angling through the trees. But it was faster than she was. Its claws ripped into her side, and Vic flew sideways into a tree. Her back smacked into the trunk and all the air was punched from her lungs. Pain split the right side of her body as she heaved herself back up. Blood streaked the snow when she left it behind. The thing was gone.

Vic took off running again, slower now, too slow. Her lungs pulled in frigid breaths but they came sharper and sharper.

She couldn't see more than a few feet in front of her. There were no trails, no evidence of the path she had carved into the forest. Vic moved forward blindly, hoping the road was in front of her, hoping she would get lucky, just this once, and be saved.

She longed for a weapon, a knife or a sword or a fucking machine gun. But she'd left them all at the castle with her brother and her friends and her shadow, and she had no means of defense against a creature she couldn't name. All she could do was keep going.

Vic didn't have any warning this time.

The beast collided with her from the side. She felt jagged teeth sink into the flesh of her right thigh, and she screamed. Its jaws clamped tight around her leg, the monster threw its head from side to side, and Vic's body followed. Her scream came out like a sob.

The thing dropped her in an instant and drew back into the shadows beyond her vision.

Vic sobbed when she looked down at her leg. Blood poured from deep holes, and Vic knew it had torn something important.

Gritting her teeth, Vic tried to pull on the bind. She hated using Aren's magic, hated relying on him, hated dragging herself even deeper into his clutches. But at the end of the place where she'd felt the magic before, there was nothing.

There was no response. She was alone. Even Aren had turned his back on her.

A horrible thought made its way through the tangle of panic and pain. Aren could be responsible for this. Even now, he could linger in the forest nearby, waiting to place her final moments in one of his ruby-red stones, numbered and ordered, ready to be called upon when he needed to draw power from her pain. Was this how he had killed her mother? Had the Orcan sent to kill Meredith taunted her, played with her like half-wanted food?

Vic struggled to her feet. She couldn't run anymore. Her leg almost gave way when she put weight on it. She hobbled through the forest clutching the trees for support, biting back a cry each time she leaned on her right leg.

She was trapped.

She had been so stupid, coming into the forest. She knew it wasn't Henry. It couldn't have been Henry. She had known that, hadn't she? But she'd come anyway, because—even after weeks at Avalon—she refused to accept her own limits. Vic hadn't understood how powerless she was. She should have stayed in the car. She should never have gone to Avalon.

Vic screamed as loud as she could. Her voice was ragged in the empty air, cold and desperate and searching. Vic screamed for salvation. She screamed for Henry, she screamed for Xan, she screamed for Max. She even screamed for Meredith, like she would return from the dead, strong and resolute, to save her only daughter. Vic screamed for someone, anyone, to help her.

The forest met her cries with silence.

No one would come this time. No one would save her. Vic had landed herself in this mess, through her ignorance and her foolish insistence that she could handle whatever the world threw at her, and she would suffer the consequences of her hubris.

Vic squinted through the trees for any chance of escape. Her vision blurred. Even in the dark, she knew the blackness creeping across her vision came from the inside. Vic sobbed harder as she screamed for help she knew wasn't coming.

She started screaming with rage now, on the off chance that Aren Mann might hear her. She screamed every obscenity she knew, in as loud a voice as she could muster, intent on leaving a reminder of his wickedness. Every time he replayed this memory, he'd hear Vic's condemnation. He would have no choice but to listen.

When she turned, Vic saw the beast again. It sat on its haunches a few yards away from her with unnatural stillness. Like a dog awaiting a command, Vic thought wildly.

"Please," she said. She knew it didn't care.

The creature tilted its head to the side in confusion.

Perhaps it didn't know that word.

"Please," Vic repeated in a softer voice.

Its skeletal mouth peeled open.

"Please," it said back to her in her own voice. Its teeth clicked together as it spoke.

Vic whimpered.

The thing lunged forward at her. She tried to pry it off as it pinned her in the snow, but it was too strong. And she was too weak. Blackness clawed toward the center of her vision. She couldn't hold on to consciousness much longer.

Vic let out a rasping scream when she felt its claws rip into her stomach. She was burning. She was on fire. Her back, almost numb with cold, pressed into the snow as an unbearable heat burned across her abdomen.

She gasped as the monster disappeared again.

Vic rolled over onto her front and fought to push herself back up. She felt a sickening emptiness and realized some of her intestines had fallen out.

She tried to cram them back in. They were hot and wet against her frozen hand.

They wouldn't stay inside her. Vic clutched them to her belly as she pulled herself onto her knees. With her other hand, she pushed herself up until she stood on shaking legs.

Blood pooled in the snow around her. Her blood.

Vic limped into the forest.

She didn't know where she was going.

Away, she thought.

Her vision darkened further as she stumbled. Only pinpricks left, there in the center, like a telescope's sight.

She didn't have the energy to scream.

The creature sat watching her out of the holes where its eyes should have been. Empty, emotionless sockets fixed on her.

Waiting for her to die.

Vic couldn't move. She couldn't see.

Her vision went black a second before her knees hit the frozen ground.

She couldn't stop herself from falling face-first into it. She barely registered the impact.

Vic sank into the snow and felt herself flicker out like a candle.

XXIX

Arachni are so named for their resemblance to the common spider, though they have six legs instead of eight. Their limbs are thin and muscular, making them adept at jumping large distances, and quick, fierce fighters. Their weakness is the chasm mouth, as the soft palate provides direct access to the brain. Any weapon that destroys brain function will be lethal to the arachni.

—From the archives of E. Matthew Stephens (1947)

Maybe it was a trial run, Xan considered as he watched a spidery shape dart along a rooftop. The arachni resembled a skeleton pulled in six different directions—a pale head at the center of its body with spiny legs twitching out from the middle. Each taloned leg pulled the body along independent of the others and gave the creature a jumpy, disjointed appearance. It sank into a squat atop the pointed roof. Then it leaped into the air and landed on the nearby lawn, crushing the Orcan that Sarah Garza was fighting. She shouted a sound of disgust and thrust a surge of fire toward the spider's face. She missed and hit one of the creature's legs. It lurched backward, its injured leg curling toward its center. The creature's face split from forehead to chin as its mouth peeled open in a shriek. Sarah stood her ground and screamed back at it.

Xan threw the stake this time. The point lodged in the creature's open mouth, killing it instantly.

"That one was mine!" Sarah cried as Xan ran up beside her.

He tugged the spear from the creature's skull, bracing his foot against one of its legs.

"There's another one behind you."

"Thanks!" she shouted over her shoulder as she drew a short sword from the ether and moved toward another arachni crawling toward her in the darkness. She buried her shoulder in the arachni's body like a linebacker and impaled it as they both fell. Sarah tended to favor aggressive offense when fighting, more a raging bull than anything cautious enough to take note of its surroundings. Xan had tried to train this impulse out of her for years, but Sarah couldn't shake her instincts. The strategy brought her some success against Orcans with less mass, but one of these days it was going to get her in trouble.

As Sarah clambered to her feet, a wraith swept down on her from the sky, and she screeched. She jabbed her blade upward and growled in frustration when the wraith remained undeterred. It grabbed her from behind and lifted until Sarah's feet left the ground. While she dangled in its hold, its claws reached under her arms toward a strip of stomach left exposed with her arms raised. Wraiths, like many Orcans, preferred to eviscerate their prey.

Xan ran toward Sarah as a jet of flame flew toward her from the right. Sarah crumpled to the ground as the wraith caught fire.

May Lin appeared with both hands encased in flame, emanating a threatening glow through the darkness. She knelt at Sarah's side, and the flames disappeared. May reached for Sarah's face, and Xan twisted away to lodge the stake in an approaching arachni's mouth.

When he looked back, the two witches were embracing, locked at the lips like there weren't a dozen Orcans on either side of them.

With an angry grunt, Xan cast a spear toward an Orcan at Sarah's back. The two women pulled apart with befuddled expressions on their faces.

"Eyes on the fucking monsters!" Xan yelled. "Idiots," he added under his breath.

Sarah looked at him with a stupid smile, happy as a pig in shit. She leaped to the side to bury a knife in another spider's face, while May shot a streak of fire toward a pair of wraiths hovering overhead.

Xan was tempted to follow after them, break them apart so they wouldn't get themselves or anyone else killed, when a creaking roar split the night. His eyes shot to the sound, and Xan watched as Max used his magic to wrench a dilapidated auto body shop out of the ground. With a subtle shift of his cane, Max threw the building across the square. It roared through the air like a rocket and landed on a huddle of Orcans with an explosive crash. The ground shook, and Xan bent his knees to steady himself.

Dead Orcans lay scattered at the heart of the fighting. The Sentinels mowed through the beasts as they descended. A winged creature dove toward the crowd and was incinerated by a jet of bælfyr before it came within striking distance of the Sentinels. The few Orcans capable of summoning fire of their own shot fits and spurts of it back at the advancing witches, but they were outnumbered.

Another horrible grinding, and Xan turned to watch Max pick up what looked like a post office and launch it at an approaching cloud of flying Orcans.

It was a bloodbath.

Mann could not possibly have expected the Order to be overcome by a few hundred or so Orcans. The scale might be unprecedented, but defending against this—the onslaught—was as much the mission of the Order as any of their duties. They were prepared for Orcan war, had been since long before Mann himself was an Elder. Mann knew their ways, knew their training, he should have known they could handle this. He should have known they would mobilize to neutralize the threat before it spread. Even with diminished numbers, the Sentinels could have taken on twice this many Orcans without suffering serious casualties.

Xan skewered two arachni as he tried to understand what Mann was planning.

Until it hit him.

Mann hadn't chosen this place because there was anything special about it. He hadn't unleashed an army of Orcans to destroy a town for its own sake. There was no hidden message in his choice of location or scenery. Mann wanted the Order to come. He wanted them all to come. He wanted the Sentinels to do what he knew they had trained to do—contain the Orcans before they could move anywhere more populated.

That was the point.

The Orcans weren't here for any reason having to do with this place or these people. They were a distraction. Mann wanted the Sentinels in one place. Mann wanted the Sentinels away from the castle.

It was a trap.

Of course it was.

It was a trap the Order was destined to fall into. The possibility of an Orcan horde sweeping through the Order's territory would never go unanswered. Mann had predicted their behavior exactly—they sent everyone to the front. All available manpower went toward eradicating the threat.

Xan forced his way forward. He needed to get to Max. Mann must have been drawing them away from his true target.

He thought of the castle, nearly empty as the Sentinels pulled out and the recruits were sent to safety. Anyone with a position integral to the Order was sent to the safe house in the event that the Sentinels all left at once. Who remained in the castle? Servants, a skeleton crew, maybe a Mage or two unwilling to uproot their work.

A human woman with curly black hair.

The bottom of Xan's stomach dropped.

Had she left when the others did? What were the odds she was still in the castle?

Xan swore. She should have fled when he told her to. She should have left the castle the night she arrived.

It made no strategic sense that Mann would want anything to do with Vic. Xan never would have predicted Mann would single her out the way he had. The possibility that Mann wanted her, that he wanted to draw her away from the Order while they were distracted, rattled Xan. But even if she wasn't part of Mann's plan, even if her presence was an accident, she wasn't safe near the castle if Mann meant to target it.

Xan had to get back. He had to find her.

Shooting another pulse of fire at a descending wraith, Xan pushed his way through the horde toward Max. Orcans tangled with the Sentinels on the ground, and weapons flew on a makeshift battlefield lit by scattered fires. He felt it then, as he did whenever witches gathered, the crush of magic on all sides. Chaos filled the air, choked him, pressed against his windpipe and begged to be used. The energy that made them fractious and unpredictable in civilized company only helped the Order on the battlefield. It made them stronger, wilder. It ripped them out of their heads in a way Xan could never train. He tamped down the desire to lash out as he fought his way toward Max, at the center.

"I have to get back," he said as he sidled up beside Max. "I think Mann wants us here. I'm worried he's planning something to do with the castle."

"A trap?" Max asked without taking his eyes from a pair of Orcans in front of him. The fighting hardly ruffled Max, though a faint spattering of Orcan blood dotted his otherwise pristine overcoat. He held his cane at shoulder height, and the Orcans on the ground circled around him, wary of getting too close.

Orcans were attracted to magic, to the power of it. The Order had long suspected that witches made tastier meals than humans. As a result, many Orcans, particularly summoned Orcans unfamiliar with the ways of the Earthen world, were drawn toward those beings most likely to kill them. Yet even Orcans knew to steer clear of Max. They hovered at his periphery, and he struck out at them.

"Don't you think?" Xan grunted as he gripped another wraith with a shadowed hand and squeezed until it stopped moving.

"Take some of the squads with you. You'll need to clear the castle."

"They're too slow. I can get there faster on my own."

Max sent a jet of bælfyr at an approaching wraith. "I'll send a warning to evacuate," he said. "And I'll be there as soon as I secure the situation here."

Xan grabbed Max by the shoulder as a thought, hidden in the back of his mind throughout the months they'd prepared for such an attack, bubbled to the surface. He hadn't dared broach the subject before.

"Don't let the other Elders kill the survivors," he told Max in a low voice. "Find another way to keep them quiet."

Max caught his eye and nodded. "I will, Alexandros. Now hurry."

It was hundreds of miles to the castle, where Xan would walk into an unknown situation. He had no idea what might await him, and if he moved as quickly as he could, he would expend most of his energy just getting there. It was unlike him to fly into a situation he didn't understand and wasn't prepared for. But tonight he had to. It was a trap he walked into willingly. Just as the Order could never turn its back on the Orcan horde, there was never any chance of Xan staying here. He would never leave Vic to fend for herself.

With the release of a tightly held muscle, like a sigh at the end of a long day, Xan shifted into shadow and bolted.

XXX

In the darkest moment of human experience comes an opportunity. No one knows how a hand extends from the darkness and who gets the pleasure of the choice. But every once in a while a human finds it within himself to become something greater.

—Terrance Vern, *Theories on Transmogrification*
(New York, 1999)

She fell.

And fell.

And fell.

As if falling in a dream.

Her body had no weight, nothing holding it together. But it was heavy and tumbled over itself as she sank.

She never jerked awake. Never felt plush comfort beneath her and the relief that this had all been a fantasy.

This time. It was not a dream.

It was real, and she was   falling.
Falling and falling.

Deeper into herself.
Into a well in the unexplored caverns of her mind.

The space around her thickened as she fell.
      Gray and thick, like smoke pouring from a late-summer
fire.

She choked for breath, only for the vapor to fill her lungs.
      Cold.
      Shards of ice froze the blood in her veins.

An unintelligible wailing rent the air.

Screaming on all sides of her, overwhelming, the wails of the
dead and the dying. The air itself cried at her for relief.
All around her, screaming.

Formless shapes swirled alongside her. Were they others like her,
she wondered, falling through the nothingness?

She did not remember how she got here.

She did not remember anything.

Her descent slowed as the substance around her grew thicker. She gulped for air, but none came.

She hit the ground.

No different from the air around her, but it must have been the ground, because she stopped falling.

She lay gasping on the floor, in a desperate hunt for air she couldn't find.

Black spots clouded her vision as she suffocated.

How many times was she going to die today?

Her arms and legs grew heavy against the ground, as if she were bound. She struggled to pull away from the gray mass, but her efforts were as futile as a fly's, stuck in a web.

She fought and fought and fought and managed to squirm onto her stomach. She flattened her palms on the ground and pushed it away.

Her arms shook as she heaved herself up, and the atmosphere pushed down upon her like an open hand—pushing her back to rest, forcing her against the formless floor.

She wrenched herself up until she found herself staring down at a pair of hands.

She recognized those hands.

Those were her hands.

There was a sickle scar on the index finger of her left hand.

She remembered getting it.

She cut herself by accident while helping make dinner. So little she'd pulled a polka-dotted stepstool from beneath the kitchen sink. She stood barefoot on the flimsy thing and cut vegetables. She was seven. Eight?

Meredith had been there.

Meredith.

Her mom.

She could picture her. Honey-haired and full of energy. Mom had soft hands, which her own resembled more with every passing year, and she would grab her face with a palm on each cheek to plant kisses on her forehead.

Oh, how she loved her mom. Mom was the sun, and she the helpless planet caught in her orbit. She would have danced circles around her her whole life.

Mom had a big toothy grin across her face. When Mom smiled hard—and she always did—you could see her gums at the top real easy.

But Mom's smile faltered when Vic cut herself. One fast slice and blood. She'd cut deep. Mom ran across the kitchen and pressed a towel into the cut to stop the bleeding. Mom held it, hard, saying *I'm sorry darling* over and over.

She remembered crying. Not hers, she didn't think. These were someone else's sobs.

It was Henry crying.

Henry.

He was little then, too. Even smaller than she was, in a high chair on the other side of the kitchen. Kicking little tyrant feet and screaming.

He cried when he saw the blood, or maybe his sister's reaction to it. She was scared and in pain and it frightened him.

She realized that she didn't want to scare him. She had to act brave so Henry wouldn't be scared. She was learning then, little as she was, how to behave.

When she got scared, Henry got scared.

She had to stop.

She couldn't be scared, and she couldn't be in pain. She needed to make Henry stop crying. She could handle a little cut like this, couldn't she?

"Wic!" he called, because he couldn't wrap his tongue around the *vee* sound yet. "Wic!" he wailed from his plastic throne. Because that was her name, Vic, and he couldn't stand to see her hurt. He screamed loud and shrill until she went to him and wrapped her uninjured hand around his pudgy baby one and smiled.

"It's okay, Henry. See?" Vic held up her towel-wrapped hand. "I'm okay."

He smiled a gap-toothed grin at her, and she was okay. That time, she was.

But Vic wasn't so sure anymore, as the past came back to her, that she would ever be okay again. And the more she remembered, the more certain she became. The castle. Leaving. The monster in the woods. Blood in the snow. Her blood.

It was all over. It was done. She tried to protect Henry, and she failed. She lost it all to the thing in the forest, to the Order, to the Brotherhood, to a world she didn't understand.

Despair as thick as smoke clogged her throat.

How dare they take that from her?

Henry and her life and everything that made her unique. Everything irreplaceable, unrepeatable, about the life she'd lived.

How dare they?

It was hers.

They couldn't have it.

Rage choked her.

Vic threw her hands against the floor. Again, again she pummeled it, until she realized that it was not solid. It was the same vapor that was filling her lungs, woven into a tight structure.

She started pulling at it. Grabbing handfuls of strings and tearing them out, as if she could dig herself free of this cage if she gathered enough of it in her hands. She tore bits and pieces apart and cast them aside as they came undone in her palms. A threadbare blanket of ash fell in front of her.

She pushed her body through the hole she'd torn.

Inside it was darker, like the strings pulled tighter around one another. She was going deeper, not climbing out.

She pushed forward into complete darkness.

Her mouth opened on a breathless gasp.

Someone was here with her.

She felt the presence before she saw it.

The outline of a person sat in the darkness, their edges visible only because they were made of a different material than the wispy smoke surrounding them. Darker, solid. Another bug caught in the web.

When Vic pulled back in surprise, so did they. Vic watched, waiting for the stranger to do something, to move, to attack. They did nothing but sit still, waiting for her, in turn, to do the same. When she leaned forward, the other person leaned in toward her.

And they were eye to eye, inches from each other in the gloom.

A pair of red-rimmed irises stared back at her through the darkness.

Two points of light, the color of blood but twice as angry, trained on Vic's face.

She screamed. But there was no air to make a sound.

The thing moved backward from her as the shape of its face lengthened on the bottom, its mouth falling open like it, too, was screaming. Its horror a mirror to hers.

Vic heard nothing, only watched the thing as it watched her, screaming in the dark.

XXXI

The witch's overall abilities are limited by their physical body, and each practitioner has a finite reservoir of ability. Overextending oneself, over the course of days or even months or years, can lead to exhaustion and, in extreme cases, death.

—William Ruskin, *A History of the Acheron Order*
(New York, 1935)

V ic shot forward.

She gasped for air and clutched her throat. She felt as if a strange substance filled it, though she caught gulps of crisp, clean air.

She noticed the darkness first. She raised a hand in front of her face and squinted at the shape of it moving through the air.

The snow she noticed second. A dusting of fresh flakes lay across her body, delicate as powdered sugar. She shook the snow from her arms and felt the ice bite into her then, felt the sharpness of the raised hair across her skin.

It took Vic a moment to recall why she lay on the forest floor. When she did, her hands shot to her abdomen, remembering broken skin and horrible, unsurvivable pain. Frozen fingers probed the exposed skin at her belly through gashes in the fabric of her clothing. But the skin underneath was smooth and unbroken. Everything was on the inside where it belonged, and she gasped with relief.

As her eyes adjusted to the darkness, she saw that something had cleared the trees around her. They lay scattered like broken matchsticks, spiraling out from Vic's prone form like they'd been blown back from her. Perhaps Xan had come after all. He would be strong enough to fell the trees. But whoever had come had left Vic there, and Xan wouldn't have walked away.

Vic pulled herself to a seat with a grunt, though her muscles burned with the effort. Her joints ached as if they'd been still too long. She had no idea how much time had passed while she slept.

She listened for signs of the creature as she squinted into the shadows.

Though the forest lay as quiet as it had when the creature first appeared, Vic felt a new life behind the silence. She couldn't measure it with any of the senses she knew well enough to name. But she felt the forest breathing against her ear.

She didn't have to think to understand why that was. The knowledge of her change sat bone-deep, certain as a hum under her skin. Every cell in her body was just a little bit different.

Vic spotted a crumpled mass on the ground and approached it warily. A smattering of snow sat atop what appeared to be a stone, oddly shaped and alone.

She reared back when she realized what it was. The creature's body lay curled on the frozen ground. On its back with its legs pulled toward its body, its skin blackened and shriveled. Burned beyond recognition and frozen in perpetual agony. Its muscles seized from the fire and stuck that way. The bleached bone of its face melded into the snow underneath. When Vic stepped closer, her motion disrupted the fragile form, and one of its legs crumbled into ash.

Vic couldn't think of anything capable of doing that.

She walked away, stumbling blind through the forest until she saw the road. Vic did not know how long she had wandered, and she did not question how easy it was to find her path out of the forest now that she was not looking for it. Ice crunched underfoot as she stepped onto the asphalt.

The car sat exactly where she'd left it, still running on the side of the road. The headlights cut through the night and reflected off the ice like moonlight on water. The driver's-side door hung wide and welcoming. Vic crossed to it and climbed inside.

The car was almost out of gas.

Vic wrapped her hands around the steering wheel. Dried blood stained her fingers and filled the cracks in her skin. She'd been leached of her color by the cold and the fear, and her hands, so pale they were almost purple, didn't look like her own. Vic threw the car into reverse. The tires spun on the ice, then the car jammed backward as if shoved by an invisible hand. Vic ignored the odd tug behind her breastbone and pulled onto the road. She couldn't see through the ice coating the windshield, but she didn't need to.

The road carved forward into the night, and Vic followed it. It felt as if only seconds had passed before Vic spotted the entrance. She could see it now, changed as she was, a gap in the woods. Vic banked right without slowing down and buffeted onto the tiny lane. Moments later a familiar form loomed from the darkness.

Avalon Castle, the great sleeping dragon. Waiting for her.

The castle lay dormant tonight, with its windows dark against the black sky. Vic left her things behind when she got out of the car. She trudged up the staircase and shoved the massive doors. They gave way under her palms and pulled themselves open to admit her.

A burst of warm air hit her frozen skin, and Vic prickled with discomfort. She took the same route she'd taken every morning, her footfalls hammering through the empty halls.

Her thoughts swam past her in a muddle of confusion. She couldn't pick one out, couldn't decipher any of them. She felt tired and worn out, exhausted and unable to think.

Vic did not stop to admire the paintings on the walls. She did not notice how they changed in the moonlight, or how she would parse more details if she looked upon them now.

When she reached the door to her and Henry's apartment, she walked past it without slowing, for she no longer had a key. She passed the stairs she would have taken to Sarah's rooms. She passed the library and the courtyard and wound down the staircase to the training wing.

She didn't think about where she was going or why, other than to follow the vague sense of safety she thought she'd find in the small office off the Sentinels' lounge.

In the load-out room, the weapons racks had been cleared. She did not stop to consider why.

A man's voice spoke behind her.

"You." There was anger in that voice, and confusion.

Vic stopped but did not turn. She knew that voice.

"How did you get back into the castle?" Nathaniel demanded. "You were supposed to be gone. You were supposed to be dead."

So he'd known about the Orcan in the woods. Vic had been right; Nathaniel was working with Aren. She should have felt vindicated, but she only felt tired. Vic closed her eyes. She would sort this out in the morning. She'd climb onto the couch in Xan's office and sleep, and tomorrow she could handle Nathaniel.

A strange odor hit her lungs. Organic and acrid, it burned the hair inside her nostrils as she inhaled. Something like rotten eggs and smoke, sulfur and gunpowder.

She looked at her feet.

Black and yellow sand dappled the floor, spread haphazardly like baking flour. Vic's gaze snagged on the image as the wheels of her fogging mind fought to make sense of it.

"What are you doing?" Vic's voice sounded distant, gone from her. She needed rest.

Nathaniel moved behind her. More powder hit the floor.

"You had to come back, didn't you? God, this is all your fucking fault. If you hadn't come into this castle, none of this would have happened."

His voice drew closer and a hard hand clamped around Vic's upper arm. She didn't fight as Nathaniel dragged her forward. She was too tired to fight.

"You know what? This is better, actually. A poetic end to the whole thing. Everything will be wrapped up nicely when they get back."

Vic stumbled, but the hand around her arm held her upright. In some thick part of her brain, Vic realized that she did not want to go with him. Whatever Nathaniel planned to do next, she did not want to be a part of it.

She scanned the wall as he pulled her from the equipment room, but she couldn't get her eyes to focus. Her left hand closed around a dagger hanging on a hook by the door. It was short, only the length of her hand, but she clutched the handle as Nathaniel pulled her out of the room. She knew how to hold it, how to use it, but Vic had never stabbed a person before.

"None of this would have happened if you had stayed away," he was saying. The odd terseness in his voice waned as he grew more agitated. "If you had done what you were told and left this castle, I wouldn't be here. None of us would be here, if you had listened. But no. You had to push. Push and push and push."

They were halfway down the training hallway. He must have come here already, because a line of powder trailed in front of them like a venomous snake.

"And Shepherd let you do it. He let you trample our traditions and our rules. And this is where we end up. If it weren't for you showing up here, poisoning our Elders against our ways, I would never have had to go to *him*. I would never have agreed to this. But you gave me no choice. Do you have any idea how humiliating that was? After everything he's done, to go groveling? But of course you don't. Your kind never thinks about the bigger picture. You never think of anyone but yourself."

Nathaniel shook Vic as he spoke, and she realized he wasn't talking about her, not really. He'd projected a personality onto her, complete with villainous intent, and now Vic would have to suffer for it. With a wave of his hand, the door to the Arena swung inward, and he pushed Vic inside. It was a mark of how addled she felt that the drop didn't even cross her mind.

"You're just like your mother. You know she was a whore, right? She fucked both of them. Shepherd and Mann. At the same time.

Well—" He shot a cruel smile down at Vic. "Not at the exact same time, I don't think. But you know what I mean. And you'll do the same, I can tell. You think I don't see the way Max looks at you? That's the only reason he let this go on so long. He put us all in this predicament because he never got over Meredith. And look, here comes her replacement!"

Aren and Max and Meredith. It all came back to them. Anger shot to the surface of Vic's muddled mind. Nathaniel threw the past at her like it meant a goddamn thing. He'd tried to kill her, at least once, and he thought the sexual habits of a long-dead woman worth mentioning in the aftermath? He thought it mattered somehow, who fucked whom, when there was blood on the line. He was going to try to kill her again, and he had convinced himself it was warranted because of his own delusions about Vic's interest in middle-aged men. How dare he. *How dare he.*

The blade in Vic's hand shot forward, and she went with it. It registered, dimly, that she had not moved. The knife had moved her, and she didn't understand. The blow was clumsy. It struck into Nathaniel's shoulder, and blood poured forth, coating Vic's palm and gushing between her fingers. The dagger slipped from her soaking hands as she pulled it free of his flesh, and Vic watched it clang to the floor. Nathaniel released her as he shrieked and clawed at the wound, before he twisted and hit Vic across the face.

Her body swung backward at the force of the impact, but anger reigned inside of her. Here was the reason for her suffering. In the castle. In the woods. Everything that had happened—all the pain she felt as her body was torn apart—was this man's fault.

Vic hit him, on purpose this time, with a closed fist. She felt the crunch of his orbital bone as it broke, felt the eggy texture of his eye against her knuckles. He screamed again, and she might have broken her hand, if the throbbing pain there was any indication, but Vic did not stop.

She scrambled for the knife, intent for the first time in her life on killing someone. Not taking him down, not protecting herself. She wanted to tear him apart.

She was out of control. Manic rage spread through her like a fire, heating every piece of her, a wild animal twisting and snapping at the bars of its cage. Vic couldn't think past pure fury.

You're a vicious little creature, aren't you? came Aren's voice in the back of her mind. *That's okay—so am I.*

The sound hit Vic harder than a fist. That one, most unwanted part of her remained unchanged. Aren still hid inside her mind, waiting for a moment to speak. Her hand extended forward for the knife, and Vic saw it for the first time—the mark on her wrist. Dark as a tattoo and identical to the mark she'd drawn with her blood when she unknowingly created it.

Vic's distraction lasted an instant, but it was enough. Nathaniel kicked her, and she went to her knees—hard. Before Vic had a chance to think, he kicked her again between her shoulder blades. Vic fell forward and hit the stone steps, sliding down the incline on her side.

The dagger clattered against the stone when she lost her grip on it again.

Sorry, pet.

Fuck you! Vic shouted at the voice in her mind as she tumbled. She shuddered to a stop halfway down and panted, unable to catch her breath. With her face against the steps, Vic struggled to pull herself up. Where her palms met the stone, it fractured. Splits in the rock spread from Vic's hands like veins.

Her gaze met Nathaniel's when he followed the sound of breaking stone, and shock flared across his face.

"He did it. He actually fucking did it."

Nathaniel started to laugh. Cruel joy bounded off the stone, harsh and unhinged and with no humor at all. He shook his head in disbelief.

"Oh, well," he announced with a crazed shrug. "I've already broken the rules. Might as well add witch-killing to the list."

Nathaniel pulled a rod from the pocket of his slacks, longer than Vic's dagger and cast iron. He pointed the conduit at her, and Vic froze.

"Do you remember what lives under the castle, Ms. Wood?"

Vic remembered very well. She remembered the laetite breaking free of its cage. She remembered rows of razor-sharp teeth aimed at Henry and the fear that coursed through her at the sight.

There were Orcans under the castle. Lots of them.

Nathaniel smiled at the dawning horror on Vic's face.

"You do."

But they weren't near the lift. No, Nathaniel had brought Vic to the Arena. And if Nathaniel did not intend to take Vic down to the cages, then he must mean to bring their occupants up.

Nathaniel was going to set the Orcans loose inside the castle.

Vic scrambled for the knife, but she was hurt and slow. The metal in Nathaniel's hand glowed red a second before she felt the impact. A burst of energy hit her shoulder like an electric pulse. Her teeth rattled and she grunted in pain. Above her, one of the arching windows shattered. Bits of broken glass fell around her like wedding rice.

Vic was getting tired of being knocked around.

That's it, Aren said. *Get back up.*

Vic stuck her hand out farther. She heard the warning hiss this time as Nathaniel prepared the spell. But she couldn't move her hand—another few inches and she'd have the knife. This time the pain hit her forearm as she stretched. She convulsed, but it didn't hurt as bad as the first strike. The blade slid toward her of its own accord. Her hand closed around the slippery handle as she heard one of the Arena doors crash open. She didn't look to see if anyone entered.

"You had to make this difficult, didn't you? We'll see how your belligerence serves you now. I doubt *they* will have much patience for backtalk."

Vic rose on unsteady feet, clutching the dagger as she stared at the man intent on killing her.

When she met Nathaniel's mud-brown eyes, so full of loathing, something strange happened. His irises flared like living lights, like glowworms writhed within his corneas. The Lumen, Elder Thompson had called it, which distinguished witches from the rest of the world.

Vic wondered what her eyes looked like now.

"You've broken your oath, Nathaniel."

Xan.

Vic found him on the opposite side of the Arena and felt a rush of relief. She'd thought she'd never see him again, she realized. As she fell in the forest, Vic had thought she'd never see this man again. But here he was. And he looked murderous. His voice was calm, but dangerous. Low and menacing, like he was expending the barest amount of energy to speak and saving all the rest of it to rip Nathaniel apart.

Surprise crossed Nathaniel's face before he composed himself.

"The more the merrier." He attempted bravado, but Vic could tell Xan's arrival had shaken him. "It's a shame Shepherd isn't here."

"How long have you been working with Aren Mann?" Xan asked as he approached. He didn't seem panicked, only measured. Cool and calm, like Vic would have expected. When Nathaniel said nothing, Xan continued, "It's obvious Mann lured us out of the castle, but why—"

"He's going to open the cages," Vic shouted.

Fear flashed in Xan's face for an instant. And Vic felt it then, too. If Xan was scared, Vic was terrified.

The rod in Nathaniel's hands glowed white this time, and he pointed it at Vic in warning. Xan approached with hands open. A plea for peace or preparing for a fight, it could have gone either way.

"You don't have to do this," Xan said.

"You gave me no choice," Nathaniel spat. "I've worked for the

Order longer than either of you has been alive. My family has served for centuries, and I'm supposed to sit back and watch Shepherd destroy it? I tried to stop this where it all started. A Made on the Council? I tell you. It was always a ridiculous proposition. It was only ever going to lead to ruin."

Xan grew closer, but he was too far. Twenty, thirty feet away. Why wasn't he hurrying?

"This will give the Order a chance to rebuild. To reinvent itself the way it used to be, the way it ought to be. The beasts won't touch the archives, they're warded. Only the present will end. It's a cleansing, and it's past due. Those of us loyal to the true Order can rebuild it. Mann promised me that much."

"You can't control him," Xan warned.

No one can, Aren whispered in Vic's ear. *You know that. Don't you, Victoria?*

Nathaniel shifted the conduit in his hands away from Vic, and Xan took the opportunity to pounce. He turned to shadow in a blink, and a cloud of darkness sped toward Nathaniel.

But Nathaniel was ready for that, and a beam like a streak of lightning hit Xan's darkened form. Vic screamed, and Xan was a man again, like he'd fallen out of shadow at the strike. He knelt on the stone floor, forced back into solidity, and there was blood. All Vic saw was the blood, and a red haze filled her vision. Rage like nothing she'd felt before flooded her mind, her thoughts, her everything.

She turned to Nathaniel as he fixed the heated wand on the powder lining the room.

"We have to start over," he said, panic in his voice. "The Order will destroy itself if I don't."

But his words fell off in a garble as the skin of his throat split. Lengthwise, beginning below his jaw, the column of his neck opened like he'd swallowed a piece of glass and it was tearing its way out from the inside. Down to his sternum, opening Nathaniel like a zipper, and hot red blood streamed from the wound as he fell to his knees, gasping around broken skin. A gutted fish still screaming for water.

Nathaniel was dead before his face hit the floor.

But it was too late.

A wall of fire shot from the conduit as he fell, and it hit its mark.

All around Vic, the powder ignited.

XXXII

Wraiths possess no physical form and can be killed
only by burning with bælfyr.
—From the archives of E. Thomas Stanley (2007)

BANG.

On the other side of Vic, BANG. Deafening explosions followed the lines Nathaniel had drawn. Vic fell to her knees as the ground rattled underneath her, and she stumbled to stand. Xan shifted into a form midway between man and shadow and sent a jet of water toward the powder leading into the training hallway. He meant to extinguish the fire before it reached the lower levels, but it was useless. Nathaniel had prepared the space too thoroughly. It was too late to stop what was coming. All they could do was get out of the way.

BANG.

The ground trembled as more of the powder detonated. Under them now. The fire had gotten into the lift's shaft, Vic was sure. Into the cages.

From deep under the castle, roaring blows shook the foundations.

The floor rolled with each new explosion, so hard Vic worried the castle would crumble. The noise grew distant as the fire spread lower.

Within seconds, the sound was deep enough that Vic barely heard it. But the ground swayed beneath her.

Soon other sounds followed from the deep. Growls and shrieks rumbled under her feet. The sound of metal tearing apart. Heavy footfalls climbing closer.

But Vic stood transfixed, staring at the corpse in front of her. There was so much blood. It spread like a carpet around Nathaniel's body; surely all the blood he'd held inside of him now seeped across the stone. It ran in rivulets over the edge of the landing, a waterfall of crimson heading for the Arena floor.

She had done that. No question about it, Vic had done that to him. She knew it like she'd known everything since she woke up—in her bones, under her skin. She'd ripped Nathaniel apart from the inside, split him like an Orcan would its victim. Her rage had fled when she struck, and now Vic stared at the horrific white of his bloodless skin with a blankness she had never felt before.

Should she feel guilty? She didn't.

Vic jumped when Xan reached her and forced her gaze away from the man she'd murdered. Vic wondered if he'd noticed the holes in her clothing, the half-dried blood staining the black fabric, making it shimmer in the light. Vic supposed he didn't need to see any of that to understand what had happened to her. All he'd have to do was look in her eyes. He'd see the Lumen, and he'd know.

And Xan was okay, Vic noticed with a start. Where had he been hurt? Where had the blood come from? She'd seen him go down— she'd seen red. But Xan stood in front of her looking solid and strong, and Vic couldn't make sense of what was happening.

He held her eyes for an instant before tugging her toward the exit.

Vic fought for balance as they hurried over shaking ground. She slipped in the pooling blood and flung a hand forward for Xan. He was shadow at the edges, as he'd been the night he fought the manananggal, and Vic's fingers sank into his form as she grabbed him. She pulled herself upright as Xan shoved her into the hallway.

The training area was destroyed. A mess of rubble and fire blocked the main exit, and the smoke choked Vic as she stared. With his back to Vic, Xan raised both arms toward the double doors leading to the Arena.

Xan put his palms flat against the runes cut into the heavy wood. Judging by his frown, something was supposed to happen.

"What is it?" Vic asked, her voice a rasp.

"He broke the wards," Xan said. "We can't seal in the Arena."

"Can you fix it?"

Xan shook his head as he rushed to the nearest wall and repeated the action on a set of smaller runes. When he touched the markings, they flared gold. Then the runes nearby followed, sparking a chain reaction that left the ceiling aglow.

He hurried back to Vic and pulled her away from the wrecked hallway.

"Nathaniel didn't mess with the wards surrounding the castle," he said, pulling her down another corridor. "Only the ones keeping them in the Arena."

"I don't know what that means," Vic said, looking back at the ruins of the training area as they disappeared around the corner.

"They're stuck inside the castle. The Orcans can't get out."

"But people live here," Vic said, thinking of the dining hall full of people and running faster. Where was Henry? She turned to run toward the other side of the castle, where the apartments were. Where everyone she knew lived. "We need to help them."

Xan grabbed her arm and pulled her in the opposite direction.

"You're drained, Vic. You're not helping anyone tonight."

Vic growled in frustration, and the hold on her arm tightened. Behind them came the sound of breaking stone as something wrenched its way through the castle walls.

"I need to get you to safety." She wanted to argue with him. She wanted to insist that she could fight, she could help. But her thoughts kept drifting away from her. Vic couldn't hold anything in her mind still for long enough to vocalize it.

With a plaintive look behind her, Vic followed him, wondering dimly if Xan could dislocate her shoulder tugging her along like this.

"God, you're slow," Xan yelled when Vic rounded a corner an instant after he did. He put an arm behind her back and pushed, as if he could shove her faster than she could run.

"Hey!"

"You are so . . ." Xan searched for the right word as they ran up a staircase. Something nasty that would perfectly summarize how annoying he found Vic. "Corporeal," he spat.

A noise behind her made Vic turn, and she screeched as something resembling a giant spider skittered up the spiral stairs toward them. Its pincers, sharp and dripping with thick globs of saliva, snapped open and shut as it crawled up the wall.

"Here," Xan grunted, and he shoved Vic into a hallway off the landing. He spun her around and through a doorway. The door slammed shut behind them, submerging them in darkness.

But Xan did something with his hands and the wards on the wall began to glow. They lit the room enough for Vic to see the outline of Xan and the space behind him. It was an office, smaller than Max's and less cluttered.

"Some of the ranking members have rooms with extra protections," Xan said on an exhale. "You'll be safe here."

"I fucking *hate* spiders," Vic said.

She could still hear the arachni crawling around the hallway. Its claws scratched at the walls as it climbed around the door, snuffling at the cracks. A shadow at the threshold had too many legs. Vic held her breath in some wild attempt to stay quiet. When the tip of a spiny leg found its way through the crack in the door, Vic flinched, and a wrenching sound like metal bending in the wind filled the hallway, followed by a far too loud and far too wet crunch.

Had Vic done that?

She leaned against the door and slid until her ass hit the floor.

Xan knelt in front of her, his hands on her. He pulled her wrists away from her body, looking at the bloodstains on her hands. His fingers slid over her torso and thighs, looking for injuries that weren't there anymore. She'd healed in the forest, just as Max said Mades always did.

"You were hurt," she said, her voice ragged. "Nathaniel hit you."

"I'm fine," Xan grumbled. "He stunned me."

Vic reached for his shoulder, where the fabric of his clothing was torn over a cut that was about three inches long. She hovered her fingers over the wound. It wasn't deep, and it had stopped bleeding.

"I saw you bleed," Vic said. "And I killed him."

"I know you did, sweetheart. You're not yourself right now."

"Will I ever be myself again?" she asked, and a horrible empty feeling of loss hit her out of nowhere. Vic knew the answer—they both did. *No,* Xan would say, if he could bring himself to be honest and cruel. *Not the way you used to be.*

"What was it?" he asked instead. The shadows in her periphery danced.

Xan had eyes like broken glass on asphalt, like Vic remembered. Only brighter now, at once mystical and real. They glowed in the dim like crystals tossing moonlight. She'd never seen anything like it.

"Something in the woods," she said, and an emotion passed across Xan's face. His brother had been killed by a forest demon, she remembered. "A kind of mimic I didn't recognize. It had Henry's voice."

Xan's fingers froze on the sides of her arms, but he said nothing.

"Nathaniel said 'He did it,' when he saw my eyes," Vic said. "I think he meant Mann."

Xan frowned.

"Like he thought Mann orchestrated the whole thing. Someone had to. Maybe he had me Made on purpose, like he did to himself."

"Where are you hurt?" he said, and his hands wandered over her arms and neck.

Everywhere, Vic wanted to say. She was hurt everywhere. She was broken and she would never get better. She shook her head as if to clear the memory.

Xan's gaze fell to the gashes in her clothing, to the lines of flesh visible beneath them, and Vic pulled her hand over to cover the exposed skin.

"I was fixed when I woke up."

Something flared in Xan's eyes, and his palms landed on the sides of her face. Big and warm and rough against her cold skin, and Vic shivered. She felt naked, unearthed, like her whole body was awake for the first time in her life, and everything she felt was right on the surface.

Vic had always thought that time had made her tough. All her wounds had scabbed over and scarred, but today they were torn open, bleeding, and full of dirt. She felt remade in their image, a walking wound left to fester. But something else hummed under her skin—tangling with the pain and fear—a kind of newfound energy, a wild, untamed thing.

"Why did you come back to the castle?" Vic asked.

"I needed to find you," Xan said, quiet, almost dazed.

"I wasn't supposed to be here," she said.

"You're never where you're supposed to be."

Vic swallowed. "I thought I was gonna die," she whispered. "I think I might have."

"You didn't," he growled, as if the prospect made him angry.

Vic must not have looked convinced, because Xan held her face tighter, his grip almost bruising and his eyes intense as they locked upon hers.

"Listen to me," he said through his teeth. "You did not die."

But she'd come so close to death it glittered on her skin. A cold weight settled on her like snow and all she could think was the hypothetical. What if she hadn't woken up? What if that was the end? What if, what if, and a million regrets.

Vic turned her face to kiss the inside of Xan's palm. She watched his eyes as she did it, saw the heat in them, the fire.

"Vic," he said, warning in his voice.

Her lips moved against the rough skin of his palm. His other hand closed around the back of her head, holding her there.

The last time they were alone she'd run from this look in Xan's eyes—like he wanted her, like he needed her. For the first time in Vic's life someone had put her first. She'd felt treasured, and it terrified her. She'd fled the castle because of that look. It beckoned her closer while he sent her away, and it woke a part of Vic that had lain dormant for a long, long time. It was a promise of pain to come, because needing someone the way Xan invited her to need him would only leave Vic alone, abandoned, watching a closed door and waiting for someone who would never come home.

But she'd almost died today. It didn't matter what Xan said; a part of her *had* died. The cowardly part, she hoped. And tonight she wanted to be brave. She wanted to want. She wanted to let herself be carried away by the wanting, taken somewhere she didn't have to think and fear and worry about everyone and everything all the time.

As soon as the thought occurred to Vic it ran from her, like a car speeding downhill with no brakes, and she was along for the ride. What Vic wanted, she did not know. But she wanted it more than anything. It gnawed at her insides how badly she wanted it, how badly she needed to feel alive right now. She became a creature made of want, and her mind was not hers anymore.

The drapes on the window across from Vic caught fire.

The hand around the back of Vic's head tightened, and maybe Xan meant to let her go, but she went toward him like he'd called for her. She missed his mouth, so she kissed his face. Xan grunted under his breath, and maybe he spoke, but Vic wasn't listening.

She felt a spray of mist on her left side as the flaming curtains were extinguished. She smelled smoke, but she didn't care.

Xan made a sound like a groan of pain as Vic's lips scoured his cheek, and his fingers closed around the back of her neck. She kissed his cheekbones, the bearded skin of his jaw, moving too fast for finesse but intent on touching everything she could. She was desperate by the time she found his mouth.

Her front teeth hit his when Xan parted his lips, and their tongues collided. She felt his exhale against her own, and she wanted to sigh, but she couldn't spare an instant away from him. Vic's hands, shaking, moved over his body of their own accord, as if she could grab all of this man, fold him up and hold him inside her. She felt the muscles on top of his shoulders, which were hard and stern, and let her hands slide down his chest, exploring with an urgency completely foreign to her.

Before she knew what she was doing Vic had climbed on top of him. She straddled him, pressing her hips against his like she could mold the two of them together by sheer force of will.

Xan made a sound in the back of his throat at the movement, and Vic felt her hips roll.

She pulled his bottom lip between her teeth, and he swore.

And then Vic wasn't the only one moving. The hand behind her neck tugged her forward, crushing their mouths together. Xan deepened the kiss, sliding his tongue into her mouth with a fervor that matched her own, and Vic felt her hips buck under her.

She was rubbing herself against him, moving fast like she would die right here, right now, if she stopped moving for even an instant. Xan was hard underneath her, and he groaned into her open mouth as she moved.

A strong arm slid behind her back and ground Vic's chest against his.

He said her name under his breath, and it sounded like a curse.

Was he scared, too? Vic wondered. Did he feel more alive right now than he had in years?

Vic might have said his name; she might have said any number of things. She wasn't paying attention. All she could think about was the pressure building between them. Two people alone in a dark room, doing things they should have done weeks ago. His voice rumbled against her mouth, speaking garbled words where their tongues tangled. His breath was a hum against hers, his energy meeting and expanding on hers, and Vic was overwhelmed by the newness. Everything she could remember paled in comparison to the heightened tension in her muscles, the demand running over her nerves. She was on fire, and the burn felt better than anything else could.

There was a roaring in her ears, a sound like a freight train bearing down on them, and Vic was going up and up and up to the edge. With a grind of his hips and a squeeze of the muscled arm behind her back, Xan pushed her off it.

The orgasm hit her like a blow, and all the muscles in her neck were tight and long as she weathered it. All around her Vic heard crashing, and she wasn't sure what was real and what wasn't. Her head fell back as she felt, for the second time that day, that she was in the process of being rewritten.

Xan's face pressed against the crook of her neck, and he made an agonized sound against her skin as he followed Vic over the edge. She had a handful of his hair in her fist, and Vic kissed the side of his neck as he came.

He stayed against her neck as both of their breaths fell heavy and hard, slowing as they waited for the wave to ebb. The furious energy that had overrun Vic calmed, and she forced her fingers to open, dropping the stranglehold she had on his hair.

Xan raised his eyes to meet hers. They were flaring now, full of magic. Bright and alive, and Vic wondered what her own looked like at that moment.

She moved back, away from him, and Xan helped her to the ground until she sat, and he pulled his arm away from Vic's back slowly, like he wanted to stay there.

Vic noticed the wonder on his face, a mild kind of confusion, and she understood that they both were surprised at their own loss of control.

She blinked in the sight of the room around them as her thoughts began to clear. The window on the opposite wall was shattered, and the ceiling had caved in behind a heavy desk, dusting everything around them with broken stone.

"Did I do that?" Vic whispered, her voice rough.

Slowly, Xan nodded, his eyes still locked on her face.

From the distance came the unmistakable sound of a human scream.

XXXIII

The borith typically measures between one and two meters long. It has no eyes or ears. Orifices at the base of its tentacular arms serve both digestive and reproductive functions. These orifices also release a venomous mist when the borith is frightened, which causes severe burns when it contacts human skin. The borith is not susceptible to death by dismemberment, as it can regenerate limbs seemingly endlessly. Some form of magical disintegration, for instance bælfyr, is necessary.

—From the archives of E. Matthew Stephens (1947)

P anicking, Vic stared at Xan, who met her concerned gaze with his own. She hastened to stand, adjusting her clothing with shaking hands. She wobbled a little, and Xan steadied her.

"We need to go," she said. "There are still people here."

He rubbed her back before releasing her, looking reluctant. Vic faced the door and eased out the muscles in her hands. She felt reinvigorated but still exhausted. Drained, that was the word Xan had used. She knew from lessons that using too much magic too quickly could be fatal, especially for Mades.

Vic swallowed, and Xan's eyes followed the movement of her throat. The intimacy of the exchange settled hard over Vic. She was vulnerable, raw, and he was helping her. Knowing eyes caught the expression in hers, and Vic thought he understood the gratitude she couldn't voice.

"Where should we go?" Vic asked. "The apartments?"

Xan shook his head and stepped in front of her. "Front door," he said, his voice almost a grunt. "Anyone looking to escape will head that way."

He put his hand on the doorknob and turned to Vic with a determined expression. The Chief Sentinel was back, though worry lingered in his eyes.

"You're gonna move fast, okay?" Xan said. "Faster than you've ever moved before. Straight to the front door. You need to get out of the castle."

"No, I want to help—"

"You need to get out," he repeated. "If you lose me, keep going."

Vic couldn't think about leaving Xan behind. She wouldn't, if it came to that. He had come back for her, and they would leave together. She would help him get the others out—that was the only way she would leave. But Vic nodded anyway, because Xan wouldn't open the door if she didn't.

"Stay behind me," he said, and he flung the door open.

In the hallway, the crushed corpse of the arachni held Vic's gaze for the instant it took her to realize she'd puke if she looked any longer. Peeling her eyes away, she followed Xan when he started running in the opposite direction.

Sound filled the castle. Orcans tore through the halls, sniveling at doorways, looking for a meal. The roar overwhelmed Vic, and she struggled to focus on what she needed to hear: the approach of feet nearby, people who might need help.

But the screaming had stopped. Vic tried not to dwell on what that might mean.

When the wall veered left, they followed it. Another long corridor stretched in front of them, and Vic recognized one of the paintings. They were on the first floor, near the dining hall. The exit was close, maybe two or three hundred meters away.

Something rattled out of an apartment ahead of them, running so quickly it couldn't slow when it hit the hallway. Its legs went out from under it—there were too many of them, all akimbo in the air as the creature stumbled—but it didn't need to right itself. It clung to the walls on sticky feet and faced them.

It was as tall as the ceiling, with a squat, crab-like body and a long, serpentine neck that bent and twisted to keep its head level no matter how the body moved.

Xan ran forward, untouched by the panic clawing up Vic's throat, and unsheathed a dagger from his belt. The creature gnashed at him with pointed teeth. With its neck so long, it could bite him without Xan getting a clear shot at its abdomen, and Vic knew its only weakness lay in thin ridges between belts of iron-hard armor covering its belly. But before the thing's teeth could reach him, Xan dropped into a slide, like a runner crossing home plate. As he glided under the Orcan, Xan raised his dagger, slicing twice lengthwise.

A gush of brown liquid doused Xan as the beast brayed and fell on its side. Xan eased out from under it and jogged back to Vic.

Its blood sizzled and steamed on Xan's skin. He leaped over the lifeless Orcan and encouraged Vic to follow. She eyed its open mouth as she passed, teeth sharp and gleaming with rotten black at the center.

They were nearly there. One more hallway, and they'd be at the exit.

But when Vic rounded the corner, she slammed to a stop.

There was blood on the floor.

Red blood.

Human blood.

In steaks across the floor and down, leading into a meeting room off the main hallway.

Xan tried to pull Vic away from it, but she shook him off and followed the trail of blood.

Too much blood. Too much for one person.

In the darkened corner of the room something hunched. With sinking horror Vic recognized the laetite. White skin, spiked and sharp. Nearly human arms, tipped in claws as long as her hand. A face like a blooming flower, full of teeth and blood.

Vic refused to recognize the sound when it hit her. Chewing, bones breaking, the wet smacking of flesh against teeth. She stood in the doorway and stared at the monstrous shape in the corner, and the thing underneath it, the crumpled mess of blood.

She recognized the cloak as the garment the servants wore. But the person's face was out of view, blocked by the laetite sitting on its chest.

Vic stared at the pile of bodies beside it. Not just one servant, but several.

They had almost made it out.

Xan tugged on her arm again, and the movement made the laetite's head jerk up.

It spun toward Vic with its mouth stretched wide in a roar, displaying rows and rows of blood-dripping teeth.

The window behind it exploded.

"We have to go," Xan said in her ear, but Vic couldn't drag her eyes from the creature as it climbed up from the servant's body.

There were cracks in the wall near the window now, like the castle was breaking apart. The fissures spread, loud as screams, toward the creature, forcing it to step away. One of the servants' bodies fell into the crevasse.

"*Now*, dammit," Xan shouted, and he pulled Vic backward into the entrance hall.

The air was full of smoke. Something big was on fire.

Black clouded Vic's vision and she coughed.

But Xan's hand clung to her arm, and he tugged her through the murk.

Vic sprinted toward the hazy outline of the front door's archway. She didn't take her eyes from her escape, and she did not see the Orcan coming.

A beast with a body like a squid streaked through the air in front of Vic, and Xan's hand was torn away from her arm. Vic fell with the strength of the pull and screamed for Xan, who lay under the Orcan that attacked him, a borith. Two other boriths descended upon Xan's prone form, and Vic ran forward—unsure how to accomplish it but determined to free him. He was pinned to the floor, and they were going to kill him if she didn't do something.

Until Xan's form slipped out of reality.

In an instant, he became the shadow she'd seen so often. With no transitory form, he flicked out like a light. A second later, the creatures surrounding him were flung back. A gust of wind like a hurricane hit Vic, and she stumbled as Xan solidified beside her.

He had a deep burn on his arm, several inches wide and oozing, which Xan appeared not to notice as he squared up. His eyes roamed the smoky room, looking for more enemies to fight. Vic spun beside him, searching for the exit now that she'd lost her bearings.

She had less than a second's warning.

All around them, a crowd of Orcans gathered.

There was no pause. No delay. No moment of hesitation before they pounced.

The creatures came at them in a fury, all intent on the same goal. They would tear her and Xan apart.

Vic took a hurried gasp before the monsters were thrown back by a wall of shadow. The blast stunned them, threw them aside like insects slapped out of the sky, but they weren't dead, and they would get back up.

"New plan," Xan announced as the creatures began to rise. They stirred around Vic and Xan, pulling themselves up on knobby, bestial legs. "You run. I'll hold them off."

He pushed her in the direction of the door and ran toward the Orcans.

But Vic couldn't move. She stared as Xan advanced on the throng like the god of death delivering vengeance. At the edges he blended out of shape, and shadows concealed his form.

Tendrils of darkness carrying magic struck the beasts as they pounced, but Xan couldn't get them all. A handful of Orcans grew close enough to attack him, and they ripped and tore at his shadowed form.

Vic couldn't watch. She couldn't look away.

She couldn't leave.

Not when this was her mess as much as his.

Vic ran behind Xan, unarmed and unsure how to help.

But she was not powerless. She didn't know how to control her newfound abilities, but Vic trusted that somewhere, deep inside, she could figure it out.

She threw herself at an Orcan before it reached Xan's side and tackled it to the ground. It fell with a screech, and Vic landed on top of it. A face like a mantis's looked up at Vic, dazed for an instant before its pincers began grabbing at the air in front of her.

Not knowing what else she could possibly do, Vic punched it.

The massive insect's head crumbled with the crunch of a breaking exoskeleton. Vic pulled her fist from the hole she'd made and tried not to gag at the thick liquid oozing off her knuckles.

Vic clambered to a crouch as another creature closed its jaws around her elbow.

Here was where the instinct kicked in.

It came out of Vic fast. The whole thing must have lasted less than a second, but time slowed to a crawl as she felt a bundle of thread unwind within her chest. A single string plucked from the mass seemed to exit through Vic's sternum. The skin at the exit point contracted around the thread, which thrummed with life as it wriggled in the air. Vic felt the knot inside of her twist as it made room for more to follow.

The thread went where Vic thought it ought to, and it lashed at the Orcans like a whip. Where it made contact, they burned. It hit their bodies like a flame, and they fell. At the same time, the floor split again. With a deafening roar, stone broke in the center and

"I had it under control. Why would I stay behind if I couldn't handle it?"

"I thought you were being noble," Vic said. "Stop laughing! There were like a thousand of them!"

"There were twelve of them."

Twelve, Vic mouthed. "Twelve is a lot of monsters!"

"You know we don't keep the really deadly Orcans in the castle. Those were like kindergarten Orcans."

"Kindergarten? Fuck you. Fuck this place." Vic threw her head into the snow, balled her hands into fists, and screamed.

Beside her Xan's laughter filled the air, and Vic wanted to throttle him.

When he regained control of himself enough to speak, Xan turned to Vic and said, "In the future, when I give you an order, I expect you to follow it."

Vic blew a raspberry at him, and he burst into a new chorus of laughter.

He poked Vic in the side and said, "I'm glad you're alive, you little hellion."

His eyes dropped to Vic's lips, and he was going to kiss her again. Vic wanted him to. They were alive. They'd made it out of the castle, and Vic felt delirious with her own luck. Xan leaned in until their faces were only inches apart when Vic remembered the rest of what had happened.

"Do you think anyone else made it out?" she whispered.

Xan didn't back away, though he frowned.

"No, I don't."

"Why did you stop me?" Vic asked. "Right after Nathaniel opened the cages, I wanted to go find people."

"You wouldn't have survived going into the thick of it," he said, matter-of-fact like he had no doubts about it. "I was already worried you'd overextended yourself."

"You could have left me. You could have gone on alone."

Xan tilted his head slightly, looking at Vic with that too-observant expression, too aware of her. "I made my decision," he said.

"I don't need protecting," Vic said. *Not anymore,* she thought.

Xan huffed a laugh. "No, I was the one that needed protecting. You tried to maul me back there."

Vic's face went hot as hellfire. Had she ever blushed before in her life? Today was full of unwelcome firsts. Xan must have caught her mortified expression, because he laughed again. He shrugged, but his shoulders looked tight and tense.

"I get it," he said. "I tried to explain, but things like that happen when you're newly Made. It's nothing to be embarrassed about. The change affects your impulse control."

But there was something else he wasn't saying to her, and Vic opened her mouth to ask.

A rumble in the distance made Vic jump, and she twisted toward the road.

Xan groaned as he pulled away from her, and Vic felt colder instantly. Xan stood and extended a hand to pull her up. She followed with considerable clumsiness, until they stood shoulder to shoulder facing the driveway.

Now that the fighting had ended, Vic felt the day's events in her body. Every cell ached. Her joints and muscles and her face felt stretched and tired. Her legs shook, and Xan put an arm behind her back to steady her.

A row of armored cars tore down the narrow lane. At least ten of them.

But her gaze stuck on something overhead.

A speck against the night grew larger as Vic stared, until it took the form of a black bird. A raven. It flew directly at her, and Vic put her hands above her head on instinct. But before it could hit her, the feathered wings stretched farther than they ought to have been able, and the creature grew in size until it unfolded into the shape of a man. Into Max, to be precise. He landed on the snow-covered cobblestones and strode toward Vic without missing a step. She stared dumbfounded at him.

Max brushed quick hands over her shoulders. "Are you hurt?"

Vic caught his eyes as they drifted in front of her, and Max stilled. She saw surprise there as he registered the Lumen. Vic wondered how many shocked looks she would receive before the end of this.

She shook her head as Xan spoke.

"Nathaniel was working with Mann. They tried to kill her. First with something in the woods, probably a mimic. Then she came back to the castle as he was opening the cages. I found them in the Arena, right before he destroyed the training area."

Behind Max, the vehicles bearing the Sentinels pulled to a stop. Doors opened quickly, and Sentinels filtered out, looking rumpled and curious as they watched Max, Xan, and Vic. They wore combat uniforms of heavy black coats and utility pants, though most were streaked with dirt and detritus and looked distinctly the worse for wear.

"The massacre was a distraction so they could get the castle."

"Massacre?" Vic asked. "What happened?"

"An Orcan attack," Xan said. "A village near the border."

"Is Henry okay?" Vic asked, looking to Max.

"He's fine." Max patted her arm. "He's with the other recruits at the safe house."

Vic released an enormous sigh. She hadn't even let herself worry that Henry had been inside the castle.

"But why would Mann want the castle?" Vic asked. "It was almost empty, just servants."

Max was shaking his head. "There's a chance he only wanted to deal us a figurative blow. Disrupting our stronghold makes the Order look weak, makes him look stronger by comparison," he said, and Vic hated the idea that all *that*—the blood lining the hallway—amounted to nothing more than a chess move. *Make the Order look weak.* Could that really be it? "He might have done more than release the Orcans. We won't know until we get inside."

"We need to clear the castle," Xan said. "Check for survivors, see if we can restore—"

"Yes, yes," Max agreed, eyes on Vic. "We need to talk first."

"She needs to rest," Xan said.

"You'll rest after," Max told her. "We need to talk."

"Look at her," Xan said. "She's dead on her feet. We can do this later."

"There isn't time."

For a tense moment, Vic thought Xan might hit Max. He glared at the older man before crossing his arms in front of his chest and standing firm beside Vic. Max paid no attention to Xan. He watched Vic, his face torn between sympathy and curiosity. War had finally come to the Order, and Max looked ready to fight.

"Tell me what happened."

The Sentinels crowded in around them, eager to hear for themselves, and Vic's voice shook as she recounted the events in the forest. A few gasped at her description of being Made, and an instant later Sarah and May pulled out of the crowd to stand next to her.

Vic didn't have the urge to cry, though she wondered if she should. She ought to sob and scream and break things. She described as much as she remembered in a torn and crinkled voice. It was the best she could do.

Max's expression shifted from shock to horror to what she guessed was pride. Xan did not move a muscle as he stared forward, his face blank. Such a shift from the man laughing in the snow.

When she told them what had happened once she returned to the castle, angry sounds came from the gathered Sentinels.

"He's dead," Xan cut in when she got to the part in the Arena.

Vic shivered and a coat fell over her shoulders. She turned to see May placing it there and mumbled thanks. May's expression sobered when their eyes met.

"Nathaniel admitted to setting the mimic on me," Vic said. "That must be how it knew my brother's voice."

"I had the same thought," Max said. "It isn't easy, but some Orcans can be trained. Small things, like repeating a voice."

Vic imagined Nathaniel teaching the thing in the woods to sound like her brother. Tossing it chunks of raw liver when it got the exact tenor of his cries correct. She wanted to scream.

"I assume you understand what happened to you in the woods," Max said.

That was a strong word for it. Vic knew the name of what had happened. She had fallen; she had been Made. She had gotten back up a different person, one who had seen death and lived to tell the tale. But no, she didn't understand. Vic nodded. "Nathaniel thought Mann had me Made on purpose," she said, and some of the Sentinels made sounds of surprise.

Max watched her carefully as he raised a single eyebrow. "It's possible," he said in a grim voice. "You are important to him."

"Why?" Her voice was barely a whisper.

"Because your mother was important to him," Max said simply. "The Order is at war. Today was a warning shot."

The faces around Vic sobered at Max's words. He took one of Vic's hands and held it. On the back of his, Vic saw something she hadn't noticed before. A tattoo of a raven inked into the smooth skin between Max's knuckles and his wrist. As Vic watched, it twisted under his skin. She supposed it had been there the whole time, and she had only now noticed it. Magic, Vic thought, continued to confound her.

"What happens next is up to you, Victoria. If you want to stay, as a witch this time, you—"

"I want to stay," Vic interrupted, her jaw set. Fury lined her veins, lacing her words. "I want to gut the bastard."

Max smiled.

The eyes in the mirror were not her eyes.

Vic was filthy. Dried blood, mud, and soot streaked across her face. The snow caught in her curls had melted, and her hair hung limp around her ears.

But Vic paid little attention to any of that. She focused on her irises. Crimson, blood red, and gleaming. Right where a deep, dark brown had always sat.

Vic had seen many versions of the Lumen since her arrival at the Order's safe house. The Elder who had let her, Sarah, and May inside. The Sentinel who came to call Sarah and May to a meeting. The witch who led Vic to the small quarters she'd been assigned. All of them had pleasant-enough eyes. Blues and greens and browns, subtle variations on the human iris. Sarah's eyes had a soft golden glow, while May's were a stormy gray-brown.

Only Vic had eyes the color of violence.

She watched them in the mirror of her sleeping quarters. The safe house, it turned out, was more of a bunker. Concrete walls, deep underground. They'd driven in through a hole in the mountainside and taken an elevator to the base. A honeycomb of tiny individual rooms connected a handful of operations bases impenetrable by weapons known to man or magic.

Vic hunched over the bathroom sink, her hands tight around the metal counter surrounding it. Everything in her quarters was metal—metal sink, metal shower, metal walls. Easy to clean; all you needed was a hose.

The room boasted a thin bed with a bare mattress and sheets carefully folded atop it. Vic had been given standard-issue Sentinel garb upon her arrival and told that the Order would remain here while the castle was inaccessible. They would return whenever the Sentinels cleared it, to whatever was left.

Vic had snuck out once already, which she found more difficult in the cramped hallways underground than in the oversize castle. But she hadn't gone far. Xan's quarters, a few doors down from hers, had been left unlocked. She crept inside while he showered and stole a dagger from the weapons belt he'd brought in with him. Xan had hung it neatly on a hook by the door. He was basically begging Vic to take it.

There must have been a weapons room here, but Vic lacked the energy to find it. Xan would notice the blade missing, and he'd yell at her tomorrow. But he probably would have yelled at her anyway. She might as well earn it.

Vic needed a shower. She needed to wash the muck of Orcan and blood and dirt from her skin. She needed to cleanse herself of this never-ending day. But there was one thing she needed to do first.

As if he heard the unspoken invitation in her thoughts, the voice in the back of her mind spoke up.

You did great today, Aren told her. *I'm impressed.*

Vic stared at the red eyes in the mirror as if they were his, as if she could tell him with a glare how sick of this she was. She didn't want to talk to him. Didn't want to give him the satisfaction of her curiosity or her condemnation or her fear. She just wanted him gone.

I was distracted during the ending. What did I miss?

"I'm done with you."

Don't say that. You and I have a long future ahead of us.

Vic picked up the dagger from its place on the counter. She weighed it in her hand, getting a feel for the balance of it in her left palm. She was far from ambidextrous, but she could make do with her nondominant hand.

What is that?

"You know what it is." She turned the tap on, and cool water filled the bottom of the basin.

It won't work.

"I don't know that I believe you."

Why do you want to get rid of me so badly?

"I don't like you."

That's rude.

"You've killed people. Hundreds, thousands. I don't know, it doesn't matter. You do it without remorse, and you'll do it again."

Doesn't it bother you when people tell you how you feel?

"Are you going to lie to me and tell me you're torn up about it? Will you cry fake tears at the loss of innocent life? All those murders that circumstances just forced you to commit?"

Would it be easier for you if I killed people because I like it, if I felt nothing for them? If I took a sick sense of pleasure from the act, would you have an easier time accepting who I am?

"You hurt people on purpose. Your reasoning is irrelevant."

Naïveté does not suit you, Victoria.

"I'm not interested in your excuses."

I do what I do because it is necessary. Because it must be done. There are elements at play here more important than the protection of a few innocents.

"That's twisted."

I haven't hurt you.

Vic remembered the forest, that thing tearing into her, the knowledge that she had risen from the snow-covered ground as someone fundamentally altered. She looked at the eyes in the mirror and knew that he had hurt her worse than anyone else ever had.

I only ever wanted to show you how powerful you are.

Vic eyed the bind-mark on her wrist like a surgeon eyeing a tumor. About the size of a nickel, but she didn't know how deep the sigil extended into her skin. It curled along the outer edge of her arm, over the bone. Avoiding any major veins, that was good. She angled the blade in her left hand until the tip came up against the thin skin.

You were supposed to be powerful, more powerful than your mother, more powerful than me or Max. You were supposed to be strong.

"I am strong."

I can make you powerful.

"I'm good."

And she dug the blade in.

Xan kept his knives sharp, she would give him that. Vic barely felt the point break the skin. But a piercing pain followed an instant later.

She turned the knife to the side and tugged until she tore a gash the length of the mark. For a split second, the slash was bloodless, white, before crimson flowed from the cut like water breaking a dam.

You are just like your mother. Stubborn. Meredith convinced herself she understood the whole world, but all she saw of it was the inside of a gilded cage.

Blood wept streaks from Vic's wrist, and she pulled her lip between her teeth. Tears fell from the corners of her eyes as she failed to shut out the pain.

Meredith thought that everything came down to a narrow conception of good and evil. She thought she could see everything through a lens she learned in Sunday school.

The skin all over Vic's body felt light and prickly as the blood rushed from her extremities to the wound she sliced into her flesh. She'd cut an L shape; halfway done now.

You've repeated some of her mistake. It made her weak, made her miss things.

Vic sped her pace as the sink filled with blood. Bright and burning and the exact color of her eyes. It swirled around the drain.

Someone knocked on the door outside, and Vic ignored it.

You don't have to follow her. She never meant to dig a grave deep enough for two.

Finally, Vic finished the square. Four cuts, each as deep as the muscle, connecting around the bind-mark.

Then again, perhaps we are all doomed to repeat the mistakes of our parents.

Gritting her teeth, Vic slid the flat side of the blade along one of the edges of the square and dug. As if to separate a line of fat from a steak, Vic teased the knife back and forth between her skin and her muscles. She bit back a scream at the pain, at the difficulty of carving her own flesh.

The knocking at the door grew louder, as someone started banging against the metal, rattling the door in its frame.

The sins of the mother are to be laid upon the children. The Bard knew it, I know it, you know it.

Back and forth, it took too long to tear the skin from her wrist. Until finally it was connected by only a thin piece of fascia. She eased the blade against it and pulled.

Perhaps it's a fate none of us can truly—

And it was finished.

Vic threw the tainted piece of skin into the bloody basin and fell, sobbing, to the floor.

She curled into the small space under the sink, ignoring an unnatural pressure as her own wild magic spread throughout the room. Magic sat heavy in the air around her, energy like a fist pushing her to the ground. Dark strands of the stuff wove around Vic as she pulled her knees to her chest and pressed her left palm against the wound in her wrist, squeezing until she saw stars. She held herself tight and waited for the pounding of her blood to recede.

It took her a moment to realize the pounding wasn't only in her mind. And there was yelling, too.

There was someone at the door, she remembered. Someone had come for her. Her first thought was of Henry, whom she hadn't seen since the day before. Her little brother, her closest friend, and someone she had no idea how to face right now.

"Vic!" someone shouted through the door, the voice angry and booming.

Xan.

When she could force her eyes to look she noticed feet in the gap under the door. Xan was standing in the hallway, waiting for her.

Vic was curled up on the floor, hiding from the world and falling apart, and he was waiting outside her door.

Pain and fear and cold, crippling exhaustion rumbled through her like an uneven breath, and Vic bit down a cry against the back of her hand.

She wanted Xan to come inside. She wanted him to knock the

door down and rush in and hold her together while she broke into a million unrecognizable pieces.

She wanted him to run. To turn his back on her and leave this moment unwitnessed. To let her keep her weakness private like it always had been. The lights in the room went out—snuffed by magic Vic didn't understand well enough to control.

"Vic!" he yelled. "Answer me, goddamn it. What are you doing in there?"

Vic's old instinct won out.

"I'm fine," Vic called, and her voice sounded cold and distant. She choked against a rising sob. Magic wound around her skin like a weight, suffocating her, pushing Vic further into herself, forcing her to stay still and small.

Xan made a sound of frustration. "You start training tomorrow," he said. "Max's orders."

"Fine," Vic said. She poured all her energy into sounding as normal as possible, though a pleading voice in the back of her mind begged Xan to hear the strain in her tone. Begged him to understand what she wasn't saying, to come help her without her having to speak the request.

"Are you okay in there?" She heard him moving behind the door, heard his hand turn the handle like he was anxious to get inside. "I can feel magic—what are you doing?"

"I said I'm fine!" Vic snapped. "Leave me alone."

He stilled.

"Get some sleep."

Vic watched the twin shadows under the door disappear as he walked away from her.

Her head fell onto her knees, and she let shaking sobs overwhelm her.

It was pitch-black around her now. Not the pleasant darkness she'd come to associate with Xan, but something richer, darker, and meaner. Something that came from inside her, stamping out the light, and Vic couldn't feel where her own body ended and the darkness began.

Training started tomorrow, he'd said. For real this time.

Vic smiled into the blackness at the realization. She belonged at Avalon Castle now—whoever she was.

XXXV

People think the world grew tame over time. When humans built rail lines to carry them into uncharted territory and laid concrete wherever they could. People think that because they can see the landscape, because they can draw it on a map and photograph it from a satellite, they can control it. They think that humans know the nature of each creature that makes this world its home.

But they're wrong. The world remains as wild as it always was.

When the untouched landscape shrank as humans ate the world around them, chaos evolved. Instead of searching out Orcans in the dense forests surrounding communities, as they had in centuries past, the modern Order hunts them in sewers, in abandoned tunnels beneath civilization, in the wreckage humans leave behind. The wild is not conquered at all. It is transformed.

Humans speak of the world as if they need to save it. But the earth will outlive them all. It will force roots through concrete and breed organisms capable of thriving in harsher and more inhospitable climates.

Humans think they understand the world around them, but they are wrong. They are always wrong. Their ignorance of the world they inhabit will provide precious little comfort when they realize the wild never had a use for them anyway. Humans are the only ones who need saving.

—From the archives of E. Maximus Shepherd (2025)

T he thrum of the crowd as they took their places reminded Aren of his early days. Before he learned the truth behind the teachings of the church, he had an assigned seat in the front row. Every Sunday the Manns filtered into their pew before the service started. Aren watched his father prepare his sermon at the lectern and dreamed that one day, hopefully not too far in the future, he would take that hallowed place. Aren would be the one to stand tall before the congregation, to beat his palm against the ancient book, to hear the clamored concord of the crowd. They would look to him, one of these days, and he would provide answers. From his place on the polished oak came this sound as the flock prepared to sit and worship. Greetings, hallelujah.

Today was a good day.

The Brothers gathered somewhere new this morning. The Order's attempt to keep the nearby location of their so-called secure annex from him had been doomed from the jump. He'd heard where they were within minutes of the recruits arriving.

The Order's failure to anticipate Aren's movements gave him the freedom to appear here in person. For the first time in ages, and for some of them the first time at all, Aren stood in front of his Brothers and smiled down at them.

They sat atop overturned logs on the forest floor, a pit fire melting the snow at their feet. Aren loosed a sigh of relief. He had not expected it to work out quite this well. Allying with Carver was a risk, he knew that. Carver had paid a higher price for Aren's success than he'd expected—the Elder's body made food for Orcans before it went cold.

He called the crowd to order with a raise of his hands. Their numbers were growing. The Order's ineptitude over the past weeks had been a boon to the Brotherhood.

"Welcome!" Aren called, and the hum fell low. "Tonight is dawn for our new order." A shout from the crowd mirrored Aren's enthusiasm. "Yes!" he echoed, pointing to the man who'd yelled. "This is exactly what I want to see. Today is a good day."

Aren let a touch of his buried Southern accent slip into his speech. He pulled his vowels up enough to convey ease, let the beats hit slow and rhythmic. They loved it. As much as the Order scorned Aren's common background, they flocked to the evidence of it. His connection to the lowly man made Aren exotic. Although he doubted they would appreciate the display half as much if he couldn't turn it off. Aren dabbled in normalcy, put it on like a well-loved coat and surrendered it when he wanted to pass among them as an equal. He had donned the disguise for years, ever since he arrived at Avalon Castle more than two decades past. It wore like a second skin.

"As we gather and celebrate, the Acheron Order is floundering. The castle is overrun with Orcans. All their servants are dead. It will be days, weeks even, before they regain control of their fortress."

Cheering cut through the empty forest. Young men turned to their friends and laughed. Aren recognized each of them, of course. He picked all his Brothers by hand—curated his collection in private before inviting them to a meeting. He knew their names, backgrounds, habits, and hobbies. He even knew most of their parents. Max might have succeeded in keeping Aren from physically entering Avalon, but Max's coup failed to stifle Aren's influence.

"You all understand why this happened, don't you? You understand, better than the Order does, what their problem is: They've made themselves weak. First, by allowing entrance to those who do not deserve the honor. And second, by shutting themselves off from the core of the ability that binds us all. Those who call themselves Elders have kept Order members from their own abilities for so long they no longer remember how to exercise them. They have forgotten the old ways. They see Orcans roaming their hallways, and they run! They run and they hide and they wait for someone to come and clean up the mess."

It was a tricky business, working the insiders. Aren toed a fine line between making each of them feel included in the Brotherhood's vision and sharing so much information that he made himself vulnerable. His one-on-one visits were the bread and butter of Aren's leadership. People valued those who reminded them of their own importance. Remember their names, reassure them of their significance. Assemblies such as these functioned more as opportunities for the Brothers to feel connected than to further any strategic goal.

He would visit a few of them tonight. Tell them a detail he withheld from the group. Bid them not to tell the others. They would feel important, selected, respected recipients of coveted knowledge. It would work marvelously. It always did.

"The Order is weak. They cannot protect you. They cannot protect anyone. How could you expect them to protect the people you love when they cannot guard their own home? The Order is frightened. They fear what they ought to control. If they knew—as we know—

how to summon the ways of old, they would not turn and run. No, they would fight—as you would fight—to protect that which is theirs. They would cast out the undeserving and rebuild. They would forge a new legacy on the foundations of the old. They would recapture the greatness the Order once possessed, before it fell to the inclinations of humans.

"One day," Aren promised, "the Order will recognize its folly. They will see the harm in what they have done, and they will beg *us* for forgiveness. And what will we say when they are on their knees before us?"

"No!" came the crowd's resounding answer.

"No," Aren repeated softly. "We will not forgive them. Because what they have done is unforgivable. The Acheron Order reduced a millennium of power to rubble in a single generation. They allowed humans—frail, hapless humans—into the sacred Order simply because they had stumbled upon access to the Veil. Because they had fallen into magic they could not control, magic they could never hope to harness. Humans are not made for it. Their bodies cannot contain it, and the attempt can only hurt them. Only we who have it in our blood understand the power that it holds.

"The Order's mistake, so long in coming, will be its undoing. Everything that happens now is a result of that failure, and the Order are the only ones to blame. They brought themselves low, and they will know soon enough what the consequences will be for such a mistake."

The air grew quiet as Aren's voice dropped.

"You all understand that this is not a permanent setback. We have won the battle, but the war is only now on the horizon. The Order will recover from this blow. They will gather their soldiers and seek us out. Now that we have acted against them, they will strike back at us with force. They will redouble their efforts to find those within their midst who remain loyal to our cause."

Aren's gaze swept over the members of the crowd in question. The Brothers who stayed hidden within the Order's ranks nodded back to him. They knew their roles in all of this. Informants, some of them, while others were tasked with more direct action against the Order. They knew their positions were the most at risk. Traitors within the Order's ranks walked a dangerous path now that open war had begun.

"They will come for us, and we will be ready when they do. We will not allow their weakness to infect us. And we will not allow it to spread. For all that the Order has prepared for war, we know better than they do what is coming, and we will not stop. We will not rest until the Order is gone, until the new order is built and the undeserving are cast out for the final time."

Some of them smiled at Aren's vision of the future.

"When they strike at us, we will strike back. And when they hide from us, we will find them. We will not rest, we will not wait, we will not stop, until we have won. And we will win."

Like worshippers awaiting a benediction, they perched on the edge of their seats.

"Rise, Brothers, and prepare. War is here."

Aren watched with satisfaction as they stood. His gaze hung on a single face, shining up at him from the crowd.

"For the glorious dead shall rise," Aren called.

"And we shall meet them!" the crowd responded in unison.

All the pieces had fallen into place; history would repeat itself. Balance, the way of all things, had returned to the world. If Aren valued balance at all, he would have found it beautiful. He would have marveled at the universe's talent for symmetry, if he had cared enough to notice it. But Aren only saw a kind of poetic justice in it. Nothing was ever truly new, was it? They would play the same game, over and over, until one of them won.

Max remained at Avalon, as he always would. Aren sought his own legacy away from the Order, as they had known he would from the beginning. And Meredith, well, Meredith remained only in the children she had left behind, so they would play their mother's part on her behalf. Torn, as she always had been, between the two men who sought the fate of the world.

"From the gates of hell, we will march," Aren called.

Max had won the daughter, for now. But Aren had the son, and he planned to keep him.

When Henry Wood caught him watching, Aren smiled, and the boy joined in the chorus as it replied.

"And reclaim what they have stolen from us!"

Yes, this would do nicely.

ACKNOWLEDGMENTS

This story started four years ago, while I was tucked in a cabin in Vermont and hiding from law school. Since then it's passed through a thousand capable hands on its way to yours (beloved reader, whoever you are). I couldn't thank them all if I tried, but I'll try.

My editors, Natalie Hallak and Imogen Nelson, for helping me tell the story I always wanted to. Sorry I fought with you so much—I'll agree faster next time. The teams at Ballantine and Penguin Random House who carried this book over the finish line: Ivanka Perez, Kara Welsh, Jennifer Hershey, Kim Hovey, Pam Alders, Loren Noveck, Erin Korenko, Hasan Altaf, Jeanne Reina, Aarushi Menon, Ralph Fowler, Jennifer Garza, Brianna Kusilek, Taylor Noel, and Kathleen Quinlan. I am endlessly grateful for all of you and the work you've done to help me bring this dream to life.

My agent, Caitlin Mahony, who told me right away that we could make this work, and who has always lived up to that promise. Suzy Ball, who took it to the UK and forced my writing upon the English. The entire team at WME, including Abby Johnson and Frankie Yackel, who saw potential long before I did.

My friends, family, and support system, without whom I would be nowhere. Raquel, who stays up late reading every draft I send her. Emily Caldwell, whose feedback I prize above all others (I'll add sex in the next one, I promise). Emily Vernon, for her infinite willingness to talk about books. Amy, who told me to get my head out of my ass and focus on what mattered. Anni, who doesn't judge me for not knowing how to spell. Angélica, for telling me to stop messing around and sell the damn thing. Maggie and Fiona, who went out of their ways to help me understand the publishing industry. Mom and Dad, who raised me in a house full of books. I would thank the cats, Lyndon and Lady Bird, but to be honest they just got in the way.

Teacher's pet that I am deep inside, I could never forgive myself if I failed to mention the educators who taught me how to write: Wyatt Bingham, Gaby Diaz, Ginny Ballard, Peter Chen, Noah Messing, and Linc Caplan among them.

And finally . . . John, JT, my love. I think you know none of this would have happened without you. Thank you.

ABOUT THE AUTHOR

LIZA ANDERSON is a recent graduate of Yale Law School and a not-so-recent graduate of the University of Texas, where she was the editor in chief of *The Daily Texan*. She has a background in media law and journalism. She lives in Austin with her husband, two cats, and a small army of houseplants. *We Who Have No Gods* is her first novel.

liza-anderson.com
TikTok: @LizaAndersonBooks
Instagram: @LizaAndersonBooks

ABOUT THE TYPE

This book was set in Garamond, a typeface originally designed by the Parisian type cutter Claude Garamond (c. 1500–61). This version of Garamond was modeled on a 1592 specimen sheet from the Egenolff-Berner foundry, which was produced from types assumed to have been brought to Frankfurt by the punch cutter Jacques Sabon (c. 1520–80).

Claude Garamond's distinguished romans and italics first appeared in *Opera Ciceronis* in 1543–44. The Garamond types are clear, open, and elegant.